The pain he causes is rivaled
only by the pain he holds inside.

Taenaran began to relax into the Song's driving
rhythms, matching footstep, slide, and sword thrust to
the cadence of the inner melody. It was in that moment
that Arvaedra's sword began to inexorably slow—or
Taenaran's own attacks began to speed up. It was difficult to tell. All he could see was the deadly beauty of two
blades meeting in the air. Time lost all sense of meaning. For the half-elf, there was only the silver streak of
Arvaedra's sword and the answering ring of his own
steel. He was enmeshed in a symphony of battle.

Keith Francis Strohm weaves a dark tale of
honor, loyalty, and courage, filled with the fierce
determination found only in the hearts of

THE FIGHTERS

FORGOTTEN REALMS

THE FIGHTERS

BLADESINGER

KEITH FRANCIS STROHM

Wizards
OF THE COAST

The Fighters
Bladesinger

©2006 Wizards of the Coast, Inc.

Cover art by Raymond Swanland
Map by Todd Gamble
First Printing: April 2006
Library of Congress Catalog Card Number: 2005928133

9 8 7 6 5 4 3 2 1

ISBN-10: 0-7869-3835-8
ISBN-13: 978-0-7869-3835-3
620-95021740-001-EN

U.S., CANADA,	EUROPEAN HEADQUARTERS
ASIA, PACIFIC, & LATIN AMERICA	Hasbro UK Ltd
Wizards of the Coast, Inc.	Caswell Way
P.O. Box 707	Newport, Gwent NP9 0YH
Renton, WA 98057-0707	GREAT BRITAIN
+1-800-324-6496	Save this address for your records.

Visit our web site at www.wizards.com

Dedication

To the Davidsons—Robin, John, Demarie, Parker, and Carson—for offering shade beneath the desert sun; and to the God who brought us together:

Adoramus te. Glorificamus te. Gratias agimus tibi propter magnam gloriam tuam. Domine Deus, Rex coelestis.

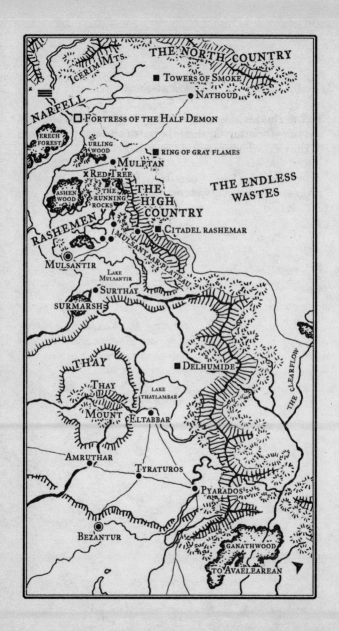

Deep the heart's yearning for fairest Cormanthor,
for the bright leaves of home, where the sun's kisses fall
upon jeweled crystal spires,
and summer winds blow through ancient oak bowers;

Soft the heart's turning through the long sigh of years,
to the glades of Varaenae, where the Eadulith flows
with moon-stippled grace,
and lilaenril blooms within night's dark embrace;

O fairest of homes!

Sharp the heart's churning for that now-distant road,
for the vale of Ny'athalael, where the dryads still sing
of root-hidden beauty,
and silver streams carry their songs to the sea.

O Cormanthor, Hail!

Through the heart's discerning, in shadow and flame,
we carry the song of your glory within;
Remember us dearly, your sons and your daughters,
'till we come once again to your soil.

To the bright, golden leaves of our home!

—from "Aelrindel's Lament"

The Year of the Unstrung Harp
(1371 DR)

Deep among the jagged teeth of the Icerim
Mountains—where wild winter winds shriek
fell tidings and the snow-blasted dead claw
at their ice-blue tombs—an old woman sang.
Harsh-throated and cruel, the terrible song
echoed among the frost-rimed boulders, not
drowned out by the wind but amplified, carried
like the rumor of war or pestilence, until
even the iron heart of the mountain trembled
before it.

Yulda, hathran and sister to the Witches
of Rashemen, threw a gnarled hand against
the stone wall of the mountain, and the deep
rumble of an avalanche answered. A sharp
bark of laughter escaped her. No going back
now, the witch thought with a thrill. Snow,
ice, and stone sealed the treacherous path she

had followed—as she had planned. The spell was simple for one such as her, steeped in the ancient ways of the wychlaran. The very stones and trees of Rashemen were alive with the presence of ancient spirits known to her people as telthor. Those same spirits, shaped by centuries of wild storms and harsh winters, were eager to accede to her request.

The heaving subsided after a few moments more. Yulda started forward, her thick, furred boots crunching across the thin layer of ice-encrusted snow. On any other night, in any other place, the witch would have used the moon's own light to guide her way. Here, in the wilds of the Icerim, with thick clouds blanketing the sky, she gathered her power and sent a golden ball of light ahead on the path she followed. The raking wind tore through her black robes until they rustled around her like the shadow of dark wings, but she paid it no mind. Simple cantrips to keep the cold at bay were one of the first things the witches taught their most junior ethran, or apprentices, and now her devotion to the arcane lore of Rashemen offered her protection enough from the predations of winter.

Thinking of the ethran brought Yulda back to her own apprenticeship, so many decades ago it seemed lost in the fog of time. She had been young and unsure of herself then—all too eager to please the other hathran. It wasn't until she had mastered the witches' arts and became a hathran herself that she began to see the hypocrisy behind her sisters' existence.

For all of their talk of keeping the law and defending Rashemen, the wychlaran were nothing more than glorified hedge witches, like those unproven who, through their own weakness, did not choose the harsh discipline and study of the hathran. The word of a Rashemi witch may be law, but they rarely spoke such a word without deliberation, relying instead on the Iron Lord and his dull-witted thugs to order things. The vremyonni, too, stung her pride like a thorn. Those male spellcasters known as the Old Ones, laboring in their secret cavern strongholds away from the eyes of the hathran, were an affront to the true dignity of the wychlaran.

Yulda had long since seen the error in such a system. Working through ale-addled men instead of ruling as they should was exactly the reason that the wychlaran were so ineffective. After centuries, danger still threatened Rashemen from its borders. Let the men, and especially those damned secretive vremyonni, truly understand their place in the natural order. Only then would Rashemen attain its true destiny!

A rumbling cough interrupted Yulda's thoughts, and the witch cast around for the source of the disturbance. There, high on an escarpment, shimmering within the golden witchlight, crouched a Rashemi snow tiger. With another deep-throated rumble, it bounded down the steep slope, muscles rippling beneath a pelt of purest white, and halted before the black-robed witch. Up close, the snow tiger shimmered and glowed with its own incandescence, betraying its incorporeal nature.

Yulda pulled back her hood and gazed upon the creature from beneath the confines of her stark white mask, the symbol of her status as a hathran. Even here, poised on the threshold of plans that would mean her own death at the hands of her sisters if discovered, she was hesitant to remove it. She had worn the mask for far too long to cast it off so easily.

"Excellent work, my *dmizny*, my Fleshrender," Yulda purred at the spirit tiger in a voice that held none of its earlier harshness. Truly excellent work, she thought. Without the presence of her telthor companion, she would never have found the cavern that held the key to her plans.

Fleshrender let loose a long growl then fell into place by Yulda's side as the witch continued on her way. She sometimes wondered what the telthor did when not directly in contact with her; one look at its baleful eyes usually convinced her that she really did not want to know. It was enough that the two were bound together in this dark purpose.

The path led through several old rockfalls, cluttered with ice and drifts of snow, and up a series of steep slopes. Yulda trudged onward for another candle's length, wheezing as she navigated the relentless course. The witch had just climbed over the shattered corpse of an ice-slain tree when her shimmering, golden witchlight winked out of existence, plunging her into total darkness.

She cursed loudly as her knee banged against the frozen stone before her, then laughed at the absurdity of it all. The dispelling of her magic should not have come as a surprise. The witch had, after all, chosen this place for a reason. During the course of its troubled history, Rashemen became the battleground of warring nations, whose mighty spells even now held sway over portions of the land. Yulda knew that no magic would function at all beyond this fallen tree and across a broad sweep of flatland, until the spellcaster reached the entrance to a small cavern at the base of a natural outcropping of stone.

The witch reached into her robe, pulled out a small torch, and lit it with some flint and steel. The flame guttered beneath the heavy wind but continued to cast fitful light. With a sharp motion to Fleshrender and a mental command to wait here, Yulda hurried along the path toward the cavern. Walking through this area devoid of magic set her teeth to itching; she felt only half alive, as if something precious and vital were missing. The torch nearly went out a few times along the way, but she finally arrived at the cavern entrance, breathless from the buffeting of the wind.

Yulda dropped the torch and bowed her head to avoid banging it on the uneven stone as she entered the cave. Immediately, she let out a sigh of relief as her mystic senses returned. In the dying light of the torch, she could see a shadowed path leading toward the back of the cave. Following it, she stood at last before a wall of stone inscribed with several glyphs. The witch sang softly, almost humming, and purple light flared from the glyphs before the wall shimmered and faded away.

She stepped through and made a sharp gesture with her hand. At once, flames erupted from wooden torches placed roughly in iron sconces around the cave. The gray stone of her rude demesne rippled with incandescent fire as the crystals embedded within the rock caught the newly created light. Normally she would stare at such a spectacle, marveling at the delicate interplay of elements. Tonight, however, she was driven by a dark and terrible purpose.

Ignoring the sharp stalagmites that jutted up from the uneven stone floor like the gray teeth of a giant frost troll, Yulda deftly made her way to the back of the cave, past hastily strewn fur rugs and the detritus of past experiments. She finally stopped before a large alcove covered in darkness so thick that even the combined illumination of the torches could not pierce it. With another word, she banished the darkness—

—and gazed upon the naked form of a vremyonni, held spread-eagled by four obsidian chains that pulsed with a baleful green light. The Old One was ancient even by the standards of his brotherhood. Deeply weathered flesh sagged on the wizard's decrepit bones, drooping toward the floor like melted candle wax. Faint tufts of silver hair sprouted from the creased lines of the man's skull; only his thickset eyebrows and flowing white beard bespoke the Rashemi blood beating sluggishly within his chest.

He stirred at Yulda's approach, gazing up at her with eyes that still shone brilliant gold, despite his treatment. The witch nearly stopped in her tracks. Power resonated from him, sharp and bright, so different from her own magic. She felt a wave of desire crest over her all at once—wild and desperate. With an iron discipline honed by nearly a century of study, the hathran mastered her body's need.

The Old One was dangerous still. His lore was deep; it burned within him, the very animating force that pumped each beat of his ancient heart. It had taken all of her cunning to lure the wizard into her trap and overwhelm his arcane defenses. She would not falter now and allow a single misstep to ruin her plan—not when she was so close.

"Have you reconsidered my offer?" Yulda asked in a voice not far from the purr she had offered her telthor companion earlier.

The vremyonni ignored her, staring steadily into her eyes.

"Where is the boy?" he asked at last, his deep, rumbling bass echoing in the frigid cave.

"The boy?" she replied with little comprehension—then she remembered the wizard's pupil, a lad of less than twelve summers, with soft, smooth skin and golden hair. "Ahh ... I remember now. He's dead."

The news seemed to deflate the vremyonni even more than his cruel bonds. The Old One bowed his head, but Yulda stepped forward and pulled the sagging wizard's head up violently to face her.

"I will have your secrets, old man—and those of your pathetic brotherhood." She nearly screamed the last words.

He gazed at her for a few moments then said softly, almost whispering, "Before I will betray the very oaths that give me life, I would see the face of my captor."

Yulda stepped back as if struck. No one gazed upon the naked face of a hathran, least of all a man, yet her path these past decades had led her far beyond the ways that blinded her tradition-bound sisters. Reaching carefully, almost tenderly, up to her mask, the witch slowly removed it, revealing the weathered lines of her own countenance. She watched as the Old One's face changed—first in disbelief at the moment of recognition, then in horror as his gaze fell upon the gaping hole where Yulda's left eye should have been, a hole that now pulsated with an obsidian energy that seemed to draw the very light of the cavern into it.

"You . . ." the Old One stammered. "What have you done?"

The question hung in the air between them, and for a single moment Yulda felt free of the compulsion that had driven her for nearly half a century. The horror of her own actions came alive within her and cried out for justice. Here was an open door, an opportunity to step from her treacherous path.

The moment passed.

With a snarl, the hathran threw her white mask to the floor and shattered it with a single stomp of her booted foot.

"I have done what I must," she finally answered the vremyonni's question. "Now," she asked almost sweetly, "what will you do for me?"

"I will never betray the oaths of my brotherhood," the Old One said, "especially to a durthan pawn."

At that, Yulda laughed, a terrible sound, like the cawing of a crow.

"Do you think I have anything to do with that dark sisterhood?" she asked at last, nearly spluttering as she tried to catch her breath. "The durthan are nothing more than toothless crones. They scurry and scuttle in the shadows of the Erech Forest, clutching their little secrets and spinning webs of intrigue like bloated spiders, too full of themselves to realize true power.

"No," the witch continued, drawing blood as she ran a sharp nail down the Old One's gaunt cheek. "I am far more than wychlaran. I am free—and nothing will stop me before I have worked my will upon the world."

"Then I am truly sorry," the vremyonni replied. "The freedom you have is a terrible burden. Who can survive it?"

The Old One's words were spoken mildly, but their sorrowful tone awoke a fierce flame within Yulda's heart. Who was this broken wizard, this *man*, to feel sorrow for her? She turned from him and with a single shout sent an arcane message spinning across the breadth of Rashemen to the one person she trusted. The witch's forces would begin to gather. Her time was at hand.

"If you will not offer me the power that I seek," Yulda said fiercely as she returned her attention to the captive wizard, "then I will reach into your very heart and rake for it."

Quietly at first, and then with greater intensity, the witch gave voice to the spell that had taken her eye to learn. Black power billowed from her ruined eye socket like smoke, forming a cloud that gathered around the chained Old One. A final shouted incantation sent the cloud rushing at the chained wizard with enough force to extinguish the guttering torches. The cave plunged into darkness as the Old One's screams kept company with the night wind.

In deep winter, night in the Icerim Mountains lasted a very long time indeed.

CHAPTER 1

The Year of the Lion
(1340 DR)

Aelrindel watched as the river burned.

He stood utterly still beneath the arching canopy of leaf and branch, caught in that silent space between breaths, that moment when life and death cease their endless dance, poised in a single embrace—watching.

Flaming wrecks of wood and iron floated aimlessly across the river's broad back, caught in its bloodied current. Thick plumes of oily smoke rose from the shattered hulks like incense to a dark god, their black and terrible shapes bruising the soft spring sky. On the far bank, obscured by the columns of smoke, trebuchets and small catapults stood in various stages of disarray—the castoff toys of a malicious giant. Everywhere, the bloated bodies of the dead and dying bobbed sickeningly in the water as a shadowed convocation of crows cawed raucous symphonies before plunging downward to feast.

Aelrindel watched it all with eyes that had gazed upon a hundred mortal lifetimes of joy and sorrow, had witnessed the world's fragile beauty suspended on a single silken strand of time, spinning out across the ages on an unending pilgrimage—and refused to look away.

"Animals," a voice to his left barked, interrupting Aelrindel's sorrowful reverie. "Filthy barbarians, that they would kill and leave their dead to rot in the sun." The words were harsh, sharp edged despite the lilting, cadence with which they were delivered.

The golden-maned elf turned a thin, angular face toward his companion, squinting almond-shaped eyes against the rapidly brightening day. The exclamation hung in the cool morning air. He heard the anger in his friend's voice—and more. The weight of history pressed down upon their hearts, of centuries spent in war and strife with the humans in this part of Faerûn. Even though an uneasy peace had reigned for nearly as long, the memory of sword and steel, wrack and ruin, lay across a generation and more of his people. Anger, sorrow, and bitterness—for the bright weavings of the *Tel'Quessir* cast into shadow, the songs stilled, and if he was honest with himself, for the extinguishing of human life—clung to the spirit of his people like a feeding wraith.

"Peace, Faelyn," he said at last, placing long, graceful fingers upon his companion's shoulders. "We are here as eyes and ears, not swords."

Faelyn scowled, but held his tongue. The elegant, angular cast of his features was sharper than Aelrindel's, more severe, like blades cutting through the air. Faelyn wore his thick, raven-black hair pulled back in the style of the *laeriaen*, bound with the finely wrought silver clasp that identified him as a bladesinger.

As he gazed at his friend, Aelrindel felt a prick of sadness. From as far back as he could remember, Faelyn had been a true companion and sword-brother, steadfast and loyal, but where Aelrindel opened his heart to the world in studied contemplation, seeking wisdom, the dark-haired bladesinger perceived only threat from almost every aspect of life. It had always been so. Though both of them had been forged by centuries of training as living weapons for the defense of their people, blood, war, and unrelenting pride had tempered Faelyn into a bitter metal indeed.

Aelrindel's hand moved from his friend's shoulder to his face, tracing the light webbing of scars that marred the otherwise bronze perfection of his skin, and was surprised to note a small shock of white hair beginning to grow at his temples. Had it truly been so long, he thought, since they were both *tael*, apprenticed to their masters and learning the rudiments of their art?

Faelyn reached out and gently put a stop to Aelrindel's exploration.

"You rebuke me, *kaer'vaelen*. Without words, you rebuke me," Faelyn said, casting his gaze to the ground.

Aelrindel heard the accusation. *Kaer'vaelen*. First Hilt of the bladesingers. This is what lay between them. It was a hard thing, a stone that had dragged on their friendship ever since Cauladra Brightwing had passed her sword, and her authority, to him before she journeyed to the groves of Corellon Larethian.

He was about to respond when a soft cry sounded in the morning air. Faelyn's head shot up and his hand strayed to the sword sheathed at his side.

The cry came again, just as soft. This time, Aelrindel's sensitive ears caught the direction of the sound. Without a word, he stepped out from beneath their hiding spot, confident that his companion strode right behind him, and moved in search of it.

The sun had risen over the site of battle and Aelrindel counted at least a score of bodies that had washed ashore and nearly twice that many lay dead and bloodied upon the ground. Carefully he picked his way down the slope that led to the heart of the destruction, avoiding the snapped points of blades, congealed pools of blood, and the feathered shafts of spent arrows that sprouted from the slick earth like gruesome flowers.

His senses were alert for the slightest sound, as, he knew, were Faelyn's. Death often called more than just crows to its sickening feast. So it was that the figures leaping from behind a small jumble of rocks and small boulders did not surprise the two elves.

There were nine of them, Aelrindel noted, adorned with mismatched armor—pieces of metal, strips of boiled leather, and hardened cloth. All were human, though barely recognizable as such beneath the gore and grit that covered their skin. Some were missing teeth or fingers, and one, a particularly emaciated figure whose bones stood out beneath a thin layer of skin, had only a single ear. They held steel in their hands—a motley collection of pitted swords, bloodied axes, and evil-looking dirks—and had a hard glint around the eyes.

Aelrindel felt his lithe form relax, the tension brought on by surveying the destruction of human war melted away beneath the promise of action. Distantly, somewhere deep within his heart, the elf heard the gentle strains of the Song begin.

"What have we here?" one of the scavengers, a burly man with a grizzled beard and a wicked scar running from temple to throat, asked in exaggerated good humor. "Two pretty maids from the lands of the bleedin' elves?"

His accent was short and clipped, difficult for Aelrindel to understand.

"*N Tel'Quessir* scum!" Faelyn proclaimed behind him.

The First Hilt held up his hand, to leash his friend's anger as much as to show these rude humans that they meant no harm.

"We are here in peace," he said slowly in the human tongue. His own mouth formed the unfamiliar syllables slowly. "We do not seek to hurt you."

That last brought a round of harsh laughter from the brigands.

"Been no peace in this land for quite some time," a weasely faced man barked out.

"An' that's just the way we like it, isn't it, lads?" the burly human asked, to the roaring affirmation of his companions. He moved closer to Aelrindel, close enough that the elf could make out the blackened stain of rot on his teeth; his breath stank like carrion. " 'Tis you who should worry about getting hurt," the burly human said with a cruel smile. "Now hand over your swords and the pretty little things that you and your 'lass' here no doubt decorate yerselves with."

Aelrindel simply stood there, watching the man's smile slowly fade as the elf made no move to comply with his commands.

The grizzled human took a step back.

"Kill them," was all that he said—was all that he would ever say again.

Twin elven blades sang from worn leather scabbards, catching the sunlight along their gleaming lengths. A single spray of blood erupted from the burly human's throat as Aelrindel's sword, unleashed at last, cleaved through muscle and bone in a single cut. The man fell, headless, to the ground.

Behind him, Aelrindel heard the sound of Faelyn's Song, and joined it with his own in fearsome harmony. Four more scavengers fell within moments. A fifth, the weasel-eyed man, began to cast a spell. The First Hilt parried a clumsy axe swing and caught the rhythm of the wizard's spell. It was one with which he was well familiar. Using his free hand, the bladesinger mirrored his opponent's casting then sent his considerable power out to surround the overmatched wizard, binding it to himself. Argent energy flew from the human's outstretched hand only to fizzle into nothingness as the bladesinger quenched the spell.

The brigands were obviously fearful now. Their earlier swagger gave way to wariness, and Aelrindel could see two of them already surveying their escape routes. Using skills honed from centuries of combat, the two elves wove a deadly net of steel from which none of their opponents could escape. Two more scavengers fell. One threw his dirk hard at Faelyn. Aelrindel batted the makeshift missile away with the flat of his own blade, while his companion slid forward to drive the point of his weapon into the man's chest. The second, perhaps the most skilled fighter of the lot, parried the snaking steel of Aelrindel's blade twice before a quick feint left his guard open. The bladesinger took the advantage, and the man fell backward with a deep tear in his stomach.

The remaining two humans dropped their weapons and began to plead for their lives. Still holding his blade easily in one hand, the First Hilt pointed a slender finger away from the battleground.

"Go," he commanded, "and leave the dead to the gods."

The two babbled their thanks and hastily retreated, tripping repeatedly over one another as they ran up the slope and back toward the human settlement. Only when they moved out of the range of his elf sight did Aelrindel start cleaning his blade. Once it gleamed again, free of the blood of his enemies, the bladesinger held it flat between both of his hands, bowed low in the way of the *laeriaen*, and placed it back within its scabbard.

"They deserved to be punished for what they did—attempted to do," Faelyn said when he, too, had finished the ritual.

"I know, my friend," he replied, expecting another session of wrangling with his embittered companion, "but we shall let the humans deal with them."

"Eyes and ears indeed . . ." came the reply, with a surprising hint of humor.

Aelrindel laughed softly at the jest. It was good to laugh.

The child's cry came again, breaking the moment. It was close, just beyond the jutting rocks from which their attackers had leaped. Aelrindel gave his companion a final smile then moved toward the sound. As he drew near, he saw a pile of corpses, each bloody and awkwardly bent. When the wailing came again, the bladesinger knew that it originated from beneath the corpses. He motioned Faelyn to help, and between them, the two bladesingers carefully separated the dead from their eternal embrace. The bodies were cool and stiff.

There, cradled in the rigored arms of a woman and protected from the elements by the press of bodies and a simple bloodied cloth, lay a screaming child. Its skin was red and splotchy from its exertion and its tiny fingers were balled into fists, beating the air in obvious fear and frustration.

Aelrindel gazed at the creature for a long moment, noting by the cast of its distorted face the moon elf blood that flowed within its veins. That and something more.

Or less.

The child had a roundness to its face, a solidity to its tiny frame that bespoke of other parentage, human parentage, if Aelrindel could judge these things right. It was one of the *a Tel'Quessir*, the Almost People. He sighed for the wailing child, caught forever between two worlds, and now, but a little while after its birth, already standing at the doorway to the gods' realm. He reached out his hand and stroked the child's cheek. Pale blue eyes opened wide, and the babe made a soft, surprised sound.

It stopped crying.

Aelrindel knelt before the child and started reaching for it with both hands.

"What do you think you're doing, Ael?" Faelyn asked, the incredulity behind the question clearly reflected in his voice.

"We cannot leave the child here to die," Aelrindel responded, not taking his eyes from the babe.

"Why not?" Faelyn continued, "Let the gods care for it. It is—"

"An abomination?" the First Hilt interrupted bitterly.

Faelyn swore. "Gods, Ael! Do you think I really believe that?"

Aelrindel shook his head—though there were some among their community who did see the *a Tel'Quessir* as abominations.

"Even so," Faelyn went on, "we cannot take this child in. Remember the Oath. We are what we are. Besides, it is an ill-omened foundling. The signs—"

"Damn the signs, Faelyn. I know them well: 'Born from battle, bad for luck.' Those are nothing but superstition," Aelrindel said with finality.

Inwardly, though, he sighed. Faelyn was right. No one had ever brought an outsider to the community, yet what were thousands of years of tradition in the face of this one helpless half-elf child? He had made his decision.

He reached out again to the foundling.

"Ael, don't." He could hear the strain in Faelyn's voice.

"Enough," Aelrindel snapped in a voice full of command. "The choice is mine, Faelyn, and I have made it."

From the corner of his eye, he saw his friend respond to the tone of command, stiffening as if he'd been struck.

"As you wish," came the flat response.

Kaer'vaelen.

It would always lie between them.

Aelrindel reached out to the child and gently, with great care, gathered the foundling into his arms. Staring into its soft, wide eyes, he didn't see the glint of anger flash across then settle in Faelyn's eyes.

All around them, the river burned.

CHAPTER 2

The Year of Wild Magic
(1372 DR)

Taen shivered beneath thick blankets.

Bitter, ice-tinged air blasted the camp again and again, like the unrelenting breath of a white dragon. Despite his best efforts, fur, wool, and quilted cloak could not keep the chill at bay. Gathering what protection he could, he stumbled toward the dying fire. Tongues of red-gold flame swirled madly beneath the wind's hard lash, casting a riot of shadows across the camp. Unbidden, Taen's vision penetrated night's shifting shroud to reveal the uneven lumps of his companions, huddled under their own blankets and shivering in obvious misery. Their cursing reached his ears despite the wind's dreadful moaning and the sharp snapping of tree limbs.

Winter in Rashemen, he thought as he idly

poked at the burning logs with a soot-covered piece of wood, is as hospitable as the first layer of the Abyss. Six days from Mulptan and the raging weather had begun its assault. Snow and ice storms became constant companions. Shortly before dusk on the ninth day, a great wind had begun to blow, forcing them all to slow their pace and bend beneath its force. Even Borovazk, their Rashemi guide, had grown concerned. Throughout their journey, the normally brash ranger had gently chided their softness, poking fun at the group's complaints about harsh weather. When the wind had raised its deep-throated voice and howled through the snow-covered crags and across the rolling hills, however, Borovazk had grown quiet. "Is *nyvarskiz*," he had finally shouted so that they could all hear him. "Ill wind. Very dangerous." With that, he had put a halt to their travel, so they had made hasty camp amidst the uneven stones and ancient trees, miserably waiting out the storm.

Still, Marissa had asked them to come, driven by her connection to nature and, she had said, the secret promptings of her god. They had followed her across the eastern realms of Faerûn, then north through the harsh, unforgiving lands of the Rashemi. All of them had followed, as she had no doubt suspected they would.

"Where is she?" a gravelly baritone voice asked from the shadows behind him.

Taen dropped another log on the fire and turned to see Roberc gazing up at him. The broad-chested, thickset halfling danced from foot to booted foot, shivering in the cold despite being buried beneath several layers of fur skins. The gleam of the fighter's mail caught Taen's eyes in the dancing firelight. Not for the first time, he found himself wondering if the halfling ever removed his armor.

"I don't know. She went off into the trees after we set camp. You know how she is," Taen answered after a few moments.

Wild, he thought to himself. Restless the way a wolf is restless—or the wind. As usual, such thoughts threw him into turmoil. Marissa *was* restless, almost half wild, more comfortable with wood and stone than flesh and blood, yet a part of him yearned to lose himself in that wildness, to cast off the weight of memory and the certain knowledge of his own failure. Easier for a man to cast off his shadow, Taen knew.

Roberc swore, interrupting his bitter thoughts. "I'm glad that she feels free to go for a stroll while the rest of us freeze to death."

For a moment, Taen was shocked by the halfling's blasphemy, but only for a moment. There was little softness in the fighter, and none of the lighted-heartedness or playfulness found in others of his race. Thick stubble covered much of his chin and cheeks save for a single swath of blistered skin near the left corner of his mouth. The puckered flesh looked red and angry even now in the shadow-filled camp. When the halfling smiled, which was rarely, it never reached his deep-set eyes; they were gray and hard as river stone.

The fell wind gusted again, whipping the length of Roberc's salt-and-pepper hair in all directions. The fighter cursed once more against the bite of winter and brought two scarred fingers to his mouth. He whistled sharply once, then again. Almost immediately, there came a deep, echoing bark from somewhere close in the darkness beyond the fire. A few moments later, a large brindle hound came into view, running straight for the halfling.

The deep-chested dog came to a stop immediately in front of the fighter. Thick, panting breaths blew steam into the frigid air, and its long pink tongue lolled out of a short, powerful muzzle. The hound stood completely still, its thick-boned torso standing nearly above Roberc's head at its shoulder. A thick layer of studded leather barding covered most of the dog's rough outer coat, but Taen could still make out the curled length of its tail.

"Come, Cavan," the halfling said in a commanding voice. "Since we can't sleep, we might as well patrol. There's no telling what lurks about in this blasted land."

Taen watched, not for the first time, but always in amazement, as the hound cast his slightly angular head to the side questioningly then proceeded to lie down, allowing Roberc to mount. Once Roberc had secured himself, the fighter spoke another command and Cavan leaped to his feet, taking off into the darkness at a brisk gait.

Roberc was right. The night remained too cold for sleeping. Yet it wasn't the harsh breath of winter that kept Taen from sleep. Were he in the jungles of Chult or the feather bed of the finest inn in all of Waterdeep, sleep would still escape him when this mood descended upon him like a dark cloud, and the ghosts of his past whispered accusations with the voice of the wind. They surrounded him, pressing in on all sides, yet these haunting recollections held more than simple weight. "Bitter are the blades of memory." He had heard the *el'tael*, the swordmasters of Avaelearean, say that often enough. In those days, he had never known how much they had understated the truth of it. Would that he still lived in such ignorance. He'd lived through hundreds of battles and suffered wounds too numerous to count, yet none hurt near as much as those he carried within his heart. Tonight, beneath the lidless eye of the moon, with the wind raging like a banshee through the trees and stones, these wounds ached with a fierce intensity.

Taen ran a calloused hand across the rounded expanse of his head, shaved clean except for the single braided length of blond hair that reached to the center of his back, and let out a curse as his fingers touched the ever-so-slightly pointed tip of his ear. Here was the ultimate cause of his sorrow, the seed from which the razor-sharp thorn of his memories had sprung—not what he had done, but what he *was*.

Half-elf.

A Tel'Quessir.

Born of two peoples and claimed by none. A failure, unable to master the arts of the *laeriaen*. An exile.

A murderer.

The half-elf shivered at this last thought. Carefully, he threw a few more logs onto the fire and tried to absorb as much warmth as he could from the blaze. Sparks from the burning logs flew up into the dark sky. Taen gazed into the night long after they had disappeared, alone with his thoughts.

And the wind.

The wolf watched Taen with emerald-green eyes.

It sat on its haunches beneath the rippling limbs of trees. Moonlight bathed its furred pelt, catching flashes of silver across its shoulders and neck. It lifted its elegant muzzle and sniffed the night air redolent with the scent of prey. For a moment, its sleek muscles tensed, ready to carry it forward into the hunt.

Only for a moment.

Marissa Goldenthorn, druid and servant of Rillifane Rallathil, asserted control of the wild instincts coursing through her heart. Roberc and his war-dog were patrolling the far side of the woods, and she caught the musky scent of their Rashemi guide from within the camp. That left only Taenaran.

Taen, she corrected herself. The half-elf only cursed and carried on when she used his full name. For nearly seven years they had traveled together across the length and breadth of Faerûn, sometimes toward wealth and adventure, but always away from the past that rode the young half-elf like the Rashemi night hags of legend. He had shared some of the details over the course of their time together, whispered reminiscences during unguarded moments around the fire or when they were both deep in their cups. When that thrice-damned blightlord had taken her arm, Taenaran had held her in the night when the fever dreams wracked her broken body and spoke to her of his own loss.

Of Talaedra and the night that changed his life forever.

Marissa looked down at her wolf form and began to lick at the stub of her left leg. Even now, three years later, the missing limb still caused her pain. The priest had done the best he could, but the corruption of Talona's blight went beyond the power of the human, and it would not heal cleanly.

It was this loss, she supposed, that had bound her so closely to Taenaran. Both of them were incomplete, missing something essential to who they were. As she gazed upon the wounded half-elf, so obviously hounded by the wraiths of his past, the druid wanted nothing more than to cast off her form and go to him, to offer him the comfort that he had once offered to her.

Too much lay between them—history, blood, guilt.

And, Marissa thought sadly, not enough.

A rustling sound in the branches above caught the wolf's attention. Gazing up, Marissa saw a large, ghostly white raven alight on the tree. It peered down upon the wolf with an angry reddish eye before letting a harsh caw echo out into the night.

Marissa understood. The ill wind had finally passed and with it the glacial chill in the air. She barked a series of commands to the albino bird, confident that her magic would cause the raven to comprehend her wishes. With a final caw, it flew from the branch and headed toward the camp.

With the dying of the winter wind, her companions

could once more enjoy a restful night's sleep. They were only a few days from the lip of Immil Vale, then a few more to the heart of their journey—the Red Tree. Rashemi tales and legends spoke of the tree, found near the heart of Immil Vale, as a source of mystic lore and spiritual consolation. For months she had felt an inner pull toward Rashemen. Troubled by these thoughts of entering this forbidding land, Marissa had gone to the Silver Grove of Haneathaer, the Great Druid, for help in discerning this call. There, in a dream filled with strange wonder, her god had spoken to her, asking that she make pilgrimage to the ice-filled land of Rashemen and offer herself to the spirits of the Red Tree. The dream had ended after that. Rillifane had given her no other explanation, and she needed none.

The druid remembered her dream as if it had happened yesterday rather than months ago. Filled with pride and love for the god who had chosen her, she had asked her companions, brooding Taenaran and dour Roberc, to journey with her. They had both said yes—each for his reasons of his own, she knew.

At first, the harsh, snow-covered land of Rashemen had daunted her, but now, after nearly a month traversing its broad back, she saw its beauty. Nature's bounty touched every part of Faerûn, but here in Rashemen, the very land itself was alive and aware. Power suffused the entire landscape—from root-tip to mountaintop. The very air itself thrummed with the sacred, wild energy of creation.

Marissa nearly howled at the sheer joy of it, giving voice to the elation she felt within. Only the silent, brooding form of Taenaran held her silent. Soon she would fulfill the call of her god, then—who knew where life would take her.

With that thought, the wolf stood on her three legs and padded with the ease of long practice toward their camp.

For the first time in several days, quiet ruled the night.

Taen nearly jumped back, startled, when the silver wolf appeared before him. He would have given a shout of warning, but the creature's shape began to shift. Fur melted, blurred, and became thick black cloth; hind legs elongated, stretching as the supine form stood on two legs. For a moment, two shapes occupied the same space—wolf and woman—until the blurring stopped, leaving the woman in its place. Only her eyes remained the same, bright, crystalline green beneath a soft, smooth brow.

She smiled at him, accenting the angular planes of her high cheekbones. For a moment, Taen found it hard to catch his breath—so much did her smile remind him of another captivating woman. He watched as the druid unselfconsciously picked small twigs and burrs out of the rioting cascade of fiery red hair spilling down from her head. Though part human, Marissa favored her elf blood. Were the druid's graceful ears visible beneath the length of her lustrous hair, Taen knew that they would be almost indistinguishable from that of a full-blooded elf.

"Taen," she said to him in a rich, warm voice, "the hag-wind has ended. Go and find some rest with what is left of the night."

He gazed at her for a moment without speaking, conscious that she knew what had been hounding him this night.

"Marissa," he began then stopped, unable to continue.

The druid came closer, drawing her robe's cowled hood over her head as she did so. She reached out mud-covered fingers to touch his furrowed brow.

"Must you torment yourself now?" Marrisa asked.

"Our journey draws to a close, and we may have need of your strength."

Taen nearly snorted.

Strength.

What strength is there in a broken blade?

"You know I cannot sleep when I am like this," he replied, trying to keep the bitterness out of his voice—and failing.

"Then perhaps I can help . . ." she began.

"No, Marissa," Taen interrupted, "I would rather see the sunrise than lay ensorcelled beneath a spell. You know this too."

He winced slightly at the tone of his voice. After all of their years together, this still lay between them. The druid meant well, and he did not wish to hurt her any more, but anger, he knew from experience, rarely found its true target.

"Very well," she said from the depths of her cowl. Taen couldn't hear any blame or hurt in her calm tones—though he was sure it lay there, hidden.

She took a step back and turned as if to go.

"I wish only peace for you," she said before drifting into the shadows of the camp like a dream.

"I know," he replied to the empty air.

Murderers, he knew, rarely found peace.

CHAPTER 3

The Year of Wild Magic
(1372 DR)

The day dawned bright and clear.

Taen rolled out from beneath his furs and squinted as the ground's crystalline snow cover caught and reflected the sunlight. He cupped a hand across his eyes and gazed out at the frozen landscape. All around them, wind-rippled drifts of snow gathered like the waves of a white ocean, trapped in a still moment of time. Ice covered the scattered pine and ash trees surrounding the camp, slowly yielding to the winter sun with chilly tears, and for the first time in nearly a tenday, he could make out the granite shoulders of the Running Rocks looming in the sky to the south. Snow covered the glacial peaks like frigid armor, running almost their entire length.

The half-elf let out a groggy curse at the bracing chill of the air, the too-bright daylight, and, most of all, the weariness that clung to his body and mind like a lodestone. Predictably, he'd tossed and turned throughout the night, unable to find much comfort in sleep's blessed oblivion. He had finally succumbed to exhaustion as the first rays of the sun bloomed pink in the morning sky, only to be awakened by Borovazk's rumbling bass voice.

"Is time for the waking, little friends!" he exclaimed. "Much ground to cover today."

Taen hated that voice—if not the man, he had to admit. The Rashemi ranger had guided them skillfully across the lands of his birth. That much the half-elf had expected. What he hadn't expected was the trust and friendship that was growing between them. As annoying as Borovazk's obvious delight in their own discomfiture was, the broad-shouldered human more than made up for it with his bravery, skill in battle, and willingness to shed his own blood in the course of protecting those who hired him. Taen knew that the others felt the same way, though he doubted they'd admit it, especially during mornings like this.

With a sigh, the half-elf began to gather up his bedroll and stow what little gear he had brought in his pack. He certainly wasn't going to give Borovazk an excuse to berate him further by being the last one ready to go.

When he had finished, Taen grabbed his pack and walked to the center of the small camp to check on the others. Roberc acknowledged his presence with a scowl and a nod of his head. The halfling stood before Cavan, adjusting the straps of the hound's makeshift saddle and drawing deeply from a long, tapered bone pipe. The pungent scent of pipeweed, carried by the crisp morning breeze, filled the half-elf's nostrils.

He looked for Marissa and found her sitting on a small outcropping of rock above the smoldering ash of their fire. The druid gazed deeply at a small yellow flower growing stubbornly in a small crack of the rock's surface. Taen didn't even bother saying good morning to the half-elf, for he knew that she could stay like that all day, contemplating but a single fiber of one of the flower's petals. Marissa had always been like that, but more so now that they had entered this wild, unforgiving land. His own preference was for more temperate surroundings, such as the lush woodlands of his . . .

Home?

No, certainly not that, he thought. Not anymore. Home was a fable, a myth—a story spun by silver-tongued bards for coin or hearth. He had no home, he had no place to lay his head, except on the rough stones and tree roots of exile.

Borovazk's booming voice, raised lustily in song, broke through the dark turn of Taen's thoughts. The ranger led their horses, two thick-muscled dun geldings and his own chestnut stallion, to the center of camp. The Rashemi horses moved placidly, but Taen had ridden one enough to know that considerable strength and endurance lay within them when needed. The ranger stopped singing when he caught sight of the gathered companions. His strong-jawed face, framed by a thick, short-trimmed yellow-blond beard, broke into a smile, revealing a full set of large, white teeth. Twin lengths of thickly braided blond hair ran down to the center of his back.

"Ah, good morning, little friends," he said, absently stroking the thick mane of his stallion as he did so. "Is good to see you awake and together. Did you enjoy our little breeze last night?"

Despite the misery brought on by yesterday's weather, Taen found himself laughing at the ranger's jest.

"If that's a breeze, Borovazk," Taen replied, "I'd hate to see what it's like around here when the weather turns ugly."

Borovazk returned the laugh. "In bad weather, mostly my people just get drunk on *jhuild*," he said, referring to the dark reddish brew that others in Faerûn called firewine. Taen knew, from unfortunate experience, that *jhuild* could drop a berserking giant at twenty paces. "This way," he continued, "we not see how bad it really is."

The half-elf shook his head in mock disbelief—though he suspected that Borovazk spoke the truth. Despite the harsh weather they had experienced in Rashemen, all of the native Rashemi he had seen dressed as if it were merely late autumn and not the depth of winter. Even now, amidst the remains of the last few days' wintry assault, the ranger wore a simple fur vest over his chain mail, with thick leather trousers and fur boots covering the lower half of his body. His only concession to the bitter cold of the Rashemi winter was a rough-spun cloak made from the white pelt of a large bear that roamed the North Country of his land. Taen could see the wicked claws of the beast hanging from Borovazk's neck and wrists, bound with a thin leather strip.

"Come," the ranger said, all jesting absent from his voice. "Morning rides on and we will miss it if we do not hurry."

With one last pat of his stallion's crest, the Rashemi swung up onto his mount. Borovazk skillfully adjusted the scabbarded short sword and belted warhammer that were his constant companions while the horse threw its head to the side and snorted, obviously anxious to be away.

Taen grumbled with what he hoped was sufficient restraint so as not to be heard and mounted his own horse. He thought he might need to interrupt Marissa from her reverie but was pleasantly surprised when the druid sidled her own mount next to his and bid him good morning. Roberc, too, was ready, mounted on sturdy Cavan.

On Borovazk's command, the group filed out of the camp and resumed their journey. What little convocations of trees and vegetation they had seen since leaving Mulptan disappeared completely by midmorning, leaving only a wide swath of windswept snow-covered plains. The horses plodded forward, sure-footed and untiring, carrying Taen and his companions through league after league of unrelenting whiteness. The half-elf would surely have fallen asleep in his saddle by midday, but the voice of their Rashemi guide cut through his fatigue and boredom. Throughout the day, it would not stop rumbling across their trail. With great vigor, Borovazk regaled them with tales of Rashemen's history—of the mysterious witches and their ages-long battle with the cursed Red Wizards of Thay; of the deeds wrought by the great heroes of the land, many somehow distantly related to the teller of those tales; and finally, of the ranger's own family, his wife and three brawny children.

By late afternoon, the group reined in their horses and dismounted for a brief rest. Pulling out cold strips of roast venison, slabs of thick-rinded cheese, and servings of a pickled root the Rashemi called *ordsk* from their saddlebags, they ate a brief meal beneath the fading light of the day.

Amazingly, Borovazk continued to spin tales. Between great tearing bites of meat and long swigs of firewine, the ranger spoke of his wife and how, after he had stumbled home drunk late one night from a gathering of warriors, she had felled him with a single blow from an oak cudgel and dragged him out to a snowdrift where he had spent the night. When he had awakened bleary eyed and groggy late the next morning, the wounded man returned to an empty home only to discover that the cudgel had split beneath the force of his wife's blow.

"That's horrible," exclaimed Marissa.

The rest of the group, having finished their meal, sat comfortably on thick wool blankets. Roberc puffed indolently on his pipe, one hand stroking Cavan's fur.

"Is indeed horrible, little witch," the ranger agreed, with more than a hint of sadness in his voice. "That cudgel was one of Borovazk's favorites!"

Taen watched as the concern in Marissa's eyes changed to disbelief then merriment. The druid began to laugh, followed soon after by Borovazk's deep-chested chuckle. Taen found himself smiling at the outrageous ranger. Even Roberc's normally taciturn face held a wry grin.

After a few more moments, their Rashemi guide stood up.

"Come," he said, wiping venison grease from his beard with a swipe of a thick arm. "Is still a while before dark. We have many more leagues to travel, and I," he jabbed a meaty finger at his own chest, "have many more stories to tell."

Taen laughed, still caught up in the lighthearted moment.

"I bet you do," Taen said as they broke their makeshift camp. "You seem to talk more than any human I have ever met."

That brought another chuckle from the Rashemi ranger.

"Tell me, Borovazk," Taen continued, emboldened by his companion's reaction, "does your wife enjoy your stories as much as you seem to?"

The ranger stopped what he was doing and cast a puzzled look at him. "I not know," he said after a moment. "My Sasha is as deaf as the stones of the Icerim Mountains." He laughed then, a full-throated guffaw, and slapped the half-elf hard on the back before mounting his horse.

Taen pitched forward, stumbling from the force of the blow. It wasn't until he sat in the saddle of his own mount and the group started forward once again that he realized he couldn't tell whether Borovazk had been kidding or not.

❀ ❀ ❀ ❀ ❀

By luck or some unasked-for blessing of the gods, the weather held over the next three days—crisp and clear, with only an occasional dusting of snow swirling and circling to the ground. In the face of such a gift, the group traversed a good deal of terrain. Taen found himself marveling at the steady, economical pace of their horses, crunching through drifts and ice with such surefooted grace. Lulled by the rolling rhythm of his mount and the now-gentle speech of the wind, he began to relax and look at the white-coated world around him, not as a thing to be endured, but as an experience to be savored. There was a beauty—a wisdom—in the broad sweep of plain and rock-strewn valleys of this wild land. Each step of his horse brought him deeper into that wildness, carried him to the heart of a mystery for which he had no name—only a sense of rock, ice, and unforgiving wind. In those moments, he thought that he could understand the pride and strength of the rough-tongued and insular Rashemi people. They were born from the very soil of wilderness, lived in harmony with its harsh rhythms, hewn and formed by its untamed forces the way rocks are shaped by the elements. They were heirs to wind-swept mountains, ice-curdled lakes, and the deep, enduring promise of the land.

Taen traveled onward with his companions. Borovazk must have sensed the half-elf's change in mood, else he, too, was caught in the grip of such reflections, for the Rashemi's stories and songs had eventually tapered off, allowing the wind-ruffled silence of the plains to replace his voice. The half-elf did not speak, dared not speak, against the vast silence of the landscape, and he knew that the others felt the same way.

Once or twice each day, Marissa would dismount and hand the reins of her horse to him. In moments, she would be running ahead of them in wolf shape, scouting their path or hunting in the fading light of day, only to return with a brace of hare, her own hunger sated.

They ate in silence.

Only Roberc seemed unaffected by their surroundings. Dozing in Cavan's saddle or drawing his blade across a whetstone, the halfling appeared to Taen as dour and as solemn as he always did. Early on the morning of their third day of silence, he drew his dun close to the halfling's war-dog and threw a questioning look down at the warrior. Roberc gazed up impassively and simply shrugged before leading Cavan into a loping run that put him well in front of the walking horses.

By afternoon of the next day, their fifteenth day out of Mulptan, the air grew noticeably warmer. Ice-covered snow gave way to wet-packed drifts, and a thin mist had begun to permeate the air. By the first fall of dusk, the horses had to slog through thick piles of slippery slush, and Borovazk eventually called an early halt to their travel.

The change in weather precipitated a change in mood as well. Taen felt free of the awe that had gripped him the past few days, as if the loosening of winter's grip had somehow loosened his tongue as well.

"Why is it getting so warm?" he asked their guide.

"Who cares," interjected Roberc as he helped his furred mount free of the leather barding that protected it. "It's just nice not to have your nose hairs freeze every time you take a breath."

"Indeed, little friends," Borovazk replied. "It will be much better for you now. We draw near to Immil Vale. Winter's heart cannot touch it. It is blessed by the gods—a gift to my people for their strength and bravery, eh?"

"How much further do we have to go?" Marissa asked.

The ranger smiled at her. "Ah, my little witch," he said with obvious affection. "You grow anxious. You not worry. Borovazk know a path that will take us into vale. Two days at most."

Taen awoke that morning feeling uneasy. Twice during the night he had been startled awake by a sound that he wasn't sure he had heard. He'd swept the area surrounding their camp during his turn at watch but had found nothing that would indicate his suspicions were well founded.

Still, the half-elf couldn't shake the feeling that something was watching him from somewhere out on the plain. That feeling grew throughout the day as they headed west toward their destination. Taen stood in his saddle and cast his glance as far as he could—but saw nothing. Finally, he indicated his suspicions to Borovazk.

The ranger nodded. "I feel it too," the Rashemi answered. "We are being followed."

From then on, they all kept a careful watch. Taen noted that Cavan threw his thick muzzle into the air and sniffed suspiciously several times, while the horses seemed unusually skittish.

The tension mounted.

Sometime after midday, Marissa's white raven flew raucously to her outstretched arm. The druid nodded as the bird continued to caw and croon. Finally, she sent it back into the air with a flick of her arm.

"We *are* being followed," she confirmed their fears. "Rusella says that there are several landwalkers keeping their distance behind us."

Taen nodded at the news. At least he hadn't been imagining things. His heart began to beat rapidly. Whatever it was behind them, the fact that they were trailing them probably meant that they weren't friendly.

Roberc drew Cavan even with Marissa's mount.

"Exactly what is behind us?" Roberc asked. "How many will we need to face?"

The druid shook her head. "I do not know," she replied.

"For all of her intelligence, Rusella *is* simply a raven."
Taen watched as she stared at the sky. "There is an easy
way to find out, though," she said after a moment and
dismounted abruptly from her horse. Before Taen or
anyone else could gainsay her, the druid took the shape of
a falcon—a bright red-gold kestrel—and launched herself
into the air with wind-swift wings. She cleaved through
the air like an arrow, soaring higher and higher, until
Taen lost sight of her.

The half-elf cursed. Then, quickly gathering the reins
of Marissa's horse, drew close to Borovazk. The Rashemi
sat thoughtfully on his stallion.

"The little witch is powerful, yes?" asked Borovazk.

"Yes, she is," Taen replied, unable to keep the worry
out of his voice.

"Then do not fear, little friend," the ranger said. "She
will return to us and we will know what is following."
Borovazk drew the curved length of his polished horn
bow from its resting place across his back.

Taen nodded but said nothing. He kept scanning the
sky, waiting for some sign of Marissa's return. A few
moments later, the sharp-noted screech of a hunting
falcon echoed across the plain, followed by a fast-moving
speck circling high in the air. The speck drew closer and
closer to the ground, until it finally alit with a rustling
of wings and pinions. The air shimmered and Marissa
stood once more in their midst.

"Ice trolls," she gasped, as if winded from her brief
flight. "Five of them. They are heading our way fast."
She grabbed the reins of her horse from Taen and swung
quickly into the saddle.

From behind him, Taen heard Borovazk say something harsh in his native tongue.

"Well, little friends," Borovazk said with a fierce grin
on his face, "it looks like we have some fun today. Ice
trolls must be very hungry to hunt this close to vale.
They do not like the heat."

"Can we outrun them?" Roberc asked. The halfling sat astride Cavan confidently, loosening the knot that held his red-hilted short sword in its scabbard. At the first mention of being followed, he had donned the gold-winged helm that he always wore into battle. It gleamed brilliantly in the midmorning sun.

Borovazk grunted. "Is unlikely that we could outdistance them," he replied. "Melting snow, slush, and mud is slippery even for Rashemi horses. No, little friends, it looks like we must fight."

Unlike many of those who adventured across Faerûn, Taen did not enjoy warfare. The prospect of battling trolls in the hinterlands of Rashemen was not a thing to set the blood singing through his veins. Still, he recognized the necessity of it—even welcomed it, if it would silence the nagging voice of doubt that whispered to him of his own failures. Protecting Marissa and his other companions from danger just might do that.

"We should find a better place to stand our ground," he said.

"Borovazk agrees," came the ranger's response. "Come, I know of such a place close by." With that, he kicked his stallion into a fast trot and motioned for them to follow.

Unlike the sheer plains they had traveled across from Mulptan, the land close to the Immil Vale rolled gently up and down. The ranger led them to the top of one such slope, carefully dismounting and walking his stallion. The ground was soft and muddy, covered with the thick slush that had been their companion for the past two days.

Taen nodded his approval as they gathered at the top of the slope. Their position gave them a good vantage point for spotting and bringing down their enemy with ranged weapons and spells, while the soft earth would slow any attack should the trolls manage to get close enough to attack.

" 'Ware their spittle, little friends," Borovazk cautioned

as he placed five dark-wooded arrows point down in the soft earth. The color of their fletching shifted from bright red to orange then back again while the ranger spoke. "It will freeze the very blood in your veins."

Even though he and his companions had fought trolls before, Taen appreciated the advice on dealing with this "homegrown" variety. Deftly, he riffled through the various small pouches hanging from his belt, sorting and sifting through the items that he would need. When he had completed that task, he turned to Marissa.

The druid had sent Rusella winging off into the distance and gazed out upon the plain. She had thrown back her hood, and her red hair rustled wildly around her face. Taen knew the measure of her power and knew that they had faced such threats and worse before, side by side. Still, he had been avoiding her since the night she had spoken to him about the past. He owed her an apology and much more; he wanted to do it now in case he never had the chance again.

The half-elf gently reached out a hand and placed it on Marissa's shoulder. The green-eyed druid gazed upon Taen and smiled. His tongue felt heavy, ungainly.

"I . . . I wanted to say thank you," he spoke finally, "for trying to help me the other night. You know I—"

"I do know," she interrupted, switching to the liquid phrases of Elvish, "but don't we have more important things to worry about at the moment, Taenaran?" Her teasing tone brought a smile to his face even as the sound of his elf-given name tore at his heart.

He wanted to reply, even started to, but Borovazk's voice boomed out across the slope.

"They have come, little friends," the ranger shouted. "Now is time to have some fun, yes?"

Taen gave the druid's shoulder a quick, final squeeze and turned to face their monstrous enemies, hoping against hope that he wouldn't have to draw his sword.

CHAPTER 4

The Year of the Morningstar
(1350 DR)

The children were throwing stones again.

Sharp-edged and round, the tiny missiles hissed through the air, biting Taenaran's skin. The young half-elf dodged as best he could, skittering through the lush undergrowth of the forest and cutting between the thick trunks of oak and ash trees that rose like woodland giants into the sky. Still, the stones found their target—for they were elf-thrown and true.

Tears spilled from his eyes as he ran, warping and bending the landscape. Taenaran tripped over an outstretched tree root and tumbled to the ground. He wanted to give voice to the hurt that was welling up inside him, but he wouldn't allow the other children the satisfaction of hearing him wail like the *voeraen*, the elf toddlers who stayed close to their mothers and fathers.

That thought nearly undid his young resolve—for he had neither blood father nor blood mother among the elves of Avaelearean, which was, he knew from past experience, the cause of today's problems. They had been playing "Hunt the Drow" in the wide forest when a few of the older children started throwing rocks at Taenaran and calling him a drider, a horrifying creature spoken of in whispers by the adult elves, made up of both drow and spider. It wasn't long before the others had joined in, so he ran—from the sharp bite of stones and the sharper bite of the Elvish words the children had flung at him like arcane arrows. "Round Ear." "Monkey Face." "*A Tel'Quessir* Bastard." These were the names that followed him wherever he went. If they weren't spoken aloud, he could see them in the eyes of the elf children, and even in the eyes of some of the adults of Avaelearean.

With a heaving sigh, Taenaran wiped the dirt from his clothes as best he could and stood up. The other elf children were still hunting in the forest, calling out his name, and worse. For once, his human heritage helped him. Though he was younger than the others, some of whom were born almost two decades ago, the half-elf's muscles were thicker and more developed. Now they carried him away from his tormentors faster than they could follow.

He ran for quite some time, through slanting shafts of sunlight and shallow pools of rainwater, down moss-covered deer tracks and winding switchbacks. Certain that he had left his pursuers well behind him, Taenaran stopped in the center of a wind-tossed oak grove to catch his breath. His chest felt tight, not from exertion, but from hurt and confusion and a growing anger that smoldered in his heart.

He began to cry once more.

Why?

Why did they treat him this way? He *was* different,

but all he wanted to be was like them—an elf. Why couldn't they see that? Even the elders, though not cruel like their children, treated him like a strange thing—as if he were a snowfall in summer—and they did not seem to know what to make of him.

He was tired of it—tired of the veiled insults and the sidelong looks. After only ten seasons among the elves of Avaelearean, he knew that he would never find a place among them unless something changed—unless he accomplished something that even the most tradition-bound elder would be forced to recognize.

It was then, beneath the rustling leaves of an elf grove, with blood from a dozen cuts trickling down his skin, that the half-elf made his first vow.

By the time he reached the sprawling tree home of his foster father, Taenaran had locked away his tears.

Music filled the elf-wrought bower, spilling wild and free like a swirling spring rainfall. Aelrindel's calloused fingers skipped and danced across the golden strings of the dark yew harp, calling forth note, phrase, and sprightly theme. The elf's eyes were closed, his sight and senses turned inward as he followed the trail of his song through his heart's twisting path. He was often like this—lost in the music. Whether he held a sword or a harp, both were weapons in his hands and gates to another realm.

When at last the elf opened his eyes and saw his *arael'vae*, his heart-son, standing before him, he ended the song abruptly. Dirt and mud were caked on the lad's leggings and tunic. His shoulder-length hair clung to his head, matted with bramble-burr and mossdew. It was Taenaran's blood, however, running like red tears down the length of his shoulders and arms, which aroused a familiar rush of pity and anger in the elf's breast.

Aelrindel placed the yew harp gently on the window-sill and prepared to go to the half-elf. For in times past, when the boy would come home ragged and crying, he would launch himself into his father's arms, seeking comfort.

This time, though, was different.

Something in the cast of the half-elf's eyes stopped Aelrindel's motion. He saw resolve and steel in their amber depths—and perhaps something of the adult that Taenaran would become. The elf grieved, for in that moment he knew that his relationship with his son had changed forever. Even though, Aelrindel thought, it was ever the way between fathers and sons, still he grieved.

"Who did this, Taenaran?" was all that he said—though carefully.

The half-elf might be only a decade old, the merest babe by the standards of the elves, but he held within him human blood and was already sprouting like a young sapling. He did not wish to wound the boy further by treating him as a complete child.

Taenaran gazed at him, eyes red with the aftermath of tears.

"Does it matter?" came his son's response.

Aelrindel frowned at that but could not gainsay the youngling's words. In truth it did not matter. The elf children had always been cruel with their games where Taenaran was involved—and that likely would continue. He had spoken with the elders and parents of the community, and those who felt pity or compassion for an *a Tel'Quessir* foundling spoke, in turn, to their young.

Yet children were, after all is said and done, still children.

"They will never accept me," Taenaran said, breaking through the elf's thoughts.

Aelrindel tried to respond, tried to say that such acceptance would come in time, but his son cut him off.

"They will never accept me," the half-elf said in a steady voice, "unless I do something to make them accept me."

The elder elf raised a pointed eyebrow at his son's assertion.

"What," Aelrindel asked with true curiosity, "will you do?"

Taenaran inhaled deeply then hesitated a moment before replying.

"I wish to become a bladesinger like you," Taenaran said. "Like my father."

Aelrindel stood for a moment—speechless and stunned—before pride bloomed within his heart like a lilaenril blossom in spring. Half-elf the boy may be and bastard born, yet it was *he* who had the shaping of him. Though wounded by the prejudice and spite of others, still the lad's roots grew strong and true. He was proud in a way that only fathers can be and thought, for just a moment, how much his decision by the side of a burning river had changed his own life.

Taenaran gazed up at him, grave and silent, obviously waiting for his reaction. When he gave it, Aelrindel pushed down his paternal instincts and became First Hilt.

"The Way is difficult," he intoned solemnly, "and more difficult for you than for the others." He spoke truthfully, for such a desire as his son had revealed deserved the truth.

Taenaran's next words filled the First Hilt's spirit to bursting.

"Still," the boy responded with reserve and dignity worthy of an elder, "I would walk that path. Will you allow me to try?"

Aelrindel thought for a moment. The others would raise their objections—especially Faelyn. The rest of the *el'tael* would eventually acquiesce, for he was First Hilt. The training, however, would be challenging for

Taenaran, and many would probably push him harder than the other *tael* in hopes that he would fail. Still, he could not deny his son this chance, so whether through wisdom or folly, discernment or pride, Aelrindel, First Hilt of the Bladesingers of Avaelearean, found himself saying "yes" to a boy's dream.

That *yes* brought a shout of joy to the half-elf's lips and an end to the reservoir of bravery and pride that kept father and son distant from each other. Tears welled up in Taenaran's eyes as he launched himself into Aelrindel's outstretched arms.

"*Va*," was all Aelrindel heard as his arms enfolded the sobbing ten-year-old.

Father.

Eyes closed, he listened once more to the song in his heart.

CHAPTER 5

The Year of Wild Magic
(1372 DR)

The ice trolls charged.

Taen watched as they ran, stoop-shouldered, across the snow-covered ground—white on white, their gelid skin glistening sickly in the sunlight. Each of them carried a large warhammer in the wicked curve of their clawed hands. The trolls barked and hissed to each other in a guttural language that sounded to the half-elf like the terrible echoes of an avalanche.

Around him, Taen's companions stood ready. Borovazk sighted down the shaft of an arrow, while Roberc held the haft of a golden war axe in a white-knuckled grip. The halfling's rounded shield hung steady on his other arm. Only Taen and Marissa stood weaponless—though the half-elf could see that the druid, eyes half lidded and mouth already reciting prayers to her god, was prepared to unleash the powers at her command. Cavan growled softly as the trolls closed the gap between them.

"Just a little bit more, my friends. A little bit more," Taen heard Borovazk whisper.

They all waited, bound by an unspoken agreement to follow the ranger's lead. Still, Taen could feel the familiar rush of energy that coursed over him whenever battle drew near. His heart pounded, strength flowed through his limbs, and the world snapped into clear focus, as if he spent most of his life walking in a land of shadows and fog, made truly real only when the specter of death rose above him. *Zaen'sheaen*, the all-seeing gaze, his masters had called it—a full awareness of life and its dangers. He experienced it now, along with something else he had thought he'd left behind in the forests of Avaelearean. Something stirred in his heart—a faint melody, like the soft strains of a bard's lay sung in the depths of the night, when the cups are empty, the fire has spent its strength, and shadows fall long upon the corners of the hall.

The Song.

Taen heard it now, the heart of the bladesinger's art—heard it in a way that he rarely had studying among the elves. For a moment, he stood in wonder.

The Song, however, gave him neither hope nor strength, for he heard within its mysterious strains the voice of his failure. It mocked him—mocked his struggle to live among the elves, mocked the choices he'd made in exile, and perhaps most of all, mocked the love he still felt for *her*.

He would have shouted his defiance of that Song, but just then Borovazk's voice cut through his awareness.

"Now!" the ranger shouted and, before Taen could draw another breath, loosed two arrows at the advancing trolls. The missiles leaped from the ranger's bow like wolves coursing for their prey. Both struck true, biting deeply into the white flesh of a single troll. Red flame erupted from the site of both wounds. The troll stumbled for a moment, clutching at his side, then fell screaming to the ground. Flames continued to burn as it rolled upon the slush-covered earth.

Taen watched in horrified fascination as another of the trolls stopped before its wounded companion and launched a glob of freezing spittle from its mouth. The disgusting globule covered the wounded monster and extinguished the burning flame. The other three trolls continued their charge.

Quickly, for he wanted to make sure he caught all of the trolls, Taen reached into one of the pouches that hung from his belt and began to recite the words of a spell. Power swelled in him and he felt the presence of his armor as the spell grew, its steel threatening to unbind the forces he commanded. His skill prevailed, and the magic came. He held it within him for the span of a few heartbeats, delighting in the energy that filled every space within his being. Then, with a single command he released the spell. A simple glowing bead shot out from the tip of his index finger, growing larger as it soared toward the trolls. Fire engulfed the hapless monsters as the bead struck the ground between the fallen troll and his companions. Only four trolls continued forward.

Immediately after, Taen heard Marissa's voice chanting the words to another spell. The shape of the words were different than his own arcane language, and although he couldn't understand them, he heard within their rolling cadence—heard within the rhythmic pulse of their sounds and their silence—praise, supplication, and most of all power. When she had finished, the ground upon which the trolls ran erupted into a riot of green grass and thorny vines. The tangle of greenery reached out to grab legs, arms, and muscled torsos. Within moments, two of the trolls were immobilized within the area of the swirling plants. The remaining two fought their way out slowly, tearing out the tangling grass and thick vines by their roots.

Before they had fully emerged from the confines of Marissa's spell, Roberc gave a single command to his mount and Cavan sped down the hill toward the monsters. The halfling gave out a great battle cry in the language of his people before engaging the trolls. One of the creatures, seeing the fighter approach, lashed out with a wide sweep of its clawed hand. Roberc ducked low on the war-dog's furred back and the troll's claws swept cleanly over his head. Gold glinted in the sun as the fighter's sword bit deep into the monster's leg.

The other troll took a step back from Roberc's assault and opened its gray-toothed mouth. Freezing spittle erupted from the beast. Taen watched as Cavan struggled to turn away from the disgusting attack—and failed. Both dog and fighter were covered in the freezing goo.

Roberc screamed once in pain but pressed his attack, obviously undaunted. Three more swings of the fighter's blade brought pale troll blood spilling onto the ground. Taen was about to launch another spell at Roberc's opponents when a slight scuffling sound caused him to turn. Another troll, one that Marissa obviously hadn't seen, charged up the hill behind the companions.

The half-elf didn't have time to shout a warning. He simply threw himself in the path of the advancing beast, drawing his red-hilted sword as he did so. Closer now to a troll, Taen could see that its skin was a sickly, transparent white; beneath its gelid surface, pale blood coursed through a webbing of thick blue veins. The troll bellowed once as it swung the great heft of its warhammer. The half-elf danced quickly back from the blow, barely avoiding the crushing attack as the iron head of the hammer struck the ground with so much force that it embedded itself into the half-frozen soil. Seeing his chance, Taen darted forward, aiming a downward swing of his sword to strike the troll's outstretched arm. Silver runes flared along the elven blade as it cut through translucent skin and thick muscle.

The strains of the Song soared within his heart, joined now by the voice of his sword—his father's sword, the ancient weapon passed down from generation to generation, from the golden age of Cormanthyr, from the hands of heroes, down through the ages until finally it reached *him*. Exile. Unworthy.

The Song leached strength from his muscle, and he nearly dropped the weapon from nerveless fingers. A shout from Marissa roused him, however. The troll had finally managed to free his weapon and advanced once again. Taen retreated ever so slightly, wanting to keep the creature away from Borovazk, whose fiery arrows were making short work of the still-entangled trolls but also needing to give himself room to avoid the deadly weight of the warhammer.

Wordlessly, Marissa joined the half-elf in his battle, standing slightly to his side. The druid raised the leather-covered stump of her left arm. Purple light glowed from the spidery runes burned into the leather as a blade made entirely of flames sprang from the end of her arm. She moved forward, swinging the fiery weapon in a wide arc. Taen watched the troll give way before the druid's attack. Once again he darted forward, striking at the troll's unprotected flank. His sword sliced deeply into the creature's side and it stumbled.

Immediately, Marissa sprang into action. Her flaming blade cut once then twice, across its shoulder. The troll screamed and lashed wildly out at its attacker. The curve of its clawed hand raked against the flesh of Marissa's neck. This time, the druid stumbled back, nearly falling as she grabbed at the wound.

Taen immediately dropped his sword and hissed the words to another spell. The troll's flesh, torn by the edge of his blade, had begun to seal as the creature's ability to regenerate kicked in. He needed something fast and deadly. No sooner had he finished the words to the spell than four silver-white beams of mystic energy streaked from his hands to strike the creature full in the chest.

It screamed again at the four smoking wounds and opened its mouth, no doubt to spew forth its freezing spittle, but at himself or the wounded druid, Taen did not know. He was prepared to launch himself in the path of the attack to protect Marissa when an arrow hissed by the half-elf's head and struck the troll full in the mouth. Instead of the freezing viscous liquid he'd expected, Taen watched in wonderment as flames and thick steam erupted from the creature's mouth. With a long, gurgling sigh, the troll fell to the ground.

"Yes, little friends," Borovazk said in his cheer-filled voice, "we have much fun in Rashemen, no?"

Taen ignored the ranger for a moment and drew near Marissa. The druid, however, waved him off.

"I'm fine," she said, removing her fingers from her neck to reveal an already healing wound. Though long, the troll's claws had not cut too deeply into her flesh. The half-elf could see that she had healed most of the damage with her own power.

Confident that Marissa would be all right, Taen looked out over the battlefield. Roberc, his armor and shield bent and battered, had dismounted and now stood over the dead trolls. He poured black oil from a flask on the corpses and set them afire with the burning length of a wood torch.

Taen walked toward the halfling fighter with Marissa at his side while Borovazk set to burning the single corpse up on the hillock. The ground where the halfling stood was covered in bloodstained slush and churned earth. As they drew closer, Taen could see that both Roberc and Cavan were bleeding from multiple wounds. Marissa spoke gently to the dog, and he limped toward her, his fur caked in blood, dirt, and gore. The druid knelt before the hurt animal and reached out a slender hand, placing it along the bleeding edge of Cavan's wounds. Singing softly into the dog's ear, the druid sent healing power into the dog until Taen could clearly see Cavan's wounds close. Once they had finished burning the corpses, Taen and his companions gathered around the horses.

"Let us mount, little friends," Borovazk said. "We are not far from the vale, and I do not want to delay us any longer."

Before he mounted, Taen bent to retrieve the sword he had cast aside. Gingerly, he wrapped his fingers around the worn red hilt, as if expecting—he knew not what. As he cleaned the blade and placed it into its scabbard, only silence ruled his heart.

CHAPTER 6

The Year of Wild Magic
(1372 DR)

Fog muffled the sound of their horses' hooves.

Taen walked in silence like the others, leading his horse carefully down the steep path, following the surefooted tread of their guide. He peered through the thickening gray haze and caught only the barest hint of their surroundings in the swirling, nebulous curtain: here, the suggestion of a tree; there, a dim outline of rock or the blurred expanse of a berry bramble. Though they hadn't been walking the curving path to Immil Vale for long, the half-elf felt as if he and his companions had left Faerûn and now strode through another plane of existence. Everything took on a muzzy cast, vaporous and indistinct, as they walked through this seemingly endless expanse of gloom and fog—until Taen himself felt that he, too, must be half-made from mist, insubstantial as a wraith in this swirling dreamscape.

If he dreamed, at least it was a dream of spring.

Borovazk had been right. Whether through some divine blessing or other more natural means, the area around Immil Vale radiated warmth and life. Soon after leaving behind the remains of their battle with the ice trolls, Taen and his companions had witnessed the snow and slush disappearing, leaving only the rapidly thawing wine-dark soil that covered this part of Rashemen. Shoots and saplings had sprung up across the rolling landscape, tender, green, and tentative. The half-elf had watched them growing thicker and stronger as they neared the vale. By the time his group had reached the trailhead, they were surrounded by a riot of bud and bramble, root and tree. A gentle, misting rain had begun to fall as they set off, wordlessly, into a dream of spring.

The heady, earth-rich scent of loam filled the air, tickling his nose as each step churned the earth beneath his feet. In the silence of the journey, Taen could hear the chittering of marmots, chipmunks, titmice, and squirrels. Birdsong filled the air, distant and muted but familiar—the warble of the grosbeak and hooded crow, the twitter of the nuthatch, and the echoing attack of the woodpecker. Winter was a distant memory, an old song whose words danced across the mind, half forgotten, even as the tune remained.Taen walked on in silence, enjoying the warmth. He'd exchanged his thick leathers and wool robe for lighter clothes and a simple, homespun cloak of rough cloth. The change in weather also made the battle with the trolls seem even more distant, and for that he was very grateful. His experience with the Song unnerved him, not only because of its strength, but also because he had heard another voice in it—the sword's. Never before had he felt the power of his father's blade come alive in such a way. He had heard its voice, and it shook him to the core.

Taen didn't know what it might mean, but it couldn't be good. He thought he'd left all of that behind him in sorrow and in death. He was *a Tel'Quessir*. A failure. There was no room in his life for the Song—or the hopes of his heart. They were distant memories, reminders of what he could never be.

"How much longer until we've reached the damned tree?" Roberc asked as he caught up with Taen. The halfling's voice, normally gravely, seemed even rougher from lack of use.

The half-elf pushed down his irritation at the fighter's interruption. It was rare for his grizzled companion to begin a conversation. There was no sense in wasting this opportunity, and it offered him a chance to escape from his dark thoughts.

"One day to reach the bottom of the vale," Taen replied, recalling Borovazk's estimation as they had set out upon the trail, "and then half a day's walk to the Red Tree."

Roberc nodded and drew a long draught from his waterskin. When he had finished, he lifted it up, offering it to Taen.

"Do you know what it is she is seeking?" the halfling asked.

The half-elf reached out and grabbed the waterskin, shooting Roberc a thankful look. He took a swig, letting the cool, clear water swish around his dry mouth before swallowing.

"No," he replied after taking another drink, "but I doubt that she does either." He handed the skin back. "Such is the will of the gods, I suppose."

Roberc snorted. "The gods—" he began and looked around, as if seeking something, but never finished his statement.

Which was just as well, as far as Taen was concerned. He'd grown used to the fighter's blasphemous speech and seeming indifference to the various faiths of Faerûn.

Even so, the halfling's contempt for piety and the ways of the gods sometimes made him nervous. Taen didn't know what lay behind the fighter's attitude, despite years of adventuring together and countless nights around a fire, with only the wind and their voices to keep them company. The halfling didn't speak much about his past, about his life before he took up adventurering—and he certainly never spoke of the scarred burn near his mouth. Sometimes he would talk about an old battle or tell a story of an evening's diversion in a tavern, otherwise Roberc was a generally quiet, if dour, companion.

A mystery.

When Taen thought about it during quiet moments, it made sense. Marissa, Roberc, and he—all three of them—carried burdens hidden from the world. Their scars ran deeper than flesh, and so did their friendship. They had found each other, these individuals who, separated, would each likely fall prey to despair or the dangers of the world. Together, they offered comfort, hope, and strength, yet their burdens existed, lightened by the sharing, but not healed.

Roberc remained a mystery.

Normally, Taen would let such a mystery lie, for he often kept his own thoughts private and did not relish baring his wounds for all to see, but there was something about the vale—whether it was the ever-present newness of spring, or the feeling of walking in a fog-shrouded dream, Taen couldn't be sure—that raised his curiosity. He found himself turning back to the halfling, searching for the right words.

"What about the gods?" he asked finally after Roberc had caught him staring for the third time. "Do you believe in them?"

Roberc looked up at Taen, and the half-elf caught a glimpse, just for one moment, of fire behind the halfling's dead gray eyes.

"Of course I believe in them," the fighter answered

after a moment. "You'd have to be a half-wit to deny their existence. The gods"—he snorted this time as he said the word—"they exist just like stone, wind, snow, and fire, but they are no gods of mine. A man may just as easily dig out of an avalanche with a dirk as pry himself out from under the finger of the gods once he's put himself there. No thank you.

"You want to know what I believe in?" Roberc asked, grabbing Taen's hand and stopping on the trail. "I believe in my sword. I believe in courage. I believe that a man's life is a candle held out in defiance of the darkness, and it burns, as all things burn, for as long as there is wax, wick, and hope. I believe that in the end, darkness comes for us all—even the gods.

"Life," Roberc whispered, "is in the burning. That's what I believe."

Taen stared at his companion, held still as much by the passion in his voice as by the fierce grip on his arm. What of friendship? He would have asked this of the halfling, but just then Borovazk called for a halt, and Roberc released his grip and went forward to help set up their camp.

CHAPTER 7

The Year of Wild Magic
(1372 DR)

Marissa dismounted and knelt before the stream.

Within the sound of its burbling water she heard the voice of the spirit, the telthor as Borovazk had called it, speak to her heart. She was aware of the others gathered around her, watching and waiting from tall seats astride their tired mounts. The druid reached to her belt and drew forth her waterskin. Gently, whispering words of thanks and gratitude, she poured the last remaining drops of water from the container, mingling the fresh snow melt from her earlier travels with the clear, sweet runoff from the stream. Deep within, she felt the telthor's approval and found herself smiling as she refilled her skin.

Water spun and rose into the air like a

funnel. Slowly it bent toward the druid and touched her cheek, gently, like the soft caress of a young child. Behind her, she heard Borovazk mutter something before he dismounted and knelt before the running water. The Rashemi ranger spoke rapidly in his native tongue then stood. A moment later the water funnel straightened then gradually fell back into the stream.

The spirit's presence departed.

Marissa remained on her knees, stunned by the intimate communion she had just experienced. Truly, the gods had crafted a land of wonders when Rashemen came into being. Even the wilds of Cormyr, the land of her youth, couldn't compare to what she had experienced here in such a short amount of time. Thoughts of her childhood came back to her. Raised in Waymoot, near the heart of the King's Forest, she had spent many years wandering the deer trails and hidden paths of the woodlands while her father toiled away at his trading business, burying himself in work to forget the fog-shrouded day he had buried his wife, Marissa's mother, an elf bard from Evereska. Perhaps Marissa reminded her father too much of what he'd lost, but soon after her mother's death, he had retreated into ledgers and factor notes, pushing her away. She had grown up in the shadow of the oak and alder trees of the King's Forest, counting her years as they came from the heights of shrub-studded bluffs and the depths of root caves, fatherless and motherless—unless the moon-throated example of wolf and the night-hunting owl could be considered father and mother. The forest had raised her.

When the Circle had come for her, Marissa had been ready. Decades she had spent as an Initiate, wandering the rugged land of Cormyr, from the forbidding peaks of the Storm Horn Mountains to the stagnant heart of the Vast Swamp, watching and learning, touching and being touched by the wisdom of soil and seed, root and stone.

She would trade it all, she knew, for a few months more in this strange northern land.

"Come, little witch," Borovazk's rumbled. His touch, however, fell light upon her shoulder. Marissa looked up into the ranger's face, lined with the years and harsh weather. There was something there, a softness that she had never seen before, a chink in the armor of his boisterous good humor.

Hesitancy, she thought. Or fear.

"Is time to be on our way," he continued.

Marissa nodded and stood. She was conscious now of the others. Roberc sat easily on Cavan and raised an enigmatic eyebrow as he puffed away on his pipe, while Taen tightened and retightened the straps on his saddle. Within moments, she sat astride her own horse and waited for Borovazk to lead them forward. The change in the ranger's demeanor didn't trouble her nearly as much as the half-elf's continued withdrawal. Ever since their brief exchange during the night of the hag-wind, he'd seemed sullen and quiet—more so than usual. She had thought he'd worked past it, just for a moment, right before their battle with the trolls. However, Taen had said almost nothing to her since the aftermath of that combat. He'd even engaged the normally surly Roberc in conversation but had found little to say to her except some softly spoken morning pleasantries.

Marissa wasn't sure exactly what was going on, but she knew it would have to stop. When Borovazk started forward, she kicked her dun gelding forward, moving next to Taen's own mount.

"What is it, Marissa?" he asked after she had stared at him for a few moments without saying anything.

"Ah," she responded, trying to keep her tone light, "I see you still have a voice. I was wondering if maybe the ice trolls had frozen it solid within your throat."

The druid watched his face change, as if he'd swallowed something bitter.

"No," Taen said after another moment of silence, "it's just—"

"Just what?" she interrupted. The spring wind had picked up, blowing several strands of Marissa's red hair across her face. She brushed them back irritably. "You've barely said anything to me since we left Mulptan," she continued, "and what you have said has been ruder than a pig farmer during the slaughter." This last she had spoken in Elvish, something that she knew would make the half-elf even more uncomfortable.

With the part of her mind that wasn't running red with anger, Marissa knew that this conversation wasn't going as she had planned at all. She needed to calm down. It was just that sometimes Taenaran's tortured soul made her want to reach out to him in comfort, and sometimes it made her want to slap some sense into him. She respected his pain and knew it wasn't simply maudlin claptrap. He had a right to feel it. His life—the things he had done. It *was* painful, and real life rarely turned out like tavern tales or those sappy songs requested by moon-eyed merchants' daughters. Still, Taen needed her, and if she was honest with herself, she knew that she needed him.

"Marissa," Taen began, "I'm . . . I am sorry. You know that. I've been feeling very strange ever since we crossed into Rashemen. It's as if everything seems somehow more real here. My past. My failure. . . ." He stopped speaking.

Marissa reached out across the short distance between them and grabbed his hand. "Taen," Marrisa said softly, "you can't deny your past, or run from it, but you can be so busy trying that you end up denying your present. We are here, in Rashemen, for a purpose. Don't ignore that or the person that you *are*. Otherwise, you'll never become the person that you were meant to be."

Taen smiled, giving her hand a squeeze as he did so. "You sound like—" He hesitated.

"Her?" Marissa asked.

The half-elf nodded.

"She sounds like a very wise woman, Taenaran," Marissa said.

She released the half-elf's hand and kicked her horse into a trot. Let him sulk now, she thought. At least he knew that he didn't have to do so completely alone.

Now that she had spoken with Taen, her mind and heart felt free of the burden she had been carrying. By the time Borovazk called their halt, Marissa could think only of their destination—the Red Tree and whatever mysteries she would encounter beneath its branches.

The Red Tree stood like an ancient giant trapped between elemental forces. Its gnarled roots reached deep into the bones of the earth, seeking the marrow-wisdom of stone, while thick-boled limbs stretched toward the freedom of air, wind, and sky. Broad, ovate leaves, some of them dappled and covered with late-autumn red and gold, waved softly in the gentle evening wind. Light from the setting sun kissed the very tips of these leaves, as a noble might kiss the elegant fingers of a courtesan; they flickered and flamed beneath the dying light of the sun.

Taen stood a fair distance from the Red Tree and gazed upon its magnificence. All of Rashemen had made him feel small and insignificant beneath its broad expanse, but here, under the shadow of this ancient tree, the half-elf felt truly insubstantial. Perhaps it was simply that the Red Tree was somehow more real. Regardless, the half-elf knew that he was in the presence of a mystery older, perhaps, than some of the gods. Even dour Roberc sat in reverential silence after they had set up camp. No pipeweed or long pulls from the wineskin—the halfling simply sat, fierce Cavan laying docilely by his side, and looked thoughtfully at the giant tree.

When they had first arrived, all of them had spent a few moments alone with their own thoughts as they stood before the wonder of the Red Tree, though it had been Borovazk at the last who had indicated that they should set up camp a distance from the Red Tree. The site, he had explained, was sacred to the wychlaran, the Rashemi Witches whose mystic power defended the land. Only those steeped in the *Vyvadnya*, the Mysteries, could safely stay beneath the Red Tree's branches and benefit from its wisdom. Many others had tried, according to the ranger, and those who were fortunate died. The others, he had said sadly, spent the rest of their lives in gibbering madness or else they simply wasted away, their minds shattered beneath the Red Tree's swaying limbs.

The three men unsaddled horses, pitched shelters, and gathered what wood they needed for their small cooking fire, while Marissa wandered deeper into the woods surrounding the Red Tree to prepare for her...

Her what? Taen didn't even know what to call it. Watching the giant elemental riddle that was the Red Tree, he wasn't sure that he would ever know what to call it. Here was a mystery that, like so many other things, went beyond his mastery. He worried about Marissa. For all of her knowledge and faith, she wasn't wychlaran. She was a stranger in this land, foreign, and there was no telling what the powers of Rashemen would do if she dared step foot beneath the tree.

Borovazk didn't seem concerned, and that did much to put his mind at ease. Something had happened at the stream when Marissa had knelt before the spirit of the water, something that obviously went deeper than just the normal paying of respect to the telthor. Ever since then, Borovazk had treated the druid differently. He was soft spoken around her—almost deferential. If the

Rashemi ranger did not see any harm in what Marissa was about to do, who was *he* to gainsay him?

Yet Taen felt uneasy.

The half-elf walked quietly to where the ranger sat carving a piece of thick wood with a bronze-handled knife.

"Borovazk, are you sure that Marissa isn't in any danger?" Taen asked.

The ranger stopped his knife from cutting and looked at Taen. Borovazk's blue eyes gazed deeply into Taen's own. The half-elf grew uncomfortable beneath the weight of that stare, but he would not look away.

"Who can tell?" the ranger said at last. "Borovazk is no Old One; he has no power within to understand the *Vyvadnya*. Is witch-lore. Deep and dark. Borovazk think that the little one has more than just power within her. If she says her god sent her to the Red Tree, then Borovazk think that her god will protect her, eh. Besides," the Rashemi raised his knife to point back in the direction from which they had just traveled, "you saw what happened at the stream. Even the telthor acknowledge her. Borovazk thinks that the telthor know something we don't."

The ranger got to his feet and gave the half-elf's back a hearty slap. "No more worry, little friend," Borovazk continued. "You and I shall drink some *jhuild* and make our own witch-lore, eh?"

Taen smiled but said nothing more. Borovazk left to find his ever-full flask of firewine, leaving the half-elf alone with his thoughts. The sun had finally set. Here and there, stars glittered and gleamed in night's dark diadem. Taen stared at them for a moment, those holes in the darkness, and wondered what would happen this night. He wanted to believe the ranger, wanted to put down his fear like a weary soldier wants to put down his blade, but he couldn't. Fear was indeed a blade, and he found it embedded deep within his heart.

Cursing softly to himself, he took up a vantage point where he could keep Marissa in his keen elf sight all night long. Let Borovazk drink himself into insensibility, *he* would keep watch over the druid.

So he waited—under the dark sheet of night, with the wind in his hair and the soft hiss of leaf-whispers sighing in his ears.

CHAPTER 8

The Year of Wild Magic
(1372 DR)

Marissa touched the Red Tree.

Her right hand traced the path of deep rivulets and channels in its bark; the stump of her left hand pressed gently against its trunk. The druid had removed her glove as well as the rune-covered gauntlet she wore over the shattered skin and bone of her other arm. She was naked, skin on skin with the ancient tree. Beneath her touch, its bark felt rough—the old wood split by wind and weather and age.

The night breeze ran softly through her hair, sending shivers coursing through Marissa's body. For a few heartbeats, she allowed herself to enjoy the delicious sensation then turned her focus to the task at hand. The druid had spent the remaining light of the day in preparation for this moment, cleansing her body and mind in the clear waters of the vale, readying herself to receive whatever Rillifane had in store for her. She'd sent Rusella to the trees near her companions, and now her mind remained clear, as still as the inner pond her masters in the Circle had asked her to create when she was an initiate in order to focus her attention.

Everything about the Red Tree was magic. From the moment she and her friends had arrived, it loomed in her mind's eye, a presence she could not deny. Nor did she want to. Power emanated from every facet of its roots, trunk, and flaming leaves, and waves of divine energy crested over her, submerging her heart, mind, and will. There was almost something familiar about this power, comforting—it was like, yet unlike, the experience she had when surrounded by her god's aura.

Now, enclosed within the tree's arboreal embrace, Marissa sank deeper into that presence, surrendering the last vestiges of herself. Beneath her fingers, she could sense the slow pulse of the earth-blood flowing in the tree's great veins. Her heartbeat slowed, became that pulse, and beat in rhythm to the ancient song. Her breath deepened, took root in her belly then rooted itself deeper—into soil and rock.

She was changing.

Had changed.

She was ancient as the land and as vast as the world's forests. Hands reached to sky, caught the wind in thin fingers, and drank dew like sweet wine from the evening air. Toes curled and twisted, like a riddle whose answer wound down into the dark heart of the world—until there was only earth and shadow and the silent language of stone.

Taen watched Marissa approach the Red Tree. When she knelt before its trunk, he half expected the thing to come alive and begin speaking. Treants, those great living trees, were not unknown to him, so he waited for the thrumming sound of the deep tree-voice and the shaking of its twisted limbs.

Nothing happened.

Still, Marissa knelt in silence, and he watched her in silence. The night sounds of the vale enveloped him like a blanket. The ghostly flapping of owl wings, the high bark of the hunting fox, and a chorus of nocturnal insects filled the darkness. Amidst it all, he could hear Roberc's light snoring and the soft, tuneless humming of Borovazk as he sang his way through three skins of firewine.

Still he watched.

The moon rose and danced across the night sky, scattering pools of silver radiance across the landscape. Once he heard the heavy rustle of some game in a nearby bush, but a single growl from Cavan stilled the beast. Taen's eyes grew heavy as the night wore on. He yawned once and rubbed his face, trying to shake the lethargy that gripped him. The scent of adelpha blossoms perfumed the air. Taen breathed the heady incense deeply. His last thought was of Marissa as sleep threw its thick mantle over his head.

❧ ❧ ❧ ❧ ❧

"You have come, sister of our heart," said a soft, soothing voice.

"We had hoped you would," said another voice, warm and rich as honey.

Marissa turned—or rather the world turned and she remained. The druid sat in a place of darkness, with only a small light glowing a few feet from her. Everywhere she looked, by the illumination of that feeble glow, Marissa could see only more darkness.

Then two other women sat beside her. They were as

different as summer and winter. One was young and beautiful, the way a flower is beautiful—soft and delicate, with pale, smooth skin and lustrous black hair. She looked at Marissa, and the druid could see green eyes flashing like jewels in the dim light regarding her with open curiosity.

The other woman was old and weathered, her skin like the bark of a tree. She had thick, iron-gray hair severely pulled back in a single braid. Her eyes were brown, the color of earth, and her fingers were thin bony sticks that drummed an absent beat while they rested upon her legs.

"Who . . . who are you?" Marissa asked hesitantly. Her mind was awhirl with confusion, yet she felt her heart free and untroubled. There was no danger here, could be no danger beneath the Red Tree—or wherever *here* was.

"You should ask yourself the same question," said the old woman, her warm voice taking on an edge.

"Hush, Imsha. There is no need to harangue the poor girl," the young woman broke in. Her voice remained soft and smooth, but watching her in the soft light, Marissa caught a hint of fire in her green eyes, an open challenge.

All of a sudden, she didn't feel quite so secure anymore. She recalled a favorite saying of her teachers: "The Lion never lies when it kills." Truth was as necessary as the sun in the world, she thought, and maybe even more necessary here.

"I am Marissa Goldenthorn, daughter of Rillifane Rallathil, and a servant of nature," she proclaimed proudly.

Imsha snorted and slapped her leg with a bony hand.

"Listen to her, Tamlith," Imsha said to the young woman, "going on about her name." Then, suddenly, she leaned close to Marissa. The druid caught the faint scent of rosemary and mint. "So," Imsha continued, "you belong to Old Greenshanks, do you? Well, little kitten, his power is far from here." The old woman's eyes glowed with purplish light.

Marissa knew that she should be afraid. Imsha was right; Rillifane's power burned low in Rashemen. She wasn't sure if he could protect her now. Here. In *this* place. Still, he had asked her to come, and she would not fail him.

"Rillifane's power may be far from Rashemen," the druid responded firmly, "but there is true power in the hills and plains of this land. *He* asked me to come, and I did. If I may be of service to this power, then at *his* request I shall do so."

"Hmm ... hmm ...," Imsha mumbled. "I see that the kitten has claws."

"And sight," Tamlith added, "for she sees true."

"Is that so?" asked Imsha. "Then tell me, my tiger—who are we?"

Both women stood now, forcing Marissa to gaze up at them. She tried to stand but found herself rooted in place.

"You are telthor," she answered, after a moment of thought, "tied to the Red Tree of Immil Vale."

"What else?" asked Tamlith, expectation apparent in her soft voice.

Marissa closed her eyes to concentrate—and nearly gasped with surprise. She could still see both Imsha and Tamlith standing over her. At last, the answer came, like a fresh breeze after a winter gale.

"You are witches," she said finally, "and you've somehow transformed your essences to become linked with the Red Tree."

"Witches," Imsha barked, clearly taking umbrage with the title. "Little tiger, we are othlor, the Wise Ones of the hathran who lead the wychlaran. Still," she continued, reaching out her hand to Marissa, "you saw and spoke the truth."

"Which is more than some among us do," added Tamlith.

The druid accepted Imsha's hand and stood up, grateful for the freedom. "I don't . . ." Marissa hesitated. "I don't understand."

"You will, my dear," the old woman said, patting the druid gently on her cheek. Both of the witches were smiling now. "For there is poison at the root, and we all wither and die while it eats away at us."

"Enough riddles," Tamlith said to her companion. "Though time moves differently here, there is still much for her to do." Turning to Marissa, the young witch's smile disappeared. "Rashemen is in grave danger," she said simply. "One of our number has betrayed us and broken the *ildva*, the bond that we have forged with the vremyonni. Even now, this traitor bends her blasphemous will upon the land. She holds an Old One imprisoned and uses his very being to power her own corrupt spells."

"The *ildva* has held our land together," continued old Imsha. "Through countless centuries the vremyonni and the wychlaran have defended Rashemen from all enemies. With the ancient bond broken, we are weakened. It has kept the peace between us and prevented either group from struggling against the other for dominion of the land. Already the vremyonni refuse counsel with the hathran, suspecting us of betrayal. They scheme now within their own dark caverns, plotting the downfall of the wychlaran. Without the *ildva*, I fear for the future of Rashemen."

Marissa shook her head in disbelief. This was almost too much for her to handle. She had come to the Red Tree hoping for—what? She didn't even know, but finding herself in the middle of an arcane struggle between the ancient protectors of Rashemen was the farthest thing from her mind. She could almost hear Roberc swearing now, and the thought nearly brought a chuckle to her lips. Marissa clamped down on it fast. This, clearly, was not the time, but what was she to do?

"Why don't you just inform the other hathran of what's happened?" Marissa asked the two witches. "Why do you even need me?"

Tamlith frowned. "We do not know who she is," Tamlith said. "She is strong—and cunning. All of our auguries and oracles have been turned aside by her power. The telthor do not know whom to trust, so we asked for help.

"And you came," Tamlith said, "but we have little time. Though we do not know the traitor's identity, we can feel her power like a canker on the land. She is concentrating her forces in the ruins of Citadel Rashemar. If she unleashes her forces, Rashemen will be divided against itself. Even if the wychlaran manage to win, it won't be long until the wizardlings in Thay smell blood and come raging into Rashemen like a pack of rabid wolves."

Marissa raised a hand to her head, trying to keep the jumble of her thoughts together.

"What can I do?" Marissa asked.

The old witch smiled and drew something from the folds of her robe.

"Take this," Imsha said, indicating a knotted yew limb about Marissa's height, "to the Urlingwood. Stand before the border of that forest and use its power. It will summon the living othlor."

Marissa could only nod her head. "You just said you didn't know who to trust. What if one of the othlor is the traitor?"

"When you have summoned the othlor," Imsha replied, "I will come to them. My power is weakening, for the traitor's corruption taints the very land itself, but if the evil one is among them, I will know. This will expend all of my strength, but at least you will have the wisdom and power of the Wise Ones to guide you further."

"What of my companions?" asked Marissa.

The question drew a smile from Tamlith. "They will be your compass and your strength," the young witch replied. "Keep them close to you, especially the one who is a twisted branch. He will need tending, but there is much power in him."

"Who—" Marissa started to ask but stopped as Imsha raised a weathered hand.

"I am sorry, little tiger," the old woman said, "but we must leave you." As she said this, a thin mist began to rise, turning the darkness into a soft blanket of gray. "Will you help us in Rashemen's time of need?" she asked.

The druid looked at both telthor, watching the outlines of their bodies flicker and fade in the shifting mist. There was so much she didn't understand; so much she needed to understand. Her duty, however, remained clear. Marissa offered a quick prayer to Rillifane Rallathil then spoke her answer.

"I will help you," she declared.

Both witches bowed low to her.

"Then farewell, Marissa Goldenthorn, daughter of Rillifane, servant of nature, and sister of our heart. You have answered the land's need, and we are grateful," Imsha said.

The world shifted and darkness returned.

"Farewell, sister," she heard Tamlith say, as if from across a great distance. "Perhaps we shall meet again one day."

Then she heard no more.

Taen woke with a start. Bright sunlight poured into his eyes, burning away the distant memory of a dream—of two mysterious women whispering wisdom into his ear. He rubbed his eyes vigorously and cursed at his own lack of discipline. He'd fallen asleep.

Asleep! After he'd vowed to keep watch over Marissa through the night.

A shadow fell over the half-elf, and he nearly cried out in surprise.

"Wake the others, Taenaran," Marissa said softly. "We have much to discuss."

CHAPTER 9

The Year of Wild Magic
(1372 DR)

Wind howled through the citadel's shattered walls.

Like an ethereal wolf it ranged across the hard, cracked earth and ran beneath the shadow of crudely erected towers. The great expanse of cluttered stone passages radiating out from the ruins of the ancient keep could not stop it, nor could the jumble of rock and rotting timber thrown up in hasty defense around the once-proud heart of Citadel Rashemar. Unhindered by work of beast or man, it blew, raged, and howled.

Sitting on a pitted, stone-wrought throne in what remained of the central keep, the hag closed her ears to the wind's bitter sound. Around her, shadows clung to the high, vaulted arches and raised ceiling of the room, broken only by uneven rays of light that spilled like liquid gold from chinks and cracks in the keep's outer wall. She drew long, bony, blue-skinned fingers across the lines of her forehead, pushing the thick tangle of black hair back from the deep recesses of her ebony eyes.

She had spent most of the day receiving a seemingly endless array of reports from her minions. Goblins, ogres, and spiteful human sorcerers with their dark spells and darker ambitions had paraded before her in wave after disgusting wave. She had grown tired of their machinations and vain prattling, and the hag's mood had gone from black to murderous. Even the wind, whose sighing and wailing she normally found so soothing, did nothing but grate on her nerves.

Which was why she stood suddenly, almost leaping from the ancient throne to tower over the trio of goblins prattling on in their damned language. The hag watched with satisfaction as two of the goblins jumped back in fright, their normally dull, slack-jawed expressions replaced with expressions of overwhelming horror; their dirty orange skin paled to an almost dusty rose. She pointed a gnarled finger at the third goblin who, the hag noted with an inward snarl, had held his ground. The creature stood almost a head taller than his companions, with thin arms that hung almost to the ground. When it gazed up at her with its pale yellow eyes, she caught a glimmer of calculation, of a sly intelligence that regarded her carefully. Not for the first time, she regretted having to involve herself with these loathsome beasts.

"Mistress," it hissed in its guttural language, casting wide eyes humbly to the ground. "Giznat not mean to offend you!" The other two goblins had fallen to their knees, whimpering. "Giznat serve Great Mistress," the goblin continued, "Giznat's tribe serve too."

Rather than calming her, the sound of their pathetic mewling sent her temper rising.

"Then do not bother me with your ungrateful begging," she snapped. This sent the kneeling goblins to the floor, fully prostrate.

"Ah," said Giznat, nodding his head in agreement, "but I not have to beg if Great Mistress give Giznat what she promised—gold, jewels, and glittering things." Its voice dropped to a soft whisper, almost crooning out the last words.

The hag nearly screamed in frustration. Giznat's tribe lived beneath the abandoned village of Rashemar that sat at the base of the long hill upon which the citadel was built. In addition to providing additional bodies for her army, the filthy goblins served as her first line of defense, spotting the approach of scouts and other would-be invaders from the heart of Rashemen, as well as the occasional band of adventurers. At first, Giznat had been satisfied with the castoffs from those unfortunates that her forces had captured and eventually killed. The creature's foul mind had turned quickly to thoughts of more wealth, and it wasn't long before he had started to pester the hag for a larger share in the spoils. She knew, however, that Giznat would never be satisfied with what he received. The goblin's greed was matched only by his propensity for treachery.

"Why should I give you any more of what is *mine?*" the hag asked, adding inflection on the last word to make sure that the goblin's limited intellect would catch her meaning. She remained standing, forcing the goblin chief to crane his neck far back to gaze up at her. Its efforts gave her some small measure of satisfaction.

"Giznat could serve Great Mistress better with more treasure," he answered after a moment. "Tribe want more gold. If Giznat bring tribe more gold, then tribe know Giznat great leader. Listen to Giznat more. Serve Great Mistress better," he finished this last with a smile on his face, the wide mouth gaping open to reveal small, sharp fangs.

"Indeed," was all she answered, gazing down upon the goblin chief and his two hapless companions. She moved back to the throne and sat down, thinking. Behind her, she could sense the hulking forms of the broad-chested ogres that served as her own personal bodyguards. As always, they lurked in the shadows like statues. With one signal, the hag knew that she could put an end to the disgusting creatures before her. However, the goblins did have their uses, and she rarely enjoyed moving with undue haste.

Within the span of a few heartbeats, she had made her decision.

She stood once again.

"I have decided," she said as regally as she could muster, "to grant you your desire, Giznat."

The goblin chief looked at her with a gleam in its cold yellow eyes. She could sense the anticipation running through its tiny body.

"For your service," the hag continued, "you will receive exactly what you deserve."

She clapped her monstrous, blue-skinned hands together and spoke a single word into the vast chamber. Waves of amber energy emanated from the hag's clasped hands, surrounding the goblin chief. Giznat began to gibber mindlessly, shrieking out his fear. Behind him, his two companions watched as the amber energy passed through Giznat's skin, forming a hardened shell. The goblin chief stopped shrieking and turned to run. His lithe form seemed ungainly, however. He stumbled once then stopped, frozen in mid run. The amber shell faded completely, revealing smooth gray stone.

"You," the hag called out to one of the remaining goblins. "What is your name?"

The goblin stared at her for a moment, before answering. "Ha—Hazbik, Great Mistress," it stammered.

"Well, Hazbik," the hag said, approaching the still-prostrate goblin, "I suggest you run along to the tribe and tell the shaman he needs to pick a new chief."

Hazbik stumbled to his feet and bowed low, nearly tumbling back down to the ground. "Hazbik goes, Mistress," he replied then grabbed the remaining goblin. After a few moments of fumbling, the two creatures managed to make their way to the door.

"Oh and Hazbik," the hag called after them, "see to it that you remove this statue." She pointed to the transformed Giznat. "Please send it to your new chief as my way of . . . honoring him."

The hag didn't wait for Hazbik's reply but turned back to the throne and dismissed her ogre bodyguards with a wave of her hand. Killing the goblin chief had eased her tension somewhat, but she still wasn't satisfied. She was tired of lurking in shadows like the villain in a bad children's tale, tired of hiding in the ruins of an ancient keep, plotting and planning.

It was time to strike.

She sent a mental summons to the priestess who served as her lieutenant and walked toward the back of the vaulted chamber. There, hidden in the dirt and crumbling mortar, stood a simple circle scribed in dried blood. She stepped into the gruesome circle and spoke a single word before disappearing in a flare of purple light.

The wind's mournful wailing echoed in the vast, empty chamber.

Yulda sat in the confines of her spartan room, waiting for Durakh's arrival. She had removed the spell of seeming she had cast on herself moments after the teleportation circle delivered her here. Now she sat amidst the broken remains of once-fine furniture and the tatters of sumptuous bedding, grateful to be wearing her own skin once again. Though her spell had only been illusory, she felt far more comfortable without any such glamour. Illusion had its uses—after all, wearing the form of an annis hag made it far easier to command her growing army of monsters—but she still preferred her true form. Walking around for too long under the distorting effects of an illusion spell felt like wearing clothes that were ill fitting and confining. She always felt a moment of relief when the spell faded. Even as a master of her lore, she wrestled with the small fear at the base of her spine that the illusion would somehow end up permanent.

Yulda chuckled at her foolishness as she gathered the length of a black robe around her and surveyed the parchment laid out on the rickety desk before her. The broad, confident strokes of the cartographer stood out in the light of her room, and the witch could clearly see the path her army would take as it began to challenge the wychlaran for dominion over Rashemen. She and the priestess Durakh had spent several months crafting and birthing their plans. The forces at her command slumbered restlessly in the dungeons and caverns beneath the citadel, and each day she stayed their hand made it more difficult to control them.

Her army couldn't win in open rebellion. She found that fact as deeply frustrating as it was true. The Iron Lord and his damned warlords controlled too many forces eager to shed their blood in defense of Rashemen, so she hunkered down within the ruins of Citadel Rashemar, biding her time, consolidating her power, and waiting for the right moment to unveil her strength.

That moment had finally come.

The secret, of course, was not to focus on the martial power of the Iron Lord. He and his band of thick-headed louts would find plenty of humiliation at her hands. It was the combined might of both the wychlaran and the vremyonni that posed the single biggest threat to her plans. The only way to defeat them, Yulda knew, was to separate them—to cause a division where there had never been any before.

She thought of the Old One, wasting away in her mountain demesne, and smiled. The old fool had not revealed a single secret to her, yet she had forced him to give her something far more precious—the very essence of his power. Using forbidden lore taken from the heart of the abyss, she had managed to forge a link to the core of the vremyonni's being. Even now, the wizard's power flowed through her, a slow wave of energy that surged, crested, and surged again, supplementing her own arcane strength and fueling her spells with eldritch might.

By attacking and overpowering him, the witch had broken a bond forged centuries ago. That would certainly have an effect on the arcane protectors of Rashemen. Already she could feel their spells of divination and their oracular gifts searching the land for her. They pressed against the mystic screens both she and Durakh had erected to conceal their location—pressed but did not penetrate.

And would not penetrate so long as the vremyonni and the wychlaran were not working in concert. Beneath their combined power, not even Yulda's own heightened gifts could deceive them.

A loud knock from behind the thick stone door of the chamber brought her attention to the present.

"Chaul," she heard a husky, feminine voice say from the hallway beyond. "Are you there?"

Yulda moved aside the thick rolls of parchment and picked up a clear crystal about the size of an egg sitting on the corner of the desk. She blew on it once, and as her breath touched the crystal, its surface shimmered with milky incandescence. The light from the crystal soon faded, leaving the image of a shadowy stone hallway and a single figure standing before a door.

Durakh.

Voluminous folds of earth-brown robes covered the broad expanse of the figure's shoulders and back but hung open in the front to reveal a suit of unmarred jet-black plate mail and plate leggings. Yulda could see that the priestess's left hand still touched the haft of her mace as she stood before the door. Red runes spilled down its length, pulsating hotly in the darkness of the hallway. A thick metal bracer with four wicked-looking metal claws covered the length of Durakh's other hand, from her wrist to beyond her fingertips.

The witch trusted Durakh, as far as anyone in her position could trust another person, which is to say very little, so she had set a permanent divination spell in the hallway. Even as her alter ego Chaul, the annis hag, she still had trouble controlling the more willful components of her army. Already, three of her subordinates had tried to kill her, one through assassination and the other two with traps designed to make it look like an accident. Their bodies were staked up outside the walls of the keep as a warning—and a promise. For all that, she knew that for as long as her purpose and Durakh's remained the same, she could trust the priestess with her life.

"Chaul," the figure called out from the hall once again.

Yulda sighed at the artifice. Durakh knew her true identity. Indeed, the priestess had been the one to suggest the idea in the first place, and now they played an elaborate game for form's sake. The witch couldn't wait until the day when she would walk triumphantly through the decimated ranks of the wychlaran and reveal to them that their undoing came at her hands. The delicious agony she would see marked upon the faces of the weak-willed fools she had betrayed would make this infantile cloak-and-dagger game worthwhile.

She gestured and silver sigils writhed and flared across the door of her chamber before it creaked open, stone grating on stone. Yulda stood up to greet her guest, placing the crystal back on her desk.

Durakh Haan wore a grim face as she entered the room. Yulda regarded the cleric carefully, measuring each tic of the priestess's eyes and each indrawn breath. She was searching, calculating, as she always did with someone she deemed a threat, for some advantage, a heartbeat's span of warning that might allow her to prevail if something unexpected were to happen.

The priestess's eyes were a smoky gray, set deep within a harsh, square-jawed face. A wide-bridged nose and thick, sloping forehead easily proclaimed Durakh's orc blood, though the effect was softened somewhat by high-set, delicate cheekbones and full lips. Three scars, faded to a dull purple with age, crisscrossed the cleric's chin, traveling in ragged lines down toward her rough-skinned throat. The half-orc's hair flowed in thick brown waves around ridged ears and spilled into the folds of her robe. A thick chain hung down from the cleric's neck, suspending a circular onyx disk with a silver Orcish rune inscribed upon it.

If Durakh took offense at such obvious scrutiny, she gave no indication. The cleric bowed her head slightly upon entering and sat upon the simple chair Yulda offered. The door swung closed behind her.

"You summoned me," the cleric said, and though Yulda listened to each word carefully, she could hear no indication of irony or contempt—just a simple state-ment of fact. Durakh's voice was deep-timbred and rich, though Yulda would never use the word *warm* to describe it. To her ears, it sounded hollow and cold—like stone in winter.

An apt description for the young priestess.

A nameless sense of menace surrounded the priestess, a sense of the deep, dark places of the land, lying always in shadow. Yulda couldn't quite suppress the shiver that ran up her spine.

"Yes, I did summon you," the witch said, though whether to remind Durakh or herself, she couldn't be sure. "We have been preparing for more than a year. Are our forces ready?"

Yulda asked the question casually, in an almost friendly tone, as if the answer meant nothing more to her than if she had inquired about the weather. Her gaze, however, remained riveted on the cleric. Failure was an option.

For her part, the half-orc returned Yulda's stare before answering, though the witch knew Durakh well enough to see the telltale signs of tension in her lieutenant. It was clear to the Rashemi that Luthic's cleric felt uncomfortable beneath the lidless gaze of her missing eye—a fact that caused Yulda a fair degree of satisfaction.

"Our army is ready," Durakh answered after a moment's hesitation, "though you have caused quite a stir among the goblins with your latest ... gift. Razk nearly—"

"May the gods damn that fool of a shaman," Yulda interrupted. "Can you control him?"

The odious beast held a fair amount of power, but he was, like all of his kind, a treacherous, venomous vermin that needed an almost constant lash of discipline and bullying to insure his loyalty.

"Oh yes," the cleric answered, baring a double row of yellowed, razor-sharp teeth as she did so. "Razk desires a certain series of rites that I happen to know. He will follow my lead until such time as he receives his reward."

"See to it that he does," Yulda warned. "Without his presence, the goblins will be far more difficult to manage. What of the others?"

"The bugbears and hobgoblins wait for our signal, as does Nanraak, the wild goblin king," the priestess replied. "They will join our forces once we have begun to attack in earnest. The rest of our army gathers here.

In two days' time, we will complete all of the final preparations."

"Ah, that is good," Yulda said, moving toward the desk once more and gathering a number of maps in her hand. "Then the plan remains the same?" she asked.

"Yes," Durakh confirmed. "Several contingents of goblins, ogres, and spiders will move swiftly north and west, harrying and raiding the villages several days' ride from Mulptan, while our main force will sweep out of the mountains and strike first at the Mines of Tethkel and then, once we control the mines, will move to capture or destroy the villages and cities of Lower Rashemen."

Durakh's eyes gleamed with anticipation as she recounted the plan, and Yulda's own doubts were swept away by that cruel glance. She had indeed chosen her lieutenant wisely. The witch smiled in response.

"It is a good plan, if I do say so myself," she said to the cleric, purposefully ignoring the priestess's own integral contributions. It would not do to allow the cleric to become too sure of herself. "Are we certain that the Iron Lord will react to the village raids?" Yulda asked.

The half-orc idly fingered her holy symbol as she considered the question.

"I believe that he will," Durakh responded finally. "My spies say that he grows ever restless locked in his citadel of iron, surrounded by warlords who boast of past victories and drink themselves into oblivion hoping for future glory. Besides," Durakh noted with more than a hint of malice in her voice, "the last assassin that we sent after the Iron Lord nearly slit his throat while he slept. Once Volas Dyervolk hears of the raids, he will gather together his army of berserkers and run headlong into battle like an owlbear protecting its cubs."

Yulda threw the maps down on the table, sending several parchments skittering and rolling to the floor.

"Leaving the bulk of Lower Rashemen open to our attack. Soon," the witch said to no one in particular, "it will all be mine."

"And the wychlaran?" asked Durakh.

Yulda turned to gaze at the cleric. Though the half-orc had asked the question with the same inflection she gave everything else, the Rashemi witch heard something beneath the simple inquiry—an undertone of fear? Hope? It was difficult to tell.

Nevertheless, Yulda fixed the black point of her eldritch gaze upon Durakh.

"Leave them to me," Yulda said in a chill voice.

During the course of the past year, the witch had gathered a growing coterie of sorcerers, wizards, and hags in the wilds of the High Country. Frustrated by the yoke of the wychlaran, choked and broken by their own lust for power, they came to her, eager to trade their own freedom for the scraps from her table. There were more of them than she could ever have imagined. The wychlaran were blinded by their traditional rule of power. Carefree and overly complacent in their hereditary role in Rashemen, they could not even conceive of anyone resisting the natural order of things. There were shadows in their mirrors and weeds in their garden that would choke the very life out of them, and they did not even take notice.

Her coterie would travel with the bulk of the army, stirring up the more impetuous of the telthor and turning their arcane power against the spells of the wychlaran, and without the aid of the vremyonni, the sisterhood of the wychlaran would fall. That left only the durthan, holed up in Erech Forest, but Yulda knew that once the durthan understood which way the wind was blowing, they would flock to her banner. Then she would use them too, as she used everything and everyone in her path, climbing over the backs of their spent and lifeless corpses to attain her goal.

Durakh only nodded at the witch's admonition, her lips pursed in thought.

"There is one thing that I believe we haven't fully considered," Durakh said.

"What is that?" Yulda replied, already sensing the turn of the cleric's thoughts.

"What will Thay do as Rashemen tears itself apart from within?" Durakh asked, and this time Yulda heard true concern in the priestess's voice. "I hardly think that the Red Wizards will sit quietly on the sidelines until the dust settles."

Yulda rubbed her hands together and let out a hideous cackle.

"That is exactly what they will do, dear Durakh," Yulda said as her laughter subsided. "Those petty wizardlings and I have come to a certain ... understanding."

In truth, she would have to give up a good portion of the western border of Lower Rashemen, but that would be a small price to pay for the freedom to work without those meddling Thayans interfering. Besides, when she had finally consolidated her power, Yulda might be able to "renegotiate" her agreement.

Durakh did not seem phased by the existence of any pact with the Red Wizards, a fact that caused the witch no small concern. Before Yulda could follow her train of thought, however, the half-orc stood and cast a cold look at her.

"You are, of course, free to make arrangements with anyone you choose," Durakh said, "just so long as you do not forget our own 'understanding.' "

Despite the cleric's insolent tone, Yulda held her temper in check. Too much was at stake to let a simple lapse in discipline upset everything.

"Our agreement still stands," she assured Durakh. "Once we have disposed of the wychlaran, you may take part of the army and explore the Fortress of the Half Demon." Yulda almost shuddered. The fortress, one of the many ruins left over from the Narfell Empire, rulers of the land before the Rashemi people were formed, held the remains of an ancient portal that legends said would lead to the Lower Planes. "If you can secure the fortress and hold it," Yulda continued, "then it is yours in perpetuity."

May you die trying, the witch thought. It was, she had to admit, an elegant solution to what could become a troubling problem. Alive, Durakh could eventually become a rival for power. If she were to die on her quest, which, according to what Yulda knew of the fortress, was quite likely, it would spare her the bother of having to destroy the cleric on her own.

Durakh bowed her head slightly.

"Then I must ask to take your leave," Durakh said, "for I have much to do if we are to leave on schedule."

Yulda inclined her own head in a regal manner designed to irritate her lieutenant.

"Then you have my leave," Yulda replied. "I trust that everything will be in order." The witch turned her back on the cleric and began once more to study the maps upon her desk, confident that everything would move according to plan.

Outside, the storm continued to rage.

CHAPTER 10

The Year of the Crown
(1351 DR)

The crowd stirred.

Taenaran stopped fiddling nervously with the ties of his shirt, sensing the subtle change in the assembly's mood. He stood with the other prospective apprentices, arranged in a rough clump in the midst of the entire community, which had gathered beneath the eaves of the *arael'lia*, the heart-oak, to witness the Rite of Acceptance. Tonight, the *el'tael*, the masters of the bladesinging art, would choose from among those young elves, both girls and boys, who had been striving to prove themselves worthy of becoming apprentices. Not everyone would move on to the ranks of the *tael*, for the masters were quite selective and would choose only the best and the brightest of elves to study the ancient art of bladesinging. Ever since that day years ago when he had expressed his heart's desire to follow in his father's path and become a bladesinger, Taenaran had studied with a single-minded intensity. He'd mastered the rudimentary lore and minor cantrips of arcane magic faster than the other children and spent every night studying the names of bladesinging heroes and masters of the art. Standing now among the other hopeful candidates, the half-elf could hardly believe that the Rite of Acceptance was mere moments away!

The crowd stirred again, and Taenaran felt his stomach lurch in answer. He prayed to every god he could think of, imploring them all to watch over him tonight. The half-elf wanted to avoid the embarrassment of being passed over, but even more, he wished to avoid the disappointment that such an outcome would bring to his father.

His prayers were interrupted by the sonorous booming of a drum, struck in time to a measured beat. Silence descended upon the assembled elf community. Immediately, Taenaran and the other candidates fell to their knees as the *el'tael* processed in solemnly, the cowls of their rich, green robes cast deeply over their heads. Centuries of slow earth magic and patient cultivation had shaped the *arael'lia* from three separate trees. Now, with their trunks united and their leaf-filled bowers intertwined, they formed a massive chamber open to the gentle spring wind that blew across the length of Avaelearean. Starlight filtered through that verdant ceiling of the *arael'lia*, spilling across the line of *el'tael*.

Watching the line of masters bathed in such light, Taenaran felt bewitched, as if in this moment, he and the rest of the candidates were somehow pulled out of time, wrapped in a spell of moonlight and stars. The sense of enchantment deepened as the masters gathered around the kneeling candidates and as one pulled back their shadow-filled cowls.

Taenaran cast a quick look at his father, hoping for

some sign that would ease his tension, but Aelrindel's gaze was focused outward, upon the whole community. He never saw, or chose not to see, the hopeful look Taenaran gave him. Tonight, the half-elf realized with both fear and pride, Aelrindel wasn't his father. He was purely the First Hilt, a guardian of Avaelearean and the leader of the bladesingers, and tonight, the candidate realized, he wanted Aelrindel to be nothing less.

"Tonight," Aelrindel began, his rich voice easily filling the hall with its measured cadence, "we gather as we have gathered throughout the millennia, as we once gathered in the holy glades of fair Cormanthor."

A sigh rippled through the crowd at the mention of that ancient forest, and even Taenaran, half-elf though he was, felt a tug at his heart. On long summer nights, when the moon bathed the treetops with silver and the elven wine flowed like a rain-soaked river, the elves remembered their long-ago home in song, story, and poem. Many were the times that Taenaran fell asleep to the rich-throated harmonies of the elves of Avaelearean as they sang of the crystal-clear springs and sun-soaked glades of Cormanthor. However beautiful Avaelearean was, Taenaran knew that his adopted folk were a people in exile, longing for the land of their ancestors.

"We kept this vigil even as evil cast its long shadow upon the walls of our home," Aelrindel continued, interrupting Taenaran's thoughts, "choosing the next generation of elves to carry on the tradition of our ancient art. When the Army of Darkness ravaged the forests of our people and descended upon Myth Drannor, the bladesingers stood side by side with Captain Fflar of that high city and shed our blood for the sake of our land."

Several elves in the crowd wept openly now at the recounting of the fall of Myth Drannor. Though Taenaran knew the story well, as did every elf who stood in the Hall of the Heart-Oak, it never failed to elicit strong emotion. The city's fall was the defining moment of elf history over the past thousand years.

"It was only when the battle was clearly lost," the First Hilt intoned, "that Fflar, seeking to preserve what was best and noble of the elves, turned to Aelcaedra Swiftstroke, greatest of the First Hilts, and made her swear an oath upon his sword that she would gather the remaining bladesingers and flee, so that our sacred art would not pass from memory.

"Though her heart was burdened with the weight of Fflar's request, for what warrior would lightly turn from such a battle, Aelcaedra swore upon the captain's sword and gathered together her few remaining followers and escaped the dying city, eventually settling here."

As Aelrindel paused, the drum took up its measured beat once more.

"So," the First Hilt continued, "we have kept the oath, through the passing of the years, as other shadows have covered and fled the lands of Faerûn. Such was its strength that we remained rooted, like the oldest oak, even as the call of the Retreat sounded in our hearts. We have remained, and alone among all of the *Tel'Quessir*, even in this time of Returning, we pass on the mysteries of our art exactly as it was passed on in the oldest of times."

The drumbeat intensified, growing both louder and faster. Taenaran felt his heart respond, thrumming in rapid counterpoint.

"I come to you this evening," Aelrindel nearly sang, "as the keeper of that tradition, and I ask you, as heirs of the great oath, 'Do you stand behind these candidates as worthy bearers of our ancient art?'"

"We do," the gathered elves responded, filling the hall with their assent. Taenaran let the sound of their voices wash over him. Though he knew that some in their community objected to his presence among the candidates, none had gainsayed the will of the *el'tael*. For that, he found himself profoundly grateful.

"Then let the choosing begin," the First Hilt called out. Immediately, several deep-throated drums joined the single percussion that had punctuated the opening ritual, followed by the assembly, raising its voice in song.

Taenaran watched out of the corner of his eye as the robed masters moved through the ranks of the kneeling candidates, stopping occasionally to lay the edge of a sword upon the left shoulder of a young elf, signaling the elf's acceptance as a *tael*. The driving rhythm of the drums and the soaring voices of the assembled elves were like the rarest of wines. The half-elf found his head spinning in excitement and pride to be a part of this great tradition passed down throughout the ages. He was about to send his own voice to join the others' when he felt a sharp tap and the weight of a slender blade upon his own shoulder.

"Rise Taenaran, son of Aelrindel, and join the ranks of the *tael*," a woman's husky alto said into his ear.

Stunned, the half-elf stood up and walked unsteadily toward the other newly accepted *tael*. When he turned to face the crowd, he saw Aelrindel cast a glance in his direction. When he met the First Hilt's eyes, he was surprised to see the leader of the bladesingers nod his head and flash him a brief smile.

Taenaran's answering smile nearly split his face.

Aelrindel heard light footfalls approaching. The First Hilt sighed softly then sat down upon the high-backed chair, slipping out of the soft-soled shoes he had worn for this evening's event.

"I thought the ritual went splendidly, didn't you?" he asked, not looking up at the figure now standing before him. Centuries of training, and nearly that many years of familiarity with his oldest friend, allowed the bladesinger to identify his guest.

"Fairly well, First Hilt," came Faelyn's response.

Even without looking, Aelrindel could sense the elf's anger, barely held in check. The leader of the bladesingers sighed again, this time heavily, then cast a resigned look up at his dearest friend. Though time's palette had certainly not colored the elf further, the years since they had found the orphaned half-elf together had hardened Faelyn even more. At times like this, he thought ruefully, Aelrindel almost felt as if Faelyn were a stranger.

"Well," the First Hilt said gently, still taking in the figure before him, "you might as well say it and get it over with. You won't be satisfied until you do."

Aelrindel could see that the elf was taken aback by his words. He'd obviously come here expecting a fight. Faelyn's discomfiture passed quickly, however. His hands balled themselves into scarred fists, and he pressed forward into the room.

"You had to do it," the angered elf growled accusingly. "You had to choose him, didn't you?"

"*He* has a name," Aelrindel responded, trying to keep his voice even. "Taenaran is my son, and besides that, the boy has demonstrated a remarkable aptitude for the ways of magic—"

"Then let him become a mage," Faelyn interrupted, "instead of mocking our art with his presence."

"Taenaran mocks nothing," Aelrindel snapped then took a deep, steadying breath. He would gain little by allowing his temper to overmaster him. "The boy reveres what we have given our lives to. He has the desire to give himself in service and the potential to do so as one of us," the First Hilt continued in a more even tone. "The other *el'tael* agree."

"Puppets," Faelyn shouted, "following their master's lead."

Aelrindel felt his blood run like ice through his veins.

"Careful, Faelyn," the First Hilt warned, his tone nearly as frigid. "You forget yourself."

Never before had his friend taken such a contemptuous tone in all the years that Aelrindel had led the bladesingers. Though he was loath to do so, the First Hilt was prepared to put a stop to such an attitude—quickly.

Faelyn must have finally realized that he had overstepped a boundary, as the angry elf pulled up as if Aelrindel's words had stung him.

"Apologies, First Hilt," Faelyn said, bowing his head as he did so. "I merely meant that many of the *el'tael* supported Taenaran against their own judgment out of respect for you."

"Hmm," Aelrindel said after a moment, feeling his lips curl into a rueful smile. "Is respect such a terrible thing to offer your First Hilt?"

"No, Ael—" Faelyn, then hesitated for a moment before continuing. "It's just that, well, you said it yourself earlier. We have remained true to our oath, passing down the art of our ancestors exactly as it was done from the oldest times—until now." Anger fell from the elf's face, replaced by a look of confusion and regret that nearly pierced Aelrindel's heart.

"Never before have we taught our art to someone with human blood. It is wrong, Aelrindel." Faelyn reached out and grabbed the First Hilt's hand with his own. "Look what happened to our beloved home once we opened our borders to the humans," he exclaimed. "The Dark Horde came and fell upon us like a curse from the gods. We have lived our lives in exile here, away from the humans and the other races. This is our way, and Taenaran, for all of his gifts, has no place here. There are others who think as I do, Ael, if you'd just—"

The First Hilt held up his hand, stopping Faelyn in midsentence.

"Others may think as you do, my friend," Aelrindel said, "but that does not make them any less wrong. The gods have placed Taenaran under our care, and we would do well to fulfill that burden."

Faelyn bowed his head as Aelrindel spoke. When the First Hilt had finished, he looked once more into his eyes with a gaze that flashed fire.

"Then you will not reconsider your decision?" the elf asked in a stony voice.

"I will not," Aelrindel responded. "I have spoken, both as First Hilt and as your friend."

"So be it," the elf growled, "but your decision will lead to darkness. Mark my words." This last Faelyn nearly shouted as he turned quickly from Aelrindel and stormed out of the First Hilt's home.

A gentle rain began to fall from the sky. Aelrindel sat there in silence, his thoughts keeping watch with the night.

❧ ❧ ❧ ❧ ❧

Taenaran scurried out of the hooded figure's way, nearly slipping on the limb's wet bark as he did so. Several of the newly chosen *tael* had spent the rest of the evening celebrating their good fortune, and he had joined them for several glasses of rich elven wine—a decision that his slightly addled brain now regretted. The figure plodded onward, seemingly oblivious to the accident that it had almost caused. In the dim light of the deepening night, the half-elf caught a glimpse of Faelyn's angry face before his uncle turned and stormed out of sight.

When he entered his father's home, he found the elder elf gazing out into the darkness.

"Is everything all right, Father?" Taenaran asked.

For an instant, the elation that had filled him from the moment of he had been chosen faded, replaced by concern. If his uncle was upset, Taenaran could probably guess the reason. It didn't take a cleric to divine the fact that his father's best friend held little love for the half-breed elf—even if his father went to great pains to conceal that fact from him. He only hoped that one day his presence among the bladesingers would earn him Faelyn's respect.

Aelrindel smiled thinly and waved away the question.

"Everything is fine, my son," Aelrindel replied, and he stood up and opened his arms. "I am so proud of you!"

Taenaran stood still for a moment, drinking in the emotion of the moment, before casting himself toward Aelrindel. Though it was the First Hilt who had presided over the evening's ritual, it was his father's arms that wrapped Taenaran in their strong embrace.

"I will make you even more proud, Father," the half-elf exclaimed, "when I stand among the other bladesingers."

Aelrindel chuckled. "Of that, I have no doubt, my son," he said and stared out at the night sky once more.

CHAPTER 11

The Year of Wild Magic

(1372 DR)

The scent of wood smoke and spilled ale filled the taproom.

Taen watched a blue-gray trail of the smoke billow out from the fire crackling merrily in the center of the Green Chapel's common area only to waft and wend its way to the circular hole in the ceiling of the sod-built inn. Like all homes in the little hamlet of Urling, Green Chapel lay beneath the ground, surrounded by a grove of alder and evergreen trees. That fact took some getting used to—especially to one who grew up in airy elf bowers high above the forest floor. When they had arrived in Urling earlier that day, the half-elf stared at the circular cluster of grassy mounds rising out of the earth near the center of the grove. He'd asked Borovazk how long of a rest stop they would take before continuing their journey to Urling. When the ranger announced that they had already arrived, Taen found himself nearly speechless. It wasn't until the Rashemi had led them through a fur-covered hole, down a series of sloping passages, and into the circular antechamber that served as the Green Chapel's waiting area that Taen began to believe their good-humored guide.

The half-elf had wasted no time, however, in stowing his travel gear and soaking away the rigors of the road in the steamy waters of a stone bathing pool. A short nap and a quick change of clothes later, and Taen felt like a new person—the urgency of their journey temporarily forgotten under the creature comforts to be found in Urling's single inn. It wasn't long before he found himself returning to the common area. Now he sat around a simple, unpolished wood table, whose thick grain lay battered and scarred beneath the jostling weight of who-knew-how-many flagons, and gazed out at the lively taproom.

Shadows flickered along the dark, earthen walls of the inn, despite illumination from the burning fire, and the air was thick with boasts and the heat of so many bodies gathered and pressed into one space. In one corner, a broad-chested Rashemi beat time upon twin hand drums while another chanted and sang in the thickly accented language of his homeland. Scattered within the crowd of common folk were several fur-clad warriors, their imposing presence increased by the lengths of the axes and the swords that hung by their sides. Though rough-tongued and forceful, these warriors were treated with affection and good-natured camaraderie by the other Rashemi.

"Berserkers," Borovazk had explained while they had waited to order from their server, "from the Wolf Lodge. They are part of the fang that protects this village. Ignore them unless you want to find yourself in the middle of a wrestling match."

Despite the warning, Taen found himself carefully watching the warriors. To a person, they were lean-faced and serious, and their dark eyes ranged around the room, searching and alert. Long black braids hung in thick lengths down their backs, and their hands never strayed far from their weapons. Taen nearly spluttered in alarm as one berserker, a silver-bearded wolf, caught his surreptitious gaze. The old warrior cast back a long, icy, feral look, lean eyed and hungry, before finally turning back to his companions. The half-elf let out a breath he hadn't known he was holding, and his hands released their tight grip on the table's edge. There was a peril only barely avoided! As skilled as he knew he and his companions were, Taen did not relish having to battle a room full of Rashemi berserkers. The thought sent a shudder through his body despite the warmth of the air.

He was grateful when, a few moments later, his server returned laden with food and drink. She was a thin-set, lanky girl not far from the first flower of womanhood. Long woolen skirts hid the shape of her legs from view, and a linen blouse, covered with grease spots, hung around her frame. Thick, golden-blonde hair threatened to escape from the single braid that wound around her head like a crown; a few of the wild strands fell into her face only to be blown away in haste as she set down food before them. Crocks of thick venison stew, laden with winter vegetables and golden potatoes; trenchers of thick brown bread, piping hot and slathered with melted butter; and a seemingly endless array of earthenware mugs topped with a foamy brew found their way from her arms and on to the table with a speed and aplomb that surprised the half-elf. He thanked the server when she had finished and was rewarded with a shy smile that set a sparkle dancing in the young woman's green eyes.

How different the people of Urling's reactions were now. Like all Rashemi, the men and women of Urling were reserved around strangers, almost suspicious in their appraising glances and clipped speech. When Taen and his companions had first arrived, they were greeted with frank stares and an almost glacial politeness—until Borovazk had stepped forward and quietly spoken to his countrymen. After that, the people of Urling's attitude had thawed, and soon Taen and his friends found themselves treated as old friends. It was, he reflected, a very welcome change.

By unspoken agreement, the group ate in silence. Roberc stared at the shadows as he tucked into the mound of food before him, but the half-elf noted with a hint of dismay that Marissa barely touched her food. The druid absently stirred her stew all the while gazing out at nothing, rarely blinking. The enormity of what had happened beneath the Red Tree came crashing down upon him, shaking loose the comfort and ease he had so recently discovered.

When Marissa had first gathered the group, bleary eyed and grumbling under the dawn sun, and recounted what the telthor had asked of her, Taen wanted to shout with frustration. There was a part of him—a surprisingly large part, it had turned out—that had hoped their time in Rashemen would end soon after Marissa completed her pilgrimage. Sacred journeys made at the behest of one's god were all fine and good, but too much had happened to disturb the fragile peace he had struggled to build within himself since they had entered this strange land. He wanted a chance to return to the life he had known, even if it was filled with the bitter melody of guilt and shame. The half-elf preferred the strains of that familiar tune to the unknown song that played now in his heart.

Surprisingly, Roberc was the first one to agree to accompany Marissa. The halfling simply nodded his head after the druid had finished her tale and stood up. "When do we leave?" was all he had asked before heading off to ready Cavan for their journey. Borovazk, too, was quick to assent to Marissa's quest—though in truth Taen had suspected that raging dragons wouldn't keep the ranger from shedding his blood in Rashemen's time of need. "Borovazk go where the little sister go," he said with great dignity, and Taen wondered, not for the first time, what it was about Marissa that made others so willing to tie their fates so closely to hers.

Including himself, he had had to admit. For how else could he have explained his own presence at the beginning of their journey. So he found himself struggling—not with the decision about whether to continue on with the druid, as that choice was taken from him the moment Marissa had opened her mouth to speak—but with the reality of what this journey could do to him.

"I know what I am asking of you," Marissa said when the two of them were finally alone.

"Do you?" was all he said, all he could say in the face of Marissa's need.

"Perhaps not," she said and touched his cheek with her cool hand. "Still, I am asking." Her eyes were twin pools of light. "I do not wish to do this thing without you, Taenaran, but I will if I have to."

Her voice was soft, like a summer breeze, and Taen found his own heart warming.

"You will not have to," he said finally and gently moved her hand from his face before walking into the shadow of the trees.

Lost in his thoughts, Taen was surprised when his spoon scraped the bottom of the crock of stew; he had finished his dinner without tasting any of it. The half-elf would have called out to the server for more food, but a loud crash drew his attention. Over in the corner, two of the berserkers were locked in a martial embrace. Even from his vantage point, Taen could see the knotted cords of muscles as both fighters strained against each other. Two tables had already fallen to the floor in the struggle, but the Rashemi patrons seemed to be taking it all in stride. Many had even gathered around the fighting berserkers, calling out encouragement to the combatants.

"I thought Borovazk said this place was restful and quiet," Marissa asked, staring at the fight with obvious interest. Taen recalled that very same thing, but he said nothing. He was just glad that something had finally broken through her reverie.

"As long as I can still sleep on a soft straw mattress," Roberc opined with a lazy puff from his pipe, "then I don't care if the spirits of the dead themselves start wailing from the rafters all night long."

"Little friends," Taen heard Borovazk's voice from behind him, cutting over the din of the taproom, "Borovazk speak truth. Green Chapel is nice, quiet place ..." The ranger paused. "Normally."

Taen turned around. Unlike the rest of the group's members, Borovazk had forgone any change of clothing. Once they had arrived at the inn, he had made straight for the back of the common area, content to sit by the bar and exchange news and swap outrageous stories, all the while consuming vast amounts of the bitter, frothy ale served by the barkeep. He returned with another Rashemi in tow, a wizened figure wearing a soiled leather apron.

"Then what happened to change the ambience, Borovazk?" she asked with a laugh as another table toppled beneath the frenzied wrestling match.

"Rumors," said the stranger standing next to their guide. He wore a frown that accentuated the deep wrinkles covering his face. "Rumors of midnight raids, slaughtered villages, and dark things creeping down from the High Country. The blood of Rashemen quickens at the thought of such events happening. The Iron Lord stirs in his citadel, whipping his warlords into a frenzy, and the whole land is abuzz with the possibility of war."

Taen listened and fought down a shudder at the old man's words. Unlike Borovazk, the stranger spoke common almost perfectly, without the heavy accent and tortured syntax that marred the ranger's speech. This made the man's statement somehow more menacing.

"I will say no more of this," he continued, "until you have spoken with the othlor."

Taen blanched as the stranger finished and noted that the others had similar reactions. If there truly were a traitor among the wychlaran, then it wouldn't do for too many people to know why they were around. The half-elf was about to stammer out a protest, denying the truth of the old man's words, but the wizened Rashemi held out his hand.

"Forgive me," the stranger said. "Here I am blathering on about things you probably want to keep secret and I haven't even introduced myself." He gave them all a rueful smile, revealing several cracked teeth. "My name is Selov, and this," he continued, extending his hand to take in the crowded common room, "is my establishment."

Taen relaxed at the stranger's introduction. Once they had agreed to follow Marissa on her journey, they discussed the best place to summon the othlor. It was Borovazk who prevailed upon them to travel to Urling to meet with a certain Selov who, the ranger had insisted, held great knowledge about the ways of the wychlaran.

"Be welcome among us, Selov," Marissa said, coming to her feet, "and thank you for your gracious hospitality."

Selov acknowledged the druid's words with a bow of his head.

"I would be far happier to extend such hospitality at a brighter time in my country's life," Selov said. "Still, a single candle in darkness is worth five in the daytime, or at least that is what my mother taught me." He looked around at the group, wincing once or twice at the sound of breaking glass. "Well, perhaps we can meet somewhere a little less... active," he said and waved his hand indicating that they should follow him. "I have a private room arranged for us. One of the benefits of ownership—or so I am told."

Selov maneuvered deftly in the crowded taproom, cutting in between the gaggle of patrons and warriors with the ease of long practice. Taen followed with Borovazk, Marissa, and Roberc close behind. They turned down a small corridor off to the side of the bar and soon found themselves ushered into a comfortable round room. It was cooler in there, a relief from the dank, sweltering atmosphere of the taproom. Several torches burned brightly along the earthen wall, and the embers of a small peat fire glowed invitingly from the room's hearth.

Taen was surprised to find a large table already set with fruit, cheese, and several pitchers of nut-brown ale. They sat down and ate companionably, telling stories of their journey and asking Selov questions about the Urlingwood. The half-elf studied the wizened innkeeper carefully as they ate.

When the four adventurers had originally decided to meet here at the Green Chapel, Borovazk had informed Taen that Selov was a great wizard—a vremyonni, one of the Old Ones. The half-elf knew very little about the mysterious ways of Rashemen's arcane culture. However, sitting in the quiet of the inn, Taen found it difficult to envision Selov as anything other than a kindly publican. With his wild, unkempt hair and soiled, ale-soaked clothing, the Rashemi would have fit the description of a thousand innkeepers in a thousand cities all across Faerûn. Power calls to power, and Taen, not an unaccomplished practitioner of the arcane arts, felt nothing from the old man. If Selov was indeed a wizard, the

Rashemi disguised it well. It was only when the man spoke of the Urlingwood or recounted a tale soaked in ancient history that something seemed to change about him. Then shadows would gather around his weathered face, and the age lines creasing his skin took on a deeper cast. Silver-gray eyes would cloud with old sorrow, while Selov's voice would shake and quaver, like a dying tree in the wind. He seemed to the half-elf like a man hollowed out by loss.

For all of that, he was a gracious host and answered questions patiently. Taen was surprised when more servers came in to clear plates from the table. Time had passed by quickly as they ate. When the servers had finished, leaving only several more pitchers of ale, the conversation died. Only the fire spoke in the silence, hissing and crackling in its ancient tongue.

The lull continued for several moments, until Marissa cleared her throat.

"Well, Selov," Marissa said, "Borovazk has told us that we should meet with you before speaking with the wychlaran, and you have told us much about the Urlingwood." She acknowledged his helpfulness with a broad smile. "However, I am thinking that there is more that you haven't said."

Taen watched the shadows gather in Selov's eyes once again then disappear as the Rashemi answered the druid's smile with one of his own. When he spoke, it was directly to Borovazk, and his words made the half-elf uneasy.

"I see that you have spoken the truth, my friend. She has the *vydda*, the witch eye. Such a gift is rare," he said, this time turning to Marissa. "It sees to the heart of things."

Selov pushed back his chair and stood, taking them all in with his gaze.

"Very well," Selov said. "There is, indeed, much that I haven't said. These are dark times, and I do not wish for the wrong ears to overhear. I trust my staff here at the inn implicitly, but a shadow grows over the heart of Rashemen, and what was once noble and hale withers beneath it."

"Once, long ago—longer than I can even remember, it seems—I studied and mastered the *vyvadnya*, becoming an Old One before my thirtieth year. It was rare that one so young would ascend to the brotherhood of the vremyonni, and I felt that honor deeply, treasuring it in my heart. I was determined to live up to my reputation, to surpass all of the other Old Ones in knowledge and mastery. Such a goal became a fever, burning in my veins both day and night."

Selov paused, taking a long draught from a mug of ale before continuing. "Driven by the goad of my pride, I worked on creating a powerful spell that would, I believed, permanently drain a wizard's ability to use magic. I had hoped to use it against the damnable Red Wizards. My brothers warned me that such a spell was too dangerous to fashion, that it bent and twisted the flow of magic in a way that made it too difficult to control.

"They were right, of course," Selov continued, "but I wouldn't listen. One night while testing the spell, I lost control of the mystical forces and they turned on me. When I awoke, I discovered that my spell chamber had been almost completely destroyed and worse, I could no longer use even the simplest of cantrips. I had stripped myself of the ability to use magic. Ashamed and devastated by what I had done to myself, I fled to Urling. It was the wychlaran who convinced me that I could still serve Rashemen, even without my former power, so I opened the Green Chapel to help anyone who comes to the Urlingwood in search of wisdom from the sisterhood."

Taen listened to the man's tale with barely concealed horror. He, too, had broken beneath the weight of his own destiny—though in his case, the half-elf had destroyed more than his own life. Still, even in the aftermath of his failure, he'd retained his skill in magic. Taen's arcane power had been the only thing that had kept him from seeking oblivion. To live without that—he shuddered. It was beyond comprehension.

"A sad tale to be sure," Roberc's voice cut in from his place at the table, "but what does this have to do with helping us complete our journey?"

Taen winced at the halfling's tone, but if the fighter's pointed question angered Selov, the man didn't show it. Instead, the Rashemi shrugged and offered them a rueful smile.

"Ah," he said. "Forgive an old man his ramblings. Though I do not have the use of my arcane power, I still hold a great deal of knowledge that will be of use to you. In each of the villages and hamlets dotting the outskirts of the Urlingwood, servants and students of the hathran live side by side with other Rashemi. Had you gone to any of the other villages, it would have been far easier for the traitorous forces within the sisterhood to discover your intent. Borovazk did well in bringing you here.

"The Urlingwood itself is a dangerous place; it is death for any not of the wychlaran to enter its expanse. However, I know a . . . special place near an ancient well at the edge of the forest. If you gather there beneath the night sky, it will offer you protection against scrying and other forms of spying."

Marissa smiled at the man's words.

"Thank you, dear Selov," Marissa said. "Your assistance means a great deal to us."

"Well," Selov replied, "don't thank me just yet. There is a price for my knowledge."

Taen watched Marissa's eyebrows rise in response.

"What is that price?" Marissa asked.

Selov looked long at the druid then at each of his guests before responding.

"You must take me with you," Selov said with a smile.

Marissa caught Taen's eye, and he could read the question there. Slightly, imperceptibly, he nodded his head. Taen felt as if they sailed across a dark and stormy sea riddled with hidden reefs and riptides that could sink them at any moment. They could not afford to turn down aid.

The druid raised her mug of ale.

"Done," she said to Selov, "and gladly so."

Taen drained his own mug then several more as the conversation turned to the particulars of their journey. By the time the half-elf rose from his seat and navigated the shadow-filled corridor back to his room, it was very late. Fighting back sleep, he never saw the long-skirted servant idly cleaning by the door of the rounded chamber.

CHAPTER 12

The Year of Wild Magic
(1372 DR)

They left Urling well after nightfall.

Crept out would be more like it, Taen thought as he walked softly along the snow-covered track. No wind stirred the soft needles of the pine trees around them or rustled the lengths of wool cloaks they wore. Instead, the night air lay still—suspended, as if the world were holding its breath. The silence unnerved him. Taen found himself grateful for the creak of leather and harness, the jangle of mail, and the crunch of ice-crusted snow beneath his feet.

Stars littered the blue-black sky, burning coldly as they marched along, and the moon hung above them like a crescent pendant carved from purest silver. In the distance, the witches' wood brooded in darkness, a shadowy mass of tangled branches, thick trunks, and gnarled wisdom. Even from where he walked, Taen caught the sense of menace emanating from its shadow-strewn depths. It was as if the very trees were fixing him with a penetrating gaze, judging his life against a span of years that circled back to the first flowering of the world. He felt small and insignificant beneath the weight of that vernal stare; the thought of even attempting to steal past the vigilance of the forest's edge sent a shudder through his body. No wonder the Rashemi spoke of the Urlingwood with both awe and fear.

Not for the first time, he felt his misgivings about their journey rise to the surface. Ancient pacts broken, traitors within an arcane sisterhood, and a growing darkness within Rashemen—these had been far away from his thoughts when he had first agreed to accompany Marissa on her pilgrimage. Now he was right in the middle of a war for the soul of a nation, and even though he and his companions were on the side of good, the half-elf found the prospect of meeting the leaders of the wychlaran a little daunting. Perhaps it was the chill that he hadn't been able shake since he'd entered Rashemen's borders, or the unforgiving presence of the Urlingwood itself, but Taen felt as if somehow the power of this land threatened to twist the sense of shame and failure that had defined his life, exposing his secrets the way an ancient oak's roots can twine and twist around a house wall, pulling it down over time and exposing the inside to sunlight. Over the course of the past ten years, Taen had made an uneasy truce with his past. All of that threatened to disappear. Now all he felt was a constant sense of guilt. Of course, he thought bitterly, stealing out of Urling like a thief in the night hadn't helped his mood any either.

At Selov's insistence, Taen and his companions had dined in the common room of the Green Chapel, mixing small talk in with humorous anecdotes from their travels, playing the part of gracious guests. As the evening wore on, the innkeeper had once again invited them rather publicly back to a reserved room to enjoy some of his best wine and mead. Away from prying eyes, the group had waited, with their gear already neatly packed and stowed, ready to leave at a moment's notice. Finally, after the candles had burned low and the fires of the inn were banked, Selov gave them a sign. At once, they gathered up their gear and followed the innkeeper through a secret tunnel and out into the fields to the west of Urling.

Now Taen and his companions found themselves furtively traveling in the long, bleak silence of the night. Roberc led the group, sitting astride Cavan, who, the half-elf noted, walked easily despite the weight of rider and barding. Borovazk strode alongside the mounted halfling, his deep voice muffled and oddly gentle as he whispered some passing story to his new-found companion. Taen smiled as he thought about the unlikely pair. Whether dicing, drinking, or exchanging raucous insults, the giantlike Rashemi ranger and the diminutive fighter were becoming fast friends.

Selov followed a few steps behind, his almost skeletal frame wrapped in a thick gray cloak. The former wizard had insisted on walking without aid, even when their brisk pace had sent the Rashemi into a paroxysm of wheezing. He had waved off the suggestion that they slow down, vowing that he would not delay them. So far, Taen noted, he hadn't.

Even so, Marissa kept close to the wizened innkeeper, walking alongside him and asking questions about the Urlingwood and the telthor that he knew of in the area. Taen watched the druid as she walked—seemingly care-free and easy along the twisting path—and nearly forgot to breathe. Marissa wore the moonlight like a mantle. It spilled down the length of her hair and traced the graceful outline of her body like molten silver. Everything about her caught and reflected that light; she glittered and gleamed beneath the dome of the night sky. With the Staff of the Red Tree held lightly in her right hand, casting its own pale illumination, the druid looked like nothing so much as one of the Seldarine, or an avatar of Sehanine Moonbow, gracing this plane with her presence.

He shook his head sharply, as if to shake away those fanciful thoughts. Whatever had happened to Marissa since she had come under Rashemen's spell, it was clear to Taen that she seemed more whole than she had been ever since the blightlord had destroyed her arm. That night was a terrible one—for her as well as for him. His heart wept for Marissa as she shouted and thrashed beneath the fury of the fever raging through her body. He bared his soul to her, thinking that she would never remember but wanting to offer her some comfort, some knowledge that she was not alone in the world, that he, too, had lost something so dear it was like losing a part of himself.

What had happened next was even worse—for the druid had remembered. Now that night of intimacy lay between them, a treasured memory and a goad in his side. Taen's heart had already been given—and pierced beneath a moon just like this one.

Talaedra! He nearly cried her name out loud.

Beneath the sharpness of that grief, Taen knew that he could never give himself to another, so he and Marissa had spent the years dancing endlessly between intimacy and friendship.

Until now, he thought with a terrible certainty. Now she was whole.

And—perhaps—beyond him.

He wanted to find out *now,* in the midst of their journey to meet the wychlaran. Such was the burden he felt that it lay like a geas on his heart, but just as he began to quicken his pace in an effort to draw near the druid, Selov called a halt.

"We are close to the well," he said after a long draught from his waterskin. "There is a deer track about half a candle's walk west of here. It cuts northeast for a ways and then opens into an abandoned trade road. If we follow the track and then walk along the road, we'll come to a large oak that has been split by lightning. The well is just a short walk beyond the oak."

The others nodded, passing around a skin of wine and some salted beef before pressing on. The stillness of the deep night held as they marched onward. Taen tried several subtle attempts to draw Marissa into a private conversation, but the druid seemed distracted, answering him with simple grunts or not at all. As they picked their way carefully through the deer track, avoiding the fallen trunks of trees and the thorns of the thick underbrush, the half-elf finally lost patience.

"Marissa," he snapped. "Are you listening to me at all?"

"Hmm ... what?" the druid replied after a moment. Then, as if waking from a dream, she stopped to look back at him. "Oh, Taenaran," she said, "I'm sorry. I ... I guess I am a little distracted. It's this," she said, holding out the length of the staff she received from the Red Tree. "I can feel it—the same way I could feel the presence of the Red Tree, only this time it's gentle, like a soft whisper in my mind."

Taen nodded. "I understand," he said uneasily. Though he knew that powerful magic items could sometimes manifest intelligence and an independent will, the half-elf was more than suspicious of whatever sentience lurked within the confines of that staff.

"Look," he continued, "I know we're right in the middle of something really big here, but we need to talk." He had schooled himself against her anger, and he was prepared to defend himself on any number of grounds, all eminently logical and rational.

Instead, she simply nodded her head.

"Yes," Marissa said with a familiar twinkle in her eye—one that Taen found particularly alluring. "I have much to say to you, Taenaran of Avaelearean, but now is not the time."

He started to protest, but she cut him off. "Peace, *arael'sha*," she said gently. "Let us meet with the othlor, then"—she paused—"we shall see what we shall see." With that, she turned and walked away.

Taen stood there, stunned, and watched her go.

Arael'sha.

She had called him *arael'sha,* heart-friend, a term so laden with meaning that in the subtle Elvish tongue it had nearly a hundred uses. Somehow, with just a few words, the druid had managed to confuse him even further.

Taen shook his head and stared into the night-shrouded underbrush a moment before continuing on.

The track wended and twisted its way forward, sometimes wide enough to walk two abreast and sometimes collapsing in upon itself so much that Taen and the others were forced to move slowly, almost creeping forward, in single file. As the moon began its lazy descent, the darkness deepened. By the time they had reached the end of the trail and stepped out on to the road, it was nearly pitch black, save for the faint glow emanating from the Staff of the Red Tree.

They huddled in that darkness, waiting for Selov to scent the trail and lead them forward. When he did, there came a great stirring from the treetops. An explosive beating of wings and the harsh-throated caw of a great raven echoed in the night. Rusella, aloft and flying wildly, circled thrice around the group before alighting on the tip of Marissa's staff. The creature's albino-red eyes whirled and glared as it darted its head in all directions, calling madly.

"Something's wrong," Marissa said in between snatches of a mumbled song meant to sooth the agitated bird. "I . . . I can't understand her. She's nearly mad with fright."

That's when Taen felt it—a tightening of the silence, as if the walls of the world were shrinking in upon themselves and pressing down with an abominable weight. He gasped from the force of it, trying at last to suck air into his lungs. None would come.

A faint mist had begun to form along the ground. Taen screamed silently as it leeched the warmth from his bones. He wanted to run but couldn't. His legs remained rooted to the ground. If he didn't escape, the half-elf knew that there would be nothing left of him but the bitter, cold emptiness of the grave.

"Look," Selov hissed and pointed down the old trade road.

Shadows swirled where the old man pointed, deeper pits of darkness against a landscape of black. Points of red light stabbed out from the darkness like the embers of a long-dead fire. Taen could sense the need behind those baleful eyes, the implacable hunger of death rising up out of the night to swallow the living.

"Wraiths," Roberc said, though his voice came out as a barely breathed whisper.

As the creatures advanced, Taen could make out the dim outline of black robes flowing with each incorporeal step. There were six of them, floating silently down the road like nightmares. Even in his panic, Taen noted that the last one held a scepter in one hand while a gilded crown wreathed its shrouded head.

Roberc struggled to draw his weapon as Cavan backed away from the oncoming wraiths. The war-dog whined and yelped in a high-pitched tone as his rider fought for control.

"Enough," Marissa said at last through clenched teeth. Lifting her staff high into the air, she intoned a brief prayer. Immediately the chill disappeared, replaced by warmth and the sweet fragrance of a spring evening. Taen nearly stumbled as the terror drained from his body.

"Quick, everyone form a circle," Taen shouted. "Don't let them surround you."

As they fell into formation, the half-elf grabbed Selov and pulled him into the center of their position. Once the innkeeper was secured, the half-elf raised both hands into the air and uttered the words to a spell. At first, he stumbled over the torturous pronunciation but soon found the rhythm of the arcane formula. Of all the disciplines of magic, none were as distasteful to him as necromancy. Even when the spell worked against the forces of undeath, it still left its mark, like a bruise upon the soul. There were powers in the world, he knew, best left untouched. Still, their need was great, so as he finished the spell, Taen thrust out both arms, as if embracing the oncoming wraiths. A soft, golden radiance emanated out from the space between his arms, enveloping the advancing creatures. As the light struck the wraiths, they recoiled as if struggling against a tremendous wind. When at last the mystical light faded, three wraiths remained frozen, enveloped in a thin cocoon of golden energy.

At that moment, Marissa took a single step forward and shouted a supplication to her god. Immediately, a brilliant column of flame roared into existence, consuming one wraith in a coruscating shower of fire.

With a single command to Cavan, Roberc broke rank and charged at an oncoming wraith. The war-dog danced nimbly to one side as the undead creature thrust out a shadowy hand, allowing Roberc an opening with his sword. His blade gleamed in the dying moonlight before it plunged into the wraith's form—to little effect. The weapon simply passed through.

Roberc cursed but kept the wraith busy as Borovazk moved into a flanking position. The ranger's warhammer and sword moved in a deadly dance. Both struck the wraith hard, causing ripples in the creature's form.

Taen had time to watch his friends' battle only for an instant. Confident that they could hold their own, he returned his attention to the crown-bearing wraith now looming before Marissa. The druid fell back, barely avoiding the wraith's attack as the undead creature swung its scepter in a wide arc. It gave a soft moan, like the wind whistling through an empty graveyard, before pressing forward.

Taen loosed a series of magical bolts from his fingertips, hoping that the arcane missiles would distract the creature. The creature shuddered as the energy struck its form, but it continued to advance toward Marissa. Desperately, she swung the length of her staff at the creature. Pure white energy erupted at the point of contact, causing the wraith to fall back in pain. It glared at her from the depths of its red eyes but made no further move to advance.

Borovazk's cry of pain and anger drew Taen's attention. He watched in horror as a wraith withdrew its long, black arm from within the ranger's chest. Roberc beat madly at the undead monster with the edge of his blade, but his opponent remained focused on the wounded Rashemi. Without thought, Taen summoned the words to another spell. When he had finished, a single bolt of blue lightning sped from his outstretched hand to strike the wraith. It shuddered like an unfurling sail in the midst of a gale wind before fading out of existence.

Too late, Taen realized that casting his spell left him vulnerable to attack by the wraith lord. He managed to stumble away from the creature's first swing, but it quickly followed through with a thrust from its outstretched arm.

Taen gasped as the wraith's long fingers passed through the skin of his neck and reached deep into his being. Instantly, the world spun away, replaced by a thick haze of gray fog. He stumbled forward, anxious to find his companions, trying to avoid the follow-up blow that would surely fall, but the fog swirled around him, filling his lungs. Taen's chest burned. His heart had stopped beating, and was replaced by a single ball of white ice that sat in his chest like a lodestone. Choking and retching, he nearly didn't hear the woman's voice that called out to him from the depths of the fog.

"Murderer!" it shouted, and again, "Murderer!"

Taen wanted to protest, to deny the accusation, but he knew the truth. He was a murderer. Talaedra's face formed in the fog swirling around him.

"Murderer." This time several voices accused him— then several hundred, until the air reverberated with the word—"murderer."

"Talaedra!" he shouted—then knew no more.

Marissa's blood froze in her veins when she saw Taenaran fall beneath the wraith's attack. Fear and anger rose within her at the thought that he might be dead. She gripped the Staff of the Red Tree tightly and swung it with all her strength at the stooped form of the feeding wraith. Power flowed through the staff once again as it struck the undead monster, but this time the impact caused the wood of the staff to ignite with a flaring blast of silver energy. Whatever she had done had awakened life from deep within the wood. She could feel the whispering voice in her mind grow stronger, more urgent, until it nearly shouted ancient wisdom and ancient wrath.

Marissa fought it while she could, but the voice overcame her. For a moment, she knew the terrible power held within the still-living branch of the Red Tree, knew how to tap into it and how to unleash it on the world.

A moment was all she needed.

Raising the staff high into the air, she brought its

heel down hard on the earth, singing the words to an ancient song in a voice both her own and not her own. The ground trembled. Light exploded from the artifact, as bright as the searing light of noon at High Summer. It filled the road with its blinding rays, and against its elemental force, the wraiths had no defense. In a flash of darkness, they imploded, leaving only the memory of death behind.

Then, as suddenly as it had flared into existence, the light winked out, and darkness descended like a shroud upon the trade road.

Selov was the first to recover.

"By all the gods and the wisdom of the elders," he whispered in obvious amazement. "What have you done?"

Marissa was tired, almost too tired to stand.

"I am not sure," she said wearily, "and right now I don't care." She forced her body to move toward the fallen half-elf. "Is he—?"

"He is alive," Selov said, examining Taen carefully.

"So is Borovazk," called out Roberc.

Relief flooded through her body, giving a lift to her wearied spirit.

"Then we must hurry to the well," Marissa said. "I fear that our friends need help that only the wychlaran can provide."

Or withhold, she thought cynically.

In the distance, a lone wolf sang mournfully to the dying moon.

CHAPTER 13

The Year of Wild Magic
(1372 DR)

The goblin screamed.

Yulda, wrapped in her hag illusion, smiled at the foul creature's pain—though her eyes held little humor. She watched it beat ineffectually at the incorporeal form of the snow tiger, like a small child denying its mother's discipline. Her smile deepened as Fleshrender batted the hapless creature between its paws, purring loudly while its claws sank through the goblin's skin.

In truth, her mood was fouler than the snowstorms that battered the mountains surrounding her citadel. When word had come to Yulda, through her spy at the Green Chapel, regarding the outsiders and their peculiar journey to Immil Vale, she was incensed. The presence of the Staff of the Red Tree among the outsiders drove her beyond reason. If Durakh had not had the sense to try to calm Yulda down, the witch would have set about destroying the interlopers right at that moment—thereby revealing herself too soon. Instead, she retired to her chamber, cursing the presence of the strangers and her need of Durakh's wisdom, and began planning her next move.

Circumstances made it clear to Yulda that powerful forces were moving against her. She had spent nearly ten winters planting the seeds of her plan and nurturing its growth. A little whispered gossip here, a quiet expression of dissatisfaction there, and the subtle promise of power to those who craved it the way a dragon craves gold had done much to position her for what she was about to do. There was no way that she would let her plan wither on the vine because of some soft outsiders.

She wrestled for a time with the problem before her. It was clear right from the start that she couldn't allow the intruders to meet with the wychlaran. If those meddling telthor from the Red Tree had sent the outsiders to speak with the othlor, then it could only be because they had discovered Yulda's secret and were moving against her. But, she thought bitterly, how could she accomplish the destruction of the outsiders without it being traced back to her? It was then that a plan began to form in her mind.

She had summoned Durakh from her meditations, and immediately they set out for the abandoned crypts lying in the secret places beneath the citadel. There the evil cleric bound several wraiths haunting the forgotten tunnels to her will. Once the strangers had departed the hamlet of Urling, Yulda teleported the undead monsters right in their midst.

It was a sound plan, one that was supposed to rid the witch of the one serious threat to her plans.

And it failed utterly.

Yulda nearly screamed with frustration. Not only

had the strangers defeated the undead menace, but they also managed to evade every attempt at locating them through magical scrying. It was as if they had disappeared from the world.

Selov!

She knew that the old fool was somehow behind this. He had ever been a bootlicking lackey of the wychlaran. No doubt he used his knowledge to help the outsiders. Once she ruled Rashemen utterly, Yulda would deal with the doddering idiot herself. Until then, she would just have to try and salve her seething temper and—if she were being honest—her growing fear, in the blood and pain of her servants.

Unfortunately, Fleshrender's current plaything had stopped screaming and simply lay there like a piece of meat. Yulda's assembled minions watched with barely concealed terror. Human and goblin servants huddled in clumps, pointing and whispering at the stiffening corpse, no doubt wondering if they would be next.

The stink of their fear rose up in the vaulted room like sweet perfume. Yulda breathed it in deeply, savoring its pungent aroma. Still, it could not ease the clenching of her stomach, and the witch found herself grinding her teeth in frustration.

A curse on Selov, the blasted wychlaran, and their foolish pawns, she thought acidly.

Yulda turned to face her gathered servants. Their whispered mewling irritated her. With a sharp clap of her hands, she captured their attention.

"Leave us," she shouted at them, "and prepare for your duties!"

At that, they scattered into the shadows of the room, and Yulda drew a small sense of satisfaction from their hasty retreat.

"Not you," she called out to Durakh as the cleric started to walk down the hall to her private chamber. "We have things to discuss."

The half-orc checked her movement and turned back to Yulda.

"As you command," Durakh said in an even tone.

Careful, Yulda thought—though if she meant it as a reminder to herself or as a mental warning to the cleric, she couldn't be sure. Her world had begun to spin out of control with the revelation of the strangers' presence in Rashemen. It wouldn't take much to tear things irrevocably from their moorings, leaving her only with the ruins of a plan and the ire of the wychlaran and vremyonni pursuing her through the darkness. She licked her cracked lips before speaking.

"You know that our plan has failed," she said, more as a statement than a question.

Durakh nodded.

"Yes," Durakh replied. "I felt the wraiths' destruction." Her gray eyes met Yulda's. "It was ... unexpected."

Yulda's temper rose at the cleric's equanimity.

"Unexpected," Yulda nearly shouted. "You assured me that your undead servants would destroy them."

Durakh raised a single eyebrow in response. The scars on her chin and throat gleamed angrily in the light of the chamber.

"They were powerful," she said after a moment. "More powerful than I expected, and"—she paused, casting another glance directly at the witch—"they had help."

"Help?" Yulda asked, her voice rising. Not for the first time, she regretted the necessity of her illusion, for as Chaul the hag, she could not bring her empty eye socket to bear on the impertinent cleric.

"Yes," Durakh replied. "Could you not feel it—a wave of energy that did not originate from any mortal spellcaster?"

In truth, Yulda had felt the unexpected surge of power. Its passing echoed through the bones of the earth even as far as the citadel. She was surprised, however, that the half-orc had felt is as well. She was forced, once again, to revise her assessment of the cleric.

"It was the power of the staff," Yulda said, "though how the outsiders discovered how to tap in to the Red Tree's power remains a mystery to me."

"Have you been able to locate them?" Durakh asked, fingering the outline of her ebony holy symbol.

Yulda gazed at the half-orc warily before answering.

"I have tried spells of location and detection as well as scrying," Yulda said. "So far they have eluded my arcane eye."

Though the cleric's face remained impassive as she spoke, Yulda could sense the feeling of satisfaction that crested through her thoughts. However hard she might try and disguise it, Durakh clearly enjoyed the witch's frustration.

"Then we must assume that the strangers have rendezvoused with the othlor," the half-orc said. "The wychlaran must be protecting them from your spells."

"Perhaps," was all that Yulda said in reply.

The cleric's words galled her, even as she heard the truth in them. Soon they would come after her and try to destroy what she had worked so hard to accomplish. The witch knew that she would be vulnerable in the citadel with her forces heading out into the field.

"Even so," Durakh said, "I have tripled the outer sentries and prepared a few surprises for anyone trying to use the tunnels to gain entrance to the lower portions of the citadel. It would not do for them to catch us unawares."

"Good," Yulda replied, though inwardly she seethed at the liberty taken by her lieutenant. This was *her* citadel. Clearly the witch would have to take steps in order to reinforce that reality for the half-orc.

Yulda was about to do just that when a piercing shout rang in her mind. She nearly pitched forward from the force of it but found Durakh's strong arm holding her up.

"What is it?" the cleric asked. "What has happened?"

Yulda could hear the anxiety in the half-orc's voice, but she had no time to revel in it, for the voice in her mind rang louder.

"They dare," she said, shrugging off Durakh's support and forcing her will to clamp down on the inner alarm.

When she had first come to the citadel, Yulda spent tendays preparing arcane defenses in case anyone should try and magically breach the boundaries of her demesne. One of them had just activated.

"The wychlaran are trying to teleport something or someone into the citadel," Yulda continued. "No doubt those damn outsiders."

"Can you prevent them?" Durakh asked.

The witch shook her head. "No," she said then began to smile, "but I can do something even better."

With a quick motion to silence any further questions, Yulda closed her eyes and cast her mind into the complex web of spells she had spun over the citadel. In a moment, she located the tendrils of power that would coil and grow to teleport her enemies within the walls of the keep. Quickly she gathered her power and sent a surge of arcane energy through the webwork of her defenses. It flared and expanded once the energy met the incoming teleport spell, and Yulda felt a satisfying vibration as her magic intertwined with that of the wychlarans', shunting the location of the teleport to a place of her choosing.

Her smile broadened as she thought about the incoming invaders. Yulda opened here eyes. Durakh stood quietly to one side, her head cocked as if listening for the sounds of battle from somewhere within the citadel.

"Do not worry, Durakh," the witch said quietly, "our guests are nowhere within our walls. I've arranged a little detour for them. I doubt that they shall trouble us further."

Though she remained smiling, Yulda focused every ounce of will on stilling the trembling in her limbs. It had been several tendays since she last drew energy from her vremyonni captive, and the teleportation spell drained her severely. She had no wish for her lieutenant to see her so utterly weakened. With a single command, the witch summoned Fleshrender to her side. The telthor obeyed immediately, loping past Durakh with easy strides.

"I must return to my sanctum and replenish my power," she said briskly. "I trust you can hold the fortress until my return."

She did not wait for the cleric's response but instead whispered the words to another spell and faded quickly into the shadows.

CHAPTER 14

The Year of Wild Magic
(1372 DR)

They hovered like ghosts around the well.

Marissa spotted them first as she stumbled into the clearing, half-supporting, half-dragging Taenaran. White robes billowed and shifted in the still night air, catching and reflecting the dim starlight. Sharp eyes, like diamonds, regarded them from behind the cold, impassive mien of stark white masks. There were five of them, living statues, standing still and terrible around the stone lip of the well.

She gazed upon them with a mixture of fear and wonder. In the short time since she had unleashed the power of the staff, her mind expanded—or perhaps it shrank. The strong, implacable voice that had sung the words of power in her head remained—though it softened once again to an ever-present whisper, a sibilance of wisdom that skewed and altered her perception with each utterance. Marissa felt as if she stood with a foot in two worlds, and her spirit was the portal.

Thus, when one of the figures pointed commandingly for them to approach the well, she did so without hesitation. In the half dream where she walked, the witches were creatures of ice and silence, the very judgment of Rashemen incarnated before her. She could not—no, she would not—deny them.

As Marissa approached the assembled witches, she sketched a reverent bow, careful not to let the still-dazed Taenaran drop to the ground. Borovazk bowed deeply as well then moved to help support the wounded half-elf despite his own injuries. She watched as Roberc approached, still mounted on Cavan, his grizzled face staring intensely at the gathered witches from beneath his gold helm. Selov, she noted with little surprise, merely inclined his head to the othlor, a clear gesture of respect from one's peer.

The othlor drew back from the well and formed a circle around Marissa and her companions. From this distance, she could see that the witches' masks were not identical. Though similar in their stark coloring, each mask held a unique expression frozen on its ivory surface. Some were simple and stolid, while the exaggerated features on others crossed the border into the grotesque.

Silence filled the clearing as Marissa and her friends endured the gaze of the assembled othlor. The druid wondered what the protocol was for speaking to the wisest of the wychlaran. Her instincts told her to follow Selov's lead, but concern for Taenaran rode her like a night hag. She cleared her throat in preparation to speak but stopped as one of the witches, bearing a wide-eyed, wide-mouthed mask set in a permanent leer, stepped forward.

"Who dares summon the wisest of the Wise Ones?"

the leering witch shouted without preamble. "Who dares call us from the mastery of our lore like a shepherd whistling for his dog? We are the othlor of the wychlaran, guide and guardians of Rashemen, not servile hedge-witches who run at the beck and call of our masters. Tell us who you might be so that we shall know the names of those whose blood we shed!"

The witch's voice cracked like a whip across the silence of the clearing. Marissa flinched beneath its lash and heard Borovazk groan softly under his breath.

"Be at peace, Najra," Selov said, his soft voice a counterpoint to the angry tones of the witch. "They are friends of the land and come bearing a message of warning to the wychlaran."

The witch brought her hand down in a swift, chopping motion, as if cleaving the innkeeper's words from the air.

"Be silent, Selov," Najra spoke again. "Friends of the land would never summon their betters so rudely—nor could they unless they had help." The leering othlor drew closer to Selov. "Have you broken your sacred trust?" The witch's voice purred with surprising softness, but Marissa could hear the threat lurking beneath its silken surface like a fitfully slumbering bullette.

"I have betrayed nothing, Najra," Selov replied evenly. Though tension hung thick in the air, Marissa could feel none of it coming from the former wizard. "My loyalty is, and always has been, to Rashemen," he continued. "These foreigners bring matters urgent to the survival of our land. Will you not listen to them?"

"Bah," Najra spat out. "What silly glamour have these strangers cast over your sightless eyes? I had thought that your foolishness might come to an end once you destroyed your own powers, but 'a fool in summer is a fool in winter,' as they say. You have been a fool in all seasons, it seems. That one"—she pointed a bony finger in Marissa's direction—"profanes one of the most sacred artifacts of the land with her very touch. She is an ignorant child carrying a woman's burden, yet you follow her like a two-legged familiar eager for its reward."

Marissa bit back the retort that burned hotly behind her pressed lips. She was no child, and Selov certainly didn't deserve the tongue-lashing he was receiving. In the short amount of time that she had known him, the druid had grown very fond of the kindly innkeeper. Every natural instinct within her cried out to defend the former wizard, to shout back at the asp-tongued Najra.

She held her tongue and listened with other senses—for it was clear that something beyond a simple accusation was occurring. Holding the rough wood of the Staff of the Red Tree in her hand, Marissa's mystic perceptions deepened. There, behind a carefully built arcane screen, she *felt* the presence of a wordless, intimate bond that connected each of these women. Though they stood in silence, still they enjoyed a deep communion of spirit—one that hung just at the edge of her senses. Though the druid knew that she could penetrate the witches' mystic screen and eavesdrop using the power of the staff, she refrained. That, she reasoned, would constitute too much of a violation, and if Najra's stinging barbs were any indication, her use of the staff's power had already violated the witches' self-proclaimed sovereignty.

Nevertheless, the temptation remained. Marissa hadn't expected a hero's welcome from the wychlaran. The open hostility of their current reception, however, went beyond her understanding. Perhaps, she thought, this was a test, a way of weeding out those who were unworthy of the wychlaran's help, or the thought came unbidden, perhaps the witch Najra lurked behind the troubles of Rashemen. Could she be the traitor? Would it be that easy?

Marissa's mind whirled with the possibilities, and

through it all, she knew that Taenaran needed her help, that he suffered deeply from the wraith's touch, as did Borovazk, though the ranger fared far better and bore his wounds silently. Distracted by these thoughts, it took Marissa a few moments to realize that Najra had stopped speaking. All eyes in the clearing had fallen on her; she could feel the weight of the stares, bearing her down.

She cleared her throat before speaking.

"Wise Ones," Marissa began, "please forgive the . . . abruptness of our call. Were our need, and Rashemen's, not so great, we would never treat you so."

Marissa cast a glance at Najra. The witch glared from behind her mask but said nothing.

"Selov speaks the truth," she continued. "If you are angry, direct your anger toward us and the telthor of your land. It was they who sent us to you, bearing a message of warning. Please—"

"You lie," Najra shouted, interrupting the druid. "If Rashemen were truly in peril, do you not think that we would sense it? *We* are the defenders of this land, not some outland impostors without the sense to make their lies even remotely believable." The witch drew even with Marissa. "You are lucky that the telthor tolerate your presence in Rashemen, let alone speak with you."

The witch's anger was a palpable thing, hot and sharp edged. Marissa took a step back, despite her own mounting emotion, and struggled to regain her composure. One wrong word or heated phrase could jeopardize the future of Rashemen—not to mention doom one of the most important people in her life. She was grateful when Roberc dismounted from Cavan and walked to her side. The halfling strode slowly and purposefully to stand within arm's reach, his chain mail rattling with each step.

Najra looked askance at the warrior's approach but did not seem impressed by his show of solidarity.

If anything, it looked to Marissa as if the diminutive fighter's presence poured oil on the fire of the witch's ire. Najra drew breath to speak again, but the sound of the halfling's sword slowly sliding from its worn scabbard stilled her tongue.

"Nadir, or Nadya—or whatever your name is," Roberc began softly, in a voice that held the promise of menace, "all we have done since we have entered this blasted land is freeze and bleed. We never asked to be the bearers of apocalyptic news, and we certainly never asked to be on the ass-end of a tongue whipping that my own grandmother, dead these twenty years, could have done better."

The witch sputtered and hissed behind her mask, obviously stunned by the halfling's audacity and struggling to put words to her anger.

Roberc continued, looking out at each of the witches as he spoke.

"You all may be the most powerful of the guardians of Rashemen," Roberc said, "but you don't seem to see very well at all. We are wounded and bleeding because someone didn't want us to make it to this meeting. They sent a wraith lord and its foul servants after us in the shadow of Urlingwood, right under your noses. Why would such a thing happen if we were making this whole thing up?"

Marissa held her breath as the halfling's question hung in the air. All around her, she could sense the hum of the witches' mental communion rise to a fevered pitch. For good or for ill, Roberc had spoken the truth, she thought, and now that truth would either save or damn them all.

"You dare!" Najra shouted, finally finding her voice. "You, a stranger and a man, dare to insult the wychlaran. Sisters," she said, turning toward the assembled witches, "I demand that these outlanders be punished for their transgressions—for violating the sanctity of the Red Tree and perverting its power to summon us from our duties."

With that, she raised a pale white hand over her head and began to chant softly in the language of magic. Roberc leaped forward before Marissa could stop him, sword poised to strike at the figure. She watched the first steps of the halfling's deadly dance as if he moved in slow motion, watched the arc of the sword begin to cut downward, and watched as Selov and Borovazk inched forward, trying somehow to stop what was to come.

Too late.

Everything was too late. The witches would move against them, and even if they could survive, they would have to escape from Rashemen while they were being hunted by the wychlaran.

Taenaran would still be lost in the midst of the wraith lord's cursed touch.

For a moment, Marissa lost faith. She wondered why Rillifane would have called her to Rashemen only to have things end so poorly. Why had she come?

Then she heard a word whispered softly from across a great distance, and her heart grew strong once more. The word grew, becoming louder as it traveled, swelling across the great gap of time and space, gathering force. When it finally broke forth among them, it shattered rock and split the earth with its power, knocking everyone to the ground.

"Enough!" the voice thundered.

Marissa stumbled to her feet, clapping hands to ears in pain, as the voice echoed in the clearing and in her mind. When she had recovered, the druid looked in amazement at the shimmering form of an old woman floating above the well. Silver and golden energy coruscated around the figure, dancing and arcing in a wild circle. The others gathered around as well—all of them, including the witches, who had recovered their balance with astonishing aplomb. Collectively, they stared at the radiant presence in their midst. Squinting against the pulsating illumination emanating from the figure, it took Marissa a few moments to recognize the shimmering crone.

Imsha had come as promised.

The druid nearly cried with relief—though the telthor's first words bore little comfort.

"You fools," Imsha said. "The wolf raids the henhouse while the shepherds drink to their good fortune! How long will you sit their squabbling amongst yourselves while Rashemen crumbles around you?"

Marissa would have responded but stopped in wonder as each of the witches bowed low to the telthor—even Najra, though she seemed to struggle with it. Watching it all unfold, the druid could barely contain her emotion. Both joy and guilt warred within her—joy at the presence of Imsha and the effect that it had upon the witches—there was hope now for both Taenaran and for her mission—and guilt at how quickly she had questioned her faith in the midst of adversity.

Rillifane, forgive me, she cried silently to her god.

As one, the witches finished their obeisance and gathered together. Marissa knew that they deliberated amongst themselves in the silence of their bond, but she no longer feared. When at last one of them spoke, she was surprised to hear a voice other than Najra's.

"You rebuke us all, dear sister," the witch said.

Marissa cast a glance at the speaking othlor but could see nothing beyond the contours of her white mask, its face opened in a gentle smile.

"Well do we remember your presence among us, Imsha," the witch continued. "You were the wisest of us." The othlor spoke her words quietly, in a voice surprisingly soft and melodic.

The warm tones seemed lost on the telthor. Imsha floated above the well, her aged face still stretched in a scowl.

"I rebuke only because I must," the floating crone said, though Marissa could hear both warmth and regret in the telthor's voice. "They have *all* spoken the truth, Mahara," the crone continued, "though maybe not as diplomatically as some would like." At this last, she turned toward Roberc who, Marissa noted thankfully, had sheathed his sword. The halfling returned the telthor's gaze evenly, a thin smile splitting the grizzled contours of his face.

"Mahara," Najra hissed, "these outsiders must be made to pay for their transgression. Whether they come at Imsha's request or not, they have violated our laws. They must receive punishment."

Marissa could sense that several of the other witches agreed with Najra's sentiment but was reassured at the telthor's response.

"Be silent, Najra," the crone said harshly. "Even as an ethran, you always hated others telling you what to do—and nothing has changed. The fact that you were summoned by this woman's power," she said, pointing to Marissa, "is the sole reason for your anger. There will be no punishment. These travelers are under my protection. *I* will deal personally with anyone who harms them."

Imsha's gaze passed over the assembled group like a scythe. Marissa blanched as the crone's fierce eyes met her own. She was glad that the telthor saw her as an ally and not an enemy, for her eyes held the promise of death within their gleaming depths.

Mahara turned at last to Marissa and her companions.

"Forgive us our rudeness," the othlor said. "We do not often receive strangers in our midst, let alone into our most private of councils. The wisdom and strength of the wychlaran have in the past always proved sufficient to meet the dangers threatening Rashemen. We have become too sure of ourselves, like kings locked in our strongholds, secure in our power while the kingdom burns around us."

The witch stepped forward, bringing both of her hands together and placing them before her heart.

"Be welcome at this council, strangers." Mahara bowed low. "I greet you in the name of the wychlaran, the ancient defenders of our land."

Speechless, Marissa returned the bow, noting with relief that the others did the same. When she had finished, Rusella cawed loudly from a tree at the edge of the clearing. With three swift beats of her wings, the raven flew like an arrow to the druid, landing softly and gracefully upon the tip of the Staff of the Red Tree.

Mahara chuckled from behind her mask.

"We often say that 'one can know the heart of a person by the mettle of those she travels with.' It seems you have a fine heart, indeed." Mahara paused for a moment, surveying the group. "Come," the witch said. "Your comrades have need of some rest and healing." She eyed the still-shimmering telthor. "We will listen to what you have to say."

As the othlor converged upon her friends, Marissa cast one last glance at Imsha before she turned her attention to Taenaran. The telthor's eyes gazed upon her with tenderness.

You would have made a fine hathran, the sound of Imsha's voice broke into her thoughts. Startled, she stared back at the wizened figure. Imsha raised a hand in farewell as she faded slowly into the night. There was a sense of permanence in the telthor's fading, and a wave of sadness passed through the druid as she realized that the ancient spirit had depleted her power by appearing to the assembled othlor. Tears ran down her cheeks as she heard the telthor's final words.

Perhaps, the voice came again, *you still will*.

Darkness.

Everything was darkness—wrapped in shadow and emptiness and pain.

He breathed it in, absorbed it until the shadow became a part of him—or he became a part of the shadow. It whispered to him softly, as a lover would. A shudder ran through him at its voice, part delight and part terror. He wanted to run but couldn't. He was empty, so empty that he had forgotten what it was like to be filled with laughter, love, and life—to be whole.

There was no wholeness where he lay, only hunger and desire, a need so vast that it gnawed him from within.

He was lost within shadow, until everything around him erupted into light. He drew back, cowering and fearful at the sudden brightness of it all, at the harsh touch of its hot fingers. But there was something about that light from which he could not hide. He tried to deny it, to push it away, to return to the cool darkness that whispered to him even now:

Careful, it said. *The light burns—forever.*

Light also called to him, called his name, and called him out of the darkness that lay around him like a shroud. Taen felt his body rise through that darkness, ascending. Night fell away and became dawn. Gray fog and mist burned away beneath implacable light.

At last, he opened his eyes, blinking hard in the morning sunlight. Marissa knelt over him, cupping his hand in hers. Tears blurred his vision, but Taen thought that he could see a masked figure looming over the druid.

"Welcome back," Marissa said and gave him a gentle smile.

Taen heard the effort it took her to constrain the flood of emotion behind those simple words and returned her smile.

"Remind me," Taen said in a voice that shook with fatigue, "not to accept your next invitation to go on a pilgrimage."

Her laughter followed him as he fell into the restful arms of sleep.

CHAPTER 15

The Year of Wild Magic
(1372 DR)

Taen gazed into the well.

A stark face, fatigue etched in every curve and angle, stared back from the surface of its dark waters. Though he and his companions had only spent a few tendays traveling through Rashemen, the half-elf felt as though it had been several lifetimes since he first crossed the borders of this unforgiving land. It wasn't just the life-draining touch of the wraith lord, either—though he still felt the undead creature's hand reaching into him despite the powerful restorative magic of the wychlaran. Something deeper wore at him, weighing down his heart.

A swift slap of his hand knocked several pebbles that had gathered near the lip of the well into the water. His reflection distorted and eventually disappeared, pulled apart by the swirling ripples caused by the fallen debris. That was exactly how he felt—misshapen, pulled apart by conflicting emotions. Unlike the water, which had already started to settle, he doubted that his heart would do likewise. A frisson of fear ran down his spine at the thought that his life would be forever caught between the swirling chaos of emotions stirred up by both the wilds of Rashemen and the even wilder druid who had dragged him into its borders.

Disgusted with the maudlin direction of his thoughts, Taen gazed out at the clearing, determined to find himself anywhere else than where he was now. Borovazk and Selov sat beneath a growth of thin-limbed trees, drinking slowly from leather skins and conversing in their native tongue. The half-elf had heard about the firestorm that had erupted when they met up with the wychlaran. He knew it must have been tough for the fierce Rashemi to stand on divided ground, his loyalties torn between unwavering obedience to the will of the othlor and the strength of his newfound bond with Taen and his companions. Even from this distance, the half-elf could see that the normally boisterous ranger remained uncomfortable beneath the masked gaze of the wychlaran.

The sound of a blade running over a whetstone caught Taen's attention. He turned to see Roberc carefully sharpening the edge of his second sword. The blade gleamed in the light of the late-morning sun. Cavan rested easily by the halfling's side, staring out beyond the clearing, ears twitching at sounds only he could hear. After Taen had awoken from his sleep, Roberc had described their initial encounter with the othlor, as well as the details of their continued conversation. Imsha had apparently made a lasting impression on the witches, for they had listened intently to the news of a traitor in their midst, asking pointed questions when Marissa had finished recounting her message to them. When they had finished, the witches withdrew from the clearing, leaving the druid free to check in on Taen.

The half-elf remembered clearly the relief and confusion that had descended upon him when he had opened his eyes to the light and saw Marissa gazing back at him. That confusion deepened when he opened his eyes a second time, climbing his way out of the deep, restful sleep that resulted from the witches' healing.

He looked briefly for Marissa and found her surrounded by the othlor—all but Najra. Even if Roberc hadn't filled him in on what had occurred, it was clear that the witch held little affection for them. While the other wychlaran probed Marissa for more details regarding her conversation with the telthor of the Red Tree, Najra stood apart from the group, arms folded across her chest, glaring from behind the confines of her mask. He would have found her actions laughable in any other situation. The gravity of their message, however, erased any humorous thoughts he might have had.

A few moments later, the gathered wychlaran drew back from Marissa and formed a circle. Although he had been warned about their silent communication and had even used a similar spell before, Taen found the immobile, masked forms of the witches unnerving. They remained in that position for quite some time before finally breaking off their communion.

Taen stood as the assembled othlor signaled that he and his companions should attend them—and nearly pitched forward when the world spun around him. Although he had rested throughout most of the morning, the half-elf's body still hadn't completely recovered from the wraith-wound. Mahara had warned him that he would experience some weakness until his reserves were refreshed with continued rest.

Carefully, he made his way to where the others had

gathered, walking like a newborn foal on legs that shook with each step. Mahara inclined her head slightly when he arrived.

"It is not easy for us to accept what you have shared," the othlor began without any preamble. "We are a proud sisterhood, as you probably have gathered. That pride has strengthened us throughout generations of service to the people of Rashemen—but not without cost." She turned to look at Najra and the others before continuing.

"We have grown blind and deaf to our own mortality, to the possibility that one of our own might spin a web of darkness. Always we have looked to the durthan or the Thayans when shadows fell over Rashemen, never dreaming that it would be our shadow darkening the land's spirit. A hathran has broken the ancient oath that binds vremyonni and wychlaran. It is no wonder that the Old Ones have refused our counsel, making excuses for their absence with coldly polite words. This traitor has pierced the very heart of our land—and we suspected nothing. How long would we have remained in ignorance, were it not for your courage and generosity? *All* of us," Mahara said with particular emphasis, "our entire sisterhood, owe you a debt of gratitude."

Taen found himself surprisingly touched by the witch's admission. The Rashemi were, indeed, a proud people, used to fighting for every freedom and good thing that they enjoyed. To acknowledge their dependence on an outsider must be a bitter draught to swallow. The half-elf admired the courage and humility it took to admit that aloud. Looking around at the faces of his companions, Taen knew that Marissa and the others felt the same way.

He bowed low before Mahara and the other othlor. "We are honored by your words and by the hospitality you have shown us," he said without a hint of irony. "Let the start of our acquaintance be forgotten, and let us always remember this moment, when Rashemen's need and the wisdom of her leaders made strong the bonds of friendship between people of good will."

The words surprised him as they tumbled out. They must have surprised Marissa and Roberc, too, for both of them threw him a wide-eyed glance. Perhaps, he thought with only a touch of bitterness, he truly was his father's son—in spirit if not in blood.

"Your words are bright gems in the darkness we face," Mahara replied. "They are a gift whose worth may be beyond measure, and we accept them as such."

"Thank you," Taen responded, bowing once again before continuing, "and if the wychlaran or Rashemen ever have need of our assistance, you only need to ask and we will gladly give it."

The half-elf winced inwardly at that, wondering if, perhaps, he had stepped too far out beyond the boundary of what his companions would tolerate. He half expected Roberc to break in with a sarcastic denial, but the halfling merely looked at him with his usual sour expression. Behind the fighter, Borovazk stood beaming, his face split with a thick-toothed smile.

"Perhaps—" Mahara said then paused, looking around at the other witches, "perhaps there is something that you might do for us—a very large thing, actually." She cleared her throat before continuing, "Now that we know of the traitor's existence and the location of her lair, we must still decide on how we will deal with her. It's clear from the fact that you were attacked while on your way to warn us that our renegade hathran has quite a few spies amidst the people—and probably among the wychlaran, as well."

Taen could hear the fire burning within her voice.

"The only people we know that we can trust completely are standing in this clearing. It will take all of our power," she said, pointing to the five othlor, "to unearth the traitor's network of telltales while keeping our actions a secret. That leaves only you and your companions free to act against the betrayer of Rashe-men. Our magic can transport you to an area within the walls of Citadel Rashemar. If we can keep our knowledge of her presence hidden, then you will have a better chance of taking her by surprise.

"Make no mistake," the witch said in a husky tone, "what we are asking is dangerous. There is a very good chance that you won't succeed. Our enemy has managed to create an army of foul creatures and dark magic without our knowledge, and she has trespassed into the forbidden arts of the vremyonni. She is powerful and quite evil."

Taen thought about it for a moment only. Even if he hadn't just promised his aid, he would still agree to this mission. From the moment he set foot in Rashemen, he felt as if he were being swept along in a chaotic tale not of his devising. He was tired of fighting it, of fighting the swirling rush of emotions that bore down on him. There was only one solution—to surrender and follow the dark tide wherever it would lead him.

"I will go," he said and stepped forward, not surprised by the fact that he hadn't been the first to do so.

Marissa stood ready, her hand holding the Staff of the Red Tree before her. The druid smiled as he joined her in the center of the witches' circle.

"Little friends not escape Borovazk that easily," the ranger replied as he, too, strode forward to join them in the circle.

Taen looked at Roberc expectantly. The halfling stood at the edge of the circle, his hand resting on the hilt of his sword. The fighter gazed back at him with an even look, his eyes unblinking. For a moment, the half-elf wondered if Roberc would whistle softly for Cavan and ride away. Instead, the halfling swore loudly and tromped into the circle.

"I can't believe I'm doing this to myself again!" he exclaimed.

Taen smiled at the foul-mouthed fighter's response. They had been through a lot in the past few tendays and would likely go through a lot more. Despite everything, Roberc remained as hot tempered and sharp tongued as ever. It was nice, Taen reflected, to know that some things remained constant in a world that seemed ever changing.

"You humble us," Mahara said, interrupting his thoughts, "with your generosity and bravery. Prepare yourselves well, friends of Rashemen, for if we are to move against the traitor, we must act swiftly."

At that, the companions gathered together, inspecting their equipment and making sure that they had sufficient supplies. Taen had just finished sealing a vial of sulphurous ash when he felt a hand upon his shoulder. He turned to see Marissa smiling at him.

"Thank you," she said in a soft voice. "It means a lot to me that you agreed to help the wychlaran."

For a moment, Taen did not reply. Being in such close proximity to the druid brought all of his emotions rushing around him like a whirlwind.

"How could I say no?" he responded. Especially, he thought, when he knew that wild hippogriffs wouldn't prevent Marissa from giving her aid to the othlor. "The people of this land have no one to turn to."

Marissa held his gaze for a few heartbeats without saying anything. "Still," she responded finally, "I am glad that you will be at my side through this."

Taen nodded dumbly, knowing that his voice would betray the raw mix of feeling swirling beneath the surface of his calm demeanor. He turned as if to continue with his preparations, but Marissa's hand held firmly to his shoulder.

"Taenaran," she whispered, "I promise you that we will talk after this is all over."

With that, the druid offered his shoulder a single squeeze then walked away, returning to her own preparation. Taen watched her graceful form glide toward the edge of the clearing.

Despite himself, he could not keep a smile from alighting upon his face.

Taen stood in a circle with his companions.

The chill afternoon breeze ran ice-tipped fingers across his skin. He shivered slightly beneath its unrelenting touch and gathered his cloak around him. The familiar weight of his armor offered some measure of comfort in the dying light of the sun, but he knew from speaking with Borovazk that the citadel to which they would be teleported sat high in the Sunrise Mountains, wrapped in winter like a king draped in royal finery.

"It is time," Mahara said, interrupting his thoughts.

He watched with keen interest as the assembled othlor gathered around them in silent convocation. First one then the rest of the masked witches raised pale hands into the air. Suddenly, the clearing fell silent—neither wind nor bird nor shifting branch broke the stillness. With his own arcane senses, Taen could feel the slow buildup of mystic forces, like the gathering of power before a storm.

"May the telthor guide your steps," Mahara said then began a complex chant.

As her voice rose and fell to the rhythmic patterns that would focus and seal the power of the witch's spell, Taen's vision began to shift and blur, as if the world itself stretched and coiled around itself. He nearly jumped as he felt a hand grip his own. By its size and calloused feel, it could only be that of Borovazk. Blindly, he reached out until he could feel Marissa's shoulder; he rested his hand heavily upon it.

The flow of the arcane energy shifted violently, and

Taen knew, from his own mastery of magic, that something was wrong.

"The traitor has some sort of mystic shield repelling our spell, Mahara," Najra called out, confirming what the half-elf had already suspected.

"Whatever she has in place," Mahara shouted, "the power of the Urlingwood will not be denied!"

With that, the witch slammed both of her hands together, palm to palm. Eldritch energy roiled from her joined hands, spilling out in waves upon Taen and his waiting friends. The world lurched madly then disappeared in a single moment of violent disorientation. Taen's mind tried to rebel at the utter *nothingness* around him, but years of arcane study had prepared him for the sense of dislocation.

Half a heartbeat later, the world resolved into a faded tableau of gray stone—the suggestion of a wall, the hint of an uneven floor—then just as suddenly, it disappeared in another gut-wrenching twist out of reality.

This time, Taen counted the heartbeats spent suspended in nothingness. Though he knew that he remained linked to his companions, all sense of touch had disappeared. Clearly, something *had* gone wrong! He'd used enough teleport spells in his day to know that some outside force had forcibly changed their destination. Now he worried that they would spend the rest of their lives trapped on the astral plane.

He was just about to cast a spell of his own when the darkness shifted around him again. When the nauseating sense of disorientation abated, Taen could once more feel solid ground beneath his feet, and the touch of his companions. The darkness, however, had not parted. It covered them like an impenetrable skin.

"What in all of the Nine Hells was that?" Roberc swore.

Before Taen could answer, something skittered and hissed somewhere in the darkness beyond them.

"Borovazk not like the sound of that, little friends," the ranger said.

Taen heard the sound of the Rashemi's weapons slide from their resting places. Quickly, he spoke an arcane word into the pitch black emptiness. The world exploded into light.

And the screaming began.

CHAPTER 16

The Year of the Arch

(1353 DR)

Steel rang against steel in the forest clearing.

Sweat ran down Taenaran's face, stinging eyes and running in tiny rivulets down his back. The half-elf struggled to bring his sword into the third position, angled slightly above his head, when the silver-haired elf standing in the clearing's center called for the next attack. Arvaedra was a harsh swordmaster, and Taenaran knew that if he performed the maneuver even slightly off-center, the *el'tael*'s quick eyes would catch it, and she would pounce on him like a wyrmling on a fatted calf. All of the *tael* knew that the only thing quicker than Arvaedra's sword was her tongue.

A cool breeze swept through the clearing, rustling branches and the long green cloaks of the other masters watching from the shadowy edges of the clearing. The wind sent a soft shiver down Taenaran's spine. He tried to ignore it in the same way that he tried to ignore the cold, impassive gaze of the other masters, made worse by the fact that his own father watched from the shadows—critiquing, finding fault, noting and cataloging the imperfections and weakness in his execution of the forms. Later, when they returned home, Aelrindel would correct him gently.

The half-elf shook his head, banishing thoughts of the future. There was only this moment, this place in the Song, as the masters would say. If only it weren't so painful, he thought bitterly. Taenaran's wrist and shoulder burned with fatigue, and the muscles in his legs were trembling with exhaustion. He breathed deeply, trying to return to the *haera*, or the center—and nearly dropped the sword as his opponent's blade struck. The shock of the attack set the hilt of his sword humming; the blade turned in his hand, causing his opponent's weapon to slide with deadly speed down its steel length.

Taenaran braced himself for the stinging kiss of the blade, only to find Arvaedra's sword intervening at the last moment, flicking the oncoming blade away with a fast turn of her wrist. The half-elf let out a hiss of relief. *Tael* swords were not crafted razor sharp, but they still held an edge, enough to remind an errant apprentice to pay attention.

"Halt," the swordmaster shouted to the assembled *tael*.

Swords hissed instantly into their sheaths, as the apprentices sank to their knees, assuming the traditional sitting position, back straight, body resting on calves, and feet angled toward each other, nearly touching. She stared for a moment at Taenaran, and he nearly flinched at the swordmaster's cold glance.

"Taenaran," she said, using his name like a whip, "the rest of us were practicing the Seven Forms. Do you mind telling me what it was that you were doing?"

The half-elf sat completely still, trying to contain the feeling of shame that threatened to drown him. Though his hearing was not as sensitive as that of a full-blooded elf, still he could make out the soft, dreadful sound of snickering among the other *tael*. The tips of his ears flamed red.

Arvaedra must have heard the sound as well; she spun quickly and walked among the kneeling apprentices, her steps slow and sure, containing the promise of power, like a lioness among her cubs. Silence filled the clearing.

Taenaran risked a sideways glance toward his father and the other masters. Aelrindel stood with arms folded. There was a stillness around him that seemed to reach out and draw in everything in his path. He was impassive, a living statue. Taenaran knew, however, that disappointment lurked beneath the calm surface. He could feel it, or imagined he could, when they were alone at dinner, talking of other things. Often his father avoided discussing any of Arvaedra's discipline.

It wasn't that the silver-haired swordmaster unjustly criticized him or singled Taenaran out for punishment. All of the *tael* felt the sting of her acid-laced tongue at one time or another. There were others, however, in the community, and even among the masters, who seemed to delight in every mistake, every slight missing of the mark that he made. He knew that his father had fought hard with the *el'tael* so that he could study the art of the bladesingers. It was an honor for a swordmaster to sponsor a young elf into the Way, for the masters represented the community, and it was an awesome privilege to be chosen by the community to give one's life in its service, yet the half-elf felt that every error he made was a repudiation of his father's choice and confirmation for those who had wished to bar him from studying the art.

Taenaran had no further time for reflection, as Arvaedra had completed her rounds and stood before him once more. Wind tousled the swordmaster's hair, sending the thin strands of her ponytail waving behind her. He would have smiled at the effect, but her stern gaze rested upon him. As always, he was shocked by the signs of age in the *el'tael* before him. The tiny wrinkles around her almond-shaped eyes and the shock of silver-white hair were signs of contradiction among the long-lived elves. Among the people of the community, she was considered ancient and wise.

"You still haven't answered my question, *tael*," Arvaedra demanded at last. "What were you doing?"

She was also, he knew, quite deadly.

Taenaran met the forbidding glare as best he could. Experience told him that there were no responses that would spare him from her discipline. There were simply answers that were "less wrong." He thought for a moment then decided on the blunt truth.

"I was tired and lost my center," he explained.

One of Arvaedra's snow-white eyebrows arched high at his response. "Hmmm . . ." was all she said, then, "so Taenaran, what will you do when you are in the heat of battle, and you are tired and forget the simplest exercises of the youngest *tael*? Will you ask your enemy for a quick break before you engage him once more in battle?"

Laughter broke out among the *tael*.

"Silence!" Arvaedra shouted, turning on the culprits. "You are no better than he. At least Taenaran shows courage enough to admit what you are all either too dim or too frightened to say out loud."

She moved to the center of the kneeling apprentices. "The Seven Forms are the doorway to true mastery. You must practice them and learn them until you can perform them without thought, then"—she paused a moment before continuing—"you must forget them. They are the foundation of our art, the first notes of the Song."

She gazed out among the assembled *tael*. "What is the Song?" she asked.

For a few moments, no one answered. Taenaran could feel the tension among the *tael* mount. Every apprentice had heard the masters speak of the Song. Taenaran thought back, desperately trying to remember some of what Aelrindel had said to him about the subject. There wasn't a single apprentice who wanted to answer a question posed by Arvaedra with nothing but a blank stare.

At last someone called out, "The Song is the essence of bladesinging." It was a high-minded enough answer, Taenaran thought, something that he had heard the other *tael* mumble piously or haughtily to impress their friends and comrades.

"That is an answer that says everything . . . and nothing," Arvaedra replied with a sharp bark of laughter. "Good enough if our art were no more than wind and shadows. You." She motioned toward Taenaran with a scarred finger. "Come here."

Instantly, the half-elf sprang up from his kneeling position, fatigue and embarrassment momentarily forgotten. Much to his surprise, Taenaran found his sword already held in the First Form.

"Now," the swordmaster snapped, "attack."

For a moment Taenaran didn't respond, unsure if he had heard Arvaedra correctly. "What?" he asked finally.

"Attack," the swordmaster replied in an acid tone. "Since the *tael* do not know what the Song is, we will show them. Now, attack!"

Taenaran obeyed, driving his sword forward in the First Form's basic attack. Arvaedra parried easily then riposted an attack of her own. The half-elf quickly raised his blade and caught the edge of the *el'tael*'s weapon. The ringing of their swords echoed in the clearing.

He attacked again, aiming a low horizontal cut at

Arvaedra's legs. The swordmaster leaped easily over his blade and brought her own sword down in a sweeping diagonal cut. It continued like this, with the *el'tael* gradually increasing the speed and deadliness of her attacks. The half-elf soon found himself struggling to remember the correct parry as the elder elf swiftly moved through the Seven Forms, beginning to strike at random. Tired muscles cramped with fatigue, and the half-elf felt as if a giant sat on his chest. He was about to signal his defeat after a wicked sword thrust nearly pierced his shoulder, but as he spun desperately away from the attack, something began to happen.

Very faintly, on the edge of his perception, Taenaran heard the soft, melodic strains of music. As it intensified, he realized that the sound originated from somewhere within himself. Could it be that he was hearing the Song for the first time?

A sense of elation began to run through him, energizing tired muscles and sinew. The Song swelled within him. At first, he struggled against its rhythm, for it felt unnatural. In the midst of this inner wrestling, his form fell apart. Disciplined sword thrusts became off-balance swipes. He felt almost as if he were drunk. Several times, Arvaedra nearly disemboweled him with swift strokes of her gleaming blade, yet each time he managed to knock her thrusts away mere inches from his skin.

Finally, Taenaran began to relax into the Song's driving rhythms, matching footstep, slide, and sword thrust to the cadence of the inner melody. It was in that moment that Arvaedra's sword began to inexorably slow—or Taenaran's own attacks began to speed up; it was difficult to tell. All he could see was the deadly beauty of two blades meeting in the air. Time lost all sense of meaning. For the half-elf, there was only the silver streak of Arvaedra's sword and the answering ring of his own steel. He was enmeshed in a symphony of battle.

Without thought, he departed from the forms and slid his sword past Arvaedra's guard. The elder elf laughed wildly and raised her weaponless hand as she spun out of the way. Taenaran felt a ripple of power move through the air and strike him square in the chest. The force of the magic caused him to stumble, and he cursed himself for forgetting that steel is not a bladesinger's only weapon. He recovered his balance and advanced once more against the swordmaster. He feinted a high attack then summoned his own power. Fueled by the strength of the Song, the eldritch energy rose within him easily. He knew in an instant that this was somehow different than the spells he normally cast. As Arvaedra's sword rose to meet his attack, he released the power he had raised. Taenaran's sword, rather than presenting an obstacle, acted as a channel for his spell. Immediately, power poured forth from his blade and assaulted the elder elf.

He watched in amazement as the *el'tael* absorbed the arcane attack, dissipating its force. The half-elf wanted to follow it up with another blast, but suddenly the Song shifted in to a different key. It swelled within him once more, but this time Taenaran felt it pull at him, as if it were demanding something. He had managed to settle into its rhythms previously, but this time it wanted more than just his cooperation. This time it pulled at the deepest parts of who he was, tugging at the core of his spirit. Fear ran through him like a cataract and something within cried out against the Song's terrible need. He clawed for freedom against its power—then silence filled his mind.

Taenaran stood there for a moment, stunned, then Arvaedra's sword cut toward him almost too fast to see. With surprising force, she knocked the half-elf's sword out of his hand and slammed the flat of her blade into his face.

Light exploded behind his eyes. When at last it finally

cleared, Taenaran found himself lying on the ground with blood trickling from his nose. He heard Arvaedra's voice, as if from down a long tunnel, speaking rapidly to the gathered *tael,* as he struggled to his feet. A strong arm stabilized him when at last the half-elf managed to rise. It took Taenaran a moment to realize it belonged to Arvaedra. The elder elf said nothing as she motioned for him to return to the line of kneeling *tael,* but Taenaran could see the pride burning behind her eyes.

The half-elf wiped blood from his nose as he knelt once more. Fear and satisfaction warred within him, but even in the midst of that battle, Taenaran could not quite keep the smile from his face.

Aelrindel watched his son battle Arvaedra—and winced several times as the master nearly caught the beleaguered *tael* with a swift stroke of her blade. Centuries of battle and mastery of his art allowed the First Hilt to sense the moment when Taenaran discovered his own Song. He was surprised, at first, by the power of it—especially when he nearly managed to land a blow against Arvaedra. Tears threatened to blur the elf's vision, but he fought them back. It would not do for the leader of the bladesingers to show any overt reaction to his son's performance.

His resolve was tested, however, when he sensed Taenaran's inner struggle. Aelrindel felt, rather than heard, the moment when his son's Song fell apart, making him an easy target for Arvaedra's attack. He would have taken an involuntary step forward as Taenaran pitched toward the ground, but the sound of a voice behind him stopped the First Hilt in his tracks.

"Hmm," Faelyn mumbled as the half-elf struck the ground hard.

"He did well, Faelyn, even you have to admit that,"

Aelrindel said, not sparing his friend a backward glance.

"He did," the bladesinger agreed, "until the end. It is his human half, Ael. It struggles too hard against its death."

With that, Faelyn spun on his heels and walked away, leaving Aelrindel alone with the bitter turn of his thoughts.

The Year of Wild Magic

(1372 DR)

Death stalked the cavern.

Taen could see it clearly in the newborn light—razor-sharp teeth, a powerful, scaled hide, and a hideous cartilaginous tale that whipped around the confines of the high-ceilinged cave. It moved slowly, its broad, ridged head casting from side to side, peering down at the party with burning orange eyes. The creature's nostrils flared, sucking the fetid odor of the cave in with short snuffs.

The half-elf moved slowly, careful not to spook the beast. He watched as the creature tracked his movements, its tail weaving slowly, undulating like a charmed serpent above its head. When Taen caught sight of the barbed stinger gleaming wetly in the arcane light, he let out a curse.

"Wyvern," Roberc whispered. "Very dangerous."

Were they not in such a precarious situation, Taen would have laughed at the fighter's all-too-unnecessary comment. Though not as massive as their draconic cousins, and quite a bit more dull witted, wyverns were powerful beasts whose massive teeth and razor-sharp claws could easily eviscerate the best-armored opponent. Its poison-tipped tail, however, presented the clearest danger to them all. Assassins all across Faerûn coveted the dread creature's poison; it could kill a human in mere heartbeats.

The half-elf glanced around at his companions. Borovazk stood with axe and warhammer held steady. Taen watched as he tracked the wyvern's movements, obviously looking for a vulnerable spot in the massive beast's thick brown-scaled armor. Roberc had already dismounted and stood easily by the half-elf's side, his sword and shield ready. Marissa stood behind them, raising the Staff of the Red Tree in the air. Above them in the darkness of the cavern's heights, Rusella flapped noisily as she circled the site of impending battle.

The wyvern stopped moving and hissed again, the high-pitched noise reverberated in the massive chamber, echoing and folding in upon itself, sounding to Taen's ears like the screams of a thousand children.

"Ready," he whispered to his companions. When they all nodded, he continued. "Wait for my signal." Carefully, he reached into his belt pouch.

"Now!" he shouted and flung out his hand. Light bloomed once again from the fingertips of the half-elf's hand, this time leaping from his outstretched fingers to the creature's eyes.

With a mighty hiss, the wyvern reared up on its hind legs, unfurling nearly fifty feet of leathery, cracked wings and shaking its head to dislodge the glowing ball of illumination that pulsated between its eyes. At that moment, Borovazk let out a deep-throated cry and sprang forward. His gleaming axe cut deep into the beast's scaled hide, unleashing a flow of steaming blood that pulsed hotly from the wound, spraying him with its dark, crimson hue. The explosion of fluid did little to slow the ranger's attacks. The Rashemi gave another cry and brought the solid weight of his warhammer down upon the wyvern's left hind leg. The sound of splintering bone echoed in the cavern, soon overpowered by the beast's screaming hiss.

Not wasting any time, Roberc barreled toward the creature, whirling his short sword in a deadly arc. His first cut rebounded off the wyvern's hardened scales, but the second pierced the creature's armored hide and parted the soft skin underneath, puncturing muscle and tissue.

Though blinded, the wyvern lashed out with a sweep of its massive head. Powerful jaws snapped sharp-edged teeth mere handspans above Borovazk's head. The now-chanting ranger ducked belatedly beneath the attack, as if just realizing his danger. Taen would have called out a warning, but the wyvern's powerful tail struck downward, forcing the half-elf to skitter backward; it struck the very stone where he had just been standing with a shower of earth and pebbles.

"Are you all right?" Marissa called out.

Taen stumbled to his feet and nodded affirmatively. The half-elf knew that his light spell wouldn't hold for much longer. If they had any chance of emerging from this battle alive, they would have to finish off the wyvern fast.

Just then, the beast shifted its body, turning quickly to its left. The sudden movement caught its attackers by surprise, and Taen watched in horror as both Borovazk and Roberc fell beneath the shifting bulk of the wyvern's torso. Still blinded, it extended its wounded left leg slightly, as if searching for its attackers.

Borovazk rolled to his feet with surprising speed, avoiding the taloned claws of the wyvern. Roberc, however, couldn't quite escape. Within a heartbeat, the creature had him pinned beneath the wicked curve of its talon. The wyvern's tail rose up for a final strike.

With a ragged cry of denial, Marissa lifted her staff and cried out a prayer. Instantly, a whirling column of flame appeared above the wyvern's head and fell upon it like burning rain. The beast gave a long, bellowing hiss of pain and beat its scarred and burning wings, carrying it out of the divine flames.

Freed from the pinning talon, Roberc rolled out from beneath the massive form of the wyvern and returned to the battle. He gave a quick wave to signal his condition then advanced on the monster.

Seeing the light spell almost completely gone, Taen reached into his pouch and pulled out a small clump of fur. Grasping a thin glass rod in his other hand, the half-elf chanted the ancient words to a spell. As the power swelled and grew within him, he pointed the rod at the retreating wyvern. A bright flash of blue-white light erupted from the glass as a bolt of ragged electrical energy sped toward the beast. It struck the wyvern with a sizzling burst of power. Small tendrils of electricity spattered and arced across the length of the wyvern's dark brown torso; it shuddered briefly beneath the force of the spell before falling to one knee.

The odor of burned flesh filled the cavern. Taen nearly gagged from the acrid stench, but he pressed on. The wyvern hissed once more, fanning its giant wings in a furious fashion. Dirt and small pebbles flew up from the cavern floor, tossed wildly by the force from the beast's buffeting wings. The storm of debris stung eyes and skin, making it difficult for Taen to track his enemy's movements in the shadowy cave. It grew in intensity, fueled by the wyvern's bestial rage, the endless slapping of its wings against the dank cavern air.

The half-elf squinted against the assault, peering into the dust-filled cave. In the swirling chaos of the turbulent atmosphere, he could barely make out the shadowy bulk of the wyvern, moving to the right.

"Can you see it?" Taen called out to his companions. A chorus of voices exclaimed their frustration. "It's moving toward the right rear wall of the cave," he shouted.

"Borovazk see," the ranger returned the shout and charged toward the brown-scaled beast.

The triumphant ringing in his voice faded, soon replaced by a breathless curse. Taen ran toward the Rashemi and let out his own string of invectives. Standing to either side of the wounded beast were two smaller wyverns, their red eyes whirling in obvious agitation. Before them lay the half-eaten carcasses of a thick-furred brown bear and two unclad humans. Blood and gobbets of flesh hung loosely from their gaping, sharp-toothed jaws.

Taen had little time to process the presence of the two dead humans, as the largest wyvern took that moment to still its wings and pounce forward. Still moving forward by the force of his own momentum, Borovazk could do little except swipe at the creature's ridged head with his double-bladed axe. The wild swing struck the wyvern at an angle and bounced harmlessly off its thick scales. Untroubled by its attacker, the beast struck out and clamped its jaws down upon the ranger's shoulder. Sparks flew as the wyvern's teeth scraped across the Rashemi's chain mail. Borovazk grunted loudly as the creature's bite ripped through his armor, tearing at the unprotected flesh beneath.

Without thinking, Taen unleashed a string of arcane words and pointed his index finger at the monster. A single glistening arrow appeared out of the darkness and sped toward the wyvern, striking it squarely in the eye. The beast hissed as its eye socket bubbled and burned from the arcane acid attack. It released Borovazk and advanced upon Taen.

The half-elf leaped backward just as the monster's jaws snapped powerfully closed. He reached to his side and drew forth his father's blade, weaving it before him like a steel serpent. Taking a chance, he gazed to his left in order to see how the others fared. Roberc and Marissa stood side by side, battling the twin wyverns. The halfling bled from several wounds, and Taen could see several trickles of blood soiling Marissa's cloak. Still the druid did not retreat; she fought bravely at Roberc's side, laying about her with spell and staff to keep the beasts off balance.

One of the smaller creatures, whose left wing hung torn and ragged at an awkward angle from its body, turned swiftly and brought its needle-sharp tail to strike at its enemies. As he continued to weave his own defense, Taen watched with admiration as Roberc brought up his rounded shield to deflect the stinging attack. The point of the wyvern's barbed tail struck the shield soundly, nearly punching a hole through its metallic body with a dull ring. The halfling swayed beneath the blow, nearly losing his balance as the pointed cartilage impacted hard against his shield.

Taen had no further time to spare for his companions, however. The largest wyvern, driven beyond rage at the burning touch of the half-elf's arcane acid, launched an all-out assault against him. The half-elf ducked once beneath its snapping jaws and dived forward, curling his body into a ball and springing to his feet in order to avoid the sweeping dart of its poisoned tail. Off balance from his defensive maneuvers, Taen could not avoid the creature a third time. He cried out as the beast's stinger plunged deep within his chest. Before it could withdraw it, however, he slashed down hard at the extended tail, severing it with a single swipe.

Taen stumbled back, the tip of the wyvern barb still embedded in his breast, pulsating as it spewed its deadly toxin. The half-elf's veins ran with poison, and he could feel the cramping of his heart muscle. It was as if hot acid flowed through the pathways of his body, searing away tissue and life. He gasped once for air, trying to force his lungs to work, but they would not obey him.

He stumbled and fell to his knees just as Borovazk ducked beneath a wild snap of the wyvern's jaws and brought his own axe down on the creature's neck. The enchanted blade cut swiftly through its scale and skin, biting deeply into tissue and bone. The wyvern gave a strangled, gurgling hiss, then collapsed to the floor in a ground-shaking heap.

As the ranger turned to see what had befallen Taen, the half-elf could see the light of victory dim then disappear from the Rashemi's eyes. He wanted to see more, to tell the ranger that he would be all right, but a shimmering gray haze began to gather at the edge of his vision. The pain of his wounds floated away beneath a growing lassitude. Twice now he had come to the doorway of death. It was unlikely that he would pass this way again. A part of him raged against the unfairness of it all—that he had survived so much, only to fall in a dank wyvern cave at the edge of nowhere. Another part, however, had already begun to let go.

The gray fog deepened, drawing like a curtain before his eyes—only to disappear in a burst of light and warmth. Pain returned, like an old friend, to his body. He gasped as his lungs sucked air into their expanse, remembering what it was to obey him. He could see his companions standing around him: bloodied Borovazk, grinning despite the torn flesh hanging from his shoulder; grim-faced Roberc, cleaning his gore-covered sword and offering Taen a simple nod of his head; and standing behind them Marissa, her hand still glowing from the spell she had just cast.

"Try as you might, Taenaran," the druid said with a wink, "you can't get rid of us that easily."

Laughter rose up in him at that, and he groaned as it aggravated his wounds. Though they had removed the barbed stinger from his chest, it still ached fiercely. Carefully, they helped him to his feet, and together they explored the rest of their surroundings.

The cavern itself stretched its rounded expanse in all directions. Stalactites hung unevenly from the ceiling, their jagged lengths resembling giant, twisted teeth. The surface of the dull gray stone that made up the majority of the cavern ran unevenly—forming deep ridges that often flowed back into themselves.

"Well," Roberc asked as he peered through the shadows at the cave wall, "where have we gotten ourselves this time?"

Taen grunted at the question. Clearly they had stumbled into the wyverns' lair, that much was certain from the stench of rotting meat and the pile of splintered bones tossed around the cavern, but where exactly that might be was anybody's guess.

"I'm not sure," he admitted. "Something—or someone—interfered with the teleport spell."

"Then we could be anywhere," Marissa said. "There's no telling how far away we are from Citadel Rashemar." She sat down on a small outcropping of stone.

"Do not worry, little friends," Borovazk said, his voice echoing in the vast cavern. "We are not too far from the citadel."

"How do you know?" Taen asked the ranger. Perhaps there was hope for their quest after all.

"Listen," the ranger said, pointing his finger up toward the ceiling. "Do you hear that? Is the *prydvya*, the singing wind. It only blows that hard in the highest places of the Sunrise Mountains. Citadel Rashemar must be close."

Taen cocked his head and listened. Indeed, he could hear a high-pitched wail coming distantly from beyond the walls of the cavern. The wind's sharp wailing would need to be very strong for them to hear it deep within the cavern.

Something else registered in his sensitive half-elf ears as he listened to the shrieking of the wind—the sound of something, or someone, scurrying across rock. If he strained, he could also hear the creature's snuffling inhalations. It grew louder as he listened.

"We have company," Taen whispered softly, not wishing to alert whatever was drawing near them.

"I heard it too," Roberc whispered back. He quietly spoke a command to Cavan.

The animal cocked its head once then silently padded off into the darkness. Within moments, a high-pitched shriek filled the cavern, followed by the familiar low warning growl of the war-dog.

Taen and the others ran toward the sound, weapons already drawn to face whatever threat Cavan had uncovered. When they arrived, their light revealed the war-dog's powerful jaws clamped around the muddy wool cloak of an orange-skinned humanoid. The creature's wide mouth hung open, revealing a set of small, sharp fangs, and its deep-set eyes whirled and gleamed a sickly yellow in the arcane light. It gibbered and cried out in a harsh language that sounded to Taen like the retching and hacking of a plague-wracked human as it caught sight of the assembled companions.

"Goblin," Roberc said with obvious disgust. "They're like rodents. If you see one, there's bound to be more hiding under rocks nearby."

He then spat a series of unintelligible words at the frightened creature in what Taen reasoned must have been its own tongue. The goblin fell silent at the sound of its language streaming forth from the halfling's mouth.

Watching it cringe and cower at their presence, the half-elf felt a confused rush of pity and disgust for the goblin. Alone and even in small tribes, the creatures were usually nothing more than nuisances. Like orcs and others of their ilk, however, goblins were quite fecund and often bred like vermin. Roberc had spoken the truth—goblins very rarely ventured out by themselves, and once they gathered in significant numbers, they could present a real and powerful threat. What in the world would this one be doing skulking around a wyvern's cave?

"No hurt! No hurt!" the goblin shouted in broken, heavily accented Common, interrupting Taen's musings. "Yurz not meaning any harm to gr . . . great lords," it stammered out.

"What are you doing here?" Taen asked harshly.

"Elfling call off monster wolf," Yurz cried in a piteous tone, "then I tell all." The creature cowered further against the uneven stone wall of the cave but stopped as Cavan growled deeply at his movement.

Taen frowned and looked at Roberc. The halfling cursed softly then barked a command at Cavan. Instantly, the war-dog released the goblin's cloak.

"Don't even try and run," Roberc said and spoke once more in the creature's tongue.

When he finished, he pointed at Borovazk. The hulking ranger had drawn his bow and now aimed a sharp-tipped arrow at Yurz.

The goblin gulped audibly and nodded his misshapen head.

"Now," Taen said, "tell us what you are doing here."

Yurz whined softly before answering. "Big Chief tell Yurz to bring dragons food." He answered finally. "Yurz gather other goblins and we come here with offering. Goblins hear dragons roar and hear the sound of fighting. They get scared and run off. Not Yurz," he explained. "He more scared of Big Chief."

"Other goblins," Marissa broke in with her question. "How many of these goblins are there?"

Yurz gazed at the half-elf for a moment, and Taen

found himself growing uneasy at the look of sly calculation that passed over the goblin's face. He would have said something to the druid, but Yurz finally answered.

"Many goblins. Big army," he said, nearly cackling. "Big Chief run tribe in the man-castle. Partner with Ugly One," this last he uttered in a hissing whisper.

Whoever this Ugly One was, thought Taen, it clearly frightened the hapless goblin. "Where is this man-castle?" the half-elf asked, casting a knowing gaze at his companions. If they were close to the citadel, then perhaps Yurz could prove much more valuable to their quest than he had originally thought.

Yurz shook his head violently. "Yurz not tell," he said in an almost defiant tone, the rough orange skin of his sloped forehead wrinkling as he squinted his eyes. "Big Chief get mad. Hurt Yurz."

Roberc stepped forward and launched into a string of words in the goblin's tongue. Taen watched as the color drained from Yurz's face, but the creature stood firm.

"No!" he shouted in common. "Even if great lords kill Yurz, it still better than what Big Chief and Ugly One do!"

Taen sighed and was about to call his companions together to discuss this further when Marissa stepped forward. "Let me try," she whispered to Taen.

The half-elf nodded and accepted the druid's staff as she presented it to him with a smile and a wink. She began to chant softly before moving toward the defiant goblin, and as Taen heard the whispered prayer, he understood immediately what the druid was up to.

He watched as Marissa knelt before the goblin and saw Yurz's clear expression of distrust and fear begin to melt away at the druid's presence, replaced by a wide-eyed, almost worshipful stare.

"Yurz," Marissa said, "you know that we would never hurt you, don't you?"

The goblin nodded. "N . . . no," Yurz replied. "Pretty elfling not hurt Yurz."

"Good," the druid said, reaching out a thin hand to stroke the creature's bulging head. "We're your friends, Yurz, and friends help each other, right?"

"Oh yes," the goblin said. "Friends help each other."

"Do you want to help me and my friends, Yurz?" Marissa asked.

The bespelled goblin nodded once again.

"Good," the druid acknowledged. "Then will you take us to the man-castle to meet the Big Chief?"

Yurz gazed at the druid then out at the companions. Taen could see that the creature's former calculating stare had been replaced by a wide-mouthed smile, and the half-elf began to relax.

"Yes, Yurz take Pretty Elfling and friends to meet Big Chief. You like Big Chief and maybe he like you," the goblin said.

The druid stroked the goblin's head once more. "Thank you, Yurz," she said, and stood back up. "Well," she turned and said to her stunned companions. "It appears we've found our guide into the citadel."

CHAPTER 18

The Year of Wild Magic
(1372 DR)

Shadows shifted in the curving passageway.

Marissa blinked hard to help her eyes adjust as she and her companions followed Yurz through the twisting bowels of the mountain. She watched the goblin's bulbous head bob quickly up and down as he walked, experiencing a rush of guilt whenever he turned and cast an adoring gaze her way. Though she knew Yurz, like all of his kind, was cruel, cunning, and evil by nature, the druid always disliked overpowering the will of another creature—no matter how depraved it might be. Still, Rashemen's need beat like a war drum within her, swift and steady, its deep-noted call resonating through bone and tissue, replacing even the measured pulse of her own heart. Marissa knew that she would sacrifice far more than her own moral comfort to slake the land's need—and the thought frightened her.

Thankfully, her thoughts were interrupted by a sudden shift in the tunnel. Borovazk, Taenaran, and Roberc stood around Yurz, who sniffed the air carefully. From her vantage point, the druid could see that the trail they followed turned sharply to the left, revealing a ragged break in the tunnel wall before them. She could see an uneven passage sloping upward beyond the break, but it soon moved outside the range of her elf vision. A chill breeze blew down from the newly revealed passage.

"Passage must lead to surface," Borovazk exclaimed as he, too, inhaled the fresh airflow. "Borovazk smell snow and ice."

Yurz nodded quickly. "Oh yes," he hissed, "man-thing speak truth. This passage run out to mountain trail, then into village by man-castle."

"Then let's not delay," Roberc spoke up, his hand resting upon Cavan's broad back. "The sooner we get to the citadel, the sooner we can finish up this gods-blasted mission." He turned to Marissa and cast her a look of undisguised longing. "I haven't found myself on the tail end of a drunken binge in quite some time."

"No, no, no," Yurz replied. "We no follow mountain trail. Village empty except for goblin spies. See us coming. They not understand why Pretty Lady and friends need to see Big Chief." The goblin stamped his foot, a sight so like that of a little child that Marissa found herself stifling a laugh, despite the seriousness of their situation. "We follow this path," Yurz continued, pointing to the left, where the trail they had been following turned sharply. "Soon we get to underlevels of the man-castle. Yurz take you to see Big Chief. There be big feast. We all eat until we fall asleep."

The thought of spending an evening feasting with a tribe of goblins did little for Marissa's appetite, and she could see by the looks on her companions' faces that they felt similarly.

"I still think we should chance the mountain trail," Roberc said. "It seems far safer to me than traipsing through the warrens of a goblin tribe." *Led by a goblin.* Marissa could hear the halfling's unspoken reproach.

"It is a matter of trust," Taenaran said in Elvish, which he so rarely spoke.

Marissa nodded once to acknowledge the half-elf's words, but she said nothing. So much had happened to her since coming to Rashemen, events that had changed her in ways she was still discovering. For so long, her relationship with Taenaran had been based on mutual need, a desire to drown out the hurts of the heart with each other's presence. Now she needed—no, wanted— something else besides comfort.

Marissa knew Taenaran understood that on some level he was barely aware of, knew that he experienced it as a distance between them—for she felt it as well. Their current situation had provided them with little time to explore this new dynamic, so the druid chose her words carefully, for she did not want to drive a deeper wedge between them than already existed.

"I trust our new-found friend, Taenaran," she replied to the half-elf in their native tongue and watched as his eyes flashed once, only to be replaced by the calm, flat gaze that signaled his withdrawal behind walls so steep she had never managed to scale them. Their mission drove her onward, however, and so she had little time to worry over what her words might have done to Taenaran. Instead, she turned to the rest of her companions and said, "We should follow Yurz's lead. He has guided us well so far."

Which was the truth, she thought. Despite her initial apprehension about the depth of Yurz's enchanted devotion, the druid had found herself relaxing ever so slightly with each twist and turn of the passage. Not only had Yurz proven a knowledgeable guide, steering them clear of several dangerous sections of tunnel and carefully leading them through a cavern littered with piercers, but the bespelled creature had also helped them elude three goblin patrols. In each case Yurz had cocked his head to the side, listening, then had hastily ushered the group down a small side tunnel as a noisy band of goblins tramped through the main tunnel.

"Besides," she continued, "we might have a greater chance of bypassing the traitor's defenses if we come up from below the citadel."

She watched as the others nodded in reluctant agreement, even, she was relieved to see, Taenaran. "I don't like it," the half-elf said, "but I can clearly see the wisdom in it." He reached out and gave Marissa's shoulder a squeeze. "I trust you," he finished in Elvish. Marissa fought back tears as she watched the half-elf turn and gather his gear.

"Great," Roberc muttered, once again mounting Cavan, "that's just great. I've always wanted to spend my time skulking around goblin tunnels. It's so much better than just about anything else I could think of."

"Wonderful, little friend," Borovazk responded, clapping the halfling heartily on his back. "Now you will get your chance, eh?"

Marissa's tears turned to laughter as the halfling fighter's curse-laden response echoed in the tunnel. Wiping the moisture from her eyes, she turned to follow Yurz down the passageway.

Within her, the war drum thrummed to its implacable pulse.

Taen stood silently in the darkness, listening.

The caverns and tunnels running through the depths of the Sunrise Mountains held a rhythm and a life all their own. Within their twisting shafts and dripping grottos untouched by natural light, the half-elf could hear the echoing drip of water falling into still, deep pools; the trickle and flow of underground streams plunging mindlessly along their paths; the clattering of dirt and rock sliding down cavern walls, thrown by the subtle shifting of the earth all around them; and most of all, Taen could sense the movement of hidden creatures slithering, crawling, and running through the darkness.

He'd journeyed into enough dungeons and underground lairs to become familiar with the pulse of life beneath the earth, but he had never grown used to feeling like an intruder, an unwanted visitor from another plane of existence. To him, the darkness had a hundred eyes, each one peering at him from within the shadowy depths of the subterranean night.

"Where are they?" Roberc whispered from somewhere nearby, nearly causing Taen to jump.

The half-elf and his companions all huddled in the darkness, waiting for Borovazk and Yurz to return from scouting the tunnel ahead. Taen had extinguished his arcane light, not wanting to take a chance that its illumination would attract unwanted attention, so they waited beneath a blanket of night, relying upon Cavan's sense of smell and their own instincts to ward them against any danger.

"They will return soon enough," Marissa replied softly from somewhere to Taen's left.

The half-elf hoped so. Though they hadn't stopped too long ago, the group's constant skulking through the lower caverns of the citadel was beginning to wear upon his nerves. The fingers of his left hand twitched slightly, moving unbidden in the patterns of an offensive spell he found himself eager to use. Such thoughts, he knew, were not helpful when engaged in a mission of infiltration, but they were his nonetheless. It wasn't as if he regularly found himself following the lead of an enchanted goblin into the belly of a mountain, the half-elf reasoned—though that thought brought a wave of resentment spilling over him.

Damn Marissa and her spell of enchantment! Taen had given her his trust, and he'd meant it when he told her so, but he found their whole situation, as well as their relationship, completely frustrating. She was like a raging river, always moving on her own path, slowly wearing down anything, or anyone, that stood in her way.

The sound of footfalls padding lightly up the corridor drew Taen's attention. Cavan let out a soft growl then settled down. The half-elf relaxed at that, for at the first sign of danger, the war-dog would have immediately alerted Roberc.

"Passage ahead is clear," Borovazk whispered, "though we found signs of goblins moving through to eastern caves."

"Man right," Yurz confirmed. "Tribe patrols just passed. Yurz thinks we have only short time before they return. We must move."

Taen gestured and a soft light floated a few feet before him, scattering the darkness. He blinked a few times to adjust his vision then moved forward, following the enchanted goblin. The others fell in behind them quickly, bypassing several small side passages that ran off of the main tunnel. The uneven stone passage twisted and turned, undulating through the mountain depths like a stone serpent.

Taen doggedly followed their swift-footed goblin guide along the sharply sloping trail and across a series of thin stone ledges. Finally, after nearly half a candle's journey, Yurz stopped their march. The tunnel through which they had been traversing ended abruptly in a jagged wall of stone. Taen traced his hands across the length of the interposing stone while the others caught their breath, but the half-elf found nothing.

"You've lead us into a dead end, Yurz," he said to the goblin, not quite keeping the accusation from his voice.

Yurz shook its head violently in denial as the others gathered around. "No, elfling," the creature whined piteously. "Me not lead Pretty Lady and friends to dead end. We now at entrance to upper caverns," he said, pointing toward the ceiling.

Taen followed the direction of the creature's finger, eventually discovering a roughly circular hole that opened into the tunnel's ceiling where it met the jagged wall. Walking carefully beneath the hole, he peered up into its depths and swore softly. What had at first looked like nothing more than a heavily shadowed section of the tunnel was actually a naturally occurring chimney leading up into darkness. He would probably never have found it were it not for Yurz's knowledge of the area.

"Well, so it is," Taen said, returning to the group. "So it is." He placed a hand upon the goblin's shoulder. "Good work, Yurz."

The creature beamed, its orange skin flushing a deeper tone in the dim light. "We go up and soon see Big Chief!"

"That will be nice, Yurz," Marissa said as she drew close to the goblin, "but before we enjoy your Big Chief's hospitality, we'd like to see the inside of the citadel."

Taen watched the creature's eyes widen. "Oh no," Yurz replied hastily. "Pretty Lady not want to visit man-castle. Ugly One there." The goblin shook his head as if to emphasize the point.

Marissa sighed heavily and Taen could see her arrange her face in mock sadness. "I understand, Yurz," she said. "It's just that I so wanted to see the citadel. You wouldn't consider letting us see it as a favor to me, would you?"

Taen almost felt sorry for the hapless goblin as he

watched the creature's face trace the battle of fear and awe waged in his enchanted heart. It was clear which side had won when Yurz reached out a grime-covered hand to Marissa.

"Pretty Lady no worry," he said with eyes glistening with eagerness. "Yurz will lead her to man-castle. First we go to upper caverns then over bridge to the place of the dead. Then we be in man-castle pretty quick."

"Thank you, Yurz," Marissa said. "You are certainly a brave friend."

Taen was forced to turn away at the look of pure devotion that crossed the goblin's craggy face. As he did so, the half-elf noticed Borovazk and Roberc staring up into the chimney.

"Borovazk no engineer," the ranger said, "but he does not think that climbing up dark hole will be easy."

Taen looked at the massive-shouldered Rashemi then back at the chimney opening, and he had to agree. Though the stone inside the chimney was rough and uneven, providing several possible hand- and footholds, the width of the opening itself would make the climb very difficult for the large human. Taen thought about it for a moment. Their best possible bet was probably to send an unarmored Roberc up through the vertical passageway first. Once up there, he could find a nearby stalagmite or outcropping of rock to secure their rope to and lower the rest of the rope down the chimney. They could then go up one at a time—though Cavan did present a bit of a logistical problem.

Taen was about to verbalize his plan when Marissa strode forward with Yurz. "Listen," she said softly. "Yurz believes that there could be some sentries near the entrance to the chimney. Let me climb through the passageway in another form. I can move swiftly and remain unseen by whatever guards the entrance to the upper caverns."

Taen nodded at the druid's suggestion and noticed

the others doing likewise. Within moments, the air around Marissa began to shimmer and ripple, as if folding in upon itself. One moment Taen saw the druid clearly, and the next, a large spider, almost the size of his two hands, scuttled forward from the space where she had just stood. Yurz leaped backward at the sight of the spider, and the creature would have let out a shriek had not Borovazk moved swiftly to clamp a meaty hand over the goblin's face.

Taen reached down and lifted up the spider, carrying it to the wall just beneath the chimney. Within moments, the transformed druid had crawled into the darkness of the chimney. He whispered a quick prayer of safety to any god who would care to hear.

It was at that moment that Cavan leaped up from where he was lying down on the uneven floor of the cavern and growled a warning. Instantly, Roberc had drawn his sword and peered out into the shadows. Out of the corner of his eye, Taen caught Borovazk releasing the goblin to draw his own axe. Yurz fell backward, whimpering softly as he crawled to his feet.

Several bulbous-headed shapes resolved out of the darkness, padding closer on light feet. Taen swore again as he caught sight of them. Goblins—about ten of them. They stood about twenty feet from Taen and his companions with crude crossbows pointed in their direction.

"Stop! Intruders," one of them shouted in a voice so like that of Yurz that Taen cast a quick look behind him at the quivering goblin.

Taen could see his companions frozen, not in fear, but in preparation for explosive action; their muscles were coiled and tensed like a panther's before it springs down on its prey. The coiling expanse of the underground tunnel would, Taen suspected, likely carry the sounds of any combat to sensitive goblin ears—and that was a discovery they could ill afford. The half-elf reached slowly into his belt pouch, pulling out a small handful of dust. As the goblin sentries drew closer, crossbows firmly pointed at the intruders, Taen whispered the words to an old spell, and he gathered the arcane power at his command. Eldritch energy flooded his senses, swelling like a river pent up behind a dam. At the exact moment when Taen felt that the dam would break, he released the power, scattering sand over the heads of the approaching goblins. The tiny granules spattered and sparked when the spell activated.

First one then another of the goblins jerked as if struck sharply from behind, their bodies pitching forward, bereft of consciousness. The measured sound of goblin snoring filled the tunnel.

"That was well done," remarked Roberc, "though I do wish that you could have left one or two for the rest of us."

Taen smiled at the halfling's words, though in truth he wasn't sure the fighter had been entirely joking. "Come," he said, ushering Roberc and Borovazk back to the chimney in the rear of the tunnel, "we probably don't have too much time before another patrol stumbles upon us."

He tried to ignore the wide-eyed stare Yurz threw his way as they waited beneath the dark hole, but the goblin remained at the periphery of his vision. "Friend of Pretty Lady great wizard," he said finally, after Taen had spent considerable time pretending the goblin wasn't there and wishing that Marissa would soon emerge from the chimney. "Maybe greater than tribal shaman," he finished.

The half-elf was spared having to respond, as Marissa's rope spilled out of the chimney's darkness, landing with a muted thump on the cold gray stone of the tunnel floor. He turned and urged Yurz up the rope. The goblin stared a moment longer then leaped on to the rope, scurrying up its knotted length with the grace and skill of a seasoned seaman climbing the rigging of a tall-masted ship. Borovazk followed soon after, though the ranger needed some help sliding through the initial hole in the ceiling.

Taen and Roberc conferred for a moment regarding Cavan. The war-dog gazed up at the hole then offered Roberc a crooked stare, as if measuring the probability of a successful ascent. Taen thought for a moment. They had been in a few spots like this in previous underground explorations, but none quite so physically daunting. He did know a spell that would help reduce the war-dog's size, which might make the dog more manageable as they hauled him up the chimney. Their success depended upon Cavan's patience and cooperation, however.

A few moments later, with the help of Roberc's firm-voiced commands, a much smaller Cavan stood still and, if an animal could experience such a thing, bewildered as several lengths of rope were coiled and tied around its front- and hindquarters. Taen watched as their companions above lifted the war-dog, now the size of a large puppy, up through the chimney. When that was accomplished, the half-elf followed the always-grumbling halfling up the rope and into the caverns above.

The ogres stood like ancient trees rooted to the rough stone of the cavern floor. In the dancing light of his arcane illumination, Taen could see their dull yellow skin cracked and pitted like old bark. Both of the creatures' mouths hung open, frozen in mid roar. Teeth as thick and long as his fingers glimmered in the shifting illumination.

Roberc whistled softly when he drew near the half-elf. "You did this?" he asked, turning to Marissa. The druid had long since shed her arachnoid form and sat quiet and still in the center of the cavern.

She nodded. "They were arguing over something just

a few yards from the chimney hole," the druid said. "I didn't want their argument to draw any unwanted attention, so I crept up on them and changed form. I was going to try and use a different spell, when this"—she lifted the Staff of the Red Tree—"began to whisper to me again. I heard the words and repeated them. In moments, the ogres were petrified."

Taen shook his head. He'd seen his way around enough items and artifacts of power to know that the gift of the Rashemi telthor was unusual to say the least. In point of fact, Taen felt a great sense of unease around the staff—an experience that worsened any time Marissa described the staff's somewhat conscious actions. He had never been comfortable with the untamed power of natural magic; it refused to follow established laws and yield to the mastery brought on by rigorous study. Though he did not feel even remotely suspicious of the telthor and their gift of the staff, such power answered to its own laws.

At this moment, however, Taen said nothing. There were times to engage the enemy with persuasive rhetoric and razor-sharp logic—but wandering through a maze of caverns on your way to assassinating an evil witch bent on wide-scale domination and destruction was not one of those times. Once again, he would wait until after they had completed their mission before speaking to the druid.

Not that it would matter in the slightest, he thought with a bit of acrimony and turned to search for their guide. Yurz, who had nearly gibbered himself into apoplexy at the sight of the ogres, had finally regained some of his goblinoid poise. Now the creature stood at an opening in the far northern section of the huge cavern, beckoning with his bony fingers.

"Pretty Lady, come," he hissed. "Path to man-castle go this way."

Marissa and the others turned from their measured

contemplation of the petrified ogres and marched dutifully after the goblin. Taen gave the high-ceilinged cavern one last glance before following his friends.

Chill air blew steadily through the passages and side tunnels of the upper caverns, carrying with it a deeper bite. As they progressed, Taen watched his breath coil upward in white plumes. Here and there, moisture running down the cold, gray walls of stone curdled and formed a thin layer of ice. Even Borovazk, seemingly immune and inured to the temperature extremes of Rashemen, pulled out another fur shirt to ward himself from the deepening cold. That fact brought Taen a little comfort as he fought his teeth's chattering.

With Yurz leading them, they traversed for quite some time through what seemed like an endless expanse of hidden caves, shadow-filled tunnels, and sloping passages that threatened to trip the unwary with rocky protuberances and rough, uneven ground. Taen stumbled a few times, cursing the weariness that grew within him at each step. Their battle with the wyverns, the distance they had covered, and the stress of moving like shadows in the territory of the enemy were taking their toll. Finally, after he had knocked his shin against a stalagmite for the third time, Taen called a halt.

"We have to rest," he explained. "We'll do no good if we arrive in the citadel too exhausted to deal with the traitor. The others nodded, and Taen could see by the weary expressions on their faces that they were happy to agree.

"So we rest now?" Yurz asked. At Marissa's acknowledgement, the goblin began to hop from foot to foot. "Excellent," he exclaimed. "Yurz know perfect place to take friends for rest. Follow."

With that, the goblin skirted into a small side passage no more than four feet across. Taen and the others followed as quickly as they could. As they moved, the half-elf noticed that the surrounding air temperature grew warmer. By the time they had reached the tunnel's destination—a large circular grotto nearly thirty feet in all directions—steam wafted up into the air.

Marissa practically cooed with delight as she stepped into the cave. Taen wondered what could have made the druid so excited until he, too, entered the grotto. Glimmering stones and crystal of almost every color imaginable scintillated and flashed in the light of his arcane spell. It was as if the very stone of the earth were aflame, burning with jeweled incandescence. What's more, the half-elf noted that the tunnel spilling into the room thinned, transforming into a small ledge that circled the entire grotto. Below it, a still pool of water filled the rest of the cave. Steam drifted upward from the surface of the pool like the trickle of smoke from a sleeping dragon's nostrils.

The warmth felt good, a blessed relief from the constant cold threatening to suck the very breath from Taen's lungs. He couldn't help but let out a sigh of pleasure as the heated cavern air covered his body, wrapping the half-elf in its warm embrace. He dropped his pack and sat down on the hard ground, stretching legs cramped from the day's exertions. He could see the others doing the same thing.

Yurz remained standing, a wide-mouthed grin splitting the harshness of his face. "Friends like resting place?" he asked.

Marissa laughed as she unbound a length of hair she had plaited for their journey into the earth. "Oh yes, Yurz," she replied. "Very much so."

The enchanted creature again hopped from foot to foot, clapping his hands together as he did so. "Yurz know all the secret places of the caves," the goblin said. "We close to Flying Bridge and then"—he lowered his voice—"we enter the tombs of the man-castle."

Taen relaxed even more at the fact that they were very close to their destination. Soon, he thought, they would finish what they came to do; then he and Marissa would have time to straighten out what lay between them. The half-elf stretched as he gazed down at the waters of the pool that steamed invitingly. He was about to suggest a relaxing swim when the half-elf caught sight of a ripple in the water's surface. Looking closer, he could see a large scaled form cutting through the depths of the pool.

Taen jumped to his feet. "What is that?" he asked, pointing to the form swimming beneath the surface.

The others came rushing over, all except Yurz. "Pretty Lady and friends not worry," the goblin said. "That just the water dragon. It not hurt you—unless you go for a swim."

The others soon returned to their packs, stowing gear and pulling out the hardened trail rations they had brought with them for their journey. Taen, however, didn't trust the creature that lurked within the hidden depths of the spring-fed pool. He watched the beast, unable to fall back into the relaxed mood he had just a few moments before. As the others ate and drank, exchanging stories and laughter in the wholly unexpected comfort of the cavern, Taen wondered what the renegade witch was doing at that moment.

A loud splash echoed through the cave as the water dragon dived into the black silence of the pool.

CHAPTER 19

The Year of Wild Magic
(1372 DR)

The Old One sagged within his bonds.

More than a year of captivity, twisted and tortured by Yulda's arcane ministrations, had reduced the ancient wizard to an almost insubstantial physicality. He was nothing, a shadow, a burning ember of power wrapped in a decrepit and decaying body—which was just as she wanted it.

Yulda gestured and the shimmering funnel of energy that connected her to the dying wizard spun away into nothingness. Her body brimmed with arcane energy, stretched, it seemed, to its limits with the pulsing eldritch power that raced through her very veins. For a moment, she feared that she had taken too much, had sucked the Old One dry, reducing him to a powerless lump of flesh.

He stirred, however, moaning softly into the shadowy cavern, and her fears subsided. The old man couldn't hold out much longer. Despite what had seemed like an inexhaustible reservoir of arcane might, the Old One's strength had begun to fade. Yulda knew that she had been drawing too much power from the wizard, depleting his reserve too quickly, but it couldn't be helped. Her plans were moving forward, and she needed every ounce of eldritch might to keep her servants in line. Soon she would be able to rest, and the Old One would have a chance to regain the precious power that was all that kept his heart beating.

Soon.

But not now.

Another storm beat hard upon the rocks from which her demesne was forged. The wind moaned and shrieked with a bitter voice—one that she could hear even in the heart of the cavern. It mixed with the piteous sounds of the Old One as he wept and panted through his suffering.

"You ... you," he said through great gasping breaths, "you shall never succeed with your plan. The very heart of the ... the land rises up against ... against you."

"Shut up, old man," Yulda spat back, tired of his endless prattling. "I have already succeeded. You and those blind crones are just too stupid to realize it."

The Old One began to laugh, a great wheezing gurgle of a sound that reminded the witch of someone drowning. "Even now," the wizard gasped between great bouts of laughter, "Rashemen moves against you. You will ... will fall, and your name will be but a passing shadow, soon forgotten and never uttered on the ... lips of future generations of our people, you—"

"Enough!" Yulda shouted, smacking the wizard's face with the back of her own gnarled hands.

She felt the brittle bones of his nose shatter like dried tinder beneath the blow. With a single moan, the Old One slumped forward, bereft of consciousness; blood spurted from his face, pooling beneath him on the frozen stone floor of the cave.

The witch spat in disgust and moved away from the unconscious wizard. He was a frail and bitter man, she knew, choking beneath the shame of his defeat. His words were like flies; they buzzed and hummed around her head but could not bite. Still, Yulda thought for a moment, she probably should check in on the fate of the erstwhile intruders she had banished to the wyverns' cave.

She turned to find Fleshrender lying comfortably on the stone floor, tearing apart the corpse of a mountain hare. The telthor looked at her calmly as it ripped the rabbit's soft flesh from its bones. Despite herself, Yulda couldn't suppress a shudder at the creature's actions. Telthor, she knew, did not require sustenance to live. The beast simply enjoyed the taste of death.

Careful not to disturb her feasting companion, the witch walked toward the back of the cavern, where an uneven hunk of blue-misted ice sat on a simple stone pedestal. She knelt before the pedestal, gazing deeply into the colored ice. Almost immediately, a dim light began to pulse within its heart, growing stronger with each beat, until an unearthly blue gleam radiated throughout the entire cavern.

Shadows began to emerge in the ice, silhouettes and suggestions of a scene that resolved quickly into a clear picture at a single word from the witch. Looking in the ice, one would think it a mirror, reflecting the interior of the cave in which it sat. Yulda, however, saw with deeper eyes. The cave she gazed at stood several hundred leagues from her demesne. With a sweep of her hand, the picture began to move, searching the lair of the wyverns.

At first she thought the cave empty, for there was no sign of the wyverns or her guests anywhere. Then she caught sight of a large shape almost completely hidden as it lay slumped against a cavern wall. Yulda smiled, thinking it the collected remains of her would-be assassins, but her smile soon changed to horror as she saw the hacked up corpses of the wyverns, bloodied bodies and slashed tails intertwined as they lay still and cold in a cave somewhere beneath her citadel.

How could those gods-blasted fools have escaped their fate, Yulda raged. The meddlesome intruders could be anywhere now! She extended her arcane senses deeper, pouring her newly regained strength into the scrying spell, bridging the great distance between her and the citadel with the merest thought. She scanned the tombs and lower dungeon of the citadel to no avail. With a frown, she went even deeper, magically peering into the depths beneath Rashemar. Through empty tunnels and echoing chambers her mind ranged, skimming over the rude consciousness of half-sentient creatures slithering through the subterranean realm, until at last she found her quarry—and something else.

Something of great power.

It beat against her senses with a wild, almost uncontrolled strength, shining like a beacon in the dark. She withdrew her mind, not wishing to alert whatever power was present. This, she thought, changed everything. Could those fools have been foolish enough to bring the Staff of the Red Tree right to her doorstep? Yulda's craggy face cracked into a twisted, gap-toothed smile. Such a powerful item would only insure her success if she could bring it under her sphere of control.

It took only a few moments for the plan to coalesce in her mind. She sent an eldritch message to Durakh then called Fleshrender away from his dead plaything. Stepping into the mystic circle inscribed to the left of the stone pedestal, she disappeared.

Her last thought before the spell of teleportation activated was of the Iron Lord's citadel burning.

CHAPTER 20

The Year of Wild Magic
(1372 DR)

The Staff of the Red Tree shuddered in her
hands.

To Marissa, it felt as if she were holding a
living thing—an animal shivering in the chill
cavern air or quivering with rage. The voice of
the Staff of the Red Tree buzzed in her mind
like a swarm of angry hornets and had done
so ever since they had left the steaming pool.
It was difficult to concentrate with the presence of the Staff of the Red Tree looming over
her internal senses, but the druid managed to
mark their journey from the spring-fed cavern
to their current location—a quarter candle's
sojourn—well enough. Yurz had turned to say
something to her at several points during that
time, but Marissa could not distinguish the
goblin's voice from that of the staff's angry hum.

She had simply nodded, hoping the creature hadn't asked her anything important.

Now she and her companions gazed out at the vast expanse of a cavern. The druid shook her head, mentally forcing the voice of the staff to the back of her mind so she could examine her surroundings. Stone and shadow stretched out before her, well beyond the limits of arcane illumination and elf-sharp vision. What small portion of the giant cave Marissa could see resembled an ocean of petrified waves, their undulating crests and troughs stilled by the eyes of a giant medusa, fixed forever in this subterranean world—a world which tumbled down into the depths below her feet as much as it soared to the heights above her. The slightest sound, whether the soft scuff of boot on the rocky ground of the passage or the rhythmic exhalation of Cavan's panting, reverberated wildly in the vast chamber.

Standing at the entrance to this massive cavern, Marissa felt as if she stood upon the edge of oblivion. Normally such a precipitous location would have spun her head with dizzying fury. It wasn't so much the height that bothered her—she had spent time enough scaling high-trunked trees and out-thrust cliffs—but rather the enduring sense of nothingness, as if one step would teleport her to a place where nothing existed, neither time nor physicality. The very thought unsettled her.

Thankfully, a wide-shouldered expanse of natural stone broke up the cavern's emptiness. Dark rock, nearly as black as pitch, arced over the cave's shadow-filled depths, presumably linking their passage with the entrance to the citadel's tombs. In places, great stalactites reached down from the ceiling like giant teeth, almost touching the bridge's uneven expanse. Here and there, Marissa could make out thick stalagmites thrusting upward from the bridge toward the cavern's hidden roof. It seemed to her like a maze of hard black rock, difficult to navigate at any speed. That thought sent a frisson of unease up her spine. Anyone crossing the bridge would find it almost impossible to retreat if they faced an overwhelming attack.

The others had gathered around her, each of them casting a professional eye toward the bridge. Marissa took that opportunity to voice her concern. The others agreed.

"I was just thinking the very same thing myself," Roberc affirmed. "Perhaps one of us should go ahead and act as a scout."

"Not necessary," Yurz interrupted. "Me know quickest way across bridge. Friends follow Yurz."

Marissa caught the looks that the others cast among themselves. Clearly they still mistrusted her enchanted companion. She sighed. "Thank you for offering, Yurz, but I can send Rusella ahead," she said, indicating the raven perched upon a gray stone ledge.

"You could do that," Taenaran responded, "but anything keeping sentry in this cavern would know that something was up if it saw a strange bird flying through."

Marissa bit her lip in thought. The half-elf was right. There was only one other thing that she could do.

"I will scout ahead again and make sure the path is clear," the druid said.

Not waiting for any response, she gathered her power around her like a cloak. Years of practice allowed her to shape the image of a creature in her mind's eye, making minute adjustments. With a single thought, she filled the image with her essence, finally sealing it with a blast of divine power. In a single heartbeat she felt her body begin to change. The world shifted in and out of focus. Her bones lightened, becoming flexible, while skin stretched taught, taking on a scaly texture. In another moment, the transformation ended, and Marissa slithered forward, her serpentine body flowing easily over and around the jutting rock of the bridge's floor.

Though not completely blind, the world seemed dull and shadowy as she viewed it through small eyes that remained fixed above her jaws like tiny black seeds. She felt, rather than saw, the details of the world around her, separating and cataloging the thousands of minute scents in the cavern with a single flick of her forked tongue. Marissa searched the area around the bridge carefully, using her form's ability to distinguish changes in heat to see if anyone—or anything—lay in wait for them. Though she could sense a slight vibration in the heart of the ebony stone, the druid did not perceive any immediate threats.

Carefully, Marissa made her way back to her companions. The druid saw Yurz take a few steps back as she coiled herself up and with a single thought shifted forms.

"It looks as if we're safe," she said after a brief moment of disorientation.

"Good," Taenaran said, "then we should hurry. I doubt that our traitorous witch is in the citadel sitting on her thumbs."

Yulda gazed at the invaders from the shadows.

Hidden on a ledge high above the ebony bridge, she watched their slow progress. From the witch's vantage point, the intruders looked like nothing more than annoying insects, snow beetles creeping along an almost mindless path. Unlike the harmless beetles that infested the snow-peaked heights of Rashemen, however, the creatures below could sting—to deadly effect.

She hadn't been surprised to discover that a feckless goblin led them. Those weak-willed humanoids were always falling prey to the smallest enchantments. It did explain, however, how the invaders made it so swiftly to the underground entrance to her citadel.

Yulda would feel great satisfaction in watching her minions tear the goblin's disgusting head from its shoulders.

It was almost time. The foolish intruders had almost made it to the halfway point of the bridge. When they did, the witch would send a silent signal to Durakh and her forces. Not only would she have the satisfaction of destroying those who dared to move against her, she would also capture the artifact in their possession. Even from this distance, Yulda could sense its presence; it shone like a beacon in the darkness to her arcane senses, pulsing with immeasurable power. The witch had nearly fallen from her hiding place in shock when her eyes had confirmed what her heart had hoped for. The fools had walked into her demesne carrying nothing less than the Staff of the Red Tree.

With the Staff of the Red Tree at her side, she could tear the Urlingwood up by its roots and squash the pathetic wychlaran, who burrowed blindly like grubs beneath the forest's shadow. Corrupting the will of the Staff of the Red Tree would not be easy, but she would drain the last drops of life from her captive vremyonni to accomplish the task—and once done, she would never have to beg, cajole, or steal power from anyone else again.

The anticipation sent a pleasant tremor coursing through her body.

Cackling softly to herself, Yulda almost missed the moment when the intruders reached the appointed spot. Cursing her foolishness, the witch sent a telepathic command to Durakh, who lay in wait just behind the stone door to the undertomb on the other side of the bridge. The cleric's ogres would lead the charge, followed by her own arachnoid servants.

At that, shapes loomed out of the shadows around Yulda—wide-bodied, multi-legged monstrosities whose mandibles clacked together hungrily.

"Yes, my pretties," she cooed softly to the giant spiders, "it is time."

With a single command, she sent the monstrous arachnids scurrying down their thick, silken strands of web. The creatures' eyes caught and reflected the light from below, gleaming as they descended toward their prey.

As the door to the undertomb burst open, Yulda summoned a bright, greenish light that surrounded her body in a sickening nimbus of power. Stepping forward, wrapped in her hag illusion, she floated idly in the air above the bridge.

"Welcome to my home," she shouted at the stunned intruders, magically amplifying the strength of her voice. "Too bad you won't be alive to enjoy its comforts!"

Her laughter echoed in the cavern.

Time slowed down for Taen.

Between the moment when tall humanoid figures began to pour out of the undertomb door and the shrill, dark voice reverberated in the cave, an eternity seemed to pass. The half-elf watched in horror as broad-shouldered, long-limbed beasts with greasy yellow skin and long, tangled hair ran toward them, cutting the air with great sweeps of their thick-boled wooden clubs. A wave of foul odor wafted ahead of the beasts, stinging Taen's nose with the stench of rotten meat, rancid sweat, and offal; he nearly retched from the malodorous assault but managed to hold himself together.

From behind him, Borovazk shouted. "That voice—is Chaul, the Hag of Rashemar."

Taen could not spare long to gaze up at the where the sickly light pulsed, but when he did so, the half-elf caught sight of the green-skinned creature. It floated idly above them, shrieking out imprecations and dire threats. He would have cast an offensive spell at the beast, but the ogres were almost upon him.

Without preamble, time snapped back in step. Quickly Taen turned to the side, allowing both Roberc and Borovazk to meet the onrushing monsters. Though the beasts had the advantage in numbers, the width of the bridge worked in the defenders' favor—the ogres could not bring more than three of their warriors to bear at any given time. By now the Rashemi ranger and his halfling companion fought like an efficient construct. The moment that the wave of ogres crashed into them, they set to work. Borovazk struck high, wielding his war-hammer and axe with consummate skill. His first swing shattered an ogre's club. The beast took a step back as its hard wood weapon splintered beneath the crushing blow. That gave Roberc all the advantage he needed. The halfling sidestepped a sweeping blow from another ogre and darted forward, slicing deeply into the open flank of the now-weaponless creature. Blood spurted from the wound as Roberc's sword cut corded muscle and thick tendon, stopping only as it met bone.

The wounded ogre roared in pain, hopping back further. One of its companions stepped forward, filling the gap. Taen knew that they couldn't win a battle of attrition—despite his friends' battle skills. More humanoids emerged from behind the open door, crossbows held at the ready. Several had begun climbing the stalagmites on the bridge, obviously searching for a better vantage point from which to loose bolts.

To his right, he could sense Marissa gathering her power. The druid walked behind the furiously engaged halfling and touched him with her staff. Immediately Taen could see his skin harden, becoming thick and rough like the bark of a tree. Confident that his friends could hold the line for a few more moments, the half-elf took stock of the goblins' emerging positions and loosed a spell of his own. A ball of fire exploded behind the ogres. Goblins shrieked in pain and fear as the conflagration decimated their ranks. Two of the ogres also roared with anger as part of the magic flame licked their backs.

The half-elf would have cast a second spell, but Roberc stumbled backward from an ogre blow, almost knocking Taen over. The fighter cursed with obvious frustration. Luckily for the him, the halfling had caught part of the attack on his shield—which now hung uselessly on his arm, bent backward beyond hope.

Seeing his master falter, Cavan leaped forward, forestalling the ogre's follow-up attack. The war-dog danced neatly out of the path of the ogre's club and bit the beast on its thigh. Seeing an opportunity, Taen drew his own sword without thinking and cut downward as the monster lifted both arms to crush the animal worrying at its legs. His elven sword cut a long swath into the ogre's belly; blood, guts, and other effluvia came spilling out as the beast fell backward.

"My thanks," Roberc said as he finished unstrapping his ruined shield and jumped once more into the fray.

Taen had no time to acknowledge the halfling. Three crossbow bolts hissed past his head, and a fourth would have pierced his leg if he hadn't seen it hurtling out of the shadow at the last moment. He flung himself sideways, twisting his hips so that his legs spun over the missile in mid air. It was a defensive move he hadn't used in quite some time, and the half-elf's body protested as it landed back on the ground. There was no time to falter, however, as Taen's ogre opponent reached out a meaty hand grab him. Long fingers latched on to his shoulder with the strength of steel; he could feel his bone quiver beneath the excruciating pressure of the beast's grip.

Unable to bring his sword to bear, Taen beat his fist against the ogre's arm, trying to break the hold. It didn't work. Slowly, inexorably, the half-elf felt himself being drawn toward the ogre's chest. Once there, the beast would envelop him in a crushing hug that would grind his bones to dust.

The words to a spell fluttered in his mind. Taen shouted them out loud, but the pain of the ogre's grapple distracted him, and the spell's energy dissipated harmlessly into the air. The half-elf knew that he had only moments in which to free himself.

Suddenly the ogre pitched sideways, releasing his iron grip. Taen fell backward, his left shoulder nearly numb. Marissa stood beside him, the tip of her staff glowing faintly. The monster roared at the sight of the staff and dived forward, trying to rip the artifact from her hands. Taen called out a warning, but he soon saw that it wasn't necessary. Marissa quickly retracted the staff. Overbalanced, the ogre tripped and stumbled forward. The druid stepped to the side deftly, planted the staff against the ogre, and pushed.

The beast tumbled sideways, rolling over the lip of the bridge and plunging into the darkness below.

Taen rolled to his feet and returned to the battle, relief at Marissa's safety flooding through his body, combating some of the fatigue that threatened to slow down each parry and swing of his sword. The soaring melody of the Song accompanied him into the fray with a strength that he had not experienced since his days as a *tael*. He settled into the Song, wanting to abandon himself to it completely, but he kept waiting for that dreadful moment when it would drag at the core of his being like a blood-hungry vampire, so he fought his enemies under an uneasy truce with the Song building within him.

Behind him he could hear the druid shouting words to another spell.

Marissa watched the intricate dance of Taenaran's swordplay and marveled, not for the first time, at the half-elf's fluid style, the lithe interplay of body and steel, moving and weaving with an almost unearthly grace. Where Borovazk and Roberc met the ogres' powerful attacks with an almost equal ferocity, the half-elf seemed to flow with his opponent's energy, blending with it instead of meeting it head-on.

To an unschooled observer, it would look like nothing more than a playful dance, a choreographed piece of theater with no application to the real world, but Marissa saw within Taenaran's flowing movements the deadly art of the bladesinger. She'd seen the half-elf use his training in battle before but never like this. Marissa knew the shame that he carried within him, knew that such a burden often caused the young half-elf to fight his trained battle instincts. The result was usually a stilted attack, something that resembled the art she had seen a few times before in her life—like a pseudo-dragon resembles a full-grown wyvern—but never quite matched its purity.

Something had clearly changed for the half-elf—had been changing ever since they started off on this journey, if Marissa was honest. In combat, at least, he seemed no longer to be two persons—a gifted acolyte of an ancient and revered art, and a dishonored exile struggling to find peace—inhabiting the same skin. The druid saw in his uninhibited sword work what he must have been before tragedy and guilt had crippled him. The vision made her smile—not for the destruction Taenaran wreaked, but for the healing that so obviously had taken place.

A furtive movement off to her side caught Marissa's attention. She spun to face it just as a swarm of giant spiders dropped down onto the bridge from the darkness above. The druid cursed as the fat-bodied arachnids scuttled forward on long, spindly legs. She had been too busy focusing on the battle in front of her, not paying attention to any danger which might present itself from above.

She called out a warning as the bloated spiders attacked. One of the monsters leaped toward her, attempting to knock her down with its thick body, which looked to be nearly three feet in diameter. Marissa spun out of the creature's path and brought her staff down on its head. Blood and gore sprayed the bridge as her mystic weapon struck the spider with a meaty *thump*. The wounded monster let out a horrifying screech and scuttled backward, spinning madly in pain.

Another arachnid darted forward quickly, nearly tripping the druid. She dodged wildly out of the way, breathing a quick sigh of relief as it bit nothing but the air, mandibles clacking together harshly. Marissa's celebration was short lived, however. Two more spiders crawled over the side of the bridge. The druid managed to call fire down upon one of them. It shrieked and died almost instantly, its long legs curling inward as its body smoked and smoldered on the bridge. Its companion, however, scurried around the corpse, finally interposing the bulk of its body between her and her companions. Before she could react, three more of the creatures followed suit. She called out once more to her friends, but the press of the remaining ogres and goblins pinned them to their own defensive ground.

As one, the spiders attacked.

Two of the creatures scuttled forward and caught the druid's staff in their barbed mandibles. Desperately, she tried to shake them off, but their arachnoid strength was too much for her. The remaining two leaped forward. This time, the druid could not avoid them. One of the spiders bit down hard on the flesh of her neck. She screamed once in pain and felt the beast's deadly toxins flow, mixing with her blood. Fire burned within her breast.

Immediately, her vision swam. Horrified, she could feel the poison sapping her strength, sending shuddering spasms like shockwaves through her muscles. Dimly, she recalled the words to a spell that would burn the toxin from her system. Marissa called out the words to the spell just as another spider bit down hard upon her thigh. The fragments of her spell blew away like a candle snuffed by the wind.

"Taenaran," she managed to cry out before the darkness took her in its shadowed arms.

Taen heard Marissa's cry.

The half-elf ducked beneath the club of the last remaining ogre and looked behind him. He was horrified to see the gathering of spiders surrounding the beleaguered druid. The shock of it shattered the strains of the Song. Energy fled from his arms and legs. They felt heavy, weighed down by fatigue and fear and sorrow.

"See to her," Borovazk shouted and barreled into the lone ogre, forcing the creature back a single step.

Taen gazed at the battered and bloody Rashemi ranger just for a heartbeat before running toward the druid. Even from here he could see the angry purplish-red tracks wending toward her heart from the wounds on her chest and leg.

Poison!

Taen knew that he had only moments to scatter the spiders and let the druid drink from one of the potions he had with him. Pushing his body beyond its limits, the half-elf leaped into the air. He sailed in a wide arc, one that he knew would carry him over the menacing bodies of two spiders—

Only to rebound off of an invisible barrier.

The half-elf fell to the ground at the same moment that he witnessed Marissa do the same. He would have screamed her name, but the fall had sucked the wind out of him. Desperately he pounded against the wall, using both sword and spell, hoping to bring it down, all the while watching the spiders cover Marissa's body with their disgusting webs. Though the invisible barrier flickered and flared several times beneath his assault, the mystic wall held.

Within moments, the spiders had secured Marissa and began to scuttle up in to the shadows, crawling quickly up their nearly invisible strands of web. Taen shouted separately to his companions for help. In silent accord, Borovazk and Roberc plunged their weapons into the remaining ogre. It fell to the ground, shaking the bridge. At its demise, the few remaining goblins shrieked in fear and fell back into the undertomb.

Quickly Borovazk dropped his weapons and drew his curved long bow. With surprising speed, he loosed two arrows. The feathered shafts hissed into the shadows, pursuing the retreating spiders. Taen watched them cut through the air like hunting falcons—only to veer quite suddenly to the left, as if swatted by an invisible hand.

Taen cursed and fell to his knees.

Above him, spiders carried Marissa's web-covered form into the darkness.

CHAPTER 21

The Year of the Serpent

(1359 DR)

Thunder rumbled among the storm-wracked sky.

Chill rain fell like a hail of arrows upon those *tael* still battling in the forest clearing. The senior apprentices fought hard, their bodies carried forward in a complex dance of deadly steel. Loud gasps of breath echoed in the clearing, cutting through the silence left behind by the harsh clamor of blades, the ring of steel upon steel.

Despite a bone-deep fatigue that threatened to slow and paralyze muscles worked hard to the point of failure, Taenaran was enjoying himself. An opponent's sword snaked toward him on his left side. Without breaking stride, he flicked his own blade in a downward stroke at the incoming attack. As the weapons met, he raised his right foot and twisted his hips, using the initial momentum of his parry to carry him into a sideways flip. The maneuver allowed him to avoid a second opponent's incoming sweep toward his legs. He slid to the left, and his two opponents attacked each other.

Such was the way of *alu'dala,* the water battle. *Alu'dala* was an ancient exercise, a group combat where each participant met and blended with the attacks of all others near him. The purpose of the exercise was not so much to vanquish opponents as to flow with the energy each attack created. Among masters, the *alu'dala* could last days.

Taenaran would be satisfied if he made it through the next few candle lengths. At first, the rain had been a welcome gift, cooling off his overheated body. Now the frigid water mixed with his own sweat, running into the half-elf's eyes and making it difficult to see the whole battlefield. He barely avoided the slashing attack of a long-muscled apprentice to his right. With an inward curse at his own lapse of concentration, he sucked down a lungful of air and rolled across the rapidly muddying ground, bringing his own sword up to attack the nearest opponent. It was a difficult maneuver, one that required a great deal of coordination. The fact that he executed it perfectly brought a smile to his face—and a grimace of dismay from the defending apprentice, who obviously hadn't expected the half-elf to succeed quite so spectacularly. Even though the apprentices' blades were not honed to combat sharpness, they could still do some damage. Taenaran's sword slipped beneath his opponent's guard and pierced the elf's skin. The wounded apprentice fell backward just as one of the masters called out his elimination from the exercise.

Taenaran had little time to worry about his erstwhile enemy, as two more swords whipped at him from behind. He spun quickly, knocking both blades away in a precise parry that brought a murmur of approval from the junior apprentices and those senior *tael* who had been eliminated from the *alu'dala*.

The half-elf felt his face begin to flush. For many years, he had endured the whispered comments, the biting insults murmured behind covered faces or concealed within seeming compliments or worse. It wasn't uncommon for some of the other apprentices to target him specifically during exercises such as the *alu'dala*, purposefully trying to overwhelm the younger but stronger half-elf. If the masters saw any blatant harassment, they were quick to put a stop to it. Much more went on, however, behind the *el'taels'* backs. It was nice to receive the occasional acknowledgement of his skill.

It was even nicer, the half-elf thought, to have Talaedra witness it. Although he couldn't see the young elf maiden, and he didn't dare take a moment to look for her silver-haired beauty among those assembled, Taenaran knew that she was watching.

He didn't have too much time, however, to bask in the accolades. Both opponents, the only two remaining besides himself in the *alu'dala*, began to weave a deadly coordinated attack, seeking to draw his blade too far away during a parry so that the other could strike at his unprotected flank. He took a moment to gaze at the two enemies before him and cursed silently. Andaerean and his never-far-from-him companion, Nardual, were two of the most active antagonists during his time as an apprentice. It had been clear from very early on that the golden-haired, bronze-skinned Andaerean somehow took umbrage at Taenaran's presence among the *tael*. It didn't help that his Uncle Faelyn worked with the haughty elf apprentice privately to hone his skills. Nardual, however, never seemed to hold a personal grudge against Taenaran. He simply followed his elder companion—though out of a misguided sense of loyalty or a lack of imagination, Taenaran never knew.

He did, however, have his suspicions.

The half-elf managed to catch the sly smirk that spread across Andaerean's face before the elf lashed out with a booted foot. Taenaran's instincts cried out for him to dodge the hasty kick, but years of training had helped him identify the real threat. Nardual's weapon slashed to Taenaran's right, perfectly aligned to strike the half-elf in mid dodge. Instead, he took the brunt of Andaerean's attack, catching the elf's boot with his free arm and wrenching his opponent off balance. Nardual's sword whistled about a hand's width from Taenaran's shoulder.

Thunder rumbled in the distance, but the half-elf barely heard it. From the moment that he had caught Andaerean's boot, the world seemed to slow. The sounds of the clearing faded. The patter of rain, the rustle of wet leaves in the storm-ridden wind, the explosive breath of his attackers—all of it settled beneath the first strains of the Song. He felt it grow within him, gradually crescendoing. Nardual launched a desperate attack to give his companion a few moments to regain his footing. The elf's longsword beat against Taenaran's defense, but as the Song grew, his opponent's blade began to move more slowly. As Nardual's sword cut downward, the half-elf watched it with a sense of dispassionate observation. His own blade touched the tip of Nardual's longsword then slid down its length, stinging the elf's hand with a light rap.

The sword fell from Nardual's grip just as Andaerean returned to the fray. The now-angry elf shouted something that Taenaran, enmeshed in his inner Song, couldn't make out. Despite his ever-present unease at the Song's power, the half-elf rode his fear, mastering it like a skittish horse. He knew that if the battle ended soon, there would be little chance of the Song turning on him. He had asked his father about the Song's dreadful demands, but on that subject his father, and the other masters, were stonily silent. "This was," they insisted, "a path that Taenaran would have to walk alone."

At that moment, his opponent's blade struck out, seeking the exposed flesh of Taenaran's throat. The half-elf ducked beneath the attack and rolled forward, executing a backward slash with his own weapon. Lightning lit up the stormy sky as their blades met. In the distance Taenaran could hear the braying of the training horn, signaling the end of the exercise. Instantly, the Song faded and he stood in the midst of the clearing, panting heavily.

Nardual bent down to retrieve his sword, but Andaerean simply stared at Taenaran, his own weapon still held in battle readiness. Taenaran returned the look, trying not to let his body's trembling, brought on by the rain's chill touch and the strain on his muscles, become too noticeable.

"You performed well, Taenaran," the elf remarked coolly before wiping and sheathing his blade.

Taenaran said nothing, thrown off guard by Andaerean's words. The haughty *tael* had never spoken a kindly word to him in all the years that they had trained together.

He did not disappoint now.

The elf sniffed the air, as if scenting something foul. "Proof that even an ape, with proper coaching, can imitate his betters," Andaerean said. "Perhaps one day they will teach you to sing and dance as well."

All pleasure that Taenaran had felt at his execution of the water battle shattered beneath the cutting edge of the elf's words. The half-elf felt his anger rise like a river swollen with spring thaw. He wanted to reach out and punch that smug, superior smirk off of Andaerean's face, or at the very least, send the *tael* back home with a few bruises. He might have done so, had another, lighter voice not broke in to their small circle of conflict.

"Taenaran," the voice called out. "Oh, there you are."

Talaedra stopped in midstride, her face flushed and her breath swirling in gray clouds blown by the rain-laden wind. Her silver hair, rare among the sun elves, danced wildly in the storm, tangling and twisting where the gusts tossed its curling strands. Where in others such an unusual coloring would be a flaw in an otherwise stunning beauty, Talaedra wore it like a crown. The silver-white tint of her hair set off eyes as gray as the mists of the spring-soaked Glades of Araenvae. The effect added to the elf maiden's beauty, making her seem even rarer, like a certain moonrise that occurs but once in a lifetime.

The effect was immediate—and not unexpected. Taenaran felt his breath catch and his tongue stiffen; he stood transfixed, as if caught by the gaze of a basilisk. Andaerean, on the other hand, straightened immediately. The half-elf watched enviously as the haughty, dour lines of the *tael*'s face were replaced by a gracious and open smile. Andaerean bowed low.

"Talaedra," he said, pronouncing the young elf maiden's name with perfect grace, "it is an honor to see you again. How fortunate for us that you chose this day to come and see the *alu'dala*."

Taenaran felt a surge of jealousy as Talaedra returned the *tael*'s bow.

"Andaerean," she replied. "The water battle is always a delight to watch. You performed well," she said, eliciting another wave of jealousy that suddenly stopped and turned to amazement when Talaedra continued with a sly wink toward Taenaran, "all of you."

The half-elf's heart leaped in his chest. She had noticed his skill today. The thrill of it was almost enough to restore his earlier feeling of contentment.

Almost.

What came next, however, damped Taenaran's enthusiasm like a torrent of freezing water on a fledgling fire.

Andaerean cleared his throat. "Tonight is the Feast

of First Planting," the elf said with great formality. "I was wondering if you would grant me the honor of accompanying you to the celebration."

Taenaran winced at the elf's words, despite himself. He knew what was to come, yet even though he saw it, like an arrow speeding toward his heart, it did not hurt any less, which was why he spluttered and choked violently at Talaedra's response.

"Thank you for your offer," the elf maiden said formally, her rich voice lilting and even, "but I already have a companion for the celebration." She reached out a slender, smooth-skinned hand and laid it gently upon Taenaran's shoulder.

The half-elf nearly burst out laughing at the look of consternation and disbelief that passed across Andaerean's face, soon followed by a piercing stare full of hatred. The elf *tael* bowed low again.

"Well," he said in clipped tones, "since I have done my duty and am now assured that you would be spared the indignity of attending tonight's feast alone, I ask your leave to retire."

He spun around quickly and grabbed Nardual. The two walked briskly toward the waiting tree line, but not before Andaerean turned to look once more at Taenaran. The half-elf felt the *tael*'s hatred, like spears thrown from the angry cast of his eyes.

Taenaran groaned once the two companions moved out of sight. "Now you've done it," he exclaimed. "Andaerean is truly angry now."

"Andaerean is a pig," Talaedra spat, "whose manners, however cleverly disguised, would be more appropriate among orcs than elves. I cannot believe what he said to you."

Taenaran felt the tips of his ears burn with shame. "Then you heard what he said?" the half-elf asked. "Well," he continued, not waiting for a response, "thank you for coming to my rescue." He gave the maiden a quick bow then started to walk toward his pack.

"Where are you going?" Talaedra asked. "We haven't talked about tonight."

Taenaran stopped suddenly, as if caught in a spell. He turned to face the elf maiden, afraid that she would disappear and he would come to realize that this whole day had been nothing but a dream. "Th . . . Then you were serious about this evening," he stammered when Talaedra didn't fade from existence.

Her smile lit up the storm-clouded clearing. "Of course I was serious," she replied. "Where shall I meet you?"

"But your father," Taenaran began, "won't he be—"

"My father," Talaedra interrupted, "will be far happier knowing that I am spending the evening with an honest and good-hearted *tael*, no matter his bloodline, than if I were accompanied by a conniving and spiteful apprentice who barely conceals his own venomous heart behind a web of lies."

Taenaran simply stared, unable to respond.

"Good," Talaedra said, "I'm glad that it's settled. Why don't I meet you at the Verdant Pools and then we can walk to the celebration together?" She smiled once more then bent forward to kiss Taenaran lightly on the cheek before leaving the clearing.

The half-elf still stood there, honestly confused by what had just happened. Perhaps, he thought, this really was a dream.

Thunder rumbled in the distance, as if in answer.

Drops of water fell from rain-soaked trees, spattering Taenaran's cloak. Absently, he wiped away the few errant droplets that ran down his face. Despite the arrival of spring, the night air held a fierce chill. Above him, thick clouds shrouded the moon's illumination in a mantle of silver-gray luminescence.

None of it mattered to the half-elf. In fact, another Time of Troubles could have fallen upon the world and he would scarce have noticed—for Talaedra waited just beyond the next bend in the forest path. Friendships had been hard to come by, living as a half-blood among the elves of Avaelearean. Taenaran's friendship with the young elf woman meant that much more to him because of such difficulties. Now, however, the half-elf felt as if they stood upon the brink of something more, something deeper than friendship.

Taenaran smiled in the darkness as he scrambled up the last rise leading to the Verdant Pools. His smile turned to a curse as the worn leather scabbard he wore banged against an out-thrust expanse of rocks. Not for the first time, he wished that he could travel without the weight of his sword dragging at his side. As a student of the bladesinging art, however, he was expected to wear his sword always—as a means of being prepared for anything that might occur, as well as to remind him of his essential duty to the elf people.

When the shadows along the trail suddenly surged and shifted, resolving into several heavily cloaked figures, Taenaran prayed silently in thanksgiving that he had not, for once, shirked this discipline. The half-elf spun to his left, eliminating the possibility that his enemies could surround him by pressing his back against the rock. One of his assailants stepped forward and swung a thick-boled length of wood at him. He ducked beneath the blow and tried to draw his weapon, only to find himself caught beneath a press of bodies. Punches and kicks rained down upon him. He tried to cry out, but the violence of the attacks knocked the wind from him. When the weight bearing him down to the muddy earth disappeared, it was all he could do to crawl on all fours, gasping for breath.

"Get up, you *a Tel'Quessir* scum," a voice barked from somewhere above him.

Taenaran gazed up at his assailants, who stood around him in a loose circle. They each wore thick black cloaks and most of their faces were covered with a thin black veil, leaving only their eyes to stare coldly back at him. The half-elf wiped blood from his nose with the back of his hand before struggling to rise. His mind spun rapidly as he fought to stand. Had they discovered Talaedra? Was she safe? By the sound of their leader's comment, this wasn't an attack from outside the elf community.

"I said rise," the voice shouted again.

It was followed by the sharp strike of a booted foot against Taenaran's ribs. He doubled over in pain but refused to fall to the ground. Carefully, he tried to calm his mind and gain control of the fear that ran through his body, leeching his strength. The mind was a warrior's greatest weapon. His masters had said that often enough, and now he intended to take advantage of their wisdom.

"Stand before your betters, ape," the leader spoke again.

This time Taenaran clearly identified Andaerean as the speaker, despite his attempts at camouflage.

"Andaerean, stop this at once!" another voice cried— Talaedra's.

Taenaran cast around for the elf maiden and found her struggling to free herself from the hold of two of his attackers. She looked unharmed; fire burned within her gray eyes. Relief flooded through the half-elf. At least she hadn't been hurt.

"I wish I could stop it, Talaedra," Andaerean responded, "but I can't. This one must learn his place!"

"When my father hears of this—" Talaedra began.

"Go ahead, run to your father, Tal," Andaerean spat. "Who would believe that I had anything to do with this?" The elf looked around at the other cloaked figures. "Besides, I spent the evening before the celebration training," he continued with a harsh bark of laughter, "and a master will confirm it." Andaerean stared right at Taenaran as the others carried on his laughter.

"You filthy piece of troll dung," Talaedra shouted. "I'll—"

"Shut up!" the elf demanded, as he raised a fist and brought it down hard upon the elf woman's face. "If you want to be an ape-lover, I can't stop you, but I'll be damned if I'm going to listen to you mewl about this piece of filth!"

As the elf's fist smashed into Talaedra and she sagged against her captors, something burst deep within the half-elf. All of the anger and shame he had felt his entire life welled up within him like a magical storm. It wasn't enough that they hurt him, now they chose to hurt someone he cared deeply about.

It would end here.

With a snarl of rage, Taenaran quickly drew his sword, ducking easily away from the hands that grabbed for him awkwardly. His blade sang from its scabbard with a terrible, metallic keen. In his white-hot rage, he could not see Talaedra plant a wicked jab with her elbow into the stomach of her captor. Nor could he see her kick herself free from another of the elves and lunge forward, toward Andaerean.

All that Taenaran held before him was the sight of Andaerean's eyes—eyes that mocked and belittled him with their dismissive gaze. The multiverse slowed to a single heartbeat as the half-elf screamed his hatred at his tormentor and plunged the length of his sword directly at the elf's cold heart.

A woman's cry brought Taenaran back to reality.

Standing before him, impaled on the edge of his sword, Talaedra gazed at Taenaran with eyes widened in shock and surprise. Her mouth worked to form words but none came. Only a red stream of blood poured forth, spilling down her chin. She hung there for a moment, arms outstretched, before light fled from her eyes and Talaedra's body fell backward.

Taenaran looked at the fallen woman then at Andae-rean, whose own face registered shock and horror. He tried to say something—anything—but grief stole his voice.

Moments later, a sharp blow crashed down upon him, and Taenaran fell headlong into darkness.

CHAPTER 22

The Year of Wild Magic
(1372 DR)

She was gone.

Taen knelt on the hard stone floor of the bridge and wept silently. Tears just barely held in check glistened wetly around eyes red with grief. He had failed once again. His own deficiencies had once more caused harm to someone for whom he had cared deeply. It hadn't mattered that the Song had come to him like an old friend instead of a bitter enemy, strengthening his arm and bolstering his swordplay, rather than stealing his strength with the fear of its presence. The half-elf knew that he had stood on the threshold of everything that he had trained and striven for in his life—and it hadn't been enough.

He hadn't been enough.

Marissa was gone—likely dead—and their mission in shambles. The knot in his chest

confirmed what he already knew in the cold, dispassionate part of his mind. It was his fault. He should have
seen the danger from above, should have anticipated
the attack. Instead, he had allowed himself to get so
caught up in the joy of finding the doorway to his art
that he hadn't even heard her scream for help.

Taen saw her in his mind's eye, her skin sallow and
puffy from the spider venom, withdrawing into the darkness. In that moment, Marissa's face blurred, became the
face of another woman, wrapped in burial silk instead
of spider webbing—but just as dead.

He felt a hand rest gently upon his shoulder. "Borovazk is sorry, little friend," the ranger said, and Taen
could hear the grief hanging heavy upon the Rashemi
like a great gray burial stone, "but we must push on. Is
not safe for us to remain on bridge."

Taen looked up at the ranger and felt himself nod at
the warrior's words. The action felt foreign, different,
like the movement of a stranger. It was as if the half-elf
gazed upon his body from across a vast chasm, so that he
was at the same time within and without himself.

A sound caught his attention—high pitched and piti-
ful. It took his divided consciousness a few moments
to recognize that someone else was weeping. Surprise
turned to anger as he turned to face the source of the
sound. Yurz lay on the ground, rolling across the uneven
stone and wailing. The goblin's spindly arms flailed in
every direction as he gave voice to his grief.

Taen's grief transformed into rage at the sight of the
pathetic creature. "You," he shouted, leaping to his feet.
"You did this!"

The half-elf crossed the distance between them
quickly, almost pouncing on the bereaved goblin. Grabbing Yurz by the scruff of the neck, he hoisted the
goblin up in the air. The creature shouted in fright as
he hung above the bridge, kicking his bare, misshapen
feet in a desperate attempt to break free.

"Tell me why I shouldn't throw you off this bridge," Taen shouted. "Tell me!" He dangled the goblin over the black mouth of the chasm below. "You led us into a trap, you filthy spawn of a dung troll, and now Marissa has been taken."

"No!" the goblin screamed shrilly in protest. "Me no hurt Pretty Lady. Me friend. Not know why tribe here. Ugly One must have known." The goblin shook his head piteously.

"You lie," the half-elf hissed between clenched teeth.

His anger rose like a tidal wave within him, threatening to sweep away the last vestiges of his reason. Part of him knew that his rage at the hapless creature was misplaced, but he couldn't stop it; it exploded out of him like the fiery breath of a red dragon.

"Taen," he heard Roberc call out to him, "we have to go . . . now!" the halfling shouted.

He turned, still holding Yurz over the edge of the bridge, and saw both Borovazk and Roberc running toward the open door to the citadel's undertomb. They were right, of course; he didn't have time to vent his anger and grief on the treacherous goblin. If there was any chance of rescuing Marissa and making it out alive, they had to push on, yet he wanted nothing more than to slake his need for revenge. It would be so simple to just open his hand and watch Yurz tumble into the abyss below.

Taen knew that he wasn't thinking clearly, knew that at some level, he also hung over an abyss—one of his own making. At that moment, Yurz and he were linked. If he tossed the goblin into the chasm, he, too, would be lost forever.

What did it matter, Taen thought bitterly. Marissa. Talaedra. He always ended up destroying the very people whom he loved the most. Let the abyss take him. Perhaps he could find in the depths of its unending shadows an end to his heart's fierce burning, a final rest from the pain that had plagued him each moment of his adult life.

"Don't hurt Yurz," the goblin cried, glancing wildly at the chasm below and back to Taen. "Me like Pretty Lady. Me help find her."

Caught between his rage and despair, it took a few moments for the half-elf to process the goblin's words. "What did you say?" he asked.

"Me find Pretty Lady," he repeated, desperation causing the goblin's voice to squeak even higher. "Me know where Ugly One keep prisoners. Me lead you to her."

Taen thought about it for a moment. How could he trust this creature? Even if Yurz hadn't betrayed them—which was a big "if"—Yurz was still an evil, cunning little monster. Enchantment or not, he was loathe to trust Marissa's life to his fickle sense of loyalty.

Yet how could he squander any chance that he might actually be able to save her, to rescue her from the fate that his failures had brought upon her. He stared at Yurz, his limbs frozen with indecision.

"Taen . . . now!" he heard Roberc's voice again, this time much closer.

A sharp tug on his arm ended the paralysis. The half-elf blinked slowly, as if waking from a deep sleep. Roberc stood at his side, sword in hand. He could see Borovazk standing at the entrance to the undertomb, gazing into the darkness beyond.

Taen dropped Yurz unceremoniously on the stone floor of the bridge. The goblin quickly got to his feet and danced around him.

"Thankyouthankyouthankyou," the creature gibbered almost unintelligently, his eyes agleam with emotion. "Yurz lead you to Pretty Lady, you see. Yurz friend to Pretty Lady's friends—"

The half-elf reached out and stilled the whirling goblin with a harsh grapple. "If you so much as think a betraying thought in that ugly head of yours, I will separate it from your body so fast that you won't even know you're dead until you watch your headless corpse tumble to the floor," he said menacingly. "Got it?"

Yurz gulped audibly. "Yes," he replied in a frightened voice. "Yurz hear what bald elf say."

"Good," Taen said and pushed the goblin toward the open door to the undertomb. "Then let's get going."

The ghoul fell back against the wall.

Taen withdrew his sword from the creature's chest. The monster slid down the smooth stone of the tomb wall, the gleam fading from its undead eyes. To his left, Borovazk crushed the last two creatures with one mighty swing of his warhammer. Dried bones snapped as the weapon slammed the hapless ghouls against the ground.

"How much further?" Taen asked their goblin guide.

"We not too far away," Yurz replied. "We almost out of the undertomb."

"Good," the half-elf replied, wiping the slime and congealed blood from his sword. They had spent a long time traversing the cramped passages and chill crypts of the citadel undertomb, dodging more goblin patrols and a seeming horde of skeletons and zombies. Several times they had entered a seemingly empty room only to be beset by ravenous ghouls and even the occasional wight lurking in the shadows. Taen's arms ached with fatigue, his muscles long since pushed past the point of exhaustion. This last battle had nearly undone him. He sheathed his now-clean sword and rested briefly, his breath coming in great ragged gasps.

"Friends rest now," Yurz said, shooing Taen and his two companions to the center of the crypt. "Me search for secret way up into citadel." It was a testament to their fatigue that no one attempted to gainsay the anxious creature.

Taen dropped to the floor and massaged his sword shoulder. Borovazk and Roberc did the same, though the halfling spent most of his time cleaning the blood from Cavan's matted fur. The ranger looked around at their surroundings, unease written clearly upon his face. This room was larger than most, its smooth stone handsomely decorated with fading murals and elaborate stonework. Two of the walls were filled with human-sized horizontal alcoves, each occupied by a skeleton bedecked in ancient armor. Several sarcophagi sat in the center of the room, their heavy stone lids shattered by the force of the ghouls that had poured out of them.

"What's the matter, Borovazk," the halfling asked, "besides the fact that we're trapped in an undead-infested tomb trying to rescue Marissa from the clutches of a powerful hag?"

Taen found his temper rising as the halfling's acerbic comments filled the silence of the room. Fatigue won out over anger, however, so the half-elf bit his tongue, grasping the hilt of his sword as he did so and cursing the necessity for rest that caused them delay. Besides, he knew that Roberc would fight through every layer of the Abyss to rescue Marissa.

For his part, Borovazk ran a meaty hand through his sweat-soaked hair before answering the halfling. When he did finally speak, his usually resonant voice barely filled the chamber. "This is great resting place of heroes," the ranger said hoarsely, pointing to the walls of the crypt and beyond. "Borovazk feel sad to fight Rashemi whose bodies have been corrupted by the foul work of the hag and her witch ally. Is not right. The dead deserve honor." This last he nearly shouted.

Taen looked up and cast a measuring glance at the ranger. The skin beneath Borovazk's eyes sagged, bruised and nearly black with fatigue. The human's normally irrepressible smile had faded—when that had happened, Taen hadn't noticed—replaced now by a wide-mouthed frown. Dried blood and thick black patches of congealed slime marred the normally pale hue of his face.

At that moment, the half-elf realized that he wasn't the only one who blamed himself for Marissa's capture. Both Borovazk and Roberc held a haunted look in their eyes and a grim cast to their features. That fact unaccountably lightened his own heart, and he recalled something that his father used to say: "A burden shared is a burden lightened." He was so caught up in his own misery that he hadn't realized how deeply his companions grieved for Marissa. The half-elf began to understand—in the way that one does when light first shines in a dark place—that perhaps this was the root cause of much of his problems: he was always focused inward on himself, on his own guilt and misery.

"Don't worry, Borovazk," he said at last, resting a hand upon the ranger's shoulders. "We will find Marissa, and when we do, we shall make the witch and her hag minion pay for what they have done here."

Borovazk looked Taen in the eye, and the half-elf could see the Rashemi's desire for that revenge. "Is good to hear, little friend," the ranger responded. "Borovazk think that he is done with this little adventure soon, and he will be glad of it."

A shriek erupted from a shadowy corner of the crypt, followed by the sound of Yurz's cackling laughter. "Me find it!" the goblin proclaimed loudly. "Come, friends of Pretty Lady! Yurz find the door. We not far now!"

For what seemed like the first time in quite a while, a smile split the grim terrain of Taen's face. "Perhaps," he said to Borovazk, "our adventure will end sooner than we had hoped!"

With a grunt and a sigh of effort, the half-elf pulled himself to his feet, gathered up his gear, and strode toward the now-open secret door. Without a second thought, he walked through it.

CHAPTER 23

The Year of Wild Magic
(1372 DR)

Marissa breathed fire.

It seared her lungs; her chest burned with each labored inhalation. The druid struggled once more against the bonds that held her, but the steel chains just cut deeper into the skin of her wrist with each movement. The room was dark—it was always dark, except when the hag came. Shadow and flame defined her universe. She wanted to scream, but her voice, too, had become fire, so Marissa wept glistening trails of tears that were her only comfort.

The druid had no idea how long she'd been a prisoner. She remembered the bridge, remembered the sting of spider venom, and the next thing she'd been aware of was the cold kiss of her steel shackles and the bitter voice of the hag whispering hateful secrets into her ear. At first Marissa's mind seemed numb and sluggish—as if wreathed in a chill gray fog that drained thought and speech. She fought off the sensation, realizing at the last moment that it was merely a spell cast by her captor.

That was when the pain began—physical and psychic assaults that left Marissa barely conscious. She cried out again and again to her god for some measure of mercy but received nothing but more agony.

It was all about the Staff of the Red Tree. The hag had made that clear from the first moment. Somehow the artifact resisted her attempts at mastery, and the monster assumed that Marissa held the key. Perhaps she did, the druid thought bitterly, for even now she could hear the voice of the staff, muted, like a distant whisper, calling to her in the depths of her mind. If Marissa held the key to the staff's power, she had no idea how to access it.

She hung in the darkness, weeping, waiting for the hag's next visit. She thought now and again of Taenaran and her friends battling for survival somewhere in the bowels of the earth below the citadel. She had no idea if they were still alive or if the hag's minions had slain them. She remembered, dimly, the promise of a conversation with Taenaran, a conversation that she had put off until the end of their journey. Endings, she thought bitterly, have a nasty habit of coming when you least expect them, yet Marissa still held out hope that she and Taen would see each other again. She hung by that thin silver thread of hope over the abyss of despair as surely as she hung by the steel chains that bound her.

She was surprised, therefore, by the voice that cut through her interior wrestling. "Do not think that anyone will come for you," the voice said. "You are alone."

At first Marissa expected to see the hag, green skin and misshapen face leering out of the darkness. It only took her a few moments, however, to realize that the

voice sounded different, huskier than the hag's. Dim
light filled the room. The druid blinked hard as the
illumination aggravated her eyes. When she could focus,
Marissa saw a brown-haired figure standing before her.
At first her heart leaped at the sight of the stranger—
until she caught sight of the orc rune hanging around
the figure's neck. The stranger's scarred face and her
flat, gray eyes confirmed what Marissa suspected—the
half-orc standing before her was no sympathetic rescuer
but rather a servant of the hag.

A servant, she thought, and something more.

Power emanated from this creature. Marissa could
sense it—a darkness as deep as the Abyss filled her. If
she served anyone, it certainly wasn't the hag. That
thought sent fear knifing up her spine.

"You've caused Yulda quite a bit of trouble," the
stranger said, "you and your friends."

She drew closer to Marissa, reached out a thickly
muscled hand, and ran her fingers lightly down the
druid's cheek. The captive half-elf tried to turn her
head, but the stranger grabbed it harshly with her other
hand. Marissa could feel the barbed points of steel claws
pressing harshly into her head.

"You won't give up the secrets of your staff to the hag,"
her tormentor whispered. "I respect that." The half-orc
released Marissa's head. "You *will* reveal them to me,
or I promise you the torments I have prepared for you
will make you beg for the hag's return."

Marissa closed her eyes for a moment and prayed
desperately for strength. The voice of the staff rose
in her mind. The whole of her journey in Rashemen
flashed before her. The druid knelt once more beneath
the trunk of the Red Tree, spoke face-to-face with the
ancient telthor. The memory of that time eased her fears.
She had seen wonders and experienced moments of peace
within Rashemen of which she had never even dreamed.
If this, then, was Rillifane's will, that she should suffer

and die in the darkness, then Marissa would accept it. Who was she to enjoy the wondrous gifts her god had given her while rejecting the rest of her life, which was also from him? She knew that suffering, too, could be a kind of gift, one that brought the sufferer closer to the divine. The hierophants spoke of that often enough. Now, within the ancient citadel of her enemy, Marissa would live that reality.

With Rillifane's name ushering forth silently from her lips, she opened her eyes and gazed steadily at her interrogator. "I can tell you nothing," she exclaimed, "and even if I did know something, I would never reveal it to you."

The half-orc smiled in response, and Marissa felt her heart begin to falter once again. "We shall see," she said and placed a rough hand upon the druid's head, whispering a prayer to her god as she did so.

Marissa tried to shut out the cleric's voice, but the harsh cadence and sibilant syllables of the half-orc's whispered devotion filled the room with a dreadful cacophony. She shuddered and twisted against her bonds, writhing in pain. Though she couldn't understand her torturer's words, Marissa felt their power; it washed over her, stinging and lashing her spirit with each phrase. Her cell grew dark once more—pitch black—and chilled, as if the half-orc's spell were drawing all of the energy from the room. The chill intensified, deepened, stealing her life with each knife-sharp breath that she took. Memories of her life beneath the sun, time spent with friends and loved ones, laughter, life, joy—all of it was falling away from her into an icy void. Marissa knew with a terrible certainty that there would soon be nothing left, that she was being hollowed out, emptied, until all that remained was ice and darkness.

The druid struggled against her fate, summoning thoughts from her childhood, shouting prayers to Rillifane and any god who might hear her cry. Nothing helped. She felt herself falling. Her last thought before the darkness took her was of Taenaran.

The corridor stood empty.

Smooth, polished stone—so different from the highly decorative craftsmanship of the citadel's undertomb—caught and reflected the dim light of torches that burned fitfully in iron sconces. The passageway ended in a solid stone door shut tightly almost twenty feet in the distance. Taen and his companions stood silently in the shadows and listened for any sound that might indicate the presence of their enemies.

They heard nothing.

Taen crept forward carefully, making sure his weapon did not scrape against either wall of the small passageway. When nothing jumped out at him, he waved for the others to follow. Despite their apparent safety, a sense of unease rose up in him, like delicate fingers of ice running along his spine. Bitter experience had taught him to trust his instincts. The half-elf peered intently down the corridor.

"I don't like this," he whispered to his companions. "Something's wrong."

"You're just figuring that out now," he heard Roberc's hushed reply from behind him.

Taen's sense of unease intensified—fingers turned to sharp daggers stabbing at his back. "Wait," he blurted out as Yurz reached for the closed door before him.

The goblin froze, one long-fingered hand nearly touching the dull gray stone. On a whim, Taen closed his eyes and cast a spell of detection upon the door. Immediately, three purplish-black glyphs flared into existence on the door's stone surface. The serpentine symbols writhed and roiled like grubs suddenly exposed to the light of day.

Yurz fell backward with a yelp, but Taen could spare

the goblin none of his attention, as the power from the now-revealed glyphs hammered against the half-elf's mystic senses and threatened to overwhelm him. If any one of their group had actually laid a hand upon the door, it would have released unspeakable energy upon them all.

Taen walked toward the door with one hand extended. He gathered his own power and sent it streaming toward the door, hoping that his skill would be sufficient to dispel the protective glyphs. As the energy from his spell met the power bound up in the runes, the glowing symbols dimmed like a banked fire then flared into unmistakable life once again.

Taen swore. "That's done it," he nearly shouted.

"What do you mean?" Borovazk asked, casting a wary glance at the angrily pulsating symbols.

"I couldn't dispel the glyphs," Taen replied, "and now whoever set them here knows that someone has tried to tamper with them."

"What do we do?" Roberc asked, drawing his sword.

Taen reached into his backpack with the other and drew forth a triangular prism. "We'll have to move fast," he said. "I was hoping to hold this in reserve in case we needed it against the renegade witch, but it seems that our need is very great at the moment."

The half-elf muttered a few words over the prism. Pure white light blossomed from the clear heart of the item. "This prism should draw the glyphs' energy into itself," he said to the others. "Once those symbols disappear from the door, run through it. We've already lost any element of surprise."

The gleam in the crystal grew brighter, filling the room. At first, the purplish glow from the warding symbols polluted the bright light, bruising its argent incandescence. Gradually, however, the prism's power overmastered the glyphs. At first, their sickening light seemed to draw back, retreating from the crystal's illumination, but the pulsating energy moved toward the prism, entering its angular planes. The process took a few more moments as the glyphs gradually faded from the door's surface. Once completed, the light from the prism faded, and the room returned to normal.

"Now!" Taen shouted and drew his weapon once again.

The others ran toward the door, throwing open its bulk with a mighty heave. Within the space of three heartbeats, Taen stood alone in the corridor.

Carelessly, he dropped the prism to the floor. It bounced once on the obdurate stone then exploded into a thousand fragments. Taen would have spent another moment making sure the evil power had truly dissipated, but the sound of Marissa's screams reached his ears from the corridor beyond the door.

He made a wordless noise and leaped into the shadowy passageway—unprepared for the horror that awaited him.

CHAPTER 24

The Year of Wild Magic

(1372 DR)

The horror charged.

Twin skeletal heads, one human and one monstrous, opened their mouths as if to scream, while long, bony arms swung a gleaming obsidian axe. Taen nearly toppled as he dodged the weapon, caught off guard by the speed of the attack and the high-pitched keen that ushered from the creature's heads. Borovazk leaped forward, his own axe cutting through the air in a wicked arc. The axe edge struck armor, but was unable to penetrate the thick, silvery chain that covered the beast from shoulder to knees. Still, the force of the blow knocked the creature back a step, and Taen took that opportunity to pull back from the monster safely.

In the dim light of the stone corridor, Taen could see the glint of bone, some yellowed with age and others gleaming white, that made up their opponent's prodigious bulk. Unlike most of the skeletal creatures he had fought in the past, the bones of this monster didn't seem to fit together well. It was as if someone had scavenged parts from a host of different beasts and cobbled them together with magic. Arms that could have come from an ogre or a giant ended in hands that seemed delicate, almost elflike in appearance. Likewise, the beast's human-sized legs ended in elongated, three-toed feet. Bits of dried and desiccated flesh still clung to parts of the monster's bones. It was the eyes, though, that disturbed Taen the most. Deep within the empty sockets of the monster's four eyes, purple flames burned with flickering intensity. A chill ran through the half-elf whenever he found himself transfixed with that gaze.

There was little time to reflect on this puzzle, however, as the skeletal creature lurched forward, swinging its axe once again. Roberc darted forward as the weapon whistled over his head and drew a thick-headed mace from his belt. Two mighty swings of the weapon sent bone chips flying out from the monster's legs. Its keen changed in tone, transforming into a roar of anger. Within moments, twin sheets of purple flame exploded from the creature's eyes, engulfing Roberc in an eldritch conflagration.

Taen cried out as the flames erupted around the halfling, but he was too far away from the fighter to do anything. Behind him, however, the half-elf heard a low growl before Cavan's furred form darted forward, hurtling toward the ball of flame. The war-dog leaped toward the burning fire and yelped with pain as he entered the fiery sphere. His momentum, however, carried him through the raging inferno in moments, with Roberc's smoldering form before him.

Taen heard Borovazk's shout of rage as the ranger struck from behind their skeletal opponent. Axe and warhammer beat against the monster again and again. In the small confines of the corridor, the sound of shattering bone echoed with a sickening crunch. The monster staggered forward, its back now twisted at an awkward angle, but its axe still slicing through the air—and drew closer to the fallen Roberc.

The half-elf cursed every moment that they stood here battling this monstrosity. Marissa was somewhere nearby, held captive and obviously in great pain. They would have to end this battle soon. Reaching down to his belt, Taen pulled out a long, thin tube and broke the wax seal. Deftly, he pulled forth a thin roll of vellum, unfurled it, and began to chant the words that were written in spidery runes upon it.

Instantly the air before Taen began to ripple and shimmer with incandescence. The luminescence resolved within moments, revealing a giant fist that floated in midair. The half-elf sent the arcane fist streaking toward his opponent with a thought. It hurtled toward the monster, striking it with enough force to send it flying back several feet back and smashing it against the stone wall. It lurched forward, unsteady now on its skeletal feet—only to find itself pummeled repeatedly by the arcane force of the floating fist. Each time the spell-summoned hand struck, bones snapped like dry tinder. By the third attack, the skeletal creature toppled backward in a tangle of limbs. Its arms and legs lay twisted, yet still it shuddered, trying to stand and resume its attack.

Taen kept up his concentration, sending the fist crashing down upon the defeated skeletal monstrosity again and again. By the time Borovazk had seen to the injured halfling and his canine companion, the arcane spell had reduced its hapless opponent to a pile of splintered bone and dust.

"Are you all right?" Taen asked the halfling as Roberc

and Cavan sidled up to join the half-elf in the center of the hallway.

"I'm fine," the halfling growled in response, taking a hard swig from his wineskin and sucking down the liquid.

"Then let's move," Taen said, pointing toward the thick stone door that blocked the only other exit from the corridor. Carefully, he crept forward, alert for any signs that the door might fly open, releasing a horde of enemies that would threaten to overwhelm them.

Nothing happened.

The half-elf stood before the portal, head cocked, elf ears focused intently on what lay beyond. For just a moment, he thought he heard what might have sounded like sobs coming from beyond the door. Before he could make any further determination, however, the sounds stopped.

The silence brought a surge of anxiety racing through Taen's body. What if they were too late and Marissa lay dead somewhere beyond the doorway? That thought sent the half-elf springing into action. He was about to leap forward and muscle open the door, when he heard Roberc's voice hissing from somewhere behind him.

"Careful, Taen," the halfling whispered. "Remember the last door."

That warning froze Taen before his shoulders had reached the stone. He cursed himself silently for a fool. If he kept letting his fear for Marissa override his experience, he would end up getting them all killed. Taking a deep breath, he whispered the words to a detection spell. Once again, disturbing glyphs appeared before him, inscribed onto the surface of the door. He searched his memory for the right spell then sent his arcane power out with a word of command. When the sigils faded completely from sight, he turned to Yurz, still huddling fearfully in the corner.

"You stay here," he commanded softly, "and let us know

if anything tries to come at us from this direction."

As loathe as he was to trust their fate to this ensorcelled goblin, Yurz had proven a decent enough companion. With a sharp hand signal to the others, Taen indicated that they were ready. The half-elf took three deep breaths and launched himself against the stone door.

Marissa swam out of an ocean of shadow and into the dim light of her cell. Her eyes opened slowly, as if weighed down by lodestones. She blinked heavily, until the outline of her tormentor resolved into clear focus. Still disoriented from her return to consciousness, it took the druid a few moments to realize that something seemed different about the half-orc. The cleric's calm and confident watchfulness had disappeared, shattered, Marissa eventually realized, as the sounds of a nearby battle reached her ears, by what occurred beyond the doorway to the cell.

Now her captor knelt upon the obdurate stone floor and whispered prayers to her dark god. Purple and green energy suffused the cleric's body, eventually fading beyond sight. When the half-orc finally stood, the air was thick with divine power. The weight of it nearly gagged Marissa.

Still, hope surged within her. She was not alone! Her friends were just beyond that doorway. Marissa had never really believed the words of the half-orc, but despair had become a difficult suitor to deny in the darkness of her pain and torment.

"Do not think that this changes anything," her captor said in an icy tone. "The creature that guards that door will be more than a match for your pathetic friends."

The half-orc's words were like hot knives plunging into her chest. Marissa's hope faltered, and sadness welled up within her at the thought of Taenaran and the others lying dead beyond that doorway. Despite her best attempts at stifling them, sobs of anguish began to rack her body.

"Shut up," the half-orc commanded, punctuating her demand with a hard slap across the face. Marissa felt blood begin to trickle down from her nose. The hot liquid ran into her mouth, causing her to gag. Hands grabbed at her hair, causing the druid's head to snap back sharply. "If you make another sound," the half-orc hissed in her ear, "I will make sure that my mistress greets each of your friends personally before their blood waters the ancient stones of her altar. Is that understood?"

Marissa shook her head mutely, all the while praying to Rillifane for guidance and perseverance. When the sounds of battle stopped and silence fell beyond the doorway, it took all of Marissa's strength to not cry out. Instead, she held her breath, waiting to see who had triumphed.

Nothing happened.

For the space of thirty heartbeats the world lay in complete stillness. Nothing moved or made the slightest sound. "You see," Marissa's captor began, "I told you—"

When the stone door flew open and the world erupted into light, the druid called out Taenaran's name.

The door opened into darkness—a deep, shadow-filled haze from which ushered the sound of his name. Taen's heart leaped as he heard Marissa's voice calling out to him. They had not arrived too late to save her. Now they only had to stay alive long enough to walk out of here with the druid.

Light from the corridor behind him spilled into the room, banishing the gloom that hung about the chamber like a pall. Manacles and other more dire devices hung from the walls and ceiling. Dark reddish brown stains covered the floor, growing thicker and more numerous beneath the spiked chains that ran along the wall. Taen nearly gagged at the stench of bitter herbs and rancid sweat that soured the air.

When he finally caught sight of Marissa, trussed up cruelly by a thick chain that wrapped around her good hand and traveled up to the ceiling, where it ended in a metal bolt, the half-elf's heart skipped a few beats. Marissa's normally lustrous red hair lay matted thickly against her head, caked with dried sweat and crusted with congealed blood. Dark bruises blossomed like evil flowers beneath her eyes, and a thick stream of blood flowed from her nose.

"So," a voice hissed from out of the remaining shadows, "I see that you managed to defeat my little pet. You will not find it so easy to overcome me."

Taen drew his sword at the sound of the voice. Behind Marissa, stepping out of the shadows as one might step out of a fine robe, a dark figure strode into view. From where he stood, the half-elf could see that it was a female with some measure of orc blood. One thick hand wielded a rune-covered mace that looked to be made entirely of stone, while the other hand sported a metallic bracer from which sprouted four razor-sharp claws. The light from the hall behind him reflected dully off the half-orc's polished plate armor, throwing three purple scars running down toward the creature's throat in harsh relief. An onyx disk with a single glowing rune hung from her neck.

"Don't be too sure about that," Taen shot back, nearly quivering with rage. Here, at last, was someone at whom he could take out his frustration and anger for Marissa's captivity. He pointed the tip of his blade at the half-orc, and was surprised to see the silver runes flare into life. "We've fought our way into the heart of this gods-blasted citadel, and we're not going to stop until we've walked upon the broken husk of your corpse."

"Ahh," the cleric muttered with a mock smile, "it seems that the hero has brought a pretty speech along with him. What's next, a profession of your undying love for the captive elf?"

Taen's anger rose in him then stilled as he watched the half-orc's smile fade when she caught sight of his blade. "That's a pretty toy you have there, elfling," she barked. "I'll make it a gift to my mistress as she sucks the spirit from your body for all eternity."

"Enough talk," Borovazk shouted from behind Taen. "Ugly cleric hurt little friend. Borovazk say let's kill cleric now."

The cleric gave a half bow. "You're welcome to try," she responded then called out a single word.

Immediately, the floor beneath Taen's feet began to buckle. The half-elf looked down, alarmed to see the thick stone undulating and roiling like a wave in the surf. Quickly, he dived forward, rolling to his feet on a patch of stable ground. As he stood, the half-elf summoned arcane power and intoned the words to a spell. Blue-green lightning sped from his outstretched hand, arcing toward the cleric. Taen watched in mute astonishment as the bolt of lightning veered oddly at the last moment, striking a round glass sphere that hung on a chain around the half-orc's neck. The glass glowed briefly when Taen's spell lashed against it, finally fading as it absorbed the arcane force.

The half-elf had little time to dwell on this unfortunate occurrence as two arrows hissed by his head, cutting through the air toward the cleric. Just as it looked like they would strike the cleric, a purple flare of energy erupted, and the missiles jerked swiftly, batted away by some divine force.

Roberc charged forward, the force of his momentum blunted slightly by the shifting floor, and ducked beneath a wild swing of the cleric's mace. Swiftly, he stabbed forward with his blade, finding a hole in the juncture of his opponent's armor. The blade slid forward easily then stopped, as if striking stone. The wounded cleric shrieked in pain and fell back a step.

Though obviously not as hurt as she should have been from the ferocity of Roberc's attack, she gave the halfling a penetrating look, as if sizing up her opponent for the first time. The cleric slashed down with her claws swifter than a coiled asp. The metallic blades sent sparks flying from their contact with the halfling's armor. She reached out again, this time with her hand, and struck a blow across Roberc's face. Instantly, black power seeped out from her hands, dripping like dark acid across her enemy's face. Roberc let out a shriek and stumbled backward, madly clutching at his helm.

Taen moved forward, executing a series of swift attacks that forced the half-orc to move backward slowly. That gave Borovazk time to drop his bow and charge in with his axe. The weapon whistled sharply as it cut through the air. Twice the edge of the axe bit into the cleric's flesh, and both times divine power blunted the force of Borovazk's attack.

As the now-familiar strains of the Song began to rise within him, Taen noticed that the cleric chanted softly beneath her breath. Senses honed from decades of disciplined practice caught the edge of power in the air. Desperately, he launched himself forward, taking great swings with his sword in an effort to strike his opponent and disrupt the half-orc's spell before she completed it. As the chant rose to a hushed crescendo, he managed to complete a feint to his right then slip underneath the cleric's guard. His blade sliced open the thick flesh of the half-orc's arm. She gave a shriek of pain which turned into the final words of her spell.

A column of flame shot angrily down from the ceiling overhead. Taen saw the swirling conflagration and dived to his left, managing to avoid most of the roaring flame. Borovazk, however, was not so fortunate. Taen heard the ranger's roar of agony above his own cry of pain as the flames engulfed him. The Rashemi fell backward from the force of the spell, his cloak smoldering in the divine heat.

Taen stumbled as well, trying desperately to catch the breath so quickly sucked from his lungs by the unearthly blast of heat. The misstep cost him dearly. His opponent leaped forward, bringing her stone mace down hard upon his unprotected shoulder. The half-elf felt bones grind and snap beneath the force of the blow and nearly dropped his weapon from the pain. Even worse, the red runic inscriptions upon the mace flared into life, sending a series of crimson energy pulses into Taen's face. He screamed as the pain from a thousand needles lancing his eyes swept through him. For a moment, a curtain of darkness fell over the world, and he stumbled forward, blinded by the cleric's mystic mace. Thoughts of Marissa at the mercy of this vile tormentor filled Taen's mind, bringing with them a rising flash of anger. He shook his head twice, and the world resolved slowly back in to place.

Borovazk and Roberc had recovered as well, and both companions pressed the cleric with deadly attacks, offering Taen a chance to catch his breath. The rigors of the past several tendays had begun to take their toll. The half-elf felt it in the sluggishness of his own body and saw it in the stiff attacks of his friends. They would need to end this battle soon. The cleric had been right; vanquishing her would be far more difficult than he had surmised originally. With a deep inhalation, Taen gathered the remnants of his power and cast another spell. Instantly, he could feel the arcane energy coursing through him, speeding reflexes and allowing him to move faster than normally possible. He had a desperate plan in mind—if only he could survive long enough to execute it.

Empowered by the magic of his spell, the half-elf

sped forward, easily moving between his companions and ducking a wild swing from the cleric's mace. Roberc stabbed upward with his sword, forcing the half-orc to block the attack with her claws. Taen spotted his opening and launched himself forward, concentrating solely on his attack. Quickened by his spell, and fueled by the power of the Song that rang in his heart, Taen leaped in the air and spun, allowing his momentum to add strength to the attack. His first blow struck the obdurate stone of the cleric's mace, forcing her arm away from her body. The attack left him open, however, and he felt the sting of the half-orc's claws as they ripped through his armor and bit deep into his chest. He ignored the pain, and with a single cry of rage, he sliced downward with all his might.

Taen's blade parted muscle, sinew, and bone as it separated the cleric's arm just above the elbow. The wounded cleric screeched in agony as her arm hit the floor with a meaty *thump*. Hot blood pumped from the open wound, spilling out in steaming pools upon the cold stone.

Unbalanced by the attack, the cleric was unable to fend off another strike from Borovazk's axe. Bone crunched and shattered as the force of the blow knocked the half-orc back several steps. Taen could see the desperation carved now upon her face. She took another step back and weakly chanted a single phrase. Immediately a glowing circle appeared around her, coruscating with silver energy. The glow intensified as arcane power surged around her.

Taen shouted a warning, sensing what was about to happen. If they didn't do something in the next several heartbeats, their enemy would escape them. He ran toward the heavily wounded cleric, hoping that his enhanced speed would allow him to reach her in time. He was surprised, then, when Cavan's furred form shot by him. The war-dog gave a deep growl as he launched himself toward the cleric. He struck the half-orc with the weight of his body, pushing her outside the confines of the circle.

The gleaming circle faded.

Taen reached the war-dog in time to see him savagely tear at the cleric's throat. His hapless opponent struck out wildly with her claws, but the wicked blades merely rebounded off of the war-dog's tough barding. With a single wet gurgle, the cleric's body convulsed once then stilled.

Taen fell to his knees and mouthed a prayer of thanksgiving to the gods.

CHAPTER 25

The Year of the Serpent

(1359 DR)

Exile.

Aelrindel sat in the darkness of his private chamber, letting that word echo ominously in his mind, as it had when spoken in the Hall of the Masters. The *el'tael* had deliberated carefully throughout the night, conscious of the delicacy of the matter before them. Although the facts as they had gleaned them from Andaerean and his cronies exonerated Taenaran as the antagonist behind the tragedy that occurred, the half-elf was still responsible for the death of another elf.

Those masters who had opposed Taenaran's entry into the ranks of the *tael* argued that such a horrifying event was a natural consequence of initiating an *a Tel'Quessir* into the art. Even those *el'tael* free from such prejudice had to acknowledge that Talaedra's death flowed from the half-elf's presence in the community.

They had pronounced their judgment: Taenaran must go into exile.

Aelrindel absently ran his fingers across the strings of the harp he now clutched close to his chest. The notes fell into darkness, brittle and out of tune. Taenaran's exile was like a sword that pierced his heart. No father should have to witness the fall of his son. It was worse than death, watching the bright, brave spirit of his child crushed beneath the weight of guilt and shame.

Grief shaped a bitter song that spilled out of the harp. A part of him wanted to stand up and announce that he, too, would go into exile. Thoughts of walking beside Taenaran, coaching and training him further, watching him grow into the hero he was destined to become, filled Aelrindel's thoughts, but the bonds of his Oath shackled the First Hilt with cruel strength. He could not abandon his duty—his people.

Even for love of his son.

The rain had finally stopped falling upon the leaf-covered bower that formed the roof of his home when Aelrindel's fingers stopped their grief-stricken dance across the harp's strings. Silence hung heavily upon the night.

Aelrindel kept vigil with it until the dawn.

Taenaran knelt before his father.

His head throbbed from the aftermath of the blow that had knocked him out, causing the walls of the chamber to shift and bend as his vision swam. As much as the wound upon the half-elf's head pained him, it could not compare to the heart-rending ache of grief and loss that followed him even into his dreams.

Talaedra was dead.

Killed by his own hand, and he himself sent into exile. The masters had pronounced that fateful word even as they turned their backs to him as a symbol of his separation from the community. He had barely heard their judgment or any of their deliberations. Throughout the course of his trial, Taenaran had felt dislocated. Everything had filtered to him as if from a great distance. In that befuddling fog, he had spent time reflecting upon his past, his years spent among the *tael,* which had been the only time that really mattered to him, and came upon one inescapable conclusion: Everything that had happened since yesterday evening must be an illusion. This wasn't his life—couldn't be his life.

Still the masters had decided upon exile. His father, overruled by the wisdom of the other *el'tael,* had been forced to do the same. Now he knelt before that same father, who had been both mentor and master, for the last time. Tears streamed down his face, making ragged tracks in the layers of dirt and dried mud that still covered his skin. He could see the long trail of tears mirrored on his father's face. Aelrindel seemed older somehow, more frail. The commanding sparkle in his bright eyes flickered dully, its normally penetrating power muted and dimmed, as if the events of the past day had stolen something essential from his essence. Taenaran could see that his hands, which wielded both the deadly length of a blade and the subtle strings of a harp with equal facility, trembled as they reached out toward him.

The sight of his father, diminished by grief, struck another blow at Taenaran's heart. He tried to speak, but the words would not come. Shame locked them in his throat with a key he could not grasp. The half-elf struggled as one would struggle with the unfamiliar cadences of an ancient spell, but tongue and mouth would not form the proper sounds. Taenaran sobbed in frustration and threw himself into his father's outstretched arms.

As he felt Aelrindel's arms tighten around him, the half-elf let out an inarticulate wail. He recalled every hateful word and spiteful action that he had endured during his life. Each memory brought with it a wave of anger, shame, and sadness that spilled out of him with racking sobs—and always Talaedra's face hovered over him. Cradled in his father's arms, Taenaran poured out that bitter cup of sorrow that had been his life, and Aelrindel drank of it, even to its dregs. The release of that emotion left Taenaran spent; his body trembled mutely as he leaned in silence against the comforting presence of his father. They sat there in silence for several moments.

When at last Taenaran felt the trembling weight of his father's hand upon his head, he pulled back and gazed at him through tear-reddened eyes. "I . . . I am so sorry," he managed to say at last in a voice husky with grief. "I don't know what happened and now"—he continued above his father's whispered reassurances—"Talaedra is dead. Father," Taenaran's voice choked on that word, "I have killed the only friend I ever had and brought shame upon our house."

"No, my son," Aelrindel spoke in a gentle tone, "it is I who am sorry, for I allowed my selfish pleasure at having a son blind me to the true pain that you were facing. I should have protected you more, stood up for you, but I was proud of your desire to become a bladesinger, and I wanted you to do it totally on your own, so that no one could accuse you of succeeding only because *I* was your father."

Taenaran shook his head, unwilling to allow his father to take any measure of responsibility. This was his failure and no one else's. If he had been stronger somehow, more like a full-blooded elf, he could have avoided this fate, but his weakness had doomed him, and now he would wander the world in exile, separated from the only home that he had ever known.

Aelrindel held him a moment longer then rose slowly to his feet. Taenaran watched his once-vibrant father struggle to stand, bowed beneath the weight of the shame that *he* had brought upon him.

"Come," the First Hilt said at last, reaching out a tremulous hand. "It is time."

Taenaran wiped his eyes and fought back a new wave of tears. "So soon?" he asked as he stood up.

"I am afraid so, my son," Aelrindel replied. "You must begin your exile before the noon sun hangs in the sky." The First Hilt moved to the rear of the chamber and brought forth a bulky leather backpack and a worn scabbard. "I have made sure that you will have enough supplies to begin your journey," he said, presenting the backpack to Taenaran.

The half-elf nodded and reached out, grabbing the backpack and slinging it over his shoulder. Though it seemed somehow lighter than it should, considering the size, number, and shape of the bulges that distorted its shape, the backpack hung upon him like a lodestone. This was it. His life would now be forever changed—and it had happened in what seemed like an instant. He wanted to run back to the room he had occupied as a little child in this house and throw himself down upon the bed and cry, waiting for his father to come and tell him that everything would be all right.

But it wouldn't.

He knew that with the startling certainty of one who had crossed the bright threshold of childhood and now walked the shadowed paths of the world. There would be no kindly parent to wipe away tears or kiss away hurt and pain. Where Taenaran walked, he walked alone.

The half-elf was so lost in the dark turn of his thoughts that he didn't grasp the significance of the weight in his right hand. He looked down and saw the well-oiled length of the scabbard Aelrindel had just offered him, and it took Taenaran a moment to recognize the worn red hilt for what it was.

"This is your sword," Taenaran said breathlessly, his previous thoughts forgotten—at least for the moment. "I cannot take this, Father. It's—"

"Nonsense," Aelrindel said, sternness creeping into his voice for the first time. "This was my father's sword, and his father's sword, and his father's sword before that, passed down to the firstborn son in our house since the founding of Cormanthor. You *will* carry this sword, and wherever you go, no matter how far into darkness you walk, this blade will serve you well."

Aelrindel reached out and clasped Taenaran's shoulder. "Your whole life does not have to be this moment, my son. You are gifted and brave. You will become a powerful bladesinger and one day use all that you have been taught to help those in need. Like the heat from the forge, let this tragedy shape your life like a blade and not destroy it, and know that I am thinking of you each and every day."

With that, his father gathered Taenaran up into his arms once more. Tears welled up in the half-elf's eyes, and this time he didn't fight them. He didn't know whether he could live as his father had predicted, but he had no choice but to try. Perhaps he would one day atone for his weakness and failure.

"Thank you, Va," he whispered into his father's ear before gathering up his sword and backpack. When the moment finally came, father and son walked out of their house together and into the harsh light of the day.

Together for the last time.

CHAPTER 26

The Year of Wild Magic
(1372 DR)

Marissa's hand ached.

The shackles holding her upright had bitten deep into her skin, tearing the flesh around her wrist. Even after several potions from her recovered backpack, the wound throbbed. She paid it little mind, however. Instead, she felt a rush of emotions wash over her as Taen and Borovazk knelt around a thin circle inscribed into the stone floor, trying to discern some way of activating the portal. Despite her fears to the contrary, the half-elf had managed to rescue her. He wasn't dead, or worse, some undead minion in her former captor's army. Rillifane had heard her prayers and blessed her, guiding Taen to where she hung, imprisoned and despairing. He had come for her, lifted her out of the darkness. Every moment she saw his face, lips pursed and eyes intently staring as he concentrated on solving the riddle of the magic portal, Marissa had to remind herself that this wasn't a dream.

"I see that you are feeling a bit better," Roberc remarked.

The halfling had tired of trying to force the portal to give up its secrets and had made his feelings well known before starting to search the length and breadth of the grim gray walls of the room. He stared at Marissa with a frank, searching gaze.

"I am feeling much better, thank you, Roberc," she responded with a genuine smile.

Marissa no longer found her companion's directness unnerving or threatening, as so many others did. In fact, the druid found a certain rude comfort in Roberc's intense demeanor. It was familiar and solid, like the stones on an oft-traveled path.

"I'm glad," he said in his usual brusque tone, though Marissa could hear the genuine concern that lurked beneath the halfling's gruff exterior. "I wouldn't want you to miss out on the rest of our little tour. Besides, we're counting on you and your staff to give us a hand against the damned hag."

At the mention of the Staff of the Red Tree, Marissa nearly leaped to her feet. "Where—" she exclaimed and cast frantically around the room looking for it. In her relief at being rescued, she had forgotten all about the staff. When she finally located it, lying on a smooth shelf along the wall, the druid wanted to weep.

She walked toward the staff slowly, despite her excitement at finding it. The druid would have run, but a sense of torpor had taken root somewhere deep within her. Marissa hadn't lied to Roberc. She was feeling much better—physically. The scars of her torment, however, went beyond flesh. The hag and her dark priestess had taken something from Marissa. The chill of her captivity had sucked something essential from the marrow of her spirit. Here beneath the citadel, trapped in the cold embrace of the earth, the half-elf felt half alive. She longed for the touch of sunlight and the caress of a spring breeze the way a wounded falcon longs for open sky and the touch of warm air upon its pinions.

When at last she reached the staff, Marissa hesitated before reaching out to touch it. It lay quiescent, silent for the first time since she held it beneath the shadow of the Red Tree. The druid recalled the layers of spells that her captors had woven over the captive artifact. She was no expert in arcane magic, but she knew the ways of the gods, and it seemed to Marissa's senses that the dark priestess had held the foundation for the "house" of spells that they had built. With the half-orc cleric's death, the house simply collapsed.

Or so she hoped.

Reaching out at last to the seemingly inert length of wood, Marissa carefully picked up the staff and cradled it in her hand. The moment her fingers closed around the length of wood, she felt an explosion of power. Light filled the room as waves of arcane energy radiated from the staff. Marissa knew that she had fallen to the ground, buffeted by the power of the staff, yet she felt nothing. The now-familiar voice of the artifact buzzed in her mind, swelling angrily as it searched through her memories, recalling what she had experienced during their absence. At times, she felt as if it clucked angrily at her, the way a mother hen would chide her chicks when they had drawn near something dangerous. She would have laughed at that, but three sets of hands grabbed her and lifted Marissa to her feet.

"Is little witch, all right?" she heard Borovazk's deep voice rumble at her.

She concentrated on the sound, and all at once the voice of the staff fell to a tremulous whisper. When she looked around, once more in control, Marissa saw all of her companions gathered around gazing anxiously upon her.

Taen's eyes were narrowed, his mouth pinched with obvious concern. "We heard you cry out and fall to the ground," he said. "Are you hurt?"

"No," she said, shaking her head. "The staff and I were just getting reacquainted. I'm sorry if I frightened you."

Grasping the staff, Marissa climbed to her feet. The room threatened to spin out of control for just a moment then righted itself. For the first time since her rescue, she noticed the absence of her avian companion and sudden fear for the little creature rushed through her body.

"Where ... where is Rusella?" she asked.

The others all looked at her with the same mask of concern on their faces, but it was Taenaran, at last, who spoke. "We don't know," he said gently. "She flew away when you were taken on the bridge. I wouldn't worry too much; if anyone can find a way out of here, it would be her." He reached out to her and grasped her shoulder gently. "Rusella will probably be waiting for us when we leave this place."

Marissa wasn't as certain, but she offered a prayer for Rusella's safety just the same. If anything happened to her companion, she would never forgive herself. Then, to draw some of the attention away from her, she asked, "How are we coming with the circular inscription?"

Marissa watched the half-elf's face fall into a frown. Taen ran slender fingers over his head before answering.

"Well," he said, "I'm sure that the circle functions as a teleportation device, and I'm reasonably certain that there are no hidden arcane traps upon it. I only wish I knew where it might lead."

Roberc stepped forward, finishing off a draught of wine before speaking. "Marissa, do you remember anyone else besides the half-orc using the portal?" he asked.

She thought about it for a moment, only partially successful in repressing a shudder at the dark memories that would haunt her for the rest of her life. "I ... I think so," she answered hesitantly at first then, "yes, I do remember. Most of the time, the hag walked through the doors and back into the citadel, but several times after ... longer ... sessions, she would use the circle."

"Does little witch know where hag go?" Borovazk asked.

Marissa shook her head. "No, I'm sorry," she said, "all I can remember her saying was that she needed to go back to the cave. If the portal leads there, then perhaps we can use it to surprise her."

"If she's there," Roberc said.

"There is that small detail," Taen commented.

The druid thought some more, trying to recall her last session with the hag. "If I'm remembering correctly, Chaul used the circle during our last session. She might still be wherever that portal leads."

"Little friend speaks truly," Borovazk said, "if evil one not have another way in to the Rashemar."

"It's a better lead than we've had," Roberc growled, "and besides, it beats slogging through this dank place, cutting our way through wave after wave of ghouls and goblins."

"Then it's agreed?" Taen asked.

Marissa nodded in agreement. Personally, she would take any chance to end this mission sooner, and she suspected that the others felt the same.

They did.

Within moments, each of them began their preparations. Marissa watched in fascination as Taen drew forth a pearl, which he then crushed beneath a heavy rock. Carefully, he gathered the crushed pearl fragments and poured them into a silver goblet.

"I need to uncover the command word to activate the portal," he said, obviously noting her interest.

"The spell I'm about to cast will take some time. You should probably rest a little bit more before we head through."

Marissa hesitated a moment before speaking. "Taenaran," she began at last, "about that conversation we need to have."

She had nearly lost him once on this journey; then their enemy captured her. Though this clearly wasn't the time for such a thing, the druid didn't want to waste another moment.

Taen stopped what he was doing at Marissa's words, stood up, and went to her. "I know," he said, drawing the slender tip of his fingers across her cheek. She shivered at his touch. "I've had that conversation a thousand times with you in my dreams," he continued. "We don't have the time now, but please understand that I *do* know."

Marissa felt his arms enfold her, and she yielded to that embrace. They held each other for a moment, a moment that she would have stretched into eternity if she had the power, before Taen kissed her lightly upon the lips and drew back gently.

"Now," he said, staring deeply into her eyes, "go get some rest. You're going to need it."

The druid nodded and walked toward a corner of the room, dazed by the memory of his lips upon hers. The warmth of their embrace remained with Marissa as she settled down in her makeshift bedroll. She was tired, the earlier torpor she felt spreading over her like the still waters of a mountain lake. When at last she closed her eyes, Marissa felt herself floating gently to the lake's bottom.

Restful sleep, however, eluded her. A series of violent visions hammered at Marissa while she dreamed. In them, she stood before the Red Tree, whose broad limbs lay bare, as if in midwinter. Its bark was desiccated, pitted and dried, hanging loosely upon its diseased trunk. The voices of the dead whispered around the twisted tree, and rich, dark blood welled up from the black soil.

Stumbling backward from the sight, Marissa could see the bodies of her companions, their bloated corpses hanging from the highest limbs, twisting in the chill wind. All at once, the tree's trunk began to split and tear with a loud cracking sound. A greenish shape began to emerge from the split trunk, headfirst like the birth of an abominable child.

Marissa recognized the face of the hag, leering out from the trunk, and she began to scream. Pushing herself free, the hag laughed at the druid's obvious terror and began to walk toward her. Pointing a sap-covered finger in her direction, the monster opened its horrifying mouth and said—

"Marissa, are you ready?"

The druid gave an awkward shout as Taen's voice lifted her from the tendrils of her nightmare. Sweat drenched her robe and matted strands of red hair to her face. She gazed around quickly, half expecting to see the hag hovering nearby.

"Is everything all right?" Taen asked, his concern for her obvious to hear.

Marissa nodded vigorously. "Yes," she said at last. "It was just a nightmare." Then she drew herself to her feet and began to gather her things. "Really," she said again when Taen hadn't moved, "I'll be fine."

When at last the half-elf had stepped away to activate the portal, she placed the small pack she carried with her upon her back. Arcane energy swirled around the magic portal, pulsing with newly awakened life.

Please, Rillifane, she prayed silently, guide our steps.

One by one, her companions plunged into the portal, disappearing in a flash of light. When at last she stepped through the mystic circle, Marissa sent one more prayer toward her god.

Protect Taenaran, she implored before arcane power consumed her.

The Old One screamed.

Yulda delighted in the foolish wizard's pain. The sounds of his agony mixed with the delicious sensation of power flowing into her, power that she sucked from the very depths of his spirit. He resisted—even now, after many months of captivity, the wizard fought her control. His will was strong, honed by decades of disciplined study and practice in the arcane arts, and it strained against the mystical bonds of her spell like a wild stallion refusing to break beneath his rider's skill. That was what made him so valuable—and dangerous.

Yulda wished that she didn't have to replenish her power quite so often. She trusted in her own skill and the demonic spell that drained the Old One's strength. Still, the procedure required all of her attention, leaving her little to spare for anything else. The hathran couldn't afford a lapse in concentration. If the damnable wizard slipped his bonds, she would lose a major source of power and be forced to deal with the combined anger of the wychlaran and the Old Ones. She wasn't ready for that.

Not yet.

The witch cursed her meddlesome "sisters" for interfering in her machinations. Dealing with those gods-blighted intruders and wrestling the secrets of the Staff of the Red Tree from her poor little captive was proving to be a far greater drain than she had anticipated. She hoped Durakh would be able to break the pathetic elf's will before too long. Even now, her forces were converging on the isolated villages and hamlets of Rashemen, killing and burning as they marched toward the country's heart. Once the battle was truly joined, Yulda would have to focus her attention on her advancing army. She would have little time to spend mastering the secrets of the staff.

The thought of her eventual victory sent a sweet chill up her back. Combined with the heady sense of imbued power, Yulda felt as if she were truly unstoppable. Soon all of Rashemen would be under her control. Then, perhaps, she would renegotiate her deal with those abominable Wizards of Thay.

Arcane energy crackled behind her, interrupting Yulda's ruminations. She felt, more than saw, the energy from the teleportation circle and couldn't suppress a sly smile. Durakh must have finally broken the mewling elf woman. She didn't even turn to greet the cleric, wanting instead to watch the Old One realize that she had defeated him.

Again.

"So, Durakh," the witch called out, "has the druid yielded—"

Fleshrender's mental warning stopped her midsentence. Durakh had not come through the portal. Yulda spun around, summoning her arcane power with a single thought.

"You!" she screamed and let loose a bolt of pure energy at her "visitors."

CHAPTER 27

The Year of Wild Magic
(1372 DR)

Taen's vision blurred.

The sudden wrenching of his body from one place to another threatened to overwhelm his senses. He shook his head briskly, as if the violent motion would snap everything back into focus. When at last he could see make out his surroundings, the half-elf saw that he and his companions stood in the midst of yet another cave—the starkness of its gray stone relieved by the glittering incandescence of tiny minerals that reflected the torchlight like thousands of stars strewn wildly by some mad god. Taen had only a few heartbeats with which to take in the undulating expanse of the small cavern before an angry growl caught his attention.

The source of that ominous sound—a rather large snow tiger peering intently at Taen and his companions—lay only fifteen feet from him toward the rear of the cave. Though the beast still reclined languorously on the floor, Taen could see its powerful muscles rippling softly beneath stark white fur—and something else. Despite the shifting light from the cavern's flickering torches, he could make out a faint illumination surrounding the tiger. The glow seemed somehow to soften the edges of the beast's outline, making it seem less than real. The half-elf was about to signal Roberc to rein in Cavan as the war-dog's muted growling reached his ears, but a woman's screeching voice interrupted him.

"You!" Taen heard moments before he saw a weathered old crone, whose black robes had served to hide her against the cave's darker rear walls, spin around to face him. The half-elf caught sight of a craggy, face and a shock of stringy snow-white hair before he realized that the crone had unleashed a powerful wave of arcane energy, which stung his honed senses with its strength as it hurtled toward him.

Taen summoned his own power and quickly erected a wall of pure arcane force to meet the incoming attack. Eldritch energy coruscated and flared along the edges of his spell, spitting scattered power as the old woman's arcane attack met the half-elf's wall. Taen blanched at the strength of the crone's assault. Though his defensive shield held, he could already make out subtle cracks that ran through the arcane wall like tiny filaments of a spider's web. Whoever she was, the crone's power was considerable. Beads of sweat started to run down Taen's forehead. Perhaps they had been unwise to leap into the dragon's den, he thought for just a moment. Then a vision of Marissa, chained and battered from her torturous ordeal, flashed through the half-elf's mind. All thoughts of caution fled like shadows beneath the lash of the sun.

"You dare invade my sanctum," the crone screeched

in a voice that sounded eerily familiar.

It took him just a moment to recognize the rough timbre—he'd heard it last beneath the citadel, before he and his companions were attacked by giant spiders. The hag of Rashemar and this decrepit witch were one and the same. Taen knew the moment the others made the connection, for he heard Borovazk's deep bass rumble out a string of curses in his native tongue, while Roberc's own invectives filled the cavern. Only Marissa remained silent, and Taen watched as her lips curled in a snarl that resembled the fang-baring of an angered wolf.

"That's right, you fools," the witch continued, occasionally lashing out with a bolt of arcane power directed at Taen's mystic wall, "you've finally discovered my secret—and too late to do anything with it. By the time those foolish othlor discover that you have failed in your mission, my forces will already be victorious, and with the power of the Staff of the Red Tree"—she pointed a gnarled finger in Marissa's direction—"finally under my control, no force in all of Rashemen will be able to stop me."

"Who says we have failed in our mission?" the half-elf spat back at the crone, hoping she couldn't see the tiny droplets of sweat that beaded on his forehead. At this point, he held his arcane defense together by sheer force of will—a will that was beginning to weaken with each successive blast of power from her outstretched hand.

The witch's laughter echoed through the stone cavern. "Who says?" she asked with a sharp-edged smile. "You foolish little elfling ... I do!" The crone leaped forward with a piercing shout.

Taen fell back a step despite himself. Now that she stood only a few feet from him, he could see with sickening horror the ruin of the crone's left eye. Black power billowed out of the gaping hole where her eye should have been. A chill ran up Taen's body, threatening to freeze his heart as he gazed into its obsidian depths. The half-elf felt something lurch from deep within him, as if the crone's empty socket were some sort of unspeakable portal—a portal that opened into the vastness of another plane and threatened to suck in his spirit, leaving him trapped for all eternity in a sea of oblivion.

Marissa's shout caused him to pull his gaze away from the witch's pulsating eye. Taen didn't know how long he had been trapped beneath her baleful stare, but it had been enough time for the crone to cast another spell. This time, a sphere of roiling purple energy erupted from the center of her cupped hands and streaked toward the half-elf's arcane wall, which collapsed with a sudden snapping sound as soon as the purple ball struck its leading edge.

"Fleshrender," the crone shouted immediately, "kill them!"

Taen fell back another step beneath the shock of his spell's destruction but felt Borovazk's powerful arms supporting him. Without missing a beat, Roberc and Cavan stepped forward to meet the snow tiger's charge.

"Is time we finished this," Taen heard the ranger's voice hiss loudly in his ear.

The half-elf cast a quick glance in his direction and nodded. All traces of levity and humor were gone from the Rashemi's normally good-natured face, and Taen found himself thankful that Borovazk was an ally and not an enemy, for in the grim cast of the ranger's jaws and the man's iron-hard stare, he could see clearly see the warrior who had killed an ice bear with his bare hands.

"Yes, Borovazk," Taen said, drawing his sword as he did so, "it is indeed time." The half-elf waited for half a heartbeat as the Song rose in him once more before he leaped into the fray.

Marissa froze when she heard the harsh tones of the old woman's voice, and her heart pounded violently within her chest. Memories swam before her eyes, visions of an ugly hag bending over her shackled body. Sweat beaded on her face, and she nearly dropped the Staff of the Red Tree from a hand that went suddenly slack from fear. It was as if she were back in the hag's vile chamber of tortures without any hope of rescue. An unpleasant echo of pain seared her flesh as the crone's voice rose to shriek defiantly at her companions.

She would have been caught in the backlash of Taenaran's spell as it collapsed before the witch's arcane onslaught, but the Staff of the Red Tree buzzed angrily in her mind, dispelling the paralysis that had gripped her spirit. Quickly she stepped away from the conflagration and gripped the Rashemi artifact tightly, eyeing the newly joined battle. Roberc's armor burned a dull yellowish-orange in the torchlit cavern as he and Cavan met the sword tiger's charge. The halfling brought his sword up to meet the beast's raking claw and cursed mightily as its incandescent flesh passed right through the metal, reached beneath his armor, and entered the fighter's body.

Marissa watched as Roberc stumbled slightly from the pain of the attack, forcing Cavan to throw himself to the side at the last possible moment to avoid biting down on his master's flesh. The war-dog recovered quickly, however, and lunged forward, deftly dodging a powerful slash of the tiger's razored claws. Cavan opened his jaws wide, prepared to bite deeply into his enemy's neck—and nearly fell in a tangle of fur and barding as his momentum carried him right through the creature. Saliva sprayed wildly as his jaws snapped together on empty air.

"Taenaran," Marissa shouted to the half-elf as she observed the battle, "the beast is incorporeal. They'll need help."

Taenaran nodded and quickly moved behind his companions. The druid heard his voice call out the words to a spell moments before twin green auras sprang to life around the half-elf's hands. Careful not to interfere with his companion's attacks, Taenaran touched both Roberc and Cavan. Immediately, the auras flared brightly then disappeared.

Marissa knew that whatever spell he had cast would help her friends—but would it be enough? Already the crone had used the distraction of the snow tiger's attack to begin a spell of her own. The druid could see black and purple energy coalescing around the crone's upraised hands as she chanted and called out in a harsh, guttural language that sounded to Marissa like the screams of a thousand banshees.

Two shimmering arrows hissed out of the shadows, streaking toward the chanting crone from Borovazk's heavy bow. Marissa hoped that the gleaming arrows would have an effect, somehow interrupting the witch's dark incantation, but the druid's hopes were dashed like an old boat slammed against the rocks in a heavy tide. Ebon power flashed forth from the witch's baleful eye socket, striking the missiles as they sped toward their intended target and instantly vaporizing them.

Marissa knew that they would all be in serious trouble if they didn't deal with the witch soon. Moving deftly around Borovazk's bulky form, the druid opened her spirit to Rillifane's power. Gratefully, she accepted the surge of divine energy and shaped it with the words of a familiar prayer. The air grew warmer in the cavern for just a moment as she reached out and pressed her palm briefly against Cavan's powerful flank. The war-dog paid her little attention, focusing instead on his enemy. He charged forward once again, but this time, the war-dog's form shifted slightly. Surrounded by a golden nimbus of energy, Cavan's muscles rippled and swelled, its body elongated and thickened—until at last it stood even larger than his snow tiger opponent.

"Roberc," Marissa shouted over the incensed roar of the incorporeal beast, "help Borovazk and Taenaran take down the witch. I'll stay with Cavan."

The halfling glanced over at his spell-enhanced mount and flashed Marissa a wicked grin. "I. Live. To. Serve," he said, sucking in great lungfuls of air between each word. He lunged forward with his sword one more time, drawing blood from the tiger with a wicked thrust of his blade then shifted to his left, allowing Cavan to take on the full brunt of the snow tiger's attack. Without another word, the diminutive fighter joined the others as they advanced on the witch.

Judging by the rippling black mass of energy that pulsated before the ancient crone, Marissa wondered whether it was too late.

Taen could sense the arcane power building in the cavern. It hung in the air, pressing down on his inner vision, threatening to envelop him like a thick funereal pall. To his left, Cavan and the ghostly snow tiger were engaged in a grisly dance. Tooth and claw shredded fur and tore through skin as the two beasts raged and spat in a tangle of violence. For now, the spell-enlarged war-dog was holding his own against the fearsome tiger. With Marissa standing a few feet behind to administer divine aid and healing, the half-elf knew he could focus on their true enemy.

He advanced slowly, with Borovazk and Roberc slightly behind and to either side. Taen's sword pulsed dully in time to the Song that beat within his own breast. He shifted his grip on it slightly as he opened himself more fully to the melody that rose within him. The crone who ruled Citadel Rashemar disguised as a hag still held her gnarled hands above her head, pouring vile energy into a growing web of darkness that pulsated before her. Now that he could concentrate completely upon the ancient witch, it took the half-elf only a moment to realize the true danger they now faced. The blasphemous syllables vomited forth by the spellcasting witch were disturbingly familiar, echoes of an infernal tongue Taen had studied years before.

The half-elf cursed himself for a fool as he broke rank and charged the crone, hoping to reach her before the portal fully opened. "Hurry," he shouted to his companions, "she summons a demon!"

Jagged stalagmites and sloping stone slowed down Taen's hasty advance. Several times, he nearly lost his balance as he stumbled across the cavern floor. He was within striking distance of the renegade hathran when the mass of roiling darkness snapped open, like the lidless eye of a crazed giant awakened suddenly from a nightmare. A blast of pure hellfire spewed forth from the open portal, nearly knocking Taen off his feet. He struggled to keep his balance as a wicked claw as long as a scythe tore through the air to strike the ground where he would have fallen.

A second blast of hellfire shook the cavern before the portal disappeared with a sudden hiss of air, like the great rushing sound of a dragon inhaling before it unleashes its breath. Taen blanched as he saw the demonic being fully revealed by the light of the cavern's flickering torches.

The creature stood nearly eight feet tall, its grotesque body resembling an amalgam of bird and demon. Thick-feathered wings, extending out into the cavern from its broad back, beat listlessly as the demon cast around the room with its twisted eaglelike head. Twin circles of fire burned from behind the beast's large eyes. As Taen and the others drew nearer, it gestured once with a clawed hand. The air rippled for a moment as a wicked sword, complete with twin serrated edges, appeared in one of its hands.

Borovazk struck first, leaping forward with axe and warhammer in hand. Seemingly surprised by the ranger's speed, the demon lashed out awkwardly with its free claw. The Rashemi twisted to his left, avoiding the razor-sharp attack and spun to bring his broad war-hammer crashing down upon the summoned demon's leg—and nearly fell to the ground when, instead of shattering the beast's bones beneath its weight, the weapon rebounded harmlessly off of the creature. The ranger cursed quickly before reversing his spin and slicing hard with the wicked edge of his gleaming axe. This time, the weapon bit deep into the demon's torso, eliciting a horrifying screech that nearly caused Taen's ears to bleed.

Unwilling to give up their temporary advantage, Roberc and the half-elf approached the demon's flank. Swiftly the halfling sliced several cuts into the crea-ture's putrid torso then cursed as the wounds slowly closed.

"Its gods-blasted flesh resists my attacks, Taen," Roberc shouted. "We're going to have to hack this vrock back to the blasted pits where it was spawned."

Though Taen heard his friend's complaint, he could spare little energy to respond. Already the Song had grown to a near-deafening crescendo within him. For a moment, fear mixed with the calm his inner music brought him. Ever since he had entered Rashemen, he'd experienced an ever-deepening awareness of the Song. Something within this land called to him, coaxed and brought forth a part of the half-elf that he had tried to run from these many years. What if he lost control—failed as he did in the practice ground and beneath the stars when his actions had killed the only woman he had ever loved or who had loved him in return?

For just a moment, the Song softened, falling away, and he heard Talaedra's voice call out his name. Taen gazed out at his companions, struggling mightily against the summoned vrock, and he knew that he could not—would not—fail them. With an ancient bladesinger battle cry on his lips, he threw himself into battle. The Song surged within him, and he felt the power flowing through him. When the vrock's black-runed sword cut through the air, seeking his flesh, Taen brought his father's blade up to meet it. As the two swords met, Taen rolled forward, anticipating the demon's other claw that raked the space he had just occupied.

He would have lunged forward to strike at the vrock's now-unprotected flank, but a new sound caught his attention. Guarded by her demon, the renegade hathran was about to unleash another spell. The gathering arcane power flared against Taen's own senses even as the witch's chanted words clashed bitterly with his Song. The half-elf stepped out of his opponent's reach and studied the hathran for several heartbeats. The spell was familiar to him, and without hesitation, he summoned his own power and tried to counter her magic.

The crone finished her chant with a triumphant shriek and opened her palm, as if casting something forth. Fueled by the Song, Taen's arcane strength reached out to surround the harnessed eldritch energy. Black bolts of force flew from the witch's hands then sputtered into nothingness, absorbed by the half-elf's counterspell. The old woman's surprised curse did little to bolster Taen's optimism, for it had taken nearly all of his power to quench her spell. Whatever she might be, the hathran possessed a power far beyond anything that Taen had yet seen.

An icy feeling began to build at the base of his spine as he leaped forward, hoping to bring the black-robed crone down.

CHAPTER 28

The Year of Wild Magic
(1372 DR)

Marissa watched the telthor die.

Even as Cavan's powerful jaws locked on to the creature's neck and bit down, the druid found herself grieving. The telthor was evil or at least twisted by the one called Yulda beyond recognition. Still, as its body stopped moving and its luminous flesh began to fade before her eyes, Marissa grieved. Here was a part of Rashemen that would never exist again, and she had a hand in its passing.

There was little time to do anything but mouth a quick prayer to her god as the battle still raged in other parts of the cavern. Quickly she checked on Cavan, whose blood-matted fur and myriad open wounds made it difficult for the war-dog to walk; the loyal hound's front left leg hung at an awkward angle. Marissa reached out and opened her heart to Rillifane, asking his blessing upon the valiant animal. Within moments, divine energy poured out of her hand, repairing torn muscle and shattered bones. Cavan offered her hand a grateful lick before he bolted toward the rear of the cavern, returning to battle once more.

The druid was about to follow when Borovazk's cry of pain caught her attention. The ranger stood doubled while the demonic being advanced upon him. Looking carefully, she could make out tiny needle-sharp spores protruding from the Rashemi's flesh. Marissa saw Roberc slash valiantly at the demon, trying to draw its attention, but to no avail. Within a few heartbeats, the demon's wicked claws would shred Borovazk.

Gripping the Staff of the Red Tree, she called forth the power of the earth, shaping it with careful prayers to her god. Immediately the cavern floor around the Rashemi began to shift and buckle. Stalagmites grew in size, joining together to form a gray wall of stone that stretched from floor to ceiling. Protected from certain death, Borovazk reached toward his belt and pulled out a flask of green liquid. Marissa watched as the ranger pulled off the cork with his teeth and downed the potion. Relief flooded through her as the needle spores fell from his skin. She almost smiled as he picked up his axe from where it had fallen, ran around the wall, and engaged the demon once more.

As battered and bloodied as her friends looked, the summoned demon looked even worse. The matted feathers of its wings were rent with several holes, and even from her vantage point, Marissa could see gaping wounds that disgorged black blood and slime. The demon, however powerful, was the least of their problems, Marissa knew. Yulda, the renegade hathran, posed the truest threat. Anger washed over her, made more intense by the voice of the Staff of the Red Tree, whose agitated buzzing reached new heights. Ever since she had carried the staff, Marissa felt as if it had grown to be a part of her. Even now she wasn't sure where her own anger and loathing ended and the Staff of the Red Tree's powerful emotions began.

Readying her own power to assist Taenaran in his fight with Yulda, the druid sensed something she hadn't noticed in the first flushed moments of battle, or perhaps this was a gift from the Staff of the Red Tree itself. Either way, the druid could now make out a thin tendril of energy that erupted from Yulda's back, stretching deeper into the shadow of the cavern beyond. In each moment before the witch cast a spell, Marissa could see power travel along that tendril until it poured into Yulda's body.

Someone or something was feeding the withered crone power—power that threatened to destroy them and all of Rashemen. It took only a moment to call upon Rillifane's gift and transform herself. She felt the familiar dislocation as the shape within her mind took form. In three heartbeats her flesh had completed its transmogrification. The sounds of battle sounded impossibly distant to her new senses, more vibration than anything else. Deftly she scuttled forward on seven legs, maneuvering around the outer edge of the cavern, crawling closer and closer to where the tendril originated. When at last she stood before an alcove completely shrouded in darkness, Marissa returned to her original form.

Gripping the Staff of the Red Tree, she summoned light. At first it did little to pierce the veil of ebon darkness that hung over the alcove, but the voice of the staff swelled and the light grew in power. The darkness tore like thin vellum. When at last she could see what lay in the alcove, Marissa nearly cried out in horror.

An emaciated, wizened old man hung spread-eagled in the air by four obsidian chains. A writhing tendril of pure energy penetrated his skull, right between rheum-glazed eyes. The captive stared at her, pain obviously etched in every line of his face; his breath came in great ragged gasps. At once, Marissa knew that this was the vremyonni, the Rashemi wizard that Yulda had kidnapped. The wychlaran thought that Yulda had merely taken the wizard to glean vremyonni secrets. She knew now that the truth was much worse than that. Whatever spell had forged this unholy bond, it was sucking away at the wizard's power and feeding it to Yulda.

She reached out in an attempt to help free the enslaved wizard—and snatched her hand back in pain as it touched a wall of energy. Her fingertips still tingled with the force of the spell. Marissa tested the wall with elemental fire and the fury of winter itself, pouring forth her god's power in an attempt to shatter the defensive wall. The druid knew that breaking whatever bond joined the vremyonni and the hathran was the key to defeating Yulda.

"It . . . it's no use," the ancient wizard gasped as Marissa struck the magical wall with the full force of the Staff of the Red Tree. "The spell is wrapped in both of our power."

Marissa shook her head in denial. "Then how I can I free you?" she asked and felt desperation rise in her voice.

The wizard coughed and sputtered for a moment before answering. "Only my death can free me now."

"No," she nearly shouted, "there must be another way!" Destroying the telthor had been horrific enough; she would not kill another part of this wild land. Not if she could help it.

The vremyonni shook his head. "There is—" he started to say then gasped in pain as the arcane conduit drew more power from him. "There is no other way, my child. I knew that the wychlaran would not abandon me. Now you must end this, and quickly."

"How—?" was all that she asked before the wizard's gentle smile silenced her.

"You know how," the vremyonni said. "The power was

given to you by the Red Tree, but only you can make this choice. Decide quickly, my child, for Yulda merely plays with your friends. If she wanted, she could destroy them with a single spell."

As if to prove the wizard's words, Marissa heard Taenaran let out a shriek of agony. She turned to see the half-elf caught in a beam of pure darkness that emanated from Yulda's empty eye socket. His flesh began to bubble and boil, as if liquefying right off of his bones. The druid's heart felt as if it were being ripped from her body. With a single cry of Taenaran's name, Marissa had made her choice.

Taen ducked beneath another swipe of the vrock's claw and rammed the point of his sword deep into its side until it grated on bone. Spinning swiftly, he wrenched his blade free, splattering the black-robed witch with gore and effluvia. The demon bellowed and leaped forward, borne slightly aloft by the strength of its wings. Three more claws slashed downward at the half-elf. Without missing a beat, he rolled beneath one, dived to the right of another, and caught the third on his blade. He moved as effortlessly as he had that fateful day in the *alu'dala,* flowing like water, raining blows down upon the vrock, and when he could get close enough, the witch herself. Abandoning himself to the powerful rhythms of the Song, he felt freer than he ever had before.

So much so that when the Song shifted beneath him, he did not resist it but followed its strains. It grew louder, more powerful—began to pull at him, yet still he flowed with it. When the crone sent pulsating green bolts of energy flying from her fingers, Taen leaped into the air, drawing his arms to his chest and spinning so that two of the missiles flew by either side of him. The third he caught on the tip of his sword, and the fourth he took square in the chest, but even that brief moment of searing pain did not slow him down.

Taen stood before the decrepit hag, sword poised to strike. The Song crescendoed around him; he could feel its need, its hunger drawing him down into its depths. It called to him—asked of him the only thing of any worth he had to give: his life. For just a moment, he hesitated. For just a moment, he resisted its pull, struggled against it the way a drowning man struggles against an implacable tide.

In that moment, the crone struck.

Power lashed out from the wreck of her eye, a beam of pure nothingness that caught Taen full in the torso. He screamed as the dark energy of the beam struck him. Agony coursed through his body—his very spirit was afire and every inch of his skin bubbled and boiled. In an instant, the vengeful cadence of the Song was stilled. Caught in the unquenchable power of the witch's eye, unable to move, Taen caught sight of Marissa in his rapidly dimming vision. The druid held aloft the Staff of the Red Tree in her remaining hand, and in that moment, the half-elf knew with utter certainty what she was about to do.

He summoned the last bit of strength remaining and screamed, "Marissa . . . no!"

Anger and desperation melted away from Marissa, replaced by a calm certainty. Choices bring their own comforts with them, she knew, and thanked Rillifane for the one she experienced now. There was so much that she had wanted to say, wanted to share with Taenaran, so much of this land she had wanted to explore, yet it was love—love of the broken half-elf and the rugged land they had traveled across—that had solidified her choice.

A single tear of regret, for words not spoken and feelings not shared, spilled down her cheek as she raised the Staff of the Red Tree above her head. She sent one last prayer to Rillifane that he would guard and guide Taenaran and her friends, before she brought the staff down hard upon a sharp stalagmite—

And everything became light.

The concussive force of the blast knocked Taen to the ground, tossing him like a paper doll in a raging storm. He lay there stunned for a few moments as his sight cleared. Desperately he cast around for some sign that Marissa had survived the explosion. The alcove where she had stood lay buried beneath layers of thick stone and rubble.

She was gone again.

He had failed Marissa once more—just like he had on the bridge. If he hadn't hesitated at the last moment, Marissa would still be alive. Despair and self-hatred rose up in him, like old friends who had departed for a long journey and returned. They accused him, called him a wretched failure and a murderer, demanded that he run away and hide in the darkness of his inadequacy.

This time, however, Taen didn't listen.

Though the faces of Talaedra and Marissa, frozen in dying, swept across his vision, the half-elf refused to despair. Both women may indeed have loved him far more than he deserved, but they both saw within him the person that he could become. He would honor them and spend the remainder of his life becoming that person. It did not spare him his grief—that cut like a vorpal blade through his heart—but it was a clean wound, without rancor or disease.

He would have wept, but a vision of the withered crone stumbling to her feet drove all sadness from him.

"Did ... did you think you could defeat me?" she spat, blood-matted hair tossed wildly around her head. "I am beyond your power even now."

Taen pushed himself painfully to his feet, though the crone's spell had wounded him badly. Suppurated flesh tore from his skin and arms as he rose, grasping his father's sword. He concentrated for a moment, held the sword aloft—and suddenly the Song sprang to life, as deep and resonant as it had in the moments before the witch's foul spell had struck.

Borovazk and Roberc stood to his left, hacking at what remained of the vrock, who had collapsed beneath the Staff of the Red Tree's final blast. There, in the flickering torchlight, in a mountain cavern locked away from the rest of the world, Taen stood with his sword raised—beyond anger, beyond grief, beyond any emotion that had distracted him throughout the long years of his half-elf life—and he Sang. Slowly, painfully, he opened himself totally to the Song. If it desired his whole life, then he would offer it gladly, as Marissa had done for him and the lives of his friends. Without another thought, the half-elf surrendered, fell down a hole so dark and deep it might well have gone on forever. There was nothing in that hole—no thought, no sense of self—only thick, unrelenting darkness.

When he emerged, it was as if he had fallen into another universe. Power flared around him and through him, lived in each measure of the Song's flow—which was also each beat of his own heart. There was no "Taen" separate from the Song and no part of the Song that was not somehow a part of him. His father's blade sensed the change as well, for it burned with an intense argent light, filling the cavern with its own power.

"You are finished!" Taen shouted at the chanting witch. "By the will of the wychlaran and the blood of my father, it is over."

The half-elf raised his sword and moved to attack.

He gathered his arcane power, but rather than cast a formulaic spell as he had done for most of his life, Taen channeled that energy, used it to speed his limbs. The world slowed around him as he gathered speed.

The crone backed away slightly to her left and shouted, "Die, you fool!" as she brought her ruined eye to bear upon him. A black beam of power shot out once again, but this time Taen leaped to the side, avoiding it. A section of the cavern floor sizzled and popped for a moment before completely disintegrating before his eyes.

Another beam lanced out at him, but this time Taen tumbled behind a long-toothed stalagmite that took the brunt of the attack. Without hesitation, the half-elf sent arcane energy surging through his sword; bolts of force leaped from the blade's tip to strike the crone. She shrieked and fell backward, turning as if to run toward the back of the cave.

Taking advantage of his newfound speed, Taen ran to the side, intercepting the haggard witch before she could reach the circle of light that had just opened in the floor behind him. Her one good eye widened in disbelief. She raised a skeletal hand toward the half-elf and spit forth the words to another spell.

Taen didn't wait for her to finish. "For Cormanthor," he cried in Elvish before leaping through the air, "and for Marissa!" Like a living spear, he hurtled toward the witch and, focusing all of his energy, drove his sword deep into the crone's empty eye socket. The witch wailed in agony as the blade bit true, knocking both of them to the ground. Black power erupted from the wound, cascading around both of them, spinning and twirling like a mini whirlwind. Taen could feel the energy burning at his already battered body, but he did not let go of the sword that impaled the now-dead crone. His agony intensified as the ebon power covered him completely.

The walls of the cavern faded, until everything, at last, was darkness.

The Year of Rogue Dragons
(1373 DR)

Taenaran stood silently in the sunlight.

All around him, the vale teemed with life. The full-throated song of wild birds filled the air, while the undergrowth stirred with the patter of tiny furred feet. A small breeze blew across the wooded vale, redolent with the rich scents of summer. The drone of bees, their bodies bloated with pollen and tossed by the wind, rose up from the lush vernal landscape.

Taenaran might as well have stood in a bare stone room, devoid of windows or doors. He felt the touch of the sun—its warm fingers sliding across his skin—distantly, as if in a memory or some long-ago dream of summer. He took in the heady fragrance of the wind without regard to its vintage, each breath mechanically drawing it into his lungs. Deep inside, he wished nothing less than to break that machine, to still its implacable, torturous rhythm.

Grief had hollowed him out, made of his heart a tomb—full of dust and shadow and a longing so deep it reached to the very marrow of his bones. Marissa was dead, yet the half-elf no longer felt anger or bitterness over his weakness, the brokenness that had caused her to die. He had become a true bladesinger now, a master of his father's art—his own art. The red-hilted blade given him by Aelrindel hung comfortably at his side. In the storm-wrought demesne of an evil witch, Taenaran had finally become true forged, made whole for the first time in his life.

At what cost?

Behind him, he could hear Roberc's dour muttering and the answering rumble of Borovazk's voice. Taenaran's two companions had remained with him during the long months spent in the witches' care, and they had followed him here, offering their strength and friendship for the final leagues of his journey. In truth, the bladesinger remembered little of the aftermath of their battle with the witch. His memory of those final moments lay in ruins. From what Borovazk and Roberc had told him during time spent resting by the hearthside, Yulda's own power had consumed her in those last moments, burning away her body—and the half-elf's flesh would have followed had Borovazk not pulled him free.

The two had tried to awaken him, plying him with healing potions, salves, and other unguents, but to no avail. He was, according to Roberc, deader than a Cormyrean soldier after a tenday's furlough." They had resigned themselves to braving the mountains in winter when a contingent of witches had appeared in the cave. The breaking of the Staff of the Red Tree had caught their attention, and Yulda's death had shattered the arcane barriers surrounding her demesne. Within moments, the witches had teleported the wounded and tired group back to the Urlingwood.

Despite the severity of his injuries, Taenaran had begun to heal under the watchful eye of the hathran assigned to watch over him. In the days and tendays that had followed, physical pain receded, leaving only the emotional scars of his loss. Even so, Taenaran had known that Borovazk and Roberc were grieving as well, and when the numbing emptiness rose up within him, the bladesinger took to the deer paths and hidden trails crisscrossing the Urlingwood, not wishing to inflict his own grief upon his companions.

Tendays had turned into months as winter vented its fury upon the land and the first bright moments of spring burst forth from the snow-covered earth. Still, Taenaran had stayed within the thickly forested Urling, not really sure what held him there, and Borovazk and the halfling remained with him. They drank and diced, hunted and fought as friends will, but by some unspoken agreement they stayed by Taenaran's side.

Finally, as the snow cover began to melt in earnest, Mahara, leader of the wychlaran, had approached Taenaran with the two fragments of wood that were all that remained of the Staff of the Red Tree.

"Please pardon my interruption," she had said softly. "You and your companions are welcome to remain in the Urlingwood for as long as you like. It is the least of the kindnesses we can offer you. Deep though I know your grief to be," she had continued, "I was wondering if you would do us one last favor?"

There was little Taenaran could have said at that moment, so conflicted was his heart. Instead, he had simply nodded his head.

"We are humbled once again by your kindness," Mahara had replied and had reached forward, offering the burned wooden fragments to Taenaran. He had reached out gingerly, as if the splintered ends would blister his fingers. He had tried not to think of Marissa as he held the ends in his hands.

"These fragments must be returned to the Red Tree," the witch had continued. "Normally one of the hathran would make the journey. However," Mahara had paused for just a moment, "the telthor have asked specifically for you to return the remains of the staff."

So Taenaran now stood in the center of the Red Vale, with the elemental tree looming ahead of him—pushed once again on a quest not of his choosing. He drew in a deep breath then sighed it out before turning to his companions.

"Well, my friends," he said, "thank you for making this journey with me, but I would ask that you let me carry the fragments to the Red Tree by myself."

The half-elf could see Roberc's frown deepen. Both the grizzled halfling and the hulking Rashemi ranger exchanged a look, but both ultimately nodded their agreement.

"Well, you are pretty damn close to the end of the journey, so I suppose we can let you go," the halfling began with a throaty chuckle. "Not even you could mess this up, Taen!"

The chuckle became a hearty laugh as Borovazk slapped the bladesinger's back with a meaty hand. Despite the grief and sadness of the past few months, Taenaran felt a smile begin to creep upon his face.

"I'll shout if I get into any trouble," he replied good naturedly then set off down the path.

Mirth and good humor vanished quickly as he drew nearer to the Red Tree. Its ancient profile interrupted the broad swath of piercing blue sky and warm spring sunlight, brooding over the surrounding landscape like some elemental giant. Taenaran could feel its power emanating from each branch and leaf tip, a deep strength that flowed from its ancient roots, tapping into a magic deeper than any he had ever experienced. It was as if the mystical Red Tree were somehow more "real" than anything else around it—including him.

Long, thick branches blew softly in the wind, enveloping him in its vernal embrace as he walked beneath the Red Tree's cool shadows. A surge of anger crested through him, and it was all he could do to keep the memory of Marissa kneeling beneath the Red Tree from overwhelming him. Taenaran hated this land, loathed every mile of its rugged landscape, for what it had taken away from him, yet he also loved Rashemen fiercely, with a strength that nearly stole his breath away. This land and its people had given him something he had never hoped to receive—himself.

Tears ran down his face as he knelt finally beneath the boughs of the Red Tree and laid the remains of the Staff of the Red Tree against its ancient, splitting trunk. A stiff wind blew up, sending broad leaves fluttering at its touch. Taenaran felt for a moment as if he were surrounded by giant serpents.

"There," he said through clenched teeth. "I have done my gods-damned duty."

He was tired of fighting the grief and the sadness, tired of the emptiness that he felt inside. With this last request of the wychlaran completed, Taenaran knew that it was time to leave Rashemen. Where he would go next, the bladesinger hadn't a clue, but he suspected it would be far from here.

He was about to stand up when the wind blew hard again, this time nearly knocking the half-elf to the ground. He closed his eyes against the sting of dirt and pebbles brought on by the strange wind, and when at last the air stilled and he opened his eyes once more, Taenaran's vision swam before him. He struggled to his feet, reaching out to the gnarled trunk of the Red Tree to steady himself. When the bladesinger's hand touched the bark, he felt a stinging shock. Instantly, his vision cleared, but what he witnessed nearly drove

Teaghean to his knees once more.

Marissa stood before him, windswept hair blowing wildly in the wind, gazing at him with her eyes slightly squinted. He remembered that look upon her face, but he never recalled her looking that beautiful. Everything about her radiated joy and contentment.

"What is going on?" he asked of her in a voice that shook with emotion.

Marissa didn't respond. Instead she lifted her hands and brought them toward Taenaran's face. The bladesinger took a step toward her then stopped suddenly, as he realized that something was definitely wrong—the druid's lost hand had somehow regenerated.

"What are you?" he asked, suspicion tingeing his voice with a harsh undertone. "Does the Red Tree mock my grief? Have I not done enough for this gods-blasted land?"

The figure of Marissa shook her head sadly and reached out her hands once more. Taenaran didn't resist as slender fingers stroked his cheek. Her touch was light, like the kiss of a soft breeze. He felt the slightest shock as her fingertips made contact with his skin.

You are not being mocked, my Taenaran. It really is me—well, mostly me anyway.

The bladesinger's eyes widened in wonder as Marissa's voice echoed in his mind. He thought about what she had said, and it became clear to him—especially given what had occurred on their journey through Rashemen.

"Somehow you've become a telthor, haven't you?" he asked.

She smiled. *Yes, my dear Taenaran. The spirit of this land has accepted my service. Imsha used the last of her essence to travel to the Urlingwood and see if she could detect the traitor among the othlor. I have taken her place.*

Grief for her passing warred with the happiness that

came with knowing somehow Marissa had found a new kind of life.

Please do not be sad, Taenaran. I don't regret a moment of what I had to do in order to save you and the others. I would offer myself again in a heartbeat. Now I will always be here to protect and serve a land I have come to love as deeply as I loved you.

Taenaran fought back tears and reached up to clasp the hand Marissa still held to his cheek. He nearly sobbed as his own hand met no resistance, passing through her form as if he had reached out to grab the wind.

Please—shed no more tears. My time with you is drawing to a close. There is much work that still needs to be done in the wake of Yulda's treachery.

"Perhaps I should remain here and help the wychlaran tie up loose ends," Taenaran suggested.

Marissa reached out with her other hand and placed it softly upon Taenaran's shoulder. *Rashemen owes you a great debt, but there are other places in Faerûn that need your help.*

He wanted to protest, to explain that he could do the greatest good here in Rashemen, but he knew deep down that it wasn't the truth. He was a bladesinger now—a vessel for the art of his people. There were many elves who would need his help and perhaps—one day—he would even find himself returning home, so Taenaran simply nodded in response.

Please watch over Roberc and Borovazk, Marissa continued, *and make sure they don't drink too much firewine!*

The bladesinger laughed at that, but his laughter soon caught in his throat as Marissa's figure began to fade before his eyes.

I must go, Taenaran. Please know that I will always be here when you need me. Thank you, my love—for everything. With that, Marissa disappeared, fading completely from view.

Slowly, Taenaran turned toward the Red Tree and bowed profoundly. "I love you, Marissa."

He rose up once more, wiping a few stray tears from his eyes before turning back toward the path that would lead away from the Red Tree and ultimately away from Rashemen. As he walked forward, Taenaran felt the hollowness of grief begin to fill with gratefulness and with the warm memories of Marissa's presence in his life. It was as if a stone had rolled away from the dark tomb of his heart, letting in sunlight and air. It was enough that Marissa's life hadn't ended in darkness and pain. It was enough that he had seen her once more—and she was happy.

It was more than enough.

Slowly, Taenaran, bladesinger and hero of Rashemen, walked down the path toward his friends.

Behind him, the raucous cawing of an albino raven echoed throughout the vale.

An excerpt

The Knights of Myth Drannor

Swords of Eveningstar

ED GREENWOOD

Horaundoon scowled into his scrying orb. A tight-lipped, crestfallen Florin strode through the streets with the two loudest Sword wenches at his shoulders, heading back to the Lion. There—and there—and there, too—behind them, the watch spies followed. Last, the Martess lass followed the watch agents.

It was enough to make the Zhentarim smirk, yon little parade. If he hadn't been so hrasted annoyed, that is. The lad seemed to have thrown off much of the influence of the mindworm, even before Myrmeen Lhal spurned him! But how?

❧ ❧ ❧ ❧ ❧

Florin peered around the busy taproom, fire rising in his eyes. There was the table, right enough, with the tavernmaster's apron spread across it to—

"Tavernmaster!" he called, letting some of his anger show. "Where are my friends, who were here with us? Did the watch—?"

"Nay, my lord," Aviathus assured him, bustling up to them. "The way of it is: they conferred, heads together—your friends, I mean—and then the hard-faced woman—ah, forgive me ..."

"Forgiven," Pennae said quickly. "Out with it, man!"

"I, uh ... yes, well ... she led them out. All but the two swordsmen, who sat right here for a time—long enough to empty a talljack of firewine between them and eat a skewer of roast bustard each—ere they went behind yon curtains and then out, with Kestra and Taeriana."

"Who," Jhessail asked flatly, "are Kestra and Taeriana? As if I can't guess."

The tavernmaster's head bobbed.

"Coinlasses, right enough," the tavernmaster said. "And the best and cleanest in the business, let me tell you! Six seasons working here, and never a—"

"Out *where?*" Pennae snapped.

"Ah. Well, 'tis my way of speech more than 'outside,' really," Aviathus said hastily, pointing at the ceiling. "Faster than saying 'up the back stairs.'"

Jhessail rolled her eyes, Florin growled, and Martess and Pennae both gave Florin "See? Someone else besides you" looks.

"*We'll* go and look for them," Pennae told Florin firmly. "A woman looking gives less offense, but can deliver more scorn to shame them back down here when they're found."

Horaundoon gasped, reeled, and shuddered. Sweat streamed down his face to drip off his chin. Four minds, now, two of them strong-willed and wayward....

Riches, he promised Agannor and Bey, showing them chests of gleaming coins and coffers glittering with gems. *Women*, he promised, splashing their minds with ivory curves, dark and mysterious eyes, alluring smiles, and languid beckonings. *Power*, he promised, and each of the two Swords saw himself stride, a great-cloak streaming from his shoulders, through palatial rooms, hurling open doors by which servants hastily knelt, to emerge into a courtyard where white stallions in gold-plated harnesses awaited, then riding forth out of a soaring castle, as folk thundered acclaim from the balconies. . . .

All theirs, the sweating Zhentarim promised, if they but willingly served him.

More splendors he conjured and thrust upon their minds, burying them in banners, glittering courts, and beautiful courtesans on beds made of coins. He saw their mistrust, reluctance, and wary fears crumble and fade—loose black earth swept away before his cleansing flood, an onslaught that lay bare eagerness leaping up bright with hope, daring hope—

Agannor, he thought. *Bey. Are you with me?*

Their roars of assent were like raging flames in his mind, searing him even as his delight grew, and sending the hargaunt into wild, clashing chimings of alarm and excitement.

Horaundoon shuddered in pain and slumped over the table with his fingers trying to pierce its edge like claws. He smiled crookedly.

Then show me your loyalty. Step onto the great way to glory I've shown you. Slay these two wenches—who are in truth foul witches seeking to enslave you!

He spun an illusion of leering, fanged fiends, revealed to be dark and gloating behind the slipping masks of Kestra's and Taeriana's ardent smiles. He was still strengthening and improving those images when Agannor snarled, snatched his dagger out of its sheath, and drove it hilt-deep under Taeriana's chin.

Pennae frowned. Until the drunkards were hauled upstairs and tossed into beds to snore the night away, the bedchambers in the Lion stood dark and empty, doors ajar, awaiting brief use by coinlasses and their clients.

From the landing where she stood, the stair continued on up to the roof, and a narrow, gloomy hall stretched before her, a surprisingly long way. Martess was already going from door to door on the left.

Pennae sighed, shrugged, and started down the doors on the right.

In the other bed, Bey backhanded Kestra so viciously across her face that her head boomed against the wall. Dazed, she had time neither to draw breath nor scream before she was choking on her own blood, slumped over the edge of the bed, dripping and dying.

The partition walls between the Lion's bedchambers were but a single panel thick, and Agannor's snarl had been unmistakable.

Pressed against the wall in one corner of the dark and vacant adjoining room, Martess listened, shuddering.

Plink. Plosh. Plink. Lifeblood, dripping. They'd just killed the two coinlasses.

Mother Mystra, preserve us all.

Agannor blinked at Bey.

"The master—he's gone from my mind!" Agannor said.

"Mine too," Bey muttered, "but I can still feel his regard. He's watching us. Seeing if we stand strong, I think."

He rose from the bed and looked down at what he'd done. He cursed, turning to the washstand and plunging his bloody dagger and hand into the full ewer of water. "We can't let the watch see *this*."

Agannor nodded and tugged forth his own fang,

looking away as Taeriana's jaw fell open in its wake, her sliced tongue dangling.

Wincing, he went to wash up, too, glancing at the closed but boltless door. "What'll we—?"

"The roof," Bey said grimly. "That stair went on up. Bundle them into the bed linens, get them up there for the crows, and use the wash water to get rid of the blood. We'll be gone from Arabel long before rats start gnawing off fingers and dropping them around for folks to find."

Agannor nodded.

"The master should be pleased," Agannor said. "Gods, such *power* he has! None of this fighting orcs for a few coppers, winter after winter, while Purple Dragons give us suspicious glares. We're going to be *lords!*" He grinned at Bey. "Any regrets?"

"Having to break from the Swords this swift and sharp," Bey said. "I'd sort of hoped to bed our own Flame-hair, sooner or later."

"Gods, yes, little Jhessail—though in truth I'd want Pennae. Now, *there's* a wench!"

"Aye, if she were safely tied down so you'd live through it," Bey said wryly. "Perhaps the master . . ."

Agannor grinned. "If we plead prettily enough?"

Pressed against the cold, hard panel, Martess shuddered. Dared she stay still and silent, to keep safe? Or she should run like nightwind to warn Pennae before they came for her?

If they caught her, it would be *her* blood dripping onto the floor—and all her friends would be doomed. These two would blame the Swords for any killings they did, falsely reporting to the watch or arranging matters so folk would think the Swords of Eveningstar were guilty.

My head is full of spells, yet I'm so helpless.

"There's another mind very close to them," Horaundoon muttered, frowning. Surely a mere coinlass wouldn't be under magic to bring her back from a slaying?

Unless she's not a mere coinlass . . .

A Harper? One of Vangerdahast's spies?

Ignoring the hargaunt's curious queries, Horaundoon closed his eyes and felt for that errant mind, putting a hand on the scrying orb to call on its energies, to make his seeking more powerful . . .

There! In the adjoining chamber there was a mind dark with fear and despair, with the glow of feeble spells riding it. One of the Sword magelings!

Charging into her mind would burn his own; even those feeble spells would burst, blaze, and sear, wrecking her mind but doing him harm he neither wanted nor dared suffer.

Horaundoon snarled and thrust himself back at the two handy mindworms, bringing Agannor and Bey out of their room in a rush. Sometimes a sharp sword is enough.

✧ ✧ ✧ ✧ ✧

Martess heard the thunder of boots through the wall and thrust herself away from it, feeling sick. Against those two she was nothing, less than nothing. She must—

The door behind her burst open. She whirled, gasping in alarm, and managed the beginnings of a shriek before Agannor's sword, his teeth bared behind it, burst into and through her, plunging like ice and driving her stumbling back.

Bey Freemantle, wearing the same wide and friendly grin she'd seen on his face so many times before, rushed in from the side.

His steel slid into her like fire, so hot against the cold of Agannor's blade that Martess couldn't breathe.

The spell she might have lashed them with, so that she would not perish without at least dealing pain to her slayers, faded unleashed as Martess Ilmra sank down into soft and endless darkness, fire and ice fading around her.

Pennae knew what that sliced-off scream meant.

Martess was dead or dying—and if the gods willed it, she'd see that Agannor and Bey followed her!

She came out of the room she'd been peering into like a dark cloak hurled along in a gale, cursing herself for leaving her sleep-dosed daggers back in their rooms. Well, she'd just have to make this a little more *personal*.

She was still four doors away from the one Agannor and Bey had ducked out of, running hard with her daggers raised, when something like a fog with fists descended on her mind.

Rolling and shaking Pennae like thunder, it struck her head from the inside thrice, a dozen times, and more, until she was sent stumbling.

Agannor grinned from ear to ear with a light like madness in his eyes. He raised his sword.

"Yes, my beauty!" Agannor hissed. "Come and play!"

His blade lashed out, flashing.

Fetched up bruisingly against the wall as the floor seemed to heave, Pennae clenched her teeth and fought for balance. Bey's sword was coming at her, too. . . .

"Alura Durshavin, you're one *strong* little tigress," Horaundoon of the Zhentarim murmured, hurling his mind against hers again.

The scrying orb in front of him flickered, enfeebled by his use. Yet even as it drifted lower, he could see in its darkening depths the thief fling herself into a blackflip, as supple as any eel he'd ever watched eluding the nets of cooks back in the keep.

His two warriors thrust and hacked at her again—and both missed. Again.

Dazed, Pennae got herself turned around and fled.

Horaundoon bore down hard. If she got to the taproom, or managed to shout an alarm down the stairwell, he'd likely lose both of his Sword minions. She was worth ten of them, but she was fighting him even now. Taming her would take all his power and attention, day and night.

Hah! Horaundoon thrust into, shook, and tumbled Pennae's mind, watching her moan and stagger. Bey was right behind her, his blade raised to—

In the orb he watched the thief thrust herself back and down, rolling into an erupting, kicking ball that had Bey toppling over her. Then she spun on one hip to scissor her legs around the ankles of the onrushing Agannor, and sent him helplessly crashing down onto Bey, shouting in fear with his sword stabbing the air.

Pennae sprang over them, or tried to, but the battering, snarling weight of Horaundoon in her mind drove her aside into a wall. She fell hard atop the two tangled, vigorously cursing warriors, rolling and kicking.

Agannor grabbed at her, tearing her leathers, and she sliced and stabbed at him viciously, managing to catch his palm briefly with the point of her blade. He shrieked in pain and snatched his hand back just as Bey's sword thrust across her stomach, slicing leather with swift ease.

Pennae twisted, heaved, and managed to win free, her sprint down the hall now a whimpering crawl that had her clawing her way to her feet and leaning hard on the wall to keep from falling. Staggering, she slid along the wall, trailing smears of blood as Horaundoon hammered in her head and Bey pounded along the hall behind her, Agannor right behind him.

The stair had a rail, and Pennae caught hold of it just in time to swing herself up and aside as a sword bit deep into the floorboards she'd been standing on moments before.

Bey hacked at her again, and again, hewing air hard enough to smash ribs and limbs if were ever to hit the leather-clad thief.

Pennae ducked, kicked his knee hard to send him staggering back into Agannor, and raced up the stairs, hoping the trapdoor at its top wasn't locked.

The gods were with her. A simple, through-two-straps bar kept anyone from opening it from above. Pennae plucked out the metal bar and smashed aside Bey's seeking blade with it, leaving the sword ringing like a bell and him shouting at the eerie pain of a numbed sword hand.

Pennae was already across the roof, the slammed trapdoor bouncing in her wake, running hard for the next roof. It was the first of seven in the block, if she remembered rightly, and at least two of those shops had wooden stairs descending from their rooftops to balconies.

She jumped, landed awry as the foe in her mind slammed into her wits just as she was launching herself, and staggered sidewise until she fetched up against a crumbling fieldstone chimney, brittle old bird nests crunching underfoot. Pennae winced. If these head-splitting, nigh-blinding attacks continued, she'd best get down to street level, where at least she couldn't die just from falling over!

Agannor shouted behind her, and Pennae hissed a curse and ran on, heading for the next roof—and the next stab inside her head.

Horaundoon frowned. Out in the open, the wench would swiftly best his two lumbering minions. He ached to finish her, to burst her mind like a egg flung against a wall . . . but—whiteblood—he'd been trying to do that for how long now? And still she fought him.

No, it was time to leave off trying to fry her wits to cast a spell that would send his orders thundering into the minds of a score of Zhent agents all over Arabel. Orders telling them it was high time they loaded their crossbows and went Pennae-hunting.

In the wake of the shrieks, shouts, and the ringing clang of swords, boots thundered on the stairs, followed by the booming of something heavy falling, twice.

"I'm going up there!" Florin snarled, struggling in the grip of the four grim, plainly clad Purple Dragons who'd risen from a nearby table to drag him down when he'd first drawn his sword.

"*No*, outlander," one of them growled into his face as they twisted and strained together in a sweating, grunting heap on the floor, "you'll *not*. Our orders—"

"Unhand Florin Falconhand, and *get back, all of you!*" Jhessail shouted, her high, usually gentle voice ringing out across the taproom of the Lion and bringing down a hush of tensely staring drinkers. She held a dagger in her hand, and bright flames raced up and down its blade. "Or I'll cast the strongest spell I know, and bring down this tavern on us all!"

The attacks—thank Mask!—had ceased, but her head still throbbed as though she'd taken a solid mace-blow. Worse than that, other men seemed to have joined the chase: men with swords and daggers and no hesitation in using them. So where was the Lady Lord's oh-so-efficient, thrice-accursed watch *now*?

Agannor stumbled along well in her wake, obviously winded, and Bey was even further back, but—*naed!*

An unwashed, stubble-faced man stepped out of an alley right in front of Pennae with a cocked and loaded crossbow in his hands. It cracked even as she flung herself aside and brought her daggers up.

A moment later, she was wringing a numbed and bleeding hand, the dagger that had been in it gone. She heard the crossbow bolt bounce and splinter on cobbles far behind her left shoulder.

"*Naed!* Hrasting bitch," the man cursed, staring at her over his fired crossbow. "How in the tluin did you step aside from *that?*"

Pennae wasted no breath in a reply, but hurried toward him, hefting the dagger in her right hand. The man cursed again and flung the crossbow full in her face to buy himself time to drag out a rather rusty short sword.

Pennae launched herself at the wall, caught hold of a stone windowsill under a crudely boarded-over back window, and swung herself back hard, boots first, catching the man in the throat at about the same time he got his sword free.

He went over in a heap, his arms twitching in spasms, and Pennae landed hard, heels first, on his ribs.

Just who was chasing her now, was—

A crossbow bolt sang past her ear with the high, thrumming whine that meant it had only just missed her. Pennae snarled and darted into the alley.

A moment later, she came out of it again, sobbing as she flew helplessly back through the air, snatched off her feet and spinning in midair with a crossbow bolt right through her shattered shoulder.

Myrmeen Lhal looked up from the stack of decrees and dispensations she was rather wearily signing. That was the *third* alarm gong.

Three patrols called in as reinforcements? What the Hells was going on?

Boots thundered in the passage.

"Asgarth?" Myrmeen called out. "What's all the tumult?"

"Those damn—ahem, those Swords adventurers! Men're firing crossbows all over Palaceside!" the lionar shouted. "Beg pardon, Lady Lord!" he added in his next breath.

"Granted," Myrmeen called, deep and loud, shaking her head in wry amusement. She'd expected the Swords of Eveningstar to get up to something after the day's gentle tongue-lashing, but so quickly? And *three* patrols-worth of trouble?

"Gods above, Azoun," she muttered, "you certainly can pick them."

Myrmeen turned back to the piles of papers. *Her* war was here, on her desk. As usual. Now where—? Oh, yes, the third request for an escort to Candlekeep. . . .

Yet if that gong rang again, the Dragons would discover the Lady Lord of Arabel charging out there at the head of the answering patrol. Oh, yes.

Myrmeen glanced down the desk at her helm, currently serving paperweight duty on the 'not yet seen' pile.

The look she gave it was a longing look.

Weeping freely—*gods*, it hurt! She felt weak and sick inside, and kept falling. Oblivion lurked like eager dark shadows to claim her, but Pennae stumbled on.

Perhaps her foe had given up on cudgeling her brains and now rode the minds of this small army of men with crossbows who kept walking damn near into her, acquiring looks of recognition on their faces though she *knew* she'd never seen them before, and firing at her.

If they'd been better shots, she'd have a belly bristling with bolts by now, or a hole through her middle large enough even for clumsy Purple Dragons to thrust their helmed heads through.

Instead, Pennae just *felt* like she had a hole that size in her, at about shoulder level. She'd spewed her guts out all over the cobbles twice now, and had nothing left inside her to heave.

Another stride . . . another . . .

Pennae wanted *so* much to lie down on her face on the cobbles and just rest—but that would mean swift death for her, with Agannor, Bey, and at least two mysterious men in leathers following her.

She was leaving a bloody trail as she trudged, and probably a solid line of tears, too. She gave up clinging spiderlike to walls, because she'd kept falling from her perches to tumble helplessly back to the cobbles.

Yes, she was beginning to hate cobbles. Very solid things, cobbles . . . keep walking, Pennae.

"Hoy!" The face belonged to a bristle-mustached Purple Dragon, with a watch badge pinned to the baldric across his breast. Others, similarly garbed, were gaping at her from behind him.

"Evening, lads," Pennae gasped. "Never seen a lass with a crossbow bolt through her before?"

Strong hands caught her as she stumbled, and the Dragon attached to them growled.

"So, maid, what befell ye, exactly?" he asked. "How came you to have a—"

"Florin!" someone distant called. It sounded like Islif.

"Hey, Florin!" someone—Semoor, for a handful of gold—even more distant chimed in.

"*Pennae!*" That nearby shout rang out like a war horn,

cutting through the sudden hubbub of Purple Dragons calling "Ho!" to each other.

As she sank into the darkness that had been clawing at her for so long—the warm, welcoming darkness—Pennae smiled.

Florin Falconhand had come for her at last.

Horaundoon shook his head in weary exasperation. So many minds, fighting his.

He wiped his sweat-slick brow with a trembling hand, sighed, and sat back. He dared not stay linked—not with the very real risk that someone whose mind he was in would die, violently.

No, he'd dismiss the two Swords warriors as lost, and just watch things unfold through the orb. At the very least, it should be a good show.

"Lathander loves thee," Semoor's voice intoned through the gurgling waterfall of cool, blessed release that was sweeping through her.

Pennae blinked and tried to cough. Gentle fingers stroked her throat as tenderly as any lover, quelling her gagging.

"Tymora loves you, too," Doust added from above those fingers. "And—hrast it—I do too."

"And Florin *really* does," Semoor said slyly.

"*Thank* you, Stoop," Florin said firmly from somewhere above them. "That's two potions, now?"

"We holy prefer to call them 'healing quaffs,' forester," Semoor said, then grunted in startled pain.

"Ah," Islif said, "just as we unwashed prefer to call *that* 'the toe of my boot, put right where it will do a pompous holynose the most good.' Clumsum, d'you think your healing spell worked?"

"Shrug," Doust said aloud, and there were several chuckles above Pennae.

"Purple Dragons stand all around us, Pennae," Florin said, his voice drawing nearer. Pennae blinked through what seemed to be tears, and could make out that he'd hunkered down on his haunches to lean over her. "They want to know what befell you. So do we."

"Martess," Pennae gasped. "Murdered. By Agannor and Bey. Chased me here. Other men with crossbows . . . also chasing. Beware someone—wizard?—attacking you, inside your head. Made me . . . fall over."

"Blood of Alathan!" Doust gasped at about the same time as Islif snarled a curse.

Then Florin said softly, "Swordcaptain, I must ask you to turn a blind eye to what we may do next. I am enraged, and am like to do my own murdering in your streets."

"Man," a gruff and unfamiliar voice replied, "three good men are down with bolts through them. An' that's just my Dragons; I hear there're shopkeepers dead, an' a little lad who was out playing in the wrong alley, too. Go do your murders!"

Departing boots thundered, and a surprised voice—Doust's—asked, "*Jhessail?*"

"Let her go," Semoor murmured. "As if you or I or anyone could stop her."

"Help—help me up," Pennae gasped. "I'm going, too."

"You, lass, are staying right here," the swordcaptain growled. "There's blood all over you, your leathers're sliced half off, an'—"

"And my task stands unfinished," Pennae hissed, clawing her way up the man's arm until she could stand. "*My* task. I'm a Sword of Eveningstar, Swordcaptain. Mayhap you've heard of us."

"Trumpet fanfare," Doust announced helpfully. There was a moment of tense silence before Purple Dragons started to guffaw, all around them. When the Swordcaptain she was clinging to started to shake with laughter, Pennae almost fell over again.

"There!" Florin shouted, pointing ahead with his sword as they pounded along a back alley made slippery underfoot by rotting cabbage leaves. A crossbow promptly cracked, then another.

Florin flung himself at the wall, taking Islif down with him, but the Dragon running behind them screamed and crashed to his face, bouncing and moaning, with a bolt quivering through his knee.

"Jhess," the forester growled, scrambling up, "you shouldn't be here! You've no armor—"

"Shut *up*, Florin," came the furious reply.

"Wait for us! We bring holy blessings!" cried two familiar voices.

Jhessail rolled her eyes. "You're shunning *me*? What about them? The happy dancing holynoses themselves?"

Islif flung her a rare grin, and Florin waved his surrender—then peered and cursed in admiration.

A weak, pale, weaving-on-her-feet Pennae ran alongside Doust and Semoor.

Together once more, the Swords trotted on, the watch lionar beside them puffing, "We've closed the gates, and called every last blade out of the barracks—the Lady Lord herself's out running around with her sword drawn, somewhere. They can't escape us! 'Tis just a matter of time...."

Islif threw him a jaundiced look, but said nothing. They ducked around a sagging, permanently parked cart and burst out of the alley.

"There!" Islif shouted, pointing.

'There' was the dark doorway of a warehouse, a

refuse-strewn threshold where Agannor had just jerked his sword out of the throat of a reeling, blood-spattering Purple Dragon. Two crossbow bolts came humming past him out of the darkness, and one took down another Purple Dragon. A war wizard stepped coolly sideways to escape the other, and went right on casting a spell.

Purple Dragons converged on Agannor from all directions. Agannor cast looks all around, saw the Swords and gave them a mocking wave, then disappeared into the warehouse. Another pair of crossbow bolts claimed another two Dragons.

Puffing along beside Florin, the swordcaptain growled, "Where're *our* bowmen?"

"Those murdering bastards could be just inside, aimed and waiting for us, know you!" another Dragon gasped as they sprinted for the warehouse door, keeping close to the walls of other buildings in hopes they'd not run up to meet more crossbow bolts.

Islif gave him a wolf's grin.

"I know. I'm rather counting on it," Islif said.

Something crashed down right in front of her, exploding into shards and splinters as it bounced and cartwheeled away. A chair, or rather it had been.

Islif looked up in time to see a grinning pair of men launch a wardrobe over a balcony rail at her.

" 'Ware!" she roared, launching herself into a full-length leap.

The crash, right behind her, was thunderous; two Dragons managed not even a peep before they were crushed flat.

Semoor, running hard, skidded helplessly in the sudden spray of blood, but kept his feet and continued on.

"What in the *tluin* is going on?" Semoor said. "They're throwing *wardrobes* at us?"

A crossbow bolt hummed out of the warehouse and spun him around, laying open his arm at the elbow as it grazed him—and took a Dragon full in the face.

"Naed," Semoor gasped. Then he shouted, two sprinting steps later, "Ho! Changed my mind! Let's have more wardrobes!"

"What *is* going on?" Jhessail gasped, as they neared the gaping warehouse door. "Who are all these foes?"

"Zhent agents," a Dragon grunted from right behind her. " 'Least those two on the balcony were."

"Were?"

"They just got 'em," he growled in satisfaction.

Florin ducked down, plucked up the splayed shards of a smashed and discarded crate, and turned.

"Fire spell?" Florin asked.

"Done," Jhessail said. She stopped and fumbled forth what she needed from her belt pouch. A Purple Dragon ran on into the warehouse, warily ducking low, then promptly screamed as two crossbow bolts tore through him.

Flame flared up from Jhessail's hand. She caressed the rotten wood Florin held out to her, then another crate proffered by Islif.

Florin thanked her with a grin, turned, and hurled the blazing wreckage into the warehouse. There its merrily leaping flames showed all watching dusty shelves filled with sacks and coffers, a dead man sprawled out on the ground, two men fleeing with crossbows, the Purple Dragon who'd stopped two bolts writhing in agony on the floor, and ...

"Where're the chains?" the ranger asked suspiciously. "Don't these high loft warehouses load wagons just inside their doors?"

Islif tossed her blazing crate into the warehouse to add more light, but shook her head.

"I see none," Islif said. "Come *on*."

Emboldened by being able to see that no crossbowmen stood aimed and waiting, Purple Dragons rushed the doorway from several directions. The Swords joined the streams of warriors, but were a little behind the first men—the ones who shouted in alarm then died, smashed bloodily to the floor, as someone unseen let fall the chains from above in great thundering heaps that buried the men they slew or struck senseless.

Other chains swung out of the dark corners of the warehouse in deadly arcs and smashed men into broken things and hurled them back into the faces of their slower fellows.

By the time Florin reached the chaos of broken and struggling men at the warehouse threshold, things were brightening in a familiar, flickering manner. He looked up.

"Get back!" he roared, catching Islif and swinging her around into a breath-stealing, jarring meeting with the onrushing Jhessail. "*Back,* everyone!"

A sword flashed above the burning crates and barrels on top of a rack high above, severing a rope—and to the thunderous *clatter-clatter-clatter* of a winch going mad, the flaming rack plunged toward the floor.

"Get out!" Florin shouted, waving his arms at onrushing Purple Dragons. "Fire!"

He was still shouting when the crash, behind him, shook him off his feet and made the entire building creak and groan. Tongues of flame spat past him, hurling shrieking, blazing men out among their fellows.

Purple Dragons cursed colorfully, war wizards threw their arms up to shield their eyes, and over the crackling roar, war horns cried fire-warnings. Once, twice, thrice, and then the bellow of Dauntless could be heard, rising above all the tumult.

"War wizards," Dauntless said, "quench yon fire! Swordcaptains, run to fetch every priest you can! *Get that fire out!*"

As the Swords rallied around him, Florin found himself face-to-face with a Dragon he knew: Swordcaptain Nelvorr.

"Sir Sword," the officer gasped, "put your blade away. The ones we're chasing are in yon warehouse." He waved his arm in a circle. "We have it surrounded, on the other side, and no one has tried to break out that way yet. If they do, they'll die."

Florin looked into the flames. The place was an inferno just inside the door, and the front wall was leaking plumes of smoke and swiftly climbing lines of flame that traced the pitch that had been used to seal cracks in the boards. To either side of the door, however, the warehouse looked untouched. There wasn't even any smoke coming from its shuttered windows.

"Are there any cellars? Tunnels?" Florin snapped.

"No," replied a voice from behind him. A voice he'd heard before. "At least," the Lady Lord of Arabel added, a wand held ready in her hand, "none are supposed to be—and my tax collectors look hard for such things."

"I'm going in there," Florin told her. A war wizard finished an elaborate spell and the fire died down noticeably.

"You surprise me not," she replied with a half smile, waving him forward. Florin gave her a smile and a nod. Then he ran, the Swords at his heels.

Smoke greeted them, thick and curling, as Florin ducked in around the eastern doorpost and led the way, keeping low with his sword out.

The Swords hastened through the thinning blue haze, peering this way and that in hopes they'd see the dreaded crossbows before a bolt found them.

The place was a labyrinth of open-sided floors; pillars with pegs embedded in them; and stacked, roped-in-place sacks, barrels, and coffers. Ramps, cobwebs, and motionless hanging chains were everywhere.

Lanterns glimmered far behind the Swords as Purple Dragons entered the warehouse. The dancing lights of flames were gone, leaving only the faint light of a few dusty glowstones, high up on the walls in their furry-with-webs iron cages.

Another pillar onward.

And another. With every cautious step the Swords grew warier; soon they'd reach this end of the warehouse. If the men they sought weren't back down the other end—and from the way the catwalks up in the roof beams ran, and from where Florin had seen that sword slicing the ropes, that wasn't likely ... They had to be somewhere here.

Close.

Waiting.

Of course, this was the lowest level. They could be anywhere behind the sacks up above, on all those dark, open-sided storage floors.

"*How* many warehouses like this does the city hold, again?" Semoor muttered to Pennae. "Strikes me you could steal stuff by the wagonload for years, and it'd not be missed."

Pennae gave him a fierce grin—then a fiercer scowl.

"Later," she whispered into his ear. "We'll talk about this later, O high-principled holy man."

Ahead, Florin threw up his arm in a warning wave. Then he drew aside against a stack of crates and pointed.

The Swords looked out at what he'd already discovered: a sea of spilled grain, fallen from sacks sliced open in some accident or other that now hung limp and empty.

A line of boot prints ploughed through them in a path that ended abruptly in otherwise undisturbed drifts of grain. Men had hurried this way then simply—vanished.

"Jhessail?"

The mageling stepped forward, her face set, until she was standing just on the edge of the grain.

"Strong magic," she murmured, spreading her arms

almost as if basking in the sun. "Like a fire, beating on my face." She took a long step sideways, shook her head, and then did the same in the other direction, returning to where she'd first been standing. "Just here."

"Like a door," Doust murmured.

Semoor bent, scooped up some grain in his cupped hands, strode along the path of disturbed grain, and when he got to its end, threw his handful forward.

Aside from a little wisp of drifting dust, it abruptly vanished, right in front of him. "The way is open," he said, stepping hastily to one side.

No crossbow bolts came hissing out of the empty air, and after a tense breath or two Semoor rejoined them.

"Agannor and Bey went this way, you think?"

Islif nodded grimly. "I think."

Florin nodded too.

"All right," Florin said. "We've not got our armor or gear, but if we go back to get them, I'm thinking the murderers will be gone forever. What say you?"

"Let's go get them," Pennae whispered. "I saw their faces, and her blood on their swords—and they tried to slice *me* often enough."

Jhessail nodded.

"They know all about us," Jhessail said. "I don't want *that* creeping back at me unawares, some night while I sleep. After them!"

The Swords turned as one and started through the grain.

There was an angry shout from behind them. "Hoy! Hold! Stand and down weapons!"

The Swords spun around, their weapons raised, and found themselves looking at Purple Dragons. *Lots* of Purple Dragons, in full battle armor, wearing helms and shields and hefting spears in their hands.

"Swords of Eveningstar, put down your weapons and surrender! *Now!*"

A hard-faced ornrion none of the Swords had ever

seen before, who bore a flame-encircled red dragon on his shield, strode to the fore. He wagged a gauntleted forefinger at them.

"We've heard all about you!" he said. "I arrest you, all of you, for fire-setting and—"

Florin regarded the ornrion incredulously.

"What?" Florin said.

"Down with your weapons, or we'll down *you*. And quick about it, or I'll seize the excuse and save Arabel a lot of bother by just butchering you like the mad dogs you are! Adventurers are always trouble...."

Trailing his sword behind him in his fingertips, Florin trudged to meet the man—who came at him like an angry storm, wading into the grain and continuing his tirade.

"You're mistaken," the forester began, "and the Lady Lord of—"

"*Horse dung,* lying adventurer! 'Tis from her tongue we all heard of your villainy! Your crossbows have murdered a dozen Dragons this night, and if her orders to try to take you alive weren't riding me, I'd—"

Florin spread his hands to show his peaceful intent— and the ornrion's hand came up and took him by the throat.

For a moment, the forester stared disbelievingly into the man's grimly smiling face. Then his fist came in with all the force he could put behind it, smashing up under the Dragon's jaw.

The click of teeth clashing on teeth was loud, and the ornrion was staring at the rafters, up on tiptoe and already senseless. His failing hand let go of Florin's throat, and the forester twisted and snatched the flaming dragon shield free of the man's limply toppling body.

"Swords!" Florin roared, spinning around with his sword in one hand and the just-seized shield on his other arm. "To me!"

Florin charged through the grain until suddenly he—wasn't there.

There was an instant of gently falling through endless rich blue mists ere Florin's boot came down on hard stone. Stone somewhere underground, by the coolness and the damp, earthen smell. The blue radiance faded—

—at about the same instant as something crashed into and *through* the shield, slamming into him hard enough to shatter its stout metal.

And Florin's arm beneath it.

Triumphant laughter roared out from ahead as the fletched end of the broken crossbow bolt that had maimed him brushed past Florin's nose, into dark oblivion.

Stumbling back as pain lanced through him, Florin wondered how likely he was to end up following it ...

The Purple Dragons charged, a shouting wave of deadly spear points.

"Get through!" Islif yelled at Jhessail and Pennae, swatting their behinds to urge them to greater haste as they plunged past her. "Stoop! Clumsum! Get in there!"

She waved her sword in defiance as she raced after them, grinning frantically as the foremost spear reached for her, perhaps the length of her own hand away from piercing her.

Then the world blinked, and she was falling through blue mist.

It blinked again, and Islif was standing in a dark stone-lined corridor with the rest of the Swords, who were clustered around ... Florin? Hurt?

"Hoy!" she cried, as she spun around to face the blue glow behind her, "weapons *out!*"

Spears were emerging from it, thrusting out of the swirling blueness with grim-faced Purple Dragons behind them. Three soldiers whose eyes widened at the sight of their surroundings.

They widened still more when Islif struck aside two spearheads with her sword and ran in past the third to backhand its wielder across the face.

He stumbled into his fellows, there was a moment of startled hopping and cursing—and Pennae came out of the dark with a startled shriek, daggers flashing in both hands, and Doust and Semoor trotting behind her.

The Purple Dragons wavered. Islif drove her knee hard into a codpiece then thrust her leg sideways, toppling that soldier into the one next to him. Pennae landed hard on their wavering spears, smashing them to the stone floor and splintering the shaft of one of them as she flung herself forward, her fists hammering down two dagger-pommels onto two helms.

The Dragons reeled, and Pennae jerked on their helms, tilting the metal down half-over their faces. They struggled under her, punching, kicking, and trying to rise—and as Islif wrenched their spears away, Semoor leaned in, plucked a mace from the belt of one Dragon, and crowned the man solidly with it, leaving him reeling.

"I've always wanted to do that," he remarked happily. "Are you going to start cutting pieces off them now?"

The Dragons were already trying to shove themselves back and away, and his words goaded them into frantic flight. Back into the blue glow, with Islif's and Pennae's chuckles trailing them.

"Now get away," Islif ordered, waving her fellow Swords to the sides of the passage. "Against the walls and *away*. I'd not put it past them to find some bows and start volleying right down this—"

A spear burst out of the mist and sailed down the passage, to bounce and skitter to a harmless stop beside Jhessail, who was helping a sweating Florin up, and easing the bent and ruined shield off his arm.

"Move!" Islif roared, as a second spear followed the first. The Swords moved quickly as a third spear rattled past them.

"Florin says there's a crossbowman somewhere ahead of us," Jhessail warned, as they hastened on together.

"Broke my arm," Florin grunted. "Never saw him."

"When do we start having fun?" Semoor complained. "Pools of coins and gems, dancing girls, our own castles… when does *that* side of adventure kiss and cuddle us?"

Behind them, the blue glow burst into a wild, blinding-bright explosion that spat lightning bolts down the passage at them, crackling and ricocheting in a chaos that sounded like hundreds of harps being smashed all at once, metal strings jangling and shrieking. In its wake, all light faded; the blue glow was gone.

"A war wizard making sure we won't return," Jhessail said grimly as darkness descended, leaving them all blind.

Doust groaned. "Now what?"

"Well," Semoor said, "we can sit down right here and pray, the two of us—and in the fullness of time be granted the power to make light to see by."

A dim glow occurred not far from his elbow and brightened, as it was uncovered and held up, to about the same strength as a mica-shuttered lantern.

"Or," Pennae told them all, holding what they could now see was a hand-sized glowstone, "we can use this." Its radiance showed them her sweet smile.

It was Jhessail's turn to groan.

"Do I want to know where you 'found' that?" Jhessail asked.

Pennae shrugged. "I *imagine* the Lady Lord, or one of her staff, will eventually miss it. Yet I doubt, somehow, she'll be able to chase after us to reclaim it."

"What happens if you drop it?" Doust asked. "Is it likely to break and go dark?"

She shrugged. "I wasn't planning on finding out."

"So where are we?" Florin gasped, his voice tight with pain. "And which way shall we go?"

"The Haunted Halls, of course," Pennae answered "In the long passage just north of the room where we found the boots, pack, and pole. See yon cracks in the wall?" The thief gestured with the glowstone. "So the fastest way out is that way—and Bey might remember the route. I doubt Agannor ever paid that much attention to the maps—but the three we're chasing went *that* way."

"After them," Florin growled. Pennae nodded.

Islif took hold of her elbow and steered her hand to hold the glowstone close to Florin, so she could peer at him.

"Healing, holy men?" Islif asked.

"Not until after we pray for a good long time," Semoor told her. "We spent our divine favor helping Pennae."

"I'll live," Florin told them tersely. "Let's get after them."

The Swords exchanged nods, hefted their weapons, and set off into the chill darkness.

They'd gone only a few paces when they came upon a discarded crossbow on the floor. Pennae peered at it.

"Not broken," Pennae murmured, "so he was out of bolts to fire."

"Bright news," Semoor grunted. They hastened on to a wider chamber that offered them a door and three passages onward. Islif went to the door, made a pocketing gesture to tell Pennae to hide the light, and opened it.

Darkness greeted her. Pennae patted her shoulder, leaned past her, and pulled the glowstone out of its pouch again. Nothing. The room was empty—and across the door on its far wall was a fresh cobweb. Pennae shook her head and stepped back out of the room. "They probably went that way," Pennae said, pointing down the passage that led to the feast hall, "but we'd best check this end, too, just to be sure. I don't fancy them leaping out behind us and slicing up Doust or Semoor."

The passage ran northwest, not far, ere turning west to a chamber that still held, along one wall, the collapsed and sagging remnants of ancient barrels and chests. In the center of the facing wall was a door—a stone affair that lacked lock or bolt—that led to a room that had been empty when they'd explored it, days back.

As Pennae neared it, she tensed and stepped back.

"A man's voice," Pennae whispered. "Unfamiliar and declaiming some grand phrases that mean nothing to me. I'd say he's working magic."

"Let's move!" Islif hissed. "In, before he finishes!" She launched herself at the door with Pennae right behind her.

The Swords burst through the door and down the short passage beyond, startling the man who stood there into looking over his shoulder at them.

It was Bey, his drawn sword in his hands.

"Get gone!" Bey shouted to someone around the corner, and ran that way.

The Swords raced after him, rounding the corner fast and ducking low, their swords up in front of them.

They were in time to see Agannor's boot vanishing through an upright, swirling oval of blue radiance the same hue as the glow that had brought them back to the Haunted Halls. An unfamiliar man in leathers was keeping Bey from following with one arm, but snatched it out of the way the moment Agannor vanished to let Bey plunge through.

Giving the onrushing Swords a malevolent smile, he followed, leaving behind the blue glow.

Jhessail cursed. "Where does *this* one go?"

"We'll see, won't we?" Pennae flung back at her, racing for the whirling portal with Islif right behind her.

Its glow swallowed them both before any of the other Swords could reply.

Ornrion Barellkor blinked again, his head still swimming. Strong hands lifted him by his armpits, helping him to sit up.

"All right, are you?" one of his swordcaptains asked gruffly.

Barellkor put a hand to his jaw and tried to shake his head—which proved to be a mistake. His head felt like it was splitting slowly open with someone's war axe firmly embedded in it. His chin felt even worse.

"I think my jaw is broken," he moaned.

"Idiot," the Lady Lord of Arabel said curtly, dragging the wincing man to his feet. "If that's all the hurt you took, Tymora must smile on you, Barellkor. Now get out of my sight before I decide to reduce you to lionar."

The ornrion stared at her disbelievingly.

"But I—but they . . ." the ornrion started. "They were the ones who murderered all our lads!"

"Horse dung, Barellkor, as I believe you're fond of saying," Myrmeen snapped. "Why don't you step over there and try throttling yon portal-blasting war wizard, instead of a gallant young forester? Perhaps you two stoneheads will succeed in murdering each other, and I'll be shut of the pair of you!"

Pennae was a little surprised not to be greeted by sharp steel the moment the blue glow faded before her.

She, and Islif, and a moment later all the rest of the Swords, were even more surprised by what they beheld in the large chamber in front of them.

On its far wall were mounted three huge, glowing and very vivid portraits of menacing, rampant monsters, all of them familiar to the Swords from bestiaries: a chuul, an ettin, and an umber hulk. To the right of them, stone steps led up to a passage stretching away elsewhere, and a coldly smiling, white-haired yet young man in black doublet, hose, and boots—looking for all the world like a minor courtier who might well be seen standing near the Dragon Throne—stood on those steps.

Floating in three green, swirling glows, and struggling to win free of them, were Agannor, Bey, and the man in leathers who'd followed them through the portal.

"These are yours, I presume?" the man on the steps asked the Swords. "Kindly slay them." He pointed at the man in leathers. "Especially that one, who had the effrontery to open one of my private portals and lead, it seems, half the adventurers in Cormyr here."

"Who are you?" Pennae asked, frowning in bewilderment. "And where's 'here'?"

"Ah. Well." The man waved a hand, and the glow behind the Swords winked out; the portal was gone. "As you've no way of ever finding this place again, there's no harm in your knowing that you stand in Whisper's Crypt. I am Whisper, one of the mightiest wizards of the Zhentarim."

"Oh, *tluin*," Jhessail said wearily. "When will all this running and fighting and killing end?"

The Zhentarim smiled at her. "When you die, of course."

THE YEAR OF ROGUE DRAGONS

By Richard Lee Byers

Dragons across Faerûn begin to slip into madness, bringing all of the world to the edge of cataclysm. They Year of Rogue Dragons has come.

THE RAGE

Renegade dragon hunter Dorn has devoted his entire life to killing dragons. As every dragon across Faerûn begins to slip into madness, civilization's only hope may lie in the last alliance Dorn and his fellow hunters would ever accept.

THE RITE

Rampaging dragons appear in more places every day. But all the dragons have to do to avoid the madness is trade their immortal souls for an eternity of undeath.

THE RUIN

May 2006

For more information visit **www.wizards.com**

HOUSE OF SERPENTS TRILOGY
By The New York Times best-selling author
Lisa Smedman

VENOM'S TASTE

The Pox, a human cult whose members worship the goddess of
plague and disease, begins to work the deadly will of Sibyls' Chosen.
As humans throughout the city begin to transform into the freakish
tainted ones, it's up to a yuan-ti halfblood to stop them all.

VIPER'S KISS

A mind-mage of growing power begins a secret journey to Sespeth.
There he meets a yuan-ti halfblood who has her eyes set on the scion
of house Extaminos – said to hold the fabled Circled Serpent.

VANITY'S BROOD

The merging of human and serpent may be the most dangerous
betrayal of nature the Realms has ever seen. But it could also be the
only thing that can bring a human slave and his yuan-ti mistress
together against a common foe.

www.wizards.com